ONCE

UPON

A

CRIME

ONCE UPON A CRIME

EDITED BY

ED GORMAN AND

MARTIN H. GREENBERG

Berkley Prime Crime
New York

ONCE UPON A CRIME

A Berkley Prime Crime Book
Published by The Berkley Publishing Group
200 Madison Avenue, New York, NY 10016

The Penguin Putnam Inc. World Wide Web site address is
http://www.penguinputnam.com

Book design by Jennifer Daddio

First Edition: June 1998

Library of Congress Cataloging-in-Publication Data

Once upon a crime : fairy tales for mystery lovers / edited by
Ed Gorman & Martin Greenberg.—1st ed.
        p.   cm.
    ISBN 0-425-16301-6

    1. Detective and mystery stories, American. 2. Fairy
tales—Adaptation. I. Gorman, Edward. II. Greenberg,
Martin Harry.
PS648.D4053   1998
813'.087208—dc21   97-31612
                                                         CIP

Printed in the United States of America

10   9   8   7   6   5   4   3   2   1

v

TABLE OF CONTENTS

Introduction

"The Sleeping Beauty." "Hansel and Gretel." "Snow White." "Rumpelstiltskin."

These are just a few of the Brothers Grimm fairy tales that have fascinated, amused, and terrified readers for generations.

While the stories themselves date back into the mists of history—the oral history of northern Europe, when tales where literally told around campfires—they were compiled and revised by Jacob and Wilhelm Grimm, and first published in Germany in 1812 and 1815.

Since that time, young and old alike have been bedazzled by these stories.

We thought it would be fun for readers to see how mystery and suspense rewriters would retell some of the Grimm stories in a contemporary context. Some of the writers chose to parallel the Grimm story exactly; others used the premise as nothing more than a starting point, and went on to write their very own stories.

Writers from Victor Hugo to Graham Greene have written about the dark and dire truths of the Grimm stories, and certainly challenged the notion that the stories are for children only.

We think you'll have a lot of fun seeing what some of our finest suspense writers have done with these tales. Just as in the original tales themselves, you'll find all the human emotions here—pleasure, passion, hatred, jealousy, greed, terror—you know, the stuff we *really* like to read about.

THE EDITORS

ONCE

UPON

A

CRIME

Gillian Roberts's novels about Philadelphia schoolteacher Amanda Pepper have a gentle wisdom and warm wit that sometimes disguises a steely gaze. In the course of her books, she tells us a great deal about the perils of education in the waning days of this century. She is no less accomplished in the short story form. Here, she takes a new look at "Cinderella."

GILLIAN ROBERTS

After Happily Ever

Not that you're likely to believe anything I say, but the reality of it is that nobody should be the least bit surprised by what she did and how she did it. Assuming, of course, that you're willing to take off the blinkers, forget the brainwashing, and comprehend that she did do it. All of it. That she has no heart. Never did.

The thing you probably don't want to know and surely don't want to believe is that despite everything you've heard about her from the cradle onward, she was and is a world-class bitch. Actually, she never lived in the world, so "world-class" is not completely accurate. She—and all the rest of us—live in what's called "Far, far away" or "Fairyland," although that is another misnomer because fairies are only one of our ethnic minorities, and such gross labeling has resulted in a lot of bickering and factions. The gremlins, to name only one other group, have threatened to relocate en masse unless recognized.

The "once upon a time" place where we live and that we simply call "here" would more accurately be described as a parallel universe. Once upon a time is now. And then. And then some.

And forever. Ever after.

I say all this because I know Earthlings like the sound of scientific precision. Like to believe you are in charge of the facts.

Yes, we know about you. Our telescopes and observatories are trained on you as a source of entertainment just the way your imaginations are tuned into us. We tell our children bedtime stories about your exploits as often as you do ours, and they are as charmed by your odd behavior as yours are by ours—although I think our behavior is much more *logical.* Try explaining the concept of "random violence" to a child who lives in "Here." You'd be laughed right out of the nursery.

I wonder if the stories we tell about you are the real truth (not that we are hung up on a single, knowable "truth," and science hasn't really caught on hereabouts). I do know that the stories you tell about us—especially about my family—are fabrications. In any case, I doubt that you have the sort of PR people and spin doctors that we do, because if you did, your stories, like ours, would be more interesting, if you'll forgive my speaking bluntly. Where are your tales of globe-circling quests, transformations of gross matter into gold, boiling oceans, ice mountains, great and near-impossible heroic challenges and deeds, giants and trolls and curses and magical rescues and revelations? Where in fact is your magic?

Where in fact is your story of the dusty girl who cleaned the fireplaces becoming queen of all the land?

Now that I think about it more, I'm sure the stories about you must be distortions and that's why they're so lacking in color, or at least have been since Attila the Hun and a few of the Russian czars. So perhaps I should be more forgiving of your tales, and I will—if you will also be tolerant as I try to clarify everything you always thought you knew about my family, so cruelly victimized by publicists and image consultants. And by their employer, my sister Eleanora.

Here's what you don't know about the part you think you already know.

There were three of us sisters—Eleanora, Lora (that's me), and my twin, Flora. You think you know all about Eleanora. She's a catchword in your world, the name for entire categories of wonderful, happy occurrences. Rags to riches. Sudden wealth. Eternal bliss. A Cinderella holiday! A Cinderella wedding! A Cinderella victory!

How ironic. And how odd that none of you seems even a wee bit suspicious of her, given that she could never even get her story straight. Check it out—you have a slew of different versions, from Disney and his singing bibbity-mice to a truly Grimm version where the dead mother's spirit provides the fancy duds. And there are a zillion variations in between.

Aren't you people ever leery of a story that won't stay put? Don't you have liars over there?

The absolute truth is: Everything you heard about my family is a lie concocted by smarmy Eleanora and her tireless team. Their theory was that the worse we all looked, the better Eleanora looked. The sanitation squad is what I call her managers, although to give them their due, they're good. They've scrubbed her image and kept it squeaky clean throughout the centuries, and I'm the living proof.

At the same time, they've clouded my rep to the point where you're probably wondering yourself why you should believe a word spoken by the nasty and ugly sister.

And having said that, may I digress for a second? When and how and *why* did we become not only vile but also *ugly* in your versions? Read what she told the Grimm boys. We're mean, but we're called "beautiful and fair of face." And then, suddenly, the story changes again and we're hideous. Isn't that overkill? Isn't that proof of her petty meanness? Does she become prettier if she makes her sisters uglier?

And we were sisters, too. It hurts, this stepbusiness. We never thought of her as a hyphenate, a stepanything. She was not yet even toddling when my mother married her father, and she was immediately one of us, the baby of the family. In fact, that was the root of the problem. Mother was so afraid of the evil stepmother cliché, she bent over backward and sideways and did acrobatics to make sure little Eleanora was never deprived of her heart's desire. Which is to say, the child was spoiled rotten, and we were all partially to blame for the misery created by the monster Eleanora became.

Eleanora. You hear that? Not once did I ever hear the name shortened, except when Dad lovingly called her "Ella sits-by-the-fire." I certainly never heard it reversed and perverted so that its bearer became a slavey, a dusty scullery maid-type creature who sat by—or was it in?—the cinders. Cinderella, indeed! Sure, she sat by the fire a lot. She was always whining about being chilly.

Poor fragile wee thing, my mother would say. Baby couldn't wear long underwear like the rest of us, because it was too "rough" for her fair skin. Instead, she'd be wrapped in fine cashmere shawls and allowed to idle by the fire with a magazine and hot chocolate while the rest of us tidied and cooked and studied like normal women.

"What do you think you are," my sister once asked Eleanora, "a princess?" And Eleanora smiled smugly and said—even though she was so small and new to language she couldn't have—shouldn't have—been thinking of the class structure of the kingdom, "I'm in training to be one." My parents laughed. For all I know, one of them taught her the line, but in any case, they were blind to how dead serious she was about it and they were blind to the accompanying outrageous excesses and because they found all of it humorous, they encouraged the delusions of grandeur the baby had from the moment she was potty trained.

It was an insult to suggest that she would have been required to do our scullery work. The actual scullery maid took care of it. All of us were pampered and privileged, only none so much as Eleanora. We were comfortable citizens of Fairyland with lots of household help. Dad was CEO of a lumber business. That job of his was my only point of conflict with him. Dad spent lots of time deciding whether ancient forests could better serve as picnic benches and fences. The results were so awful that I sometimes think that what happened to all of us was retribution for the destruction.

But of course it was not. It was all her handiwork.

Nonetheless, because of Dad, Fairyland was getting patchy. When young men were sent to find what lived in the center of the deep, dark woods, they had to spend years searching for a big enough stand, and then to squabble over which one of them could claim it.

Unicorns, no longer able to hide or to wait for a virgin to spot them, are doing draywork.

And dare I mention what became of the poor elves and gremlins and trolls and fairies? Deep, dark woods were all they knew, and once displaced, left homeless, you found them sitting on the sidewalks holding awkwardly printed pleas. A once-proud people, begging. It's heartbreaking. The only time Dad ever raised his voice to us was after Flora and I picketed his logging firm.

Dad thought Eleanora still more wonderful because she didn't join us on the picket line. She said she was too fragile. Besides, she never joined anybody, anywhere. She was indolent and self-centered, and according to her, nobody was good enough for her. Besides, she would never question the source of the gold that maintained her lifestyle. And quite a style it was.

She invented a self that was so sensitive that only the softest fabrics, the sweetest scents, the most exotic ornaments were bearable for her fair skin and delicate sensibilities. Eleanora was an expensive piece of work, but everybody wanted to please her if only to avoid open warfare, for when Sis wasn't feeling properly and sufficiently attended to, the "frail" girl bellowed and trumpeted with rage. She wasn't above throwing (other people's) things or slapping and clawing, if she thought that would speed up getting what she wanted. A fishwife, a banshee, a shrew—whatever red-faced, howling, foul-mouthed image you favor. That was the baby of our family. Your heroine.

Of course, when we speak of her profound flaws and deformities, we're not talking externals. Those, her face and figure, were outstanding, if predictable, even stereotypical. Hair like spun gold, sapphire eyes, a perfect mouth and nose, long lashes, skin like—you know the rest. Plus a tidy body. All of which items were chemically, surgically, or cosmetically enhanced. Silicone up top, liposuction down below. (We have all of it, too, you know. Costs a fortune. Only difference is it's administered without anesthesia in one second by a witch.) Eleanora was the first person in the entire Kingdom of Fairyland to have a personal trainer. Outside, she was sheer perfection. If you like that prefabricated type, of course.

It wasn't until she considered competing in the Miss Parallel Universe Contest (something she didn't get to do, thanks to the haste with which Prince Charming rushed into marriage) that she assembled the sanitation team. One of them must have clued her in to the idea that civility, even charm, could pay off, be worth the effort.

Although she never included her family in the exercise of same, I still watched with wonderment as she practiced image improvement with the determination she used to work on her waistline and hips with the trainer. I caught her practicing smiles and working with a coach to modulate her voice so it "sparkled" and "pleased." And, of course, she succeeded. She became a professional twinkler. She dazzled and pleased like mad—when she wanted to. Which was only when a person could be of use to her. When she didn't consider a person relevant to her long-term plans, she shut off the power, as if her personality were a great fountain in the sunlight that could be stopped with the flick of a switch, and as if she needed to conserve the water. Within a second there was nothing left but surly Eleanora, screaming at a maid who hadn't picked up the clothing she'd just that second dropped.

None of which is to imply that I felt particularly sorry for Charming when he mistook a professional cutie for a real human being. Frankly, the man's values were so warped he deserved whatever he got. Who uses a few dances as the basis of a betrothal? The invitations went out to every beautiful young girl in the kingdom—and that in itself caused a lot of heartache to those who didn't make the cut. But "beautiful" and "young" were it. End of qualifications. Whatever happened to brains or kindness or wisdom or talent?

Charming's father picked his mother, a former showgirl and great dancer, via the same good ol' have-a-ball method, and frankly, the prince was a prime example of what happens when youth and beauty are the sole breeding requisites. Charming's bulb was dim. His drawbridge ended a few feet short of the moat, if you catch my drift. And I say this not out of sour grapes—Flora and I were invited, as you know. We were up to the royal standards of beauty. We qualified as queenly material.

But what's to become of a kingdom when all the queen needs is looks, the ability to follow klutzy Charming (that's what we called him in grade school) without being tromped by him while you waltzed?

Or maybe it had nothing to do with dancing, just with feet. If you ask me, he didn't give a hoot about any of the above. What interested him, what turned him on was feet. The man was a mentally deficient foot fetishist. A real catch, right? Don't believe me? Consider, please, the lengths he went to, the community resources he employed in search of the foot that fit that shoe.

Which brings us to the heart of the story. The shoe. Of course it wasn't a *glass* slipper! Please! Use your common sense. Even Fairylanders like a bit of logic. I ask you, could a girl dance with anyone if she couldn't bend her foot without shattering her shoe and lacerating herself? The same goes for the golden variation in other stories—you want a future princess to stomp around like one of your stiff-footed robots in shoes that don't give? To suggest, as some do, that the word mistranslated as "glass" really meant "fur" is to suggest that we are all idiots here. Fur shoes are for snow. They make the wearer look like a hairy forest creature—the last image Miss Fragility dreamed of projecting! And did you ever think of how hot such slippers would be, how sweaty-footed a woman would be at a ball held in midautumn when the nights were soft enough to hold an enormous party outside? Do you think the prince would have cherished such a soggy shoe? Would have searched for its wearer?

Those slippers were silver threads encrusted with *diamonds*. You should have heard the carrying on after Eleanora became convinced she needed them! It all had to do with the PR guy's thing about the need to sparkle but it also had to do with research. Eleanora knew a thing or two about Charming's quirks, and that made drop-dead shoes a necessity. How else would she—literally—stand out in a mass of beautiful women? The part of her sales pitch that convinced Dad was that diamonds were recyclable, and that they'd be worn over and over by all of us and earn their purchase.

Do you wonder, then, that we were distraught when she left half our investment and her fashion statement behind her at a party? We're talking considerable cash outlay here to coat her tootsies because her feet weren't nearly as tiny as the spin docs made them out to be. We're talking *lots* of diamonds.

Flora and my shoes were linen, dyed to match our gowns. Not that we complained. Eleanora was the designated glitteree. Dad, whose resources were being drained by his younger daughter, tried to believe in the importance of the shoes. After all, if his daughter married into the royal family, it would be good for business, Eleanora said. He was heavily in debt because of the diamond-crusted slippers, so he figured that maybe they could also help him out of it.

And then, after all that, Eleanora *forgets* she's wearing a goodly portion of the family capital on her feet. Are we pretending a woman running on one high heel and one foot isn't aware of the missing shoe? Of course she knew she'd left it. And what dire event do you think would have happened if she'd turned around long enough to put the shoe back on? Nothing, that's what. But leaving it behind and rushing off into the night were dramatic, eye-catching, headline-grabbing and enough to drive a fellow with a thing for feet mad with desire. All part of her plan.

Midnight was *Dad's* curfew, you see, not some imaginary god-mother's. It was everybody's curfew in the kingdom, an understood thing, the time decent girls went home. Only some of us didn't make a grand fuss about it, and prepared to leave well ahead of time. Some of us weren't so single-mindedly intent on snagging the stupid Charming as to waltz on beyond the last song until the Great Clock chimed. And even so, we all knew that Dad would do no more than express sorrow and disappointment if we arrived home past his deadline.

So the deliberately dropped and ignored slipper was like a smack in the face to the rest of us. And I think she meant it to be just that.

But by the time the story of the shoe and the royal search hit the news next morning, the footwear had undergone heavy-duty revisions. To our amazement, the slipper was described as glass. Diamond footwear was too *elitist,* the spin docs had decided. The people wouldn't like it. The people liked humility, liked luck to be a surprise to its recipients. It wasn't attractive to have planned and schemed and been given everything to get what you wanted. The people had to like her or they wouldn't be content to remain impoverished villagers vicariously enjoying the glories of her ascendancy.

So glass it became.

And worse. A lumber executive was neither royalty nor the deserving hardworking poor. Not sexy, the PR lady said. So out with that. Since Dad couldn't suddenly acquire a title and be promoted, he was demoted to the more acceptable hardworking poor. A woodchopper. And a woodchopper couldn't buy his daughter gowns of gold and slippers of diamonds—or even glass. Hence the invention of the fairy godmother as magical provider. Dad, who was still paying for the diamonds in monthly installments plus plenty of interest, found this insulting. He even tried to have his balance transferred to the fairy godmother, but the credit company couldn't find her address.

Our house was a problem. They couldn't shrink it down to the cottage they'd have preferred, so they did the next best thing and turned Eleanora into the abused, misused, and pitiable resident of the otherwise comfy household.

"Ella-by-the-fire," Dad used to gently chide her when she indolently lolled by it, preening and lording it over us. He made the mistake of mentioning the phrase to a reporter, and damned if Eleanora, who was also there, along with her spin docs, didn't immediately twist the meaning of what he'd said. "Ella-by-the-*cinders*," she corrected the news copy to say. "Cinder Ella." And she gave the reporters a wan, sad, but forgiving smile I'd seen her practice in front of the hall mirror.

The populace adored her. If Cinderella could literally rise from the ashes like a phoenix and become a princess, then they could, too. They accepted every one of her lies, including the business about the pumpkin turning into a chariot! Tell a big enough lie and tell it often, and it'll be believed. It's true in every galaxy. I mean this one defied all common and uncommon sense: Mice into horses? Lizards as footmen? Give me a break! But the headlines said it was so, the TV shows insisted it was true—and ultimately, it was. Sis even pointed at a half-rotted pumpkin she insisted was the actual one used that enchanted night. Then she had it cast in gold. Official "Cinderella's Pumpkin" charms became a fad, and she got a percentage of each sale.

We knew it was a pack of lies, but we were too trusting, too slow on the uptake. It took us much too long to catch on to the meaning of her maneuvers, to comprehend what her master plan meant to us.

Very soon—the engagement was announced as soon as the shoe fit, and they married a few weeks later—little Eleanora was no longer a princess in training, but the real thing. She took her diamond slippers with her, insisting they were now "historic artifacts." I have no idea what that could mean. It's a foreign term. We don't have history. It's pretty much always now here, except for the "once upon a time," which means anytime not exactly now, which is what all time becomes by the time you mention it. What I did understand was that she took the diamonds, all that we had left.

We lived quietly, almost as humbly as our sister's PR men would have had people believe, although not by choice. Things kept going downhill for Dad, and Eleanora's ascendancy to the throne did not increase his business. The princess said it "wouldn't look good" (to whom?—this is an absolute monarchy) if Charming pushed business in Dad's direction.

And it was worse than that, because as Cinderella gave more and more interviews, her horrible lies about her past ruined whatever was left of our reputations. Dad's ethics were called into question, and his business fell off even more. Mother noticed an absence of callers and invitations, and Flora and my social life dwindled to nothingness. Men we'd been seeing backed off and disappeared. People were afraid to associate with us, to be tarred by the same brush. Our house became a target for vandals. Paint was tossed onto it, and windows broken by rocks. And nobody cared.

We weren't even invited to the christenings when each of the two royal sons was born. I actually thought of hiring a woman who lived deep in one of the only surviving woods. She was known for the excellence and efficiency of her curses. But she was terribly expensive and we had no money. Besides, I didn't want to sink to that level.

Our situation became intolerable. We thought of leaving, crossing the Sea of No End and braving dragons and whirlwinds and the edge of everything simply to get away. But I hated giving up without trying a different route first, a last-ditch attempt to regain the dignity and reputation that was rightfully ours.

I took the first steps in suing the princess formerly known as Eleanora for libel and slander.

Now I must say that as time had gone on, although the people of Charming's kingdom adored their fair queen, Charming himself seemed less entranced with every passing day. I'm not sure what precisely provoked it—the new crop of young and beautiful girls, Ella's ever-more-expensive wardrobe, including her fondness now for gem-studded slippers, her mean-spiritedness, which rumor has slipping out more every day, or perhaps it was that talk of her dalliances with a wandering minstrel in a vacant spinning room.

Or maybe Charming had found a fabulous new foot. In any case, the rumbles and creaks of a marriage with dry rot were increasingly heard.

Eleanora was sufficiently distressed to pay her parents her first visit in years. She didn't precisely ask for advice or help, but she did say, with a great show of sniffles, that she and Charming were having difficulties, that she feared he had strayed and that she didn't know what to do about it all, how to be a happy girl again. "Of course," she said, "I should be glad I'm safe economically. Royal families stay together. The mother of the future king is not to be tossed aside."

Well, we hadn't had a whole lot to do, impoverished and friendless as we were, so we'd been watching your planet's "soap stories," I think you call them, or is the term "the news"?—a whole lot more than was healthy. But they'd taught us a great deal, so that I was able to explain that indeed, princesses, even those who were the mothers of future kings, did get put aside and did lose their royal status. In fact, it seemed almost as much of a fad on Earth as the pumpkin necklaces were in our neck of the universe.

"Oh, that's on *Earth*," HRH Cinderella said. "Who cares what those dullards do?"

I thought she should care. "You're right," I said. "We don't divorce Here. Our ways of removing someone wearisome are more creative. The undesired—that'd be you, Sis," I went on—"could be turned to stone, or have toads come out of your mouth when you spoke, or turned into a warty crone or a flounder. Or sent to wander as a beggar for a thousand years. Or—well, why go on? We are an imaginative people, so there's an infinite list of possibilities, all much more fun than Earth's dry way of dividing up assets and making settlements and such."

I must confess, I did get a nasty pleasure out of seeing Eleanora face a future as bleak and destroyed as the one she'd crafted for us.

For reasons of her own, Flora found that moment of silence an apt time to inform our younger sister of the lawsuit I had initiated against her. Flora spoke calmly, but made it clear that all the soon-to-be former princess's dirty secrets and dreadful lies were about to be exposed. Maybe even photos of her presurgery self. Maybe enough ammunition to make the prince put her under the worst spell ever devised. Flora commented further on how interesting it would be when we ultimately were all equals once again.

When Eleanora left, she was pale with shock. For once, Cinderella had listened to what we said. Perhaps she'd even cared.

Now that was the part of the story you thought you knew, but didn't. This is the part of the story you've never heard. But it's all true. It's what happened *after* happily ever.

I should have realized that Eleanora's cunning and my naïveté would make me a loser in any encounter, but I didn't think twice when shortly after the day at our house, she sent a messenger requesting that I come to the palace so we could "talk our problems through." She said she had a solution to all our woes.

Filled with images of familial peace at last, daring even to daydream about a contrite princess admitting to the world that she had fabricated an oppressed past, a princess newly dedicated to protecting her family and introducing her kind and generous and upright family—to her subjects, I set out for the Palace in the family carriage (the one she claimed had sprung from a pumpkin shell). I was admittedly eager to see the royal dwelling, the parts of the castle that tours didn't include, and to meet my nephews. I made my heart happy and expectant, made my eyes look toward the future rather than give in to the bitter undertaste that wondered why it had taken years to gain entry to my own sister's world.

After a tour of the sumptuous living quarters and a brief visit with the two young princes who seemed, not too surprisingly, vacant-eyed and appearing to be having grave difficulties with their schoolwork, Eleanora showed me to a special pavilion where she enjoyed spending time. It was up high, atop a turret, peaceful and private as befits royalty, with only the distant sound of waterfalls and the nearby songs of birds, with blue and white striped awnings providing shade, and great tubs of flowers that must have been tended by a wizard, for I had never seen rainbow-hued blossoms such as these.

A young girl brought us cakes and sweet chilled drinks, then seated herself by the pavilion ledge to wait for further orders. I sat in airy comfort, and when Eleanora spoke, her voice sounded distant and disembodied, another melody for this magical spot.

"I am troubled, as you might understand," she said in a voice so sweet, I would have taken it to be from a stranger, were the servant girl not now asleep and Eleanora not the only other person present. "I fear the lawsuit almost as much as I fear being banished, stripped of my possessions and my sons and sent to wander."

Cinderella was about to become what she'd said she'd been, to experience the unpleasantries she claimed to have already experienced. Interesting, I thought as I sipped the drink that tasted of peach and green flashes. Painfully ironic.

"I believe we are what we decide to be," she said. She paced back and forth along the side of the terrace. She apparently had no fear of tumbling over, although the wall was barely as high as her ankle. Well, I thought, she's used to it up here. As for me, ordinary people like me never had the chance to sit in the sky this way. I felt relaxed, comfortable, and removed from all I had known in my prior life. For a moment, I wondered if there weren't a potion in my peach drink, but it seemed a silly idea, so I let it drift away along with the breeze coming off the far hills, the gentle sweep of the princess's gown as she paced back and forth and the quiet rumbles of the snoring servant.

"I believe that if you can imagine something, you can make it happen," Eleanora said. "I am what I believe I am, and I believe I am a royal princess, the once and future princess."

I closed my eyes and let her words roll over me as I waited for the significant ones, the ones that would tell me how we were going to untangle our various messes. Anyway, I'd heard variations of this speech from her before. But of what use is New Age wisdom in a place where it's always the same age, always long ago and far away or once upon a time, a combination of then and now where new is nothing special?

"I cannot believe that I am destined to leave this behind, to be shamed by my family for harmless exaggerations that elevated all of our status by getting me this position."

I opened one eye at that, to see if she was, perhaps, joking. None of us at the bedraggled, besieged homestead had noticed any elevated status these past few years. But she wasn't kidding. Her expression was tense as she paced. She stopped only when she heard a blare of trumpets. "That means he's on his way," she said. "They do that sort of thing when either of us is about to appear. I find it quite satisfying." Then she resumed her pacing and whatever her monologue was. A plea? An explanation? An apology? I waited, only half listening.

Which is why I missed most of what preceded ". . . only solution I could figure out, and frankly, this will solve all my problems, all at once." I opened both eyes wide. It was supposed to be *our* problems we were solving, wasn't it? Was this going to be the diamond slippers all over again?

I only began to grasp what she meant and what was happening after I heard another blare of trumpets, saw her look down, and then in about three quick movements, roll forward one of the enormous planters that must have been on a platform and then, when it was at the edge, push, hard against the rim of the planter.

Those small motions from the buffed princess were enough to tilt the planter off its platform.

"No!" I screamed as I ran to where she was. But it was too late. The clay and dirt and porcelain mass plummeted down, directly onto the royal head of Charming himself.

"Eleanora," I said with a gasp. "You—on purpose, you—how could—"

At which point she screamed with all the force I remembered from her childhood tantrums. Screamed and screamed and screamed.

The pathetic servant girl awoke and leaped to her feet, rubbed at her eye, and said "Your Highness?" over and over.

"*She killed him!*" Eleanora screamed, pointing at me.

"Me? I tried to stop you from—"

Half the palace's underlings rushed up the stairs to the screaming princess. The other half were audible below, keening over the late Prince Charming.

"She was jealous of us!" Cinderella screamed between sobs. "Hated me! Consumed with bitterness because nobody wanted her. So she—look what she did to my prince!"

Need we go into further detail? Do you think her subjects said, "We believe that your vile stepsister is telling the truth when she protests her innocence?"

Of course they didn't. As always, they believed their golden, shining princess, widowed at such a young and tragic age. They cherished her, protected her, made her absolute ruler until such time as one of her sons would be ready, if either boy could ever pass their exams.

Of course, the libel suit was forgotten. The remainder of the family was too terrified of the new queen's power and wrath to do anything but leave quietly in the middle of the night, and I cannot blame them.

I couldn't leave with them, of course. Instead, I sit in this dungeon to which I am eternally condemned—Cinderella was lenient, granting me life instead of an instant beheading. I am supposed to be grateful as I grow to understand what "ever after" truly means.

But still, with some hope, I ask every set of eyes that peek into my cell to listen to this story and try to right the wrongs that have befallen me. To see Cinderella for what she is and me for what I am. I've asked them to test me—to find wizards or truth potions, to loose spirits who will determine the truth.

All they do is laugh at me. I'm a joke, an easy amusement for the bored. A one-woman sideshow. Jesters do imitations of me at court for after-dinner amusement.

Up there in all her splendor Cinderella is surrounded by adoring crowds, and down here with spiders and lizards for company, I continue as I have through the millennia, unhappily ever after. Still, I tell everyone the story.

Now I've told you. Try this version the next time your kids want a bit of Fairyland as a bedtime tale. Try truth.

Or do you still believe in fairy tales?

Jon L. Breen is the mystery field's leading critic and one of its leading short-story writers as well. One never knows what to expect from a Breen story; sometimes it's funny, sometimes it's dark, and sometimes it's a combination of both, as is the following tale, based on "Clever Hans."

JON L. BREEN

CLEVER HANS

That bear sure knew how to empty a dining room.

Have I got your attention? Good. My creative-writing teacher tells me the opening hook is crucial, and I've gotten to be legendary in class for my great opening hooks. Too bad organizing the rest of the story is not so easy for me. I tend to jump around a lot. So if I get disorganized, you have to forgive me. This is a painful story for me to tell, and that may make it harder to keep on track, but the teacher also says to write what you know.

Actually, I had another hook in mind, but I threw it out: If my mother hadn't believed in horoscopes, it all might have turned out differently. But I don't think that's as dramatic, do you? And it makes me sound like too much of a mama's boy, a Norman Bates or something, you know?

But you want to hear about the bear, right? You probably wonder if the bear is the Clever Hans of the title. He isn't. I think the famous Clever Hans was a trained horse, actually, but I don't remember for sure. Anyway, no, he's not Hans, I'm Hans, and you'll have a chance to judge how clever I was. Truthfully, the bear isn't really a character in the story at all, or not an important one. He's really what the teacher calls a framing device. But I shouldn't be telling you that. I should be showing you.

No, the bear didn't actually come into the dining room. The bear was on the shore, and all the passengers on the *Fjord Explorer* with a few exceptions—I was one of those few—rushed out on deck to watch him. They told me later he was prowling along the bank looking for something to eat, tossing aside heavy boulders as if they were empty cardboard boxes. They told me watching that powerful beast from a safe distance was a thrilling experience. I'd take their word for it. I had other things to think about, like the way this cruise was going. It was almost over, and I was trying to figure out what had gone wrong and what I needed to do to make it right.

When I asked my girlfriend Gretel—yeah, Hans and Gretel, we heard all the jokes, I used to hate them but I miss them now—when I asked her on the cruise, it seemed like a great idea. I took a cruise to Mexico once a long time ago and I really liked it: five meals a day plus a buffet at midnight, plenty of gambling and entertainment, a passenger talent show where I could practice my amateur stand-up act. Gretel had never been on a cruise, but I knew she loved animals, not as pets or caged up in zoos but out in the wild where they could do their thing.

I figured on this cruise, I could do *my* thing. I'd have Gretel all to myself for a week, get her away from that guy in her office who looked like Tom Cruise—more like Ricky Nelson really, but there's not much difference, and I liked to think of our adventure as an anti-Cruise cruise. Mr. Look-alike was always trying to seduce her into going on Sierra Club hikes with him, which she turned down out of loyalty to me, but I know she really wanted to go with him.

I mentioned my mother's confidence in astrology. I've never shared it really, but the day I got the idea to go on this cruise, I was reading the morning paper and as usual took an unserious gander at my horoscope.

I was born on October 17, so that makes me a Libra. My reading for that day said, "Plan future visit to unexplored terrain. Romantic life on the upswing. Gemini featured."

Wow! Now, I told you I don't put a lot of stock in astrology. I just got into the habit of reading the stargazing column every day for fun, like a lot of you do if you'll admit it. I would have moved right on to the funnies without passing Go, but this one horoscope gave me pause because Gretel, you see, is a Gemini. Naturally, I turned next to the Gemini reading, which I quite often did because that's how it works. When you're deeply involved with someone, you read your horoscope and then you read that person's. Anyway, hers said, "You must choose between reality and illusion, the passing and the permanent. Watch for a sign of love and commitment. Libra and Capricorn figure prominently."

That settled it. I happened to know the office Sierra Club hustler was a Capricorn, because Gretel had attended a birthday party for him the week after New Year's. It was clear I had to make a move of love and commitment before old Ricky-Tom had a chance. On the back page of that same section of the paper was this ad for an Alaska cruise, seven days on the 152-foot *Fjord Explorer.* One of the sailing dates was June 18, Gretel's birthday.

I mean, how many omens do you need? The message was too obvious to ignore. I'd give Gretel a birthday present nobody could top—and derail another office birthday party where Tom-Ricky could try to make more inroads. I knew Gretel had vacation days coming, and I knew in her *laissez-faire* office she could take them about whenever she wanted. So I got on the phone to a travel agent and made the arrangements for the two of us, just like that.

It was expensive, sure, but the real-estate business—did I mention I sell real estate?—was in an up period, and I'd had a good month. By that I mean, I'd actually sold a house. Don't ask me how. And anyway, I wouldn't let money considerations keep me from ensuring my future happiness. I once lost a girlfriend because I was too cheap (forgetful, really; "cheap" was her word) to give her anything on special occasions, and when I finally got around to buying her something, a real pretty bracelet, it turned out to be a breaking-up present. I never heard the end of that from my mother.

"Typical bad timing, Hans," she said. "You must have been born with a calendar for a wristwatch," she went on, really rubbing it in. You know how mothers do—and when I tried her line in my stand-up act, it didn't even get a laugh.

So anyway, I wasn't about to make the same mistake again. Another reason the expense seemed worth it was that I happened to know old Cruise-Nelson was a major-league cheapskate, more so than I ever was. I mean, a Sierra Club hike is not exactly an expensive date, is it?

I knew the *Fjord Explorer* was a small one as cruise ships go. One of the selling points of the trip was that she (the ship, I mean) could fit through tighter passages, get closer to shore, and give a better view of the wildlife than the bigger ships. That meant nothing to me—better the local beasts be at a distance while I'm enjoying my midnight buffet—but I knew it would be a big factor for Gretel. When I called her office, I based my pitch on the whales and the eagles and the otters and the puffins and all that good stuff I knew would turn her on. I figured I could also get her off the deck and into other places for my kind of fun. Don't be dirty-minded—well, that, too, sure, but I meant the casino, which wasn't mentioned in the advertising, but I was sure they'd have to have one, even if a little smaller than on my Mexican trip. I could also blow her away in the passenger talent show with my stand-up act, which she'd never had the opportunity to see.

Of course, you already know she accepted the invitation, so there's no need to drag this part out, is there? My teacher sometimes says I spend too much space belaboring the obvious. I told him the names of three best-selling novelists who've made whole careers out of belaboring the obvious, but he wasn't impressed. While it's true short-story markets pay by the word, he told me, you can't get away with as much padding in a short story as you can in a full-length novel. You have to make every word count. Come to think of it, does this paragraph count? I think it does. It helps you understand my frame of mind, and I'm the main character of the story, really the only character with any real definition at all possibly excepting my mother, so I think it counts. I'll leave it in for now, anyway.

That night I called my mother—this is the night of the day I made the cruise reservations; is my time sequence clear?—I called her not just dutifully but also with real eagerness for a change. I thought she'd be pleased to know I'd actually used astrology to plan my next life move. But I should have known she'd find a reason not to be as happy as I'd hoped.

"Hans," she said, in that loving, long-suffering, irritating mother voice, and if you have one or had one you have to know what I mean—and you don't have to be Jewish, because we weren't. "Hans," she said, "you've done it again." That may *sound* like praise, but not the way she said it.

Feed her the straight line. Why not? "What do you mean, Mom? I've done what again?"

"Screwed up your timing, that's what. You've been doing it since you were a kid. It's uncanny how you always manage to do that. It's like when you went for your realtor's license just as the bottom was falling out of the market."

"Mom, things are looking better now. Just last week, I sold a—"

"You sold something, fine, great. And now you're planning to go on vacation just when your career is showing some potential. You're shortsighted, Hans. Why don't you just forget real estate now that it's healthy and study something else? How about black-smithing? The horse is bound to come back, right? Or maybe you can get into typewriter repair."

"Mom, give it a rest!"

No way would she give it a rest. She was launched, and once she was launched, there was no stopping her. She had to trot out all the same old stories, the ones she'd been embarrassing me with all my life. You know how mothers do. At least there was no one else to listen to them this time, just me on the other end of the phone line.

"You always applied the last lesson to the new problem, Hans, and it was never appropriate. Like that time when you were ten and the dog needed a bath and I had to do it because you forgot and you tried to make up for it by giving the cat a bath and you got all scratched and we had to take you to emergency."

"Mom, nobody ever told me—"

"Or that time you were twelve and Mrs. Hooper sent home a note that you didn't participate enough in class and I said you should always speak up and ask questions. The next Sunday you stood up in church and challenged Reverend Wellwood on his ser-mon. It was funny later, I'll grant you, but it wasn't funny at the time, Hans."

"Mom, he was preaching against astrology. I was just standing up for you. And anyway, I'm not twelve anymore. I've learned from my mistakes. This time I planned it right. This time my timing is perfect. You've always believed in those damned horoscopes, and I made my decision based on my horoscope for the day and Gretel's."

She sighed heavily. "Hans, which day's paper did that horoscope come from?"

"Today's."

"Look again."

I reached for the section of the paper where I'd seen the astrology column and the Alaska cruise ad. She was right, I had to admit. It was yesterday's paper. Yesterday's horoscope.

"That's just like you, Hans."

"So what if it is yesterday's? It's still good advice, isn't it?"

"There used to be a song, 'What a Difference a Day Makes.' Get today's. Look at it. Maybe get your money back from the travel agent."

After we hung up, I found that day's paper and turned to the astrology column. The Libra message read, "Be cautious in all arrangements. Taking the wrong fork in the road could mean disaster. Aquarius native offers wise counsel."

Okay, so you're way ahead of me. My mother is an Aquarius. It gets worse. The Gemini message said, "Beware of geeks bearing gifts"—okay, so it didn't say that, but what it did say was, "Romantic prospects cloud, but all will become clear in time. Heart's desire is closer to home."

Closer to home. Like at the next desk, right? You might think all of this was my signal to abort, and in hindsight, I might think so, too. But I'd already told Gretel, and she'd been thrilled by my thoughtfulness. It was too late to turn back now. Anyway, I didn't really believe in this astrology stuff, and I certainly didn't want to give my mother the satisfaction of being proved right. Again. Like always.

The trip was scheduled, and we were going to love the trip, and that was that.

As it turned out, Gretel did love the trip. It wasn't really what

I call a cruise, though. No casino. No talent show. No TV in the cabins. No midnight buffet, though you could get a cup of coffee and a cookie outside of normal mealtimes. What there was mainly was a bunch of naturalist lectures by zoologists, botanists, geologists—all the stuff that bored you out of your skull in school.

Of course, sharing a cabin was part of the deal. It's not as if we didn't already know each other pretty intimately. Sharing that small space for a week, it turned out, was tough. For one thing, a couple of bunks on a little cruise ship are not exactly your basic king-size bed, and bumps, bruises, and leg cramps can put a crimp in your sexual ecstasy. That the toilet and the shower shared a small space behind a semitransparent door didn't seem to bother Gretel all that much, but it bummed me out after a while, bathrooms being a more intimate and private place than even bedrooms.

We never had a table to ourselves in the dining room. They were all set for six or more, and passengers were encouraged to mix with different people at every meal. Gretel loved to chat to the other passengers, who all seemed to be tree-hugging, bird-watching *National Geographic* types like herself.

Anytime you were relaxing or taking a shower or maybe in the middle of telling a good joke to another passenger, some news of a wildlife sighting would come over the public address and everybody would go charging up on deck, binoculars swinging around their necks, cameras at the ready, to see the latest wonder. Unless it was when there was food on the table, like with the bear, I'd join the rush, too. I was a good sport. And I have to admit the first time I saw a whale breach—that means leaping all the way out of the water—it was quite a sight. But once I'd seen it, I just wanted to go below to the bar and have a drink, but all the rest of them, Gretel included, wanted to keep watching the damn whales in the hope of seeing *another* one breach. Or the same one breach again. I mean, if you've seen one . . . but if I have to explain it to you, you'll never understand.

The whales also did something called lunge feeding, a sort of synchronized swimming event for marine mammals where a bunch of them would all come out of the water in unison. Impressive, sure, but once they'd done it, they'd done it, and all you could hope for was that they'd do it again. Like a comic telling the same joke over and over, or a band playing the same song.

As you can tell, I didn't relate to all this, and while I was getting bored, Gretel was bonding like crazy with the other passengers, which was fine when they were old married couples but not so fine when they were young guys. I should say, when they were one young guy. He didn't look much like Tom Cruise or Ricky Nelson, more like Jay Leno, but the thing was he knew the name of every damn bird and sea mammal in Alaska. He was just a passenger, and the naturalists would ask *him* questions. I had Gretel in my cabin, but he had her too much of the rest of the time, and I didn't really have her that much in my cabin, if you know what I mean.

Don't get me wrong here. I'm not so fiendishly jealous that I resented Gretel making a friend with another outdoor enthusiast. But this Leno look-alike—Joe Griswold was his name—had his eye on more than the wonders of nature. He was a major-league womanizer who started leering in the presence of any attractive female, passenger or crew. Why the women couldn't see around it, I don't know—must have been his nature-lover act—but there were some other boyfriends and husbands on board who were well aware of what he was up to. There was a retired guy, a white-haired Australian tycoon traveling with a blond trophy wife, who seemed especially bothered by Joe's attentiveness to his much younger bride.

One day, we took what they call a "flight-seeing" excursion, where you get into a dinky little prop plane with pontoons and fly over a glacier. The whole idea made me nervous, but once we got up there and I realized the pilot could land on anything and the only thing that could really get us killed was a heart attack on the part of the pilot, the flying part didn't worry me that much. But I had something else to worry about. Somehow Joe Griswold wound up in the seat next to Gretel—something about helping her with her camera—with me parked in the row behind. They were in cramped quarters, and whenever there was something to see down below, they'd lean to the left or lean to the right, even though the pilot would turn the plane so you could see the same thing out of the opposite window a few seconds later. When Joe leaned across her and brushed her breasts with the back of his hand, it was ostensibly to get himself a shot of a bunch of seals lying on the ice below, but I know he had other features of the natural world in mind.

Almost every day, we went out in these little rubber boats called Zodiacs that held about a dozen people. As if our ship couldn't get us close enough to the shore, the Zodiacs would get us even closer. For me, one Zodiac ride had about the same effect as one breaching whale. Been there, done that, have another drink. But I had to climb into my bright orange life vest and make all the Zodiac outings just to stand guard over Joe and make sure he wasn't after rarer sightings than the bald eagle.

Gretel started to sense my jealousy, and one afternoon her natural serenity did a Jimmy Hoffa and she as much as told me to stay back on the ship if I wasn't prepared to enjoy the total Alaskan experience in a spirit of discovery. That was how I happened to miss the trip out on the Zodiac where an iceberg broke in half only a few feet from the boat, a scary and exciting photo op the whole ship was talking about for the rest of the day. I acted sorry I missed it—of course, I was anything but—and Gretel decided she'd been misjudging me. But our truce was a precarious one.

I was so desperate, I even called my mother when we stopped in the little town of Haines and had access to telephones. She wasn't much help, since I didn't even know what sign Joe Griswold had been born under. She could read me my own horoscope, though, this one from a *weekly* paper, which meant it ought to keep for a couple of days. My Libra message read, "Whatever comes to you, you will return in greater quantity." What that was supposed to mean applied to my current problem, I couldn't imagine. I stuck around for the obligatory lecture about my timing—I'd even managed to call Mom during her favorite TV show, though I think she got more pleasure from haranguing me than she would from Oprah and Geraldo mud wrestling.

So that's the end of the flashback, and we've backtracked to my framing device, not to confuse you with too many technical terms, and you probably think this is about the end of the story. I hope you're not too eager for it to end. In stand-up, you always try to leave the audience wanting more, and my teacher says that applies to short-story writing, too.

Anyway, we heard about the sighting of the bear over the public address, and sure enough Joe and Gretel ran out on deck with the rest of the sheep to drink in the glories of nature. Joe's camera whacked me upside the head as he leaped out of his seat, and he didn't even apologize. I felt like picking up an empty chair and clubbing him with it—that would be returning what comes to me in greater quantity, wouldn't it? Anyway, I stayed behind to enjoy my dessert. I could have enjoyed everybody else's, too, if I'd wanted to, but I wasn't really that hungry.

That night, the whole ship had a picnic on the beach. Sounds terrific, huh? Maybe you've never navigated over a pebbly Alaskan beach and tried to find a comfortable place to sit on a fallen pine log. These picnics weren't always possible on the Alaska trips, they told us, given the cold temperatures and changeable weather conditions and all, so we'd been lucky. The crew brought all the food and drink to the beach and we all sat around a fire and sang old camp songs. Only the free-flowing wine made it tolerable.

As it got darker, more and more of the passengers went back to the ship on one of the Zodiacs that were running a constant shuttle service to and from—but not Joe and Gretel. They were in their element schmoozing with the naturalists and even some of the dining-room stewards whose work for the day was done. My bet was even if it turned out to be entirely a crew party except for the three of us, we'd still be there—Joe and Gretel didn't want to leave the party, and I didn't dare. The old Aussie retiree was in the same spot I was. He was playing life-of-the-party, leading the group around the campfire in "Waltzing Matilda" and "Tie Me Kangaroo Down" while watching his wife's activities among the younger crew members with a suspicious eye.

Then Gretel stood up from the pine log we were all sitting on and announced she needed to make a trip to the ship to use the toilet and retrieve a sweater, but she assured us she would be back. When she stood up, she discovered her shorts had picked up some pine sap from the log, but she was so entranced with the Alaskan experience, she didn't even care.

Joe and I both offered to accompany her back, but she told us not to be silly, to use the time to get to know each other better. That was the last thing we wanted, of course, but Joe and I could just go behind a tree to perform the same function Gretel was going back to the ship for—the naturalists told us it was bad for the ecology, of course, but you'd have to be a pretty serious environmentalist to take a Zodiac back to the ship just for a ten-second leak.

As you know, guys don't go to the toilet in pairs or packs the way women do. But when Joe got up to look for a secluded spot, it occurred to me he might take evasive action, maybe find his way to a Zodiac and continue his pursuit of Gretel back on the ship. So I joined him on his safari, saying it might not be safe to venture into the underbrush alone, and that was how it happened we left the beach at the same time. As I found out later, some people saw us go off together. What nobody else seemed to have seen was that the trophy wife was away at the same time, and after concluding his business, Joe excused himself from me and moved toward the Australian firecracker with a wink that could have only one meaning: I could have Gretel to myself.

By the time Gretel got back to the beach, several more Zodiacs had come and gone, shuttling passengers, crew, provisions, and equipment. She found me sitting alone on our log and asked me where Joe had gone. I told her I didn't know. Maybe he'd decided to go back to the ship and turn in. Must be his age catching up with him, I suggested. Then I got her another glass of wine—just in time; the bartender was getting ready to lug his stuff back to catch the next Zodiac—and suggested that the naturalist with the guitar play "Eleanor Rigby."

When we got back to the *Fjord Explorer* with the last group from the beach, the second mate asked us if we'd seen Joe. It seemed his key was still hanging on the board where we had to leave them whenever we left the ship. That was how they could tell which passengers were still ashore. I told the mate I was sure

Joe must have come back on one of the Zodiacs, but I said I hadn't actually seen him board one.

The ship couldn't leave the beach with a passenger missing, so the crew spent a couple of hours searching with flashlights. They finally found him. It appeared somebody had crushed his skull with a big rock and hidden the body, not well enough, among the boulders and fallen trees. Several passengers and naturalists fingered me as having been seen with Joe. I mentioned the Australian lady, but apparently nobody had noticed her absence, which seemed as unlikely as it was unlucky.

I swore I hadn't killed him, swore to it in court, where they came up with all kinds of weird theories to help convict me. It seemed I'd spent the whole voyage making cracks to other passengers about what a creep Joe Griswold was. I'd even threatened to cut him a new one on the other end. I remembered the comments as light, amusing; they repeated them as sinister and menacing. Not only was I jealous of his attentions to Gretel, the prosecution said, but I was a frustrated comic who naturally resented somebody who looked like Jay Leno. My lawyer wanted to work that into an irresistible-impulse insanity defense, but I didn't let him, insisting on my innocence to the very last day of the trial.

The day the jury went out, my mother called to tell me my Libra message for the day said I'd be vindicated. That evening I had an argument with one of the guards over who played the second Darren on *Bewitched.* I said Dick Sargent. Somebody looked it up, and I was right, so I guess that was my vindication for the day. The jury came back the *next* day and found me guilty. The Libra message for that day called for an impending move.

So I moved on to the state prison, and here I am taking a creative writing class and hoping they'll catch up with the real killer of Joe Griswold and set me free. I hear there was a murder down in Australia, on that train that goes across the Great Nullarbor Plain in a straight line. Some old guy killed a fellow passenger who was too attentive to his young wife. I'd love to know the guy's name. Could it be our friend from a cruise? Could he be a serial cuckold, who got away with it last time but got caught this time? I can sympathize with him, but if he's going down for murder in Australia anyway, maybe he can get me off the hook here. Needless to say, I'm not counting on anything.

My creative writing teacher says I'm getting better. I'd like to be a pro someday, but he says that may be setting my sights unrealistically high. I should just write for my own pleasure and for its value as therapy and eventually maybe as evidence of my rehabilitation. He says prison authors go in and out of fashion, and they aren't that hot at the moment. People are really down on criminals.

Don't feel bad about it, he says. Just a matter of bad timing.

In the past decade, Joan Hess has built a best-selling readership that grows with the appearance of each new novel. Arkansas is her turf, and her weapon of choice is the pointed barb. She reads like a combination of Erma Bombeck and H. L. Mencken. There's a lot more going on in her books than most critics have been smart enough to find. Her short fiction is also richly textured. The following story is a prime example.

JOAN HESS

Heptagon

"Miss Neige," I say, tactfully using the name she prefers, "please try to open up to me before our time is over. I can understand how difficult this must be for a young woman such as yourself, but we must talk about it."

"Are you bored, Doctor? I've been many things, but never bored. Shall I entertain you with a narrative of the murder?"

I struggle to reply in a neutral tone. "Let's go back just a bit. The information I was given has led me to think that your childhood was stressful."

"I think that might be too mild a description for the torment inflicted on me by my stepmother. My real mother killed herself when she found out that my father was unfaithful to her. He claimed she died of tuberculosis, but we know better."

" 'We'?"

"You and I, Doctor." She settles back on the couch and puts her hands behind her neck, her elbows jutting sharply. From this angle I can see the nerves bunched in her neck like metal cables.

"In the mornings," she continues in an oddly detached voice, "I'm grumpy until I've had my coffee. She was always jabbering at me, pecking at me like a magpie. All I wanted was peace and quiet. There's nothing wrong with that, is there?"

"I shouldn't think so," I reply, writing the word "grumpy" in my notebook. It's a peculiar word coming from someone so young and well educated.

"She didn't agree, and was forever telling me that being

grumpy wasn't attractive. She knew how much she annoyed me—which is exactly why she did it!"

I take a moment to answer. "Miss Neige, we're not here to decipher your stepmother's motives. You are what concerns us in this session. How did you feel when your stepmother said these things?"

Her lips twitch with repressed anger. "How do you think I felt? Do you expect me to say I was grateful? I assure you I was not. She criticized me continually, but always with such subtlety that my father never noticed. He would beam at her as if she were the most beautiful and generous person he'd ever met. There were times I wanted to slap the smile off his face and make him see what she was doing to my self-confidence with her sly digs about my appearance or lack of a social life."

"You lacked a social life? I would have thought an attractive young woman like yourself would have been surrounded by suitors."

"Then you would have been wrong. As a young child, I was bashful."

"You—bashful?" I say, making a note of the word.

"After my mother's death, I rarely spoke to anyone other than the household servants. Since I was taught by tutors, I had no opportunity to make friends. By the time I was twelve, I was bashful so much of the time that I was unable to engage in ordinary social interaction. Any persistent effort to force me to do so gave me hives that only bedrest and antihistamines could relieve. Oh, yes, I was bashful. She found that *très amusant.*"

"You seem quite articulate," I say encouragingly.

"I'm not always bashful now," she says. "Despite her twisted pleasure in my disability, I eventually overcame it and made a few friends. She was quick to point out that my father's wealth and power were my two best attributes, but I refused to listen to her. I persuaded my father to give me a clothing allowance so she could no longer dress me in unflattering smocks and bulky sweaters."

I feel a distinctly unprofessional pang of sympathy for my patient. She has a lovely face, with luminous green eyes and a heart-shaped mouth. I have yet to see her smile, but I suspect she has even white teeth and a dimple. Her voice is so melodious I expect her to burst into song at any moment.

Aware that she is waiting for me to respond, I say, "It sounds as if your life improved at this point."

"Oh, yes, there were times when I was happy. When John Earl asked me to accompany him to the Harvest Ball, I was almost ecstatic. I bought a new dress and spent the day at the salon having a manicure, pedicure, and facial. The proprietor himself did my hair." She sits up and pushes her raven hair above her head in a sloppy cascade; I must admit the effect is beguiling. "While I was getting dressed for the ball, she came into my room and told me I looked like a prostitute. I replied that I was happy and that she was jealous of my youth and beauty. She pushed me, so I pushed her back. Before I realized what was happening, we were kicking and scratching each other, and our screams brought my father to the door."

"What did he do?" I ask softly.

"She began to cry and accused me of attacking her for no reason. My father chose to believe her filthy lies and ordered me to stay in my room for the rest of the night. John Earl was told on the doorstep that I'd changed my mind about going to the ball."

"You must have been disappointed."

"I certainly was no longer happy," she says with a trace of sarcasm. "I remained in my room for a month, refusing to go downstairs for meals. I was sleepy all of the time, as if I were under the influence of a hypnotic spell. My stepmother took to standing over the bed and telling me that I wasn't sleepy, but instead sluggish and self-indulgent. I couldn't help it, Doctor. Some mornings I'd force myself to get dressed, but then I'd realize I was sleepy and simply lie down on the bed."

"Do you think you might have been depressed?"

"I was sleepy, not depressed! Why can't you listen more carefully? My dreams became increasingly bizarre, until the line between fantasy and reality became blurred. Did John Earl really climb the wall to my bedroom window and plead with me to escape? Did my mother come into the room and tell me I could go to the ball if I'd wear her wedding dress? Maybe I'm sleepy now—

and you're a figment from a nightmare! If I snap my fingers, will you vanish in a puff of smoke? Shall we find out, Doctor?"

Although our fifty minutes are up, I am reluctant to end the session while she's agitated. I excuse myself, go into the reception room, and tell my secretary that I'm going to continue the session and will lock up the office when I'm finished. Upon my return, I find Miss Neige sitting on the edge of the couch, her purse in her lap and her eyes red and watery.

"Would you care for a glass of water?" I ask her.

"No," she says curtly as she puts her purse on the floor and lies back.

I want to assure her that she is not the first patient to lose her composure on my couch, but I am leery of upsetting her with unwanted solicitude. "Well, then," I say as I resume my seat, "shall we continue, Miss Neige?"

"Where was I?"

"I believe you were discussing the period in your life when you were sleepy. . . ."

"Or so I thought until one of the kitchen maids saw my step-mother putting a few drops of something in my morning coffee. The girl smuggled the vial to me, and I quickly determined that it contained an opiate. I hadn't been sleepy, Doctor—I'd been dopey as a result of her insidious scheme to further discredit me in my father's eyes. I gave the maid a few coins and asked her to replace the vial and say nothing."

"Dopey," I write in my notebook, circling it several times. Again, a strange choice of words for a sheltered young woman such as Miss Neige. I add "happy" and "sleepy." A pattern seems to be forming, as yet too indistinct for me to comprehend. "What did you do?" I ask.

"I poured the coffee out my window each morning and contin-ued to lie in bed with a languid expression on my face. After a time, my system was cleansed and I was no longer dopey. She never realized, as she prowled around my room, that I was watching her. She tried on my jewelry and smoothed my skin creams on her wrinkled face as if they could transform her. If my father had seen her scowling into the mirror on the wall, he would have realized what an old hag she really was, but she'd poisoned his mind."

"Surely he would have been concerned if you'd told him about this opiate."

"She was much too shrewd," says Miss Neige. "Somehow she discovered that I'd learned of her scheme. She accused the kitchen maid of theft and fired her, then took the vial to my father and claimed that she'd found it in my room. She convinced him that I needed to be sent to a hospital to overcome my dependency. Before I could present my side of the story, I was taken from my home and placed in a room with barred windows and an iron cot. Sadistic nurses watched my every move through a slot in the door. Other patients pinched me until my arms were covered with welts and bruises. I was allowed one hour a day to walk on the grounds, always accompanied by an attendant with thick, flabby lips and an insolent smirk. Despite my revulsion, I feigned fondness for him and persuaded him to help me escape."

"That was very clever," I murmur.

"I thought so, until I ventured beyond the fence and realized I had nowhere to seek refuge. I was afraid to be seen walking along the road into town, so I went into the woods, hoping I might chance upon an abandoned dwelling in which I could take shelter. The attendant had provided me with enough food to survive for several days. As soon as the furor over my escape had abated, I could steal clothes off a line, disguise myself as a country girl, and seek employment in some menial capacity. It was hardly the life I'd envisioned as a child, but it was all I could think to do until my circumstances changed."

"Did you find such a dwelling?"

"I do believe my mouth is getting dry. May I please have a cup of water?"

I go into the reception room to ask my secretary to bring a carafe of cold water and glasses, but she has left for the day. As before, when I return, Miss Neige is upright and clutching her purse. I see on her face the steely expression that must have been there when she was fighting her way through the woods, determined at all costs to take control of her life.

I offer her a cup of water.

She snatches it out of my hand and greedily drinks. When the cup is empty she says, "Shall I continue?"

"Please take your time, Miss Neige."

"As the sunset faded, I came upon a small cabin situated near a stream. There were no lights on inside or any indication that it was inhabited, yet I was leery of approaching. I was taught to speak French and play the harpsichord, but training in self-defense had never been included in my curriculum. Neither had breaking and entering—but it's not nearly as difficult as one might assume."

"And was the cabin empty?" I ask.

"Yes. It was very dark by then, and I had no candle or lantern. I found a pile of filthy blankets in one corner. I made a bed, ate some of the bread and cheese in my bag, and then curled up and fell asleep of utter exhaustion."

"And the next morning?"

"I was able to take a better look at my temporary home. The only furniture consisted of a crude, hand-hewn table and two benches. Bits of crockery and cutlery were scattered on the floor. I gathered them up and washed them in the stream, then did the same with the blankets and hung them on branches to dry. I spent the rest of the day whisking the floor with a clump of weeds, scrubbing grime off the windowpanes, and searching the woods for edible berries. I stayed near the cabin in case I heard bloodhounds and needed to retrieve my remaining food and flee once again. I never did, though, and came to believe that when my father and stepmother were informed of my escape, she convinced him it was for the best to leave me out on my own. I'm quite sure she secretly hoped I would be killed by a wild animal or expire from hypothermia. She would have liked that. I could envision her standing by my grave, weeping for my father's benefit while considering which trinkets of jewelry to take from my dressing table drawer."

I make a small noise meant to assure her that she has my attention. "And . . . ?"

"I knew a diet of berries and water would not sustain me much longer. The berries, in particular, made me sneezy. I was forced to rip up my slip for handkerchiefs."

"Berries made you sneezy?" I add the word to my growing list. "Isn't it more likely that you were allergic to mold inside the cabin?"

"Does it matter why I was sneezy?" she retorts with a sardonic smile. Contrary to my expectations, her teeth are as sharp as those of a fox.

"Please continue," I say, disconcerted.

"Only if you'll stop contradicting me. I do not care to be labeled by someone who knows so little about me. It's very rude, Doctor."

"My apologies, Miss Neige."

"And you understand that I was sneezy?"

"I'll record it in my notebook."

"All right, then. Keeping the cabin as a base, I commenced to explore in all directions until I found an isolated farmhouse several miles away. I stole potatoes and turnips from bins in the barn. A week later I returned, waited until the family left, and went into the house. I filled a pillowcase with candles, matches, packages of beans and rice, and a loaf of bread. I could have taken more, but it was vital that the residents remained unaware of my unauthorized visits."

"You went back several times?"

"Oh, yes, and also to other farmhouses I'd discovered. Often the houses were occupied, forcing me to rely on what I found in barns and outbuildings. But every now and then fortune smiled on me and I was able to return to my cabin with the makings of a veritable banquet. Who would have thought I'd make such a fine thief?"

It is not difficult to imagine her concealed by shadows, spying on farmers and their families. I make a noncommittal noise.

"Don't you agree, Doctor," she continues in an amused voice, "that someone of my breeding should be totally inept in basic survival skills?"

"Yes, indeed," I murmur, noticing that it's beginning to grow dark outside. I consider turning on my desk lamp, but decide to wait. "Perhaps we should move along, Miss Neige."

"As you wish."

I expect her to speak, but she gazes at the window. My tape recorder is whirring like an insect in a distant field, ready to capture our voices so I will be able to provide an accurate transcript to the prosecutor. I decide to venture into treacherous areas. "This must have been a lonely time, Miss Neige."

"But it wasn't, not at all," she says heatedly. "They began to arrive. First one, than another—each demanding a meal, a place to sleep, clothing. It was draining. I was obliged to become the nurturing figure, much as yourself. I was the doctor, the one who murmured much as you've been doing and encouraged them to relax. I had no choice. They insisted on calling me 'Doc' despite my protests."

" 'They'?" I am bewildered. There is nothing in the police report to indicate there were other occupants at the scene of the crime.

"Yes!" she snaps. "The cabin became quite crowded. I was forced to scavenge for food several times a week to keep them fed. The blankets had to be washed every day. I would leave, and when I came back, find that the fire had been doused or the table overturned. Things had been peaceful before they came, and I begged them to go away."

"Why didn't you leave?" I ask.

Miss Neige jerks around and stares at me. "And go where? Back to the hospital? Back to my stepmother's home? I had no place to go—and I wasn't willing to abandon my idyllic little cabin simply because they were there. It was crowded, but not intolerable. It's not as if we were running into each other." Her laugh reminds me of the caustic echo of a crow. "How could we do that?"

"Who were 'they'?" I ask hesitantly.

"You are such a fool."

"I am?" I don't know how else to respond.

"Yes, you are. Why should you be surprised at the number of people living in my cabin in the woods? Is there a reason I should have been alone? Did I not deserve companionship and company? Am I as ugly as my stepmother says?"

"Dear, no," I say as I hastily stand up. "You are a charming young woman, and as I said, most attractive. I'm just not clear about the . . . arrangements at the cabin."

"The murder." She says this flatly. "That's what you want me to talk about."

"Would it be too painful to discuss?"

"No." Her voice rises in pitch. "That afternoon I was sleepy, so I went out by the stream to take a nap. I made myself a nice bed of pine branches, and was dreaming of servants and food on platters when he accosted me. I awoke to find his lips pressed against mine, his hands on my shoulders, his hair dangling in my face like a cobweb. Blinded by terror, I grabbed a stone and defended myself. Only when I came to my senses did I discover that it was poor John Earl sprawled on the ground, his skull crushed by my repeated blows. Before he died, he managed to tell me that he'd spent months searching for me, starting at the hospital and then questioning local farmers until he'd been able to narrow down the area."

"How distressing."

"An interesting word, Doctor. I murdered the only man who ever pretended that he loved me. I'm not sure he really did, considering my father's position. He might have. Then again, I didn't really murder him. I'd just been jolted out of a dream, and I suspect I was dopey. Dopey can be very unpleasant. Grumpy can, too, although he is rarely violent."

Her green eyes are flickering like strobe lights. Her expression shifts as quickly; a smile becomes a smirk and then a scowl. I begin to understand what thus far has sounded like a fairy tale of a little girl, a wicked stepmother, and a cozy cottage in the woods.

"Miss Neige," I say, "our time is up."

"Call me Blanche," she says as she picks up her purse and opens it, then stares at its contents with a curiously complaisant smile. "Bashful came up with the name. He was smitten with the French tutor, although he could never bring himself to confess his feelings to her. Poor, tongue-tied Bashful. Not even Doc could help him."

I clear my throat. "I think you're as aware of your condition as I am. You have what's known as multiple-personality syndrome.

We can work together to help you find a way to balance these distinctive aspects of your—"

I stop because she's taking a knife out of her purse.

"There's one you haven't met, Doctor," she says in an insolent drawl. "Say hello to Nasty."

Bill Crider is another multiple-genre author who has written in the mystery, Western, and horror fields. His best-known (and probably best-loved) books are the gently humorous Sheriff Dan Rhodes mysteries. Some of that gentle wit is on display here, in a revision of "Little Red Riding Hood" from the wolf's point of view.

BILL CRIDER

IT HAPPENED AT
GRANDMOTHER'S HOUSE

I never asked to be a werewolf. Oh, sure, it has its compensations, but not nearly enough of them.

Take adolescence, for example. You think zits and raging hormones are a problem? Throw in the fact that you turn into a wolf every time there's a full moon, and you have a guy who's really in trouble when it comes to getting dates.

Some of you women are thinking, "Hey, no big deal. I've dated guys like that." No, you haven't. I'm not responsible for what the more or less normal teenage guy does when the moon is full, which I'm sure is bad enough. But for me it was a lot worse. Trying to convince someone that you just have a bit of excessive chest hair isn't the best way to establish a romantic relationship.

Yes, it's not easy being a teenage werewolf, and if you've ever seen that movie with Michael Landon, you know what I mean. Then there's that other movie, *Teen Wolf.* Sure, everyone loves Michael J. Fox because he's such a great basketball player, but sports never worked out that well for me. You think it's hard to dribble or throw a pass with your hands? Just try it with paws sometime.

But this isn't about a movie. It's about real life, or what passes for it in my case, and about something that happened to me when I was in high school.

It all started with a girl named Marie Grayson. I was very interested in girls at the time, in spite of the difficulties caused by my unusual proclivities, and this one had red hair. I was always a sucker for redheads, at least when I wasn't Changed. Then I was a sucker for schnauzers, but that's another story. There was one once . . . Never mind.

Back to the redhead. Marie. She also had that perfect complexion that sometimes goes along with red hair. Rhonda Fleming had it. Not to mention Maureen O'Hara. And she had long legs and green eyes and soft breasts—at least I imagined they were soft. I certainly never got close enough to judge for myself.

I did get close enough to talk to her, though, and that was good enough for me. I never really expected any more. Just an occasional smile and a pat on the head—that's all I asked.

And that's all I got, until the time, possibly inspired by having drunk one too many root beers, I talked a little bit too much and told her the truth about myself.

She laughed, of course. Wouldn't you?

"A werewolf?" she said. "You?"

We were sitting in my car, a nowhere-new 1970 Ford Fairlane, at the Root Beer Stand: "All drinks served in frosted mugs!" She was leaning against the passenger door so hard I thought she might fall out. It might have been my imagination, but I thought she was leaning even harder since my unguarded confession.

I took a sip of my third root beer from the no-longer frosty mug and nodded sadly. "That's right. A werewolf. The genuine article. It's my grandfather's fault."

"Your grandfather?"

"Right. He was the one who went to Tibet and got bitten. I guess he had no idea a bite like that could affect his genetic structure. Anyway, that's how it happened."

Her green eyes sparkled in the light from all the bulbs lining the Root Beer Stand's awning. She was drinking pink lemonade.

"So your father's a werewolf, too."

"No," I said. "My mother."

"Oh, good grief."

"I know it's hard to believe," I said. "But it's true." I took another sip of root beer. "She'd kill me if she knew I'd told."

"Kill you?"

"Well, I don't mean that literally. At least I don't *think* I do. You never can tell what might happen during the Change."

"Tell me about that," she said.

"Well, once she Changed a day early. It can happen. And, of course, she hadn't taken the usual precautions—"

"I don't mean about what your mother might do to you. I mean about the Change. That's what I want to hear about."

"Oh."

"You don't have to say it like that. I care about you and what might happen when your mother Changes too soon, but what I'd really like to know is what it's like."

So I told her. It's pretty unpleasant, and I won't go into it here, except to say that it hurts. A lot. Every part of you hurts, even your hair.

"So I've decided never to have children," I finished. "It wouldn't be fair. I wouldn't want them to go through all the stuff I've had to."

She looked at me and said, "You really believe it, don't you. You really believe that you're a werewolf."

"Why not? You think it's some kind of joke? It's not. I could prove it to you, but I won't. I'd never let anyone see me Change."

"I don't think I'd enjoy it, anyway."

"I don't enjoy it, that's for sure."

She finished off her lemonade and handed the empty mug to me. I set it on the tray that the carhop had attached to my lowered window.

Marie gave me a speculative look. "So if you're really a werewolf—"

"I am."

"—if you're really a werewolf, you're kind of like a dog, I guess."

"What's that supposed to mean?"

"You don't have to look that way. I didn't mean anything bad. I just assumed that you'd have some kind of special senses. Like being able to find your way back home if you were accidentally moved across country."

Obviously she'd been watching too many Disney movies. On the other hand, she might have a point.

"I probably could," I said.

"And I'll bet you have a great sense of smell."

"White Shoulders," I said.

"Thank you."

"I was talking about perfume."

"Oh. I'm not wearing perfume."

"I didn't mean you. I meant the girl in the car next to us. On your side."

She glanced over her shoulder. "There's an empty space next to us."

"But there's a car next to the space."

"Okay. I see it, and there's someone in it, all right. But how do I find out if you're right about the perfume?"

I shrugged. "You could ask her."

So she did. When she got back in the car, she was looking at me with something that might have been respect, but it might also have been suspicion.

"This isn't some kind of setup, is it?" she said.

"Why would I want to set you up?"

"I don't know. Guys do stuff like that. And this werewolf business just seems . . . weird."

"You should see it from where I am."

She didn't say anything, just sat and leaned against the door and thought about something. I put my empty mug on the tray. The carhop came and picked up the tray and her measly tip.

"There's someone I'd like for you to meet," Marie said after a while.

"Meet? Why?"

"I think she'd find you interesting. And maybe there's something you could help her with."

"Her?"

"My grandmother," she said.

*   *   *

There are all kinds of neighborhoods in Houston. When you drive north over the Pierce Elevated and look to the right, you see the concrete canyons of downtown. Towering office buildings glitter so close to the highway that it seems you could almost touch them if you stuck your arm out the window.

Look to the left, however, just a little farther along, and it's a different story. You can see squatty old buildings with shattered windows and decaying houses that look as if they haven't been painted since the stock market took that little tumble back in 1929.

Marie's grandmother's house wasn't in either of those places. It was out near the Galleria, in another kind of area, one that had practically been out in the country when the house was built but that was now covered up by apartment houses and condos.

It was a low ranch-style that sat on a big corner lot, shaded by oak trees with branches so heavy and thick with leaves that there was almost no grass growing beneath them. The smooth, nearly bare ground was covered with tiny acorns, and a couple of squirrels chased each other around the trunk of one of the trees.

The squirrels were funny, and I smiled, which was a mistake. The smile pulled my lips back from my teeth just a little and gave Marie the wrong idea.

"You're not going to do anything . . . funny, are you?"

I looked at her, then at the squirrels. "I'm not going to jump out and chase them, if that's what you mean. The moon won't be full for another three days. I've never Changed that early before, so you don't have to worry."

"Oh. Well, I'm sorry I said anything. I didn't mean to offend you."

"I'm not offended," I told her, but my feelings were hurt all the same.

Marie reached into the backseat for the paper bag she'd brought with her, and we got out of the car. The bag was heavy, and Marie cradled it in both arms as we went up the concrete walk to the front door. The walk, which never got any sunshine, was dark with mildew, and the bronze doorknob was black with corrosion. Since Marie's hands were full, I rang the bell.

I don't know what I was expecting. Probably someone like my own grandmother, who was in her late sixties but who looked around ninety. At least to me.

Marie's grandmother wasn't like that at all. In the heavy shade of the oaks, she didn't look much older than Marie. Her hair was almost white, but not white like my grandmother's. It was blond, the kind of blond you bought at the Walgreens in a peroxide bottle. And she was hardly wrinkled at all. Her eyes were green, like Marie's, and she was wearing a shirt that showed off her breasts almost as well as her tight Levi's showed off the rest of her. She was also wearing Chanel No. 5, but then I'd suspected that ever since we'd parked at the curb.

"Hi, Grandma," Marie said. "Here's your bag of goodies." She handed her the paper bag, and then introduced her to me as Helen Grayson.

"Pleased to meet you," I said, wondering if it was all right to lust after someone's grandmother. I was pretty sure it wasn't, but I was a teenager, and there wasn't much I could do about it.

"Come on in," she said. "I'll shake your hand as soon as I put these books down."

We followed her into the sunken den, where two walls were completely covered with bookshelves. The shelves were crammed with all kinds of books, hardbacks and paperbacks. Most of them were mysteries.

"Marie's mother and I love to read," Mrs. Grayson said.

She set the bag on a low coffee table that sat in front of a floral couch. Then she turned to me and stuck out her hand. I took it and felt almost as if a spark jumped between us. I tried not to show anything, but I probably did. I must have because out of the corner of my eye I saw Marie smirking.

"I'm really glad you could come," Mrs. Grayson said, dropping my hand. "Why don't we all have a seat, and then we can talk."

She and Marie sat on the couch, so rather than fling myself between them, which I would dearly have loved to do, I sat in an old Kennedy rocker. It was a lot like one my own grandmother had, and just as uncomfortable.

"So," Mrs. Grayson said after we were all settled, "Marie tells me that you have some . . . unusual abilities."

I looked at Marie.

"I didn't tell her anything specific," she said. "I just said that you might be able to help her out with a problem she's having."

"I'd be glad to try," I said, wondering what I could possibly do for a woman like that. Maybe her backyard needed mowing or something. I didn't much like mowing, but I'd do it if that's what she wanted. I probably would have done just about anything.

"I'd like for you to smell something," she said.

I goggled at her, and she laughed. She had a nice laugh, so nice that I almost wasn't embarrassed. Almost.

"My, what big eyes you have," she said.

I felt my face starting to burn, and I opened my mouth to say something. I'm not sure what, since nothing came out, which was no doubt just as well.

"It's just a piece of paper," Marie said. She sounded a little put out with me. "Show him, Grandmother."

Mrs. Grayson got up, smiled at me, and glided out of the room. She was back before my face had even had time to return to its normal color, and she handed me a folded piece of lined notebook paper just like the kind everyone uses in school.

I took it and unfolded it. There was printing on it, big block letters all done in pencil:

I'VE BEEN WATCHING YOU, I LIKE YOU A LOT, I THINK YOU'D LIKE ME TOO IF YOU'D GIVE IT A CHANCE.

"Uh-oh," I said.

"Indeed," Mrs. Grayson said. "It's scary, isn't it."

"The punctuation is bad, too," I said.

"I don't think that's the problem," Marie said. "There's another one."

Mrs. Grayson handed me another folded paper. I read that one, too.

I THINK YOU'RE HOT, I'VE GOT SOMETHING FOR YOU, YOU'RE GOING TO LIKE IT A LOT.

That was so bad that I didn't even feel like commenting on the attempt at poetry, which, after all, could have been an accident.

"Who wrote these?" I said.

"There are more," Mrs. Grayson said.

"And they're worse," Marie added.

I didn't think I wanted to see them. I said that they hadn't answered my question.

"We don't know," Mrs. Grayson said. "That's what I want you to tell me."

"I don't think you want me. I think you want the police."

"I've had the police. They took the other notes, but they haven't been able to do a thing. You can buy notebook paper like this all over the city, and apparently there are no fingerprints."

"How did you get the notes?"

Mrs. Grayson smiled at me, and I started getting warm again.

"That's a very good question. Someone slipped them under my back door."

"Then get the cops to watch the house. That's the best way to catch him."

"They watched. They even stayed in the house, but they didn't catch him. When they were here, he didn't show up. When they left, he slipped the notes under the back door again."

The backyard had a six-foot-high wooden fence around it. Whoever was writing the notes must have been pretty athletic.

"The police believe that whoever is writing these notes is someone I know," Mrs. Grayson said, "maybe someone from the neighborhood."

"That's where you come in," Marie said. "I thought maybe you could smell the note and tell us who wrote it."

"Oh, good grief," I said.

After they explained things, however, I realized the idea wasn't quite as dumb as it sounded. If I could pick up a scent from the paper, which I admitted was a possibility, though not a very good one since a lot of people besides the writer had handled it and since the writer had probably been wearing gloves, I might be able to match the scent to one of the neighbors. Assuming one of the neighbors was the writer. It all seemed pretty thin to me.

"It's about all we've got, though," Mrs. Grayson said. "The police are no help at all. I think whoever wrote these notes would have to kill me for them to get really interested in doing anything. To tell the truth, I'm getting frightened."

I didn't blame her. "What if it's not someone from the neighborhood?" I said. "What if it's some nut from out of town?"

"I don't think that's very likely, do you?"

"No," I admitted. And then I had another thought. "What if I do find out who wrote the notes? What are you going to do then?"

"Why, I'm going to tell the police, of course."

"That would never work," I said "Not in a million years."

"Why not?" she asked, so I told her.

Well, I didn't actually tell her. What I said was that the cops weren't going to believe some kid who said he'd smelled a man's scent on a piece of paper. I didn't add that they wouldn't believe me even if I told them that I was a werewolf. If they believed that part, they'd probably run out looking for silver bullets.

Mrs. Grayson looked disappointed, but she knew I was right.

"I'm sorry I couldn't help," I said, and I meant it.

"Maybe you still could," Marie said, looking thoughtful. She looked good that way, but then she looked good most ways. Genetics was bad news when it came to werewolves, but she and her grandmother were certainly proof that nothing is all bad.

"How?" I asked.

"Instead of the police watching the house, you could watch it."

"Me?" I said, and then I caught on. "Oh. Yeah. Me."

"Am I missing something?" Mrs. Grayson asked.

"Not really," I said.

While I was taking her home, Marie filled me in on her plan.

"You'd do it during the time of the full moon, of course. I'll bet wolves know all kinds of ways to hide out in the dark."

"It's not so dark when the moon is full," I pointed out.

"You know what I mean. You're probably very sly when you're a wolf."

I wasn't ever very sly, but of course I couldn't tell her that. I was still hoping to impress her.

"And you could still check out the men in the neighborhood," she said. "That way, you'd know who to expect, and you'd know where he was coming from."

"Let's say, just for the sake of argument, that I do this. What am I supposed to do if the guy actually shows up? Rip his throat out?"

Marie shuddered. "Would you really do that?"

"I'm not sure," I admitted. "I don't think so, though. I've sure never done anything like that before."

Well, except for a chicken one time, but I didn't think it would be tactful to mention that. It was more in the way of an experiment than anything else, and it hadn't been exactly pleasant.

So I just said, "I don't think I'd like the taste of blood."

"Yuck. I wish you wouldn't talk like that."

"You started it."

"Maybe. But what I meant was that maybe you could . . . bark at him. Do wolves bark?"

"No. And that wouldn't scare anybody, anyway."

"How about if you jumped up on him? Knocked him down, maybe, and then slobbered in his face. Growled. Showed him your fangs. You have fangs, don't you?"

I had fangs, all right, and pretty big ones, but I didn't think that would work, either.

Marie said, "He'd think she had some kind of giant watch dog. He'd probably never come back. And if he did, we could file a complaint with the police. You could identify him and say you saw him put the note under the door. It would be the truth, too, sort of."

Okay, it was possible. Barely. But so are a lot of things. I said I'd think about it. I didn't want to disappoint Marie. Or her grandmother, for that matter.

"I want to know now," Marie said.

"Why?"

"So I'll know whether to give you a kiss when we get to my house."

I didn't need to think any longer. "I'll do it," I said.

She smiled. "I thought you might."

I spent a lot of time in my room that night, sniffing notebook paper. It didn't do any good, though. Mostly, I could smell Mrs. Grayson's perfume, and there was a faint odor of something that was probably leather. You'd think that whoever wrote the notes would use some kind of gloves that would be more flexible—rubber, for example. And there was another odor, even more faint, of something that smelled like new houses. Unless the writer was a carpenter, I didn't have a thing to go on.

That didn't discourage Marie. She talked to me every day at school, and she called me in the evenings. I had to admit that I didn't mind the attention. Maybe I should have mentioned to her sooner that I was a werewolf.

On the day of the night of the full moon, she caught up with me in the hall near my locker. The hall was noisy, as usual, with locker doors clanging, guys talking loud, feet shuffling, and Marie put her mouth close to my ear so I could hear her.

"Are you going to watch the house tonight?"

Her warm breath tickled my ear, and I was afraid I might turn into a wolf right then and there, even though I'd never Changed in the daylight hours before. And I didn't that time, either, but it was a near thing.

"I guess so," I said.

"Can I come, too?"

She was fascinated with the idea of the Change, but I wasn't about to let her see it. She might think it would be exciting, but it's not. It's mostly just ugly and painful.

"No," I said. "It's too dangerous."

"Pleeease."

"Forget it. If you try to come, I won't do it."

She pouted, sticking out a lovely, full lower lip, but it didn't do her any good.

"Oh, all right," she said after a minute. "What's your plan?"

"I don't have one," I said.

And I didn't. In the first place, I didn't think anyone would show up. There hadn't been any new notes since I'd visited Mrs. Grayson, and there was no real reason to think one would arrive that evening. They had come at irregular intervals from the beginning. But I'd said I'd watch, so I would.

After school that day I went home and told my mother I was going out that night.

"I don't think so," she said. "You know the rules."

The rules were pretty standard. She and I both had agreed to them long ago. During the full moon, we stayed home, in our rooms, which had been fixed up to be more or less werewolfproof.

We didn't really need the precautions—bars on the windows, thick wall hangings, doors that my father locked from the outside—because we weren't at all like the werewolves in most of the movies you've seen. We were basically domesticated and didn't have any desire to mangle human flesh, though there were enough animal instincts to make us dangerous to chickens now and then and (as I found out later) interested in Schnauzers and the like. Mostly we spent the nights of the Change sleeping or watching TV. Even a wolf can do that.

I explained to my mother that I was just going to do a favor for a friend. She didn't think it was a good idea.

"Werewolves don't do favors," she said. "We just keep out of sight and mind our own business."

I told her that there was a girl involved, and that really set her off.

"You haven't *told* her, have you? You know what could happen if you did that. Or maybe you don't, but you certainly should. It will be the peasants and the torches all over again."

"I thought that was *Frankenstein.*"

"Don't you get smart with your mother."

I apologized and tried to explain what I was going to do.

"You're just going to watch the house?"

I said that was the plan.

"And you're sure that's all?"

I said I was sure, though I really had no idea.

"Well, I don't like the idea of a woman being tormented like that. She doesn't have protection like you and I do. Why, if a man tried that on me, I'd rip him to shreds."

I said that I didn't doubt it. "Does that mean I can go?"

"I suppose so. But you be careful. You never know who might be using silver bullets these days."

"I'll be careful."

"And get back before dawn. You know what happens if you're out at dawn."

I knew. Cinderella had nothing on us werewolves.

"And don't tell your father. I'll handle him."

That was fine with me. I wasn't sure my father had ever completely adjusted to having a werewolf wife, much less a teenage werewolf son.

"Will you need any help?"

"I don't think so," I said.

Little did I know.

The moon came up big and bright, or as big and bright as it gets in the city, and I knew about it before anyone else. Except for my mother, of course, and any other werewolves who might be around. We don't know of any. And we don't have to see the moon. The Change happens when it's raining or when there's an eclipse or when you're in a sealed basement. It doesn't have anything to do with light.

As I said, it's painful. My bones stretch, my skull changes shape, my mouth fills with sharp white fangs, and my nails become claws while my feet and hands are becoming padded paws.

Sometimes I howl.

Not this time, however. It wouldn't have been a good idea. I wasn't in my room like most of the times before. I was on a tree-covered lot, not far from Mrs. Grayson's house. I could tell by some stakes with red ribbons on them that the lot had recently been surveyed, and it wouldn't be long before someone built a house there, but right now it was perfect for my purposes.

Lots of people think of Texas in general as a part of the southwestern desert, and parts of it are. But Houston is a coastal city with a subtropical climate. One of the things that sometimes surprises people who visit for the first time is the number of trees. They're all over the place, and the ones on the lot provided me with plenty of cover for Changing.

It doesn't take long, which is a good thing considering how painful it is, and before the moon had really gotten into the sky, I was a wolf. Not a bad-looking one, either, if I do say so myself. Big, black, and hairy, true, but not unattractive if you happened to be another wolf. Or even a Schnauzer.

The smells of the city came to me much more sharply after I Changed—diesel oil, exhaust fumes, the hot pavement, and even the cool smell of the oak trees that I was sheltering among. I could feel the grass cool under my paws and hear a bird rustling in the branches over my head.

I waited until it was as dark as it was going to get and trotted off to Mrs. Grayson's. I wasn't really worried about being seen. I figured that anyone who happened to catch sight of me would think I was just a big black dog on his way home, and there were plenty of shadows to duck into if I had to escape the animal control officer.

I circled Mrs. Grayson's block, sniffing around all the houses. A couple of times dogs penned in backyards barked in alarm, but the owners didn't notice.

There were no new houses on the block. All of them were as old as Mrs. Grayson's, and I was a bit disappointed. I'd hoped that finding the owner of the gloves might turn out to be easy. Oh, well.

Keeping myself in the shadows, I got a running start and jumped Mrs. Grayson's fence. It was easy for a wolf, though I thought a man might have a problem.

I sniffed around the backyard but didn't find anything unusual. A possum had been there recently, and some squirrels were living in one of the trees, but that was all. No scent of man.

I could smell perfume, of course, but that was coming from inside the house. A back window glowed with light, and I wondered if it was Mrs. Grayson's bedroom. I wondered if she knew I was out there. Or cared.

I circled the yard three or four times and lay down by a woodpile to wait. I stretched out my paws in front of me and rested my chin on them. I was sure it was going to be a long night, and there was nothing to entertain me except the squirrels, who were asleep, and the bugs in the woodpile, who didn't interest me.

After only a few minutes, I got restless. I got up and sniffed around the woodpile, thinking that maybe bugs wouldn't be such bad companions after all. I could hear them skittering around in there, and I sniffed at the logs.

I smelled something familiar almost at once, and I realized that I probably knew who had put those notes under Mrs. Grayson's door. If I was right, he was even more dangerous than we'd thought. Several Houston women had been raped and murdered over the past few months, in ways that were remarkably similar, and the police were baffled. All the murders had occurred at the time of the full moon, which wasn't unusual for that kind of killer. The women had no connection with one another as far as anyone had been able to figure out. Up until now, anyway. I thought I'd figured it out, and all I had to do was tell Mrs. Grayson.

But there was a slight problem with that idea. Wolves can't tell anybody anything. We might look a little like Lassie, but the resemblance is purely physical. We don't have her ability to communicate. Little Timmy would just have to drown in the well if things were left to us.

I was so excited that I didn't think about that, however. I wanted to let Mrs. Grayson know that I'd solved her problem, and maybe I even had some idea that she'd be so grateful to me that she'd scratch me behind the ears. It's possible that I was even thinking that she might be wearing some kind of filmy nightgown and that I might have a chance to nuzzle her here and there while she scratched my head.

I'm sure that if I hadn't been muddled by thoughts of pleasurable rewards for my efforts, I would have heard someone coming over the fence, though he must have been awfully quiet.

And I'm sure I would have heard him sneaking up behind me if I hadn't already been scratching frantically at the back door. I might even have heard him pick up a log from the woodpile.

Or maybe I would have smelled him if I hadn't been a little

too conscious of the odor of Chanel No. 5 that oozed out from under Mrs. Grayson's back door.

I smelled him before I heard him, though, and I tried to turn. I heard him, too, but it was too late.

What I heard was his voice saying, "Good night, poochie."

And then he slammed me in the head with the log.

I don't know how long I lay sprawled out by the back door, but I'm sure it wasn't long, no more than a few seconds. We werewolves have pretty thick skulls, thicker than most dogs and humans, and that's probably what saved me.

I was groggy, and my head was beating like a timpani, but I was alive. That was all that mattered, that and the fact that the door was slightly ajar. In his rush to get inside, the man who'd hit me hadn't closed it all the way. I could hear noises from the house, as if someone were smashing furniture.

I was afraid that my legs might be too shaky to hold me up, but they worked more or less all right. I nosed the door farther open and staggered inside.

The noise was coming from the room where the light had been in the window, so I headed that way, wagging my head from side to side in an attempt to clear it. Drops of blood spattered on the tile floor of the kitchen. I was sure that wasn't a good sign, but I kept going.

Soon enough I was at the door of a back bedroom. A tall man wearing jeans, scuffed boots, and a denim jacket was throwing himself against the closet door. He had on leather work gloves, too.

"You might's well come on out of there, sweet mama," he said.

There was no sound from inside the closet, and he braced himself before slamming his shoulder into the door. He had black, oily hair, and his teeth pulled back from his lips in a fierce grimace at the crack of the wood. He looked almost as much like a wolf as I did.

"One more time, honey," he said. "And then you're all mine. It might go easier for you if you just came on out."

There was no answer from inside the closet, but I made a low noise in my throat. The man looked around. He seemed surprised to see me.

"Well, if it ain't the poochie. I didn't think I'd be hearing from you again."

He started across the room toward me. I snarled, but not very impressively. I don't suppose I was looking very wolfish. He wasn't scared at all.

"I guess I'll have to finish what I started," he said, reaching behind his back.

When I could see his hand again, it was holding a little revolver, and it was aimed right between my eyes.

Big woop. He didn't know who he was dealing with. Or what. He might be able to bash me to death with a log, though I doubted even that, and he certainly wasn't going to be able to kill me with lead bullets. My head was already feeling better, and I thought it was beginning to heal itself.

He had no way of knowing all that, however, so he pulled the trigger.

The bullet knocked me backward, and I blacked out again. I was probably out a little longer this time, because I completely missed Marie's entrance into the house. She must have come in through the garage, because she had a hatchet in her hand, and she was standing between me and the guy with the gun.

"Put the gun down," she said. "Or you'll be sorry."

The guy laughed. I didn't blame him. I almost laughed myself. But you had to hand it to Marie. She had guts.

"You're the one who's gonna be sorry," he said. "Or maybe not. Maybe you'll enjoy it. In fact, I might just leave old blondie in the closet while you and I have at it."

I couldn't let him talk to Marie like that. I stood up.

This time he was *really* surprised.

"I'll be goddamned," he said.

He was probably right about that.

I was even shakier than I had been, but this time I didn't let that bother me. I gathered what strength I had and jumped for his throat.

He shot me twice before I hit him, but not in any area as sus-ceptible as my head. We hit the floor in a pile, and two more bullets jolted into me. That made five. I wondered if he carried one under the hammer.

He didn't. I heard a couple of clicks, and then he began hitting me in the head with the butt of the gun while I tried to bite him with absolutely no success. He was jerking around too much.

The shots hardly affected me, but the blows from the pistol butt did. After all, I'd been shot in the head and hit with a log. It was a little tender.

I whined and rolled off him. He jumped up and started kicking me in the head. I howled. Maybe he *could* kill me by beating me to a pulp.

He didn't, though, because Marie split him open with the hatchet.

She told the police later that it was an accident, and I believe that it was. She threw the hatchet at him, hoping he'd be distracted and stop hurting me. How was she to know that it would turn over just right and that the blade would meet his forehead just above the nose?

When she saw what she'd done, she got sick all over the rug, and she was sitting on the edge of the bed, still heaving, when Mrs. Grayson came out of the closet.

The newspapers got it all wrong, of course, or most of them did. The way they told it, Mrs. Grayson had been attacked by a vicious wolf, and a heroic handyman had tried to save her. His own death was a tragic accident, and the severely wounded wolf had escaped. Readers should beware of vicious sneak attacks.

Geez.

I didn't escape, exactly. I must have looked dead when the cops got there, which was a lot sooner than you'd think. A neigh-bor had heard the shots and called them. I was still lying on the floor when they arrived, and they ignored me.

Marie told me later that she got me out of there and into the yard in all the confusion. Of course, the fact that Mrs. Grayson was dressed in the scanty nightie that I'd imagined for her helped a lot. The cops couldn't keep their eyes off her. I think they forgot about me for quite a while.

And then there was the dead man, another little distraction for them to worry about.

Marie told them that I'd jumped up and run out of the room on my own, and they didn't doubt her. For weeks there were wolf sightings all over the city.

Nobody actually saw me, of course. I recovered in the yard and got out of there as soon as I figured out that I was no longer needed. I'd done my part about as well as I could.

I explained my theory to Marie later, and she confirmed that I was right. The guy was a handyman, and he also sold firewood by the cord. He cut it somewhere in the country and brought it into town in an old truck, which the police had found parked several blocks from the house.

The "new house" smell I'd noticed on the paper had been sawdust, of course, and my idea was that the guy would case houses where he sold the wood. If there was a woman living alone, and she had a fireplace that she liked to use a couple of times in the winter, she was in danger if she bought wood from the wrong guy.

Marie told the police the theory, saying it was her own, and they checked it out. Four of the five women who had been killed had bought wood from the guy, according to their neighbors, and the fifth might have. There was wood in her yard, but no one knew where it had come from. So the cops could close the books on the killer.

I was upset with Marie for having been at the house, even if she had pretty much saved my life.

"I can't believe you're so ungrateful," she said.

"It's not that. But you put yourself in danger."

"I just wanted to see you Change. But you cheated. You weren't there."

"I had a feeling you might be hiding around. And I didn't want to Change there, anyway. Where did you get that hatchet, by the way?"

"I waited for you in the backyard for a long time before I decided that you weren't coming. Then I went to my car and listened to the radio for a while, thinking that if you wouldn't watch the house, I would. When I heard the shots, I came inside. I didn't know where the front-door key was, but I knew that my grandmother kept a key to the garage door in her washing machine in the garage. There was a hatchet on the old workbench that my grandfather used before he died, so I just grabbed it."

"I'm glad you did."

"I'm not so sure that I am."

She'd get over it, but I didn't say that. What I said was, "The moon's not full tonight. We could go to a movie or something."

"I don't think so," she said. "I'm still too upset about everything that's happened."

I could understand that. I'd been a little upset, too, and my mother had grounded me for a week when she saw my head. It looked fine now, however.

I was sorry that Marie didn't want to go to a movie with me. Maybe she would later on and we could live happily ever after. Or maybe her curiosity about werewolves was wearing off. I was afraid that might be the case.

I wondered if her grandmother would like to see a movie, but I didn't think I should ask. We hadn't told her grandmother about my brave confrontation with the killer, and since she'd been in the closet she had no idea that I'd even been there. Even if she'd seen me she wouldn't have known it was me. So I didn't have much leverage with her.

Oh, well. That's the way it is when you're a werewolf. You hardly ever get credit for anything. Marie and I sort of drifted apart after that, and after graduation I didn't see her again for years. We did meet again, however, but that's another story, to be told another time.

Simon Clark is a new name to most Americans, though to his fellow Brits he's well on his way to becoming as well known as Stephen King and James Herbert. While his forte is the horror story, one can see that he has a masterly touch with the crime tale as well. The following adaptation of "The Frog Prince" only adds weight to these claims.

SIMON CLARK

Now Fetch Me an Axe

Have you ever been to England?

If you have, you might have walked down any street in any town or city and passed above two thousands years of history. Beneath your feet is the twentieth-century sidewalk (or pavement, as we Brits call it). Buried beneath that will be an older one of Victorian stone slabs; beneath that, one of Jacobean cobble; and below that, one of medieval timber and so on until you reach the Roman tessellated pavement that might date back two thousand years and lay six feet down, deep enough to be insulated from the incessant tramp of stiletto, Reebok, and loafer.

Our towns and cities are built layer upon layer, the modern often concealing the ancient—and yet, to find the ancient temples, palaces, and houses (sometimes with the bones of their occupants still lodged snugly within the fallen walls), you need only dig deep enough.

In England our society, I think, is very much like that, too. Its people are composed of many different, and very distinct, layers, or classes, from the blue-collar working class to the starched collar of the English aristocrat. And like those old towns that lay beneath today's cities, you can find, buried deep within those ancient families, skeletons, too.

My name is Rebecca St. Taine—yes! that Rebecca St. Taine, authoress of the murder-mystery novel *Three Heads in a Well.* Perhaps you're one of the nine hundred thousand Americans who bought the hardcover? To see what I look like, you need only reach up onto the shelf, selecting the book with the blood red spine, and there on the back of the book is my photograph with masses of black curls tumbling down onto bare shoulders (the product of a four-hour torture session at the hands of a sadistic hairdresser), and I'm looking out at you with my much-practiced penetrating gaze of the kind I imagine Mr. Sherlock Holmes would wear when ruminating on a particularly challenging case. And beneath the photograph is the *Times* quote: *Rebecca St. Taine—the princess of crime.*

The reviewer was referring, sweet man, to my status in crime fiction, not that I was involved in any criminal acts.

That is, until now. Because, you see, I am going to be a participant in a case of murder. In fact, to be precise, I am going to be the murder victim.

The time is 11:00 P.M. My murderer will arrive in precisely one hour. As I sit here at the computer, my nervousness so great that my fingers thump the keys with enough force to leave them tingling, my mouth is dry, my heart beats faster—I'm writing all this down simply to divert my mind from what will happen at midnight. The lights are extinguished; the sole source of illumination is the computer screen that burns like an unblinking blue eye.

If I could summon the courage I could pause from my typing, look back over my shoulder. There, gazing back at me from the uncurtained patio window, would be my reflection. And I would see a very different image of me from that on the book sitting there on your shelf. No tumbling curls. My hair is tied back. No longer the shrewd gaze. Instead, frightened eyes, darting left and right, searching for the figure that will all too soon be emerging from the darkened garden.

He will want me.

And I can't help but wonder what he'll use.

A knife? A gun? His bare hands?

I can't let myself dwell on that now; if I do, this tension alone will kill me. Instead, I'm going to sit here, sip tea from my best bone china cup, and write down how all this started.

And when did it begin? Ah, believe me, that part is easy.

It began in the grandmother of all snowstorms with me using the kind of language I rarely use in my books.

Like the white rabbit from *Alice in Wonderland* I was late for a very important date. I had to drive from where I live in Old Amersham, a rural village north of London, into London itself for an 8:00 P.M. meeting with a Hollywood film producer and my agent. The producer wanted to option my book *Three Heads in a Well*. And my agent was confident of clinching the deal that evening over dinner.

Believe me, this was a deal of a lifetime. I'd dreamed of a movie being made of one of my books. I lusted for it with an intensity that was nothing less than indecent. At that moment as I drove, cursing the blizzard that reduced my speed to a slothlike crawl, there was nothing—and I mean not one single thing—more important to me in my life than winning that movie deal.

Yes, I know, avarice is one of the seven deadly sins. And within twenty minutes of setting out from home that's when I paid the price.

I drove along a deserted country lane. The blizzard, by this time, had stopped. I switched off the wipers as the rubber blades began to squeak against the glass. It was completely dark apart from the headlights of my car flaring off the snow that lay whitely smooth and unbroken across the road. No cars had passed this way. There were no houses, nor any sign of human life. Nothing but fields that bristled with snow-cloaked trees.

Even at thirty miles an hour I was driving the BMW way too fast. At only a gentle bend in the road the car slipped sideward. The steering became strangely light, as if the car had magically become airborne. Then—

Thump!

The car had slid off the road to come to rest against a massive oak. The concussion wasn't particularly massive. I was unhurt. The car, striking the trunk of the tree, had dislodged snow coating its branches, bringing down a heavy deluge upon the car.

"Damn."

I tried driving the car back up the banking to the road.

The tires turned, but the car stayed firmly stuck.

"Damn, damn, damn . . ."

I revved the engine, the BMW's tires screamed as they spun uselessly.

The car was definitely going nowhere.

I glanced at the clock on the dash. It was seven-thirty. If the car wasn't free from the snowdrift within the next five minutes I'd be late for the meeting, my name would be mud, and the producer would leave for Hollywood in a huff.

I kicked open the car door, shivered as the cold air rushed in, then climbed out to inflict upon the car my fiercest glare.

And so there I stood, in the middle of nowhere, dressed in a little black dress, jacket, stockings, and the comfortable Reeboks I'd wear for driving, my stilettos in a carrier bag on the passenger seat. *"You're hardly equipped for driving in these conditions, Rebecca, you idiot,"* I berated myself savagely. *"You've gone and got yourself stuck . . . idiot, idiot—"*

"Need any help?"

I screamed. The voice, coming from nowhere, scared the jeepers from me.

"I'm sorry. I didn't mean to startle you."

The voice was male, calm, with the polished tones of a James Bond. A man of about thirty-five, I guessed.

"Startle me? Just a little." I clutched my throat as if I could slow my own breathing, which still rushed in gasps. "I didn't notice you there."

Seeing that I had to squint against the dazzling car lights, the man moved so he was no longer in silhouette.

When I saw the face, I recoiled in shock.

It was heavily bearded; the eyes gleamed with a strange intensity. With a writer's habitual regard for detail, I let my eyes take in the ragged hobo clothes, the overcoat tied with hairy string, the man's hair sprouting weedlike from beneath an incongruous broad-rimmed fedora hat. I found myself compelled to look back into those burning eyes as they fixed on me.

I felt helpless, vulnerable. Alone.

He spoke again with a voice that seemed incompatible with that vagrant garb. "I saw the car skid. You're not hurt, are you?"

I shook my head, afraid of this sinister-looking man.

Then, taking a deep breath, I spoke as calmly as I could. "The car's stuck. You don't know if there's a public telephone box nearby?"

"Sorry, no."

"Damn, I'm going to be late."

"I'll help," he said in that polished James Bond voice. "Get back into the car."

"Why?" I asked, suddenly suspicious. "What are you going to do?"

"You reverse the car as slowly as you can while I push. Okay?"

"The car's too heavy. You won't be able to move it."

"We can only try, can't we?"

As I looked at him, clouds of vapor swirled around his head as he breathed into his bare hands.

He glanced from me to the car. "Shall we then, Miss . . . ?"

No way was I going to reveal my name. "Okay," I said, then quickly climbed into the warmth of the car, making sure the door was locked the instant I shut it.

For a moment he stared at me through the windshield, then he came to the driver's window and tapped it.

Cautiously I lowered it an inch. "Yes?"

"Perhaps I could ask for something in return for helping you?"

"Of course," I said, flustered, and fumbling a ten-pound note from my purse, pushed it through the chink in the window. "Here you are," I said in a voice that was studiously neutral. "Thank you for your help."

"And thank you for your kind offer of money, but please don't be offended if I refuse it."

"Oh?"

"I would like something else from you instead."

My hand tightened around the steering wheel. "I'm afraid I can't offer you a lift," I said lamely, rooting for an excuse. "Even if you can free the car I'll be late for a business meeting as it is."

"I would simply ask one thing from you."

A kiss. For one horrible moment I thought the wild-looking vagrant would actually ask me for a kiss. I moved my own face back from the repulsive face peering in through the glass with the scabbed lips and burning eyes.

"I'm sorry?"

"I would like to dine with you—just once."

"Pardon?" I was astonished.

"Allow me to dine with you. What do you say?"

No! Not a chance in hell, buster! Those were the words racing toward my lips as he leaned against the car, glaring in at me. Instead I paused. Here I was in a car, stuck deep in the snow. I'm alone. There's no one else who can help me. If I'm freed within the next three minutes, perhaps I can make the meeting—just.

But dine with a vagrant? I thought. That's absurd. Then, at last, I managed to swing my surprised brain into gear. Yes, accept the tramp's invitation. What does it matter, Rebecca? He doesn't know you, he doesn't know where you live. Anyway, the man is clearly insane. As soon as you drive away from here you'll never set eyes on that disgusting face again.

"Well?" he prompted.

I smiled through the glass. "I'd be delighted. When?"

"I'll call you," he said. "We'll arrange the details then."

"All right," I said, beaming an artificial smile. "I look forward to it."

"It's a date, then?"

"It's a date," I echoed pleasantly.

"Now . . . please, if you could put the car into reverse."

"Okay."

"When I nod, reverse gently back toward the road."

"I still think the car's stuck too deep."

"We'll try, madam."

"Thank you," I said formally.

He returned to the front of the car, pushed the rim of the hat up with one finger, placed both hands flat on the hood, fixed me with those eyes, then nodded.

Carefully, I eased out the clutch. The tires spun.

The man's face turned fierce with sheer effort; his eyes blazed yet more brightly; clouds of vapors jetted from his mouth as he panted.

I was right, I thought with a bitter satisfaction, the car is too heavy; it's stuck too deeply; he'll never shift it in a month of—

Wait!

The car moved backward. Suddenly the tires gripped, and I reversed the car onto the road.

My first instinct was to floor the pedal and drive away without a backward glance at the man. I was certain he would demand a ride somewhere. And once in the car beside me, what then?

But it would be so downright ungrateful to leave without so much as a thank you.

Checking once more that all the doors were locked, I eased down the window so there was a two-inch gap. "Thanks once again for your help, I really am grateful. Are you sure you couldn't use some money?"

"No, I don't want money," he said firmly. "I want dinner with you."

Despite the shiver down my spine, I smiled. "I look forward to it." As I thumbed the button to raise the window he suddenly rested his fingers on the top of the glass. I wondered whether to close the window, giving him the option of moving his hand quickly or painfully trapping his fingers.

As I hesitated he said in a low voice, "Thank you. The opportunities to have dinner with a beautiful woman are, for me, rather scant these days. You don't know how much it means to me."

I nodded; said nothing.

"You see, I once served a prison sentence for killing a man."

Now I was really ready to stomp the gas pedal, but before I had the chance to, he wished me a safe journey in that cultivated voice, then stood back from the car.

Stomach muscles tense, teeth gritted, I drove away as quickly as I dared on the snow-covered road. When I glanced in the rearview mirror, the man had already disappeared.

I made the meeting on time. The movie deal was clinched. I was happy—gloriously happy.

One month later, my mobile rang as I sat in a café with my sister.

I answered the phone. "Hello?"

"Rebecca St. Taine?" A male voice.

"Speaking."

"I'm calling to arrange a rendezvous for dinner."

"For dinner?"

"Yes, we agreed we'd meet."

"Sorry. Who is this speaking, please?"

"Your car was stuck in the snow. I pushed you free."

"Oh."

"Now, where shall we meet?"

Stunned, I said nothing.

"Hello?" he said. "Remember you promised to—"

I cut him off, then switched off the phone.

"Rebecca, you are blushing." My sister grinned. "Who was that, pray?"

"No one." I forced a smile. "No one at all."

"Mmm? Sounded like someone to me."

"Just a ghost, that's all. Now, what're you buying the boys for Christmas?"

I listened to descriptions of train sets from Hamley's, but my mind was far away. How had the man gotten hold of my name and number? And why had I described him as a ghost?

Writers cultivate any eye for detail. At least they should. And it was then a single but vibrant detail of my encounter with the vagrant came back to me. I'd not registered it consciously at the time. But it must have stuck at some subliminal level, because right then in the café, it came thundering back.

I remember the snow was unmarked except for the tracks of the car leading to the tree, with a good three-yard break where the car had actually left the ground. In a revelatory flash I realized then that the man had left no tracks as he approached the car. They suddenly began after he appeared in the dazzling glare of the headlights, as if he'd magically materialized there from another dimension.

I didn't believe in ghosts.

And I didn't believe ghosts could harm the living—not even the ghost of a murderer. But as I sat there in the café pretending to look untroubled, a current of fear sprang up within me. A fear that was cold and blue and sent a thousand pointed insect legs prickling up my spine.

We dined in a Greek restaurant in Bloomsbury, little more than a good spear's throw from the British Museum. There were eight of us: myself, my publicist, and six pet media folk who had been particularly good to *Three Heads in a Well.* Outside, fresh snow fell; the plaintive sound of a Salvation Army band playing Christmas carols in the distance shimmered on the cold night air. As the retsina wine flowed, our media party grew progressively jollier.

"Rebecca," the chat show host said, "a little bird tells me that a certain Oscar-winning actress is fighting tooth and claw for the lead role in the movie. Is my mole right?"

"She wants it," I said, smiling, "but she hasn't been offered the part yet."

"If she accepts, promise I get the exclusive when she comes to England for the promo, okay?"

"You've got it, providing—"

"Providing?" He smiled.

"Providing you run a feature on the sequel to *Three Heads in a Well.*"

"Boy, you certainly know how to close a deal, Rebecca. More wine?"

"Please."

"Rebecca"—the publicist leaned across the table—"don't look now, but I think you've got an admirer."

I did look. The instant I saw the eyes burning through the restaurant window, I knew who it was. In one second flat he opened the door and swept off the black fedora hat in a single movement; the strains of "Silent Night" from the brass band seemed suddenly overloud. I shivered as the cold air swept in through the open doorway. I shivered again when the madman fixed his burning eyes on me, and this time I knew it had nothing to do with the cold.

"Rebecca St. Taine," he said in a low voice, "you promised

me something." He let the door swing shut behind him. "I'm here to collect."

Ten minutes later, the conversation in the ladies' room, although whispered, bordered on the ferocious. My publicist's eyes glittered as she lit a cigarette. "Rebecca, darling, are you listening to a word I'm saying to you?"

"I am listening. And I'm violently disagreeing."

"Rebecca—"

"Catherine, are you asking me to dine with a lunatic who claims to have murdered someone?"

"Yes!"

"No! Absolutely not!"

"Darling, you can't buy that kind of publicity."

"*Darling,* I don't need it."

"Everyone needs publicity, honey."

"But have you taken a good enough look at him?"

"Yes. So?"

"He's filthy. He's repulsive. To cap it all, he's probably a homicidal maniac. And you want me to make small talk to him over baklava and coffee?"

"He's a colorful eccentric. And it was you who promised him a dinner date in return for helping you free your car from that snowdrift, remember?"

"Catherine, I refuse."

"Rebecca, listen. There are journalists, a talk show host, and an editor at our table. They're all going to run a story about this."

"So?"

"So, you have a choice of which story they'll use. They heard about how that homeless gentleman played the Good Samaritan and saved your life in the raging blizzard."

"Saved my life, my foot! The car was simply stuck in—"

"Rebecca, what you say when you go out there determines which story the public will see."

"Cathy . . ." I pleaded.

"The story will be either, A: Famous Writer Throws Good Samaritan Out of Restaurant; or, B: Golden-Hearted Writer Extends

Hand of Friendship to Homeless Man Who Rescued Her from Death-trap Blizzard."

I sighed. "Heck."

"So, Rebecca? Your decision?"

I glared at her as she leaned against the sink, blowing cigarette smoke into the air, a look of triumph in her eye.

I sighed again. "Okay . . . you win."

"No, Rebecca." She gave a brilliant smile. "You win. This will be front-page news."

It was.

The newspapers, radio, and TV not only covered it, they bugled it. It was one of those Christmas stories that make people feel good even in these cynical times: *THE MIRACLE OF CHRISTMAS. Homeless man who rescued celebrity is rewarded in style.* There are photographs of me (courtesy of the paparazzi who circle London like vultures around a staked cowboy); I'm smiling, pouring coffee for the man with the matted hair and coat tied with string. The tramp did not say or do anything bizarre, threatening, or sinister. He said little, answered questions politely (his table manners were impeccable); then, at the end of the evening he disappeared into the snow-rugged streets without even giving his name. What little I could glean from him was that he recognized me from my photograph in newspapers and that he'd simply trawled the directories for my number. The mystery of how he'd managed to somehow materialize next to my car without leaving footprints was left dangling. Not that I'd lose sleep over that. I had no desire to prolong my relationship with the vagrant. As far as I was concerned I would never set eyes on that repellent face again, and that was just fine and dandy. End of story.

When I pulled up at the traffic light, the car door opened and a man slipped into the passenger seat.

"Hey! What do you think you're—" I gasped. *"You again?"*

"Drive. The light is green."

"Not a chance in hell, buster. Get out of my car."

"Drive . . . please."

"I'll call the police."

That now-familiar face with matted beard, hair, chapped lips, eyes that glared into mine, leaned closer to me. "Drive."

It was dusk; cars honked behind me.

"You must drive," he said in those cultured tones. "I need to talk to you."

"What about?"

"About murder."

The eyes blazed with such intensity I found myself driving the car away as if on autopilot.

I stammered. "Why me? Surely there are—are better-qualified people to help you."

"The police?"

I actually meant a psychiatrist; however, I nodded.

"The police jailed me for killing my brother."

"Oh?"

"Don't be frightened, Miss St. Taine. You're perfectly safe."

"What do you want from me?"

"I've read your books, Miss St. Taine. You're a clever woman. You have an ability to solve particularly ingenious crimes."

"But they're made up, fictitious. You do realize that?"

"Absolutely. But I'm convinced that faced with a real puzzle, you would solve it."

"I think you're taking an overly optimistic view of my abilities. Now, if—"

"No! I have absolute confidence in you."

"Feel free to believe what you like, but I want you out of this car now." I pulled over to the side of the road, the tires crunching loudly on frozen slush.

He ignored me. Instead he said, "That night, when I was walking alongside the road and saw the accident, I recognized you immediately. As I ran down toward your car I had, call it a flash of divine inspiration, but I knew you were the only person who could help me."

"Help you? How?"

"If you have a few moments I'll tell you everything."

I sighed, relenting. "Okay, you've got five minutes."

He then proceeded to tell me his story in a straightforward, matter-of-fact way. "I have two brothers; one is forty minutes older than I, the other is one hour younger. We were identical triplets. As we grew up, we would mercilessly play practical jokes on our schoolmasters and friends—no one could tell us apart. When we left university, my younger and my elder brother chose a career in the family business. I was ambitious, but in retrospect, foolhardy. I moved to France, where I set up a helicopter leasing company. It went bust. Before I knew it, I'd lost my business, my home, and had to scrape a living working in a bar in Paris. Call it pride, but I couldn't face going home and working for my father. It would be too much like admitting defeat. In fact, I was too shamefaced to go home at all, and by the time I was in my late twenties my sole contact with my family was through my younger brother. He went out of his way to telephone me at regular intervals, and he was always the epitome of kindness, sending me money whenever he could. Then one day my brother telephoned me, asking me to meet him in Normandy, where he was holidaying in a rented Gite. He told me if he was out when I arrived I'd find the key. He went on to say that he wanted to go into business with me and that he'd repay my debts so I could start afresh. Naturally, very pleased with this turn of affairs, I drove to what was a house in the middle of nowhere. There I found a computer-printed message from my brother saying complications with the loan arrangements had delayed him, that I was to wait, but he'd be there in a couple of days."

"When did he arrive?"

"That's just it. He didn't. I stayed there five days."

"You didn't hear from him?"

"Oh, yes, he phoned me twice a day at the house, telling me all was well and to wait there."

"Then what?"

"He telephoned me on the Sunday morning and told me to return to Paris. And that he'd meet me there."

"Mysterious."

"Very. And I soon found out why. I arrived back at the lodging house to find the gendarmes waiting for me. I was wanted in England by the police." The glare in the man's eyes was replaced by one of sadness. "My elder brother had been murdered."

"Murdered?" I echoed, shocked.

He nodded grimly, the lights of passing cars illuminating his bearded face. "I was the sole suspect. I had a motive. I was broke. With my brother dead, I was next in line to inherit my father's estate."

"But at the time of the murder you were in France?"

A smile, equally grim, played upon his lips. "Ah," he said, softly. "So I believed. But according to more than twenty witnesses, I was staying in a hotel in my brother's hometown in England, where I ran up debts, loudly insulted waiters, and made a thorough nuisance of myself. So, you realize what had happened?"

I knew I should have driven to the nearest police station, where I could have made a dash for safety. But professional curiosity had gotten the upper hand, and—disregarding what happened to curious cats—I plunged in. "So your younger brother murdered your elder brother?"

He nodded.

"If he's identical to you, it was a simple matter to persuade you to leave Paris for a few days while he booked himself into a hotel, under your name, in the same town where your brother lived, then behave in a way to get himself noticed. After making several calls to you in the rented house in France to ensure you were still safely out of the way—and deprived of your alibi—he killed your brother."

Again, the solemn nod.

"But why kill your elder brother? Not your father?"

"My father is elderly. And by killing my elder brother, and framing me for the crime, he gets rid of two people who stand between him and the inheritance: my elder brother's dead; I am disinherited. See?"

"Clever."

"Very clever." He nodded. "But it didn't go all according to plan. The jury convicted me of voluntary manslaughter, not murder, for which I served five years. And also, my father's a tough old bird; he's still sprightly for his eighty years."

"And now you fear for your father's safety?"

"I do. My younger brother is greedy for his inheritance. I'm sure he'll kill again."

"That's horrible."

He shrugged. "Patricide won't be too big a step for him."

"You must go to the police."

"Ha, and how will they react to the testimony of a man who's not only a convicted killer but also a vagrant?"

"You're not going to sit back and do nothing?"

"I'm not." He gave a grim smile. "So, Miss St. Taine, what are we going to do about it?"

" 'We'?"

"We." He nodded.

"But I—"

"Listen, please, I think I know how I can dupe my brother into publicly admitting his guilt. All I need is your cooperation. Do I have it?"

I hesitated. But how could I refuse? "Okay. What do you want me to do?"

"We'll need your media contacts, and your ingenuity, to persuade my brother to appear on a TV chat show. Can you arrange that?"

"Yes, of course. But what happens then?"

"Once he's in front of the cameras, we spring the trap."

"How?"

"Just give me a few hours to make some arrangements of my own." Now he opened the door of the car. "Can I call at your home tonight?"

Again I hesitated, but I knew lives were at stake. "What time?"

"Midnight."

"Seeing as you managed to find my telephone number, I guess you know where I live?"

He gave a sudden grin. "Yes. My apologies, but it was necessary. Midnight, then, Miss Taine, and thank you." He began to climb out of the car. "Oh, by the by, do you have a door at the rear of your home?"

"Yes. Why?"

"Then I'll come to the back of your house. Oh, and please switch off your lights. I wouldn't put it past my brother to be keeping an eye on you. He'll have linked the two of us together ever since he saw the story about us in the newspaper."

"You mean—"

"Yes," he said, his voice suddenly crisp. "You might be in danger, too. Until midnight, then?" He thrust out a grubby hand toward me, which I gingerly shook. With that he climbed out of the car, shut the door, and walked quickly away into the night; soon all that remained were his footprints in the freshly fallen snow.

For a full three minutes I found myself staring at those footprints—almost as if there were somehow a message concealed within them—a very, very important message. And for the life of me, I couldn't think of what it was.

Footprints in the snow. I find myself sitting here, dreamily gazing into the glowing blue rectangle of the computer screen; the text I've written there, white as snow.

Footprints in the snow. Those four words haunt me because they contain a message for me—a message of vital importance— only I was just too dimwitted to see.

Please. Let's go back a little while; think back to when my car ran off the road and came to rest against the tree. The snow, you will recall, was unmarked, except for the tire tracks of the car leading toward the tree, and those were broken where the car had momentarily left the Earth and had, for a good three yards, become airborne. So there I was, surrounded by a moat of smooth, unmarked snow. When the man appeared by the car, it was as if by magic. I clearly recall he left no footprints as he approached the car. How could he simply materialize there? Of course he must have left prints. But how come I never saw them?

When the man left my car tonight, and walked away across the snow, coat flapping in the breeze, I noticed the footprints he left. Not that they were extraordinary in themselves; they were merely depressions in the snow, imprinted with the pattern of the soles of his boots. And yet the sight of the prints nagged away at me; they were like a faithful dog nudging at me, striving to warn me of some hidden danger.

Then, as I sat down here to wait for the man's arrival, the revelation struck me. The man who climbed into the car at the traffic lights to speak to me *was not the same man who pushed my car out of the snow, nor the same one who appeared at the Greek restaurant.* Okay, he looked the same. But it was a different man.

And that's why I realized, when I began typing this a few minutes ago, that the man—the impostor—I'd invited to my home at twelve would murder me.

How did I know that?

Because tonight he told me that he'd seen the car skid off the road, whereupon he'd simply run alongside the road, then down the banking to where the car had—

Great heaven! I nearly stopped typing then, because I've just heard the clock in the hallway chime twelve.

Midnight.

Here he comes.

My murderer.

I must not look around. I must stay here, alone in the darkened room. Behind me are the glass windows of the patio doors. They are uncurtained. Beyond them lies the snow-covered lawn, and beyond the garden fence the winter fields shrouded in darkness.

And I imagine a shabby figure approaching the house; soon he will gently tap on the glass door.

Open the door, my princess dear,
Open the door to thy true love here!
And mind the words that thou and I said
By the fountain cool in the greenwood shade.

My God, my God . . .

What am I doing? I find myself writing the first words that come into my head.

I must appear calm, composed.

But what I desperately want to do is to leave the house at a full-blooded run. I am so scared. The telephone lines have been cut, the tires on my car are slashed, my mobile telephone has been stolen. I am alone. The house lies apart from the main village. No one will hear if I scream for help. The house of my nearest neighbor is three hundred yards away. I could run there, I tell myself, but what if the man is waiting outside the door?

Surely I'm safer here.

Aren't I?

It's a full minute past midnight. He was due to be here at twelve.

Maybe he won't come.

Oh, don't worry, girl, croaks the voice in my head, *he'll be here: a shambling figure in a filthy coat tied with string; his burning eyes fixed on you.*

I crave to look back at the window. I crave it so much it hurts.

Don't do it, Rebecca. Look cool, calm, collected. . . .

The croaking voice of fear runs through my head:

Now fetch me an axe, my hinnie, my heart,
Now fetch me an axe, my own true love;
Remember the promise that you and I made,
Down in the meadow where we first met. . . .

I clench my teeth together; my imagination is torturing me; my heart feels as if it'll surely pound its way through my chest wall.

Two minutes past midnight.

Now! A tapping on the door behind me.

Dear God, O dear God—*he's here.* I pray that . . .

The TV reporter—a blond-haired man in a tweed overcoat—stands in the snow outside the thatched cottage. Snow falls from a gray sky. Police move purposefully in the background.

"Police say the man struck at midnight," the reporter said; "armed with an axe, he entered the back of the house via a patio door. The crime writer Rebecca St. Taine was alone in the house at the time. There was a struggle." The reporter turned to a woman dressed in a leather flying jacket and gloves. "Rebecca, what happened next?"

An hour later I was in the kitchen, busying myself making a meal—a particularly spicy dish of my own creation. I hefted a large joint of meat from the refrigerator. Outside in the snow, the TV news crew were coiling cables and packing cameras into steel carrying cases. The police still beavered in my study—measuring, photographing, writing notes. It would be a while before I could clean the blood from the carpet.

"When did you realize it was my brother, not me?" The voice was familiar, those same polished James Bond tones of an English gentlemen. The man's appearance, however, was very different. Now he was clean-shaven, he'd bathed, and he wore a white open-necked shirt and a pair of dark blue corduroy trousers. Many women would have described him as good-looking. And they would have found him a good catch, too. He was none other than Robert De Lacey, the earl of Elmet's son, a true blue English aristocrat. "Was it when he climbed into your car at the traffic light?"

"I didn't realize it *wasn't* you at first," I replied. "He'd made a good job of the disguise, complete with the coat tied with string and false beard."

"Mmm, he always was a clever so-and-so."

"It was only when he walked away from the car that something troubled me. You see, he left footprints in the snow."

"Footprints?" He shook his head, puzzled. "How could those arise your suspicions?"

"Because the night you pushed my car back onto the road you left no footprints when you approached the car. It was as if you'd materialized out of thin air."

"Ah," he smiled, understanding. "So how did I appear by your car?"

"I saw no prints approaching the car because"—I looked him in the eye—"because you were in the tree."

"That's correct, Miss St. Taine. I was in the tree, high among the branches."

"Up a tree? In the middle of winter? What on Earth were you doing up there?"

"In days gone by, an Englishman, when faced with disgrace, would fall on his sword."

"You climbed up into the tree to die?"

"Yes. The cold would have been as effective as a blade or a bullet, don't you think?"

"But why a tree?"

"Shame. I simply wanted to vanish. There was a hollow high in the tree trunk. I managed to squeeze inside, in the knowledge that my body would never be found. Of course, then, as I lay there, feeling drowsy despite the cold, I felt a tremendous thump."

"My car hitting the tree?"

"Precisely. I climbed down from the tree to satisfy myself that no one needed help."

"Hence the lack of prints leading to the car."

He nodded. "And the moment I saw you, I recognized you as a famous crime writer; at that instant I intuitively knew that the answer to all my problems lay with you. In fact"—he smiled— "you might say I even fell in love with you on that night."

"That cold must have affected you more severely than you first thought," I said coolly, and briskly positioned the beef on the chopping board.

He continued, "When you saw the prints left by my brother as he left the car tonight you realized something was amiss?"

"But it only hit me when I started to type up my notes." I grinned as I plucked my favorite paring knife from the drawer. "You see, I thought this experience might make a suitable story. Anyway, I suddenly realized that what the man told me tonight didn't add up. He said he saw my car leave the road, and that he simply ran from where he was standing to the car. Which was, of course, impossible. He would have left prints. I'd swear on my mother's life there were no prints. Therefore: He was lying."

"Why didn't you call the police?"

"By that time it was too late. The telephone line had been cut, the car tires had been slashed, my mobile phone had been stolen a couple of days ago—by your devious brother, no doubt. I didn't dare leave the house. I had to wait for him to come to me. My only ace was that I would have the element of surprise. He wouldn't suspect that I knew he was posing as you."

"You must have hit him hard with that old cricket bat?"

"By heaven did I! I knew I wouldn't get a second chance. I opened the patio door. Then the moment he stepped across the threshold, I walloped him one."

"Anthony's going to wake up in the police cells with one hell of a headache."

"Good. He deserves it. Now, will you pass me that bowl, please. No, not the green, the red one. Thanks."

He handed me the bowl, saying, "The police agree with your own conclusions. That my brother was going to kill you—after first disguising himself as me—and that he'd roamed the village, making sure he was seen by your neighbors. And, no doubt, he'd grown impatient of waiting for my father to die a natural death, so he'd probably repeat the charade of dressing up in the vagrant disguise and killing him, too. Of course, I'd be arrested for both murders." He watched me trim the fat from the beef. "My God, I haven't seen a piece of meat like that in months, never mind tasted it. Are you going to roast it?"

"Roast it? Heavens, no. That would be a waste of perfectly good beef. I'm going to cut it into tiny slivers, marinate it for twenty-four hours in herbs and red wine, then simmer long and hard before serving it with a sauce thickened with chilies. It's a variation of a Malaysian dish and guaranteed to turn the taste buds incandescent."

"I used to love a Sunday roast of beef when I was a child," he said dreamily. "I'd play near the kitchens, knowing that if I hung around long enough, cook would cut me a big, juicy slice of the just-roasted beef, sprinkle it with salt, then sneak it through the window to me. Sometimes it would be too hot to hold and I'd have to juggle it, still steaming, from one hand to the other. Sheer heaven."

"Well, this is going to be served oriental-style. I have friends coming to dinner tomorrow."

At that moment a Rolls-Royce pulled up outside, its massive tires cutting deep tracks in the snow.

"Uhm, Rebecca," he said, then seemed to pull himself up. "Sorry to be so familiar, Miss Taine." He smiled shyly. "My father's here to collect me. And, believe me, this is one reconciliation that is long overdue. However, I wondered if I might call you. Ahm . . ." Suddenly he seemed tonguetied. "Perhaps we can dine again sometime?"

"I don't know," I said briskly. "I'm awfully busy these days."

He blushed. "Oh, of course. I'm sorry for being so . . . ah, well . . ." He held out his hand. I shook it. "Thank you so much for helping me. Without your, ahm, accidental intervention I wouldn't be here today." Again he seemed to struggle to find the right words. "Thank heaven for the snow, what say you? Ahm, excellent . . . good day, thanks for everything."

With that he quickly left the house. A white-haired man, his father, embraced Robert at the gate and led him toward the Rolls-Royce, the rear doors of which were opened by a chauffeur. Seconds later, they were gone. I was alone again. As I had been for most of my adult life.

"From vagrant to aristocrat in twenty-four hours," I said to myself. "Now, there's a transformation you don't see every day." I paused. "And do you think he had really fallen in love with you, Rebecca?" I sighed, then briskly shook my head. "Come on, sunshine. This beef won't dice itself." I gripped the handle of the knife and positioned its keen edge against the meat. Again I pictured Robert De Lacey's wistful expression as he recalled golden days of childhood warmed by roast beef dinners in the family home.

"Okay, Rebecca," I told myself. "You're cooking Beef Malaysian for eight."

I paused, knife above the meat. Then I gave a massive grin.

"Oh, no, you're not. You're going to make a bloody good roast for two!"

Mat Coward is another British writer better known across the pond than over here. He brings a special sardonic touch to his crime fiction, a touch that can sometimes sting with fury and other times touch with unexpected sentiment. In "Old Sultan," an update of the fairy tale of the same name, he examines loyalty and honor among thieves with the same swift touch.

MAT COWARD

Old Sultan

No one had ever called Sultan a nice guy. He didn't even think of himself—on those very rare occasions when he thought about himself at all—as a nice guy.

But loyal, yes. He thought of himself as loyal, and he thought that others thought of him that way, too. You didn't have to be nice to do his job, was the way Sultan looked at it, but you did have to be loyal.

And here was the thing: It had never occurred to him that loyalty didn't go both ways. Just never occurred to him.

"So how do you know he's going to kill you?" said Wolf, and Sultan thought, What sort of dumb question is that? Wolf's in the business, he knows how these things work.

"What else is he going to do, Wolfie? Give me a pension? Throw me a retirement party? Buy me a cottage by the seaside?"

"Okay, he's going to kill you." Wolf shrugged his gym-built shoulders, his long, curly, sun-blond hair rattling around his sunbed-orange face.

"He's going to kill me," said Sultan. "That's what I been telling you, he is going to kill me, and that is just totally unfair. That is just totally out of order. Twenty-three years, one mistake, and—blam."

"The old lead handshake," said Wolf.

"He's going to kill me," said Sultan. "Is that a bastard or what?"

"He's a bastard," Wolf nodded. "Geoff Shepherd is an ungrateful bastard."

"No, no." Sultan shook his bullet-shaped, crew-cut head, spilled a little beer on his barrel chest, wiped it off with his ham hands so it flicked downward, onto his big gut, which looked like it might have been fat or might have been muscle. "No, that's where you're wrong—Mr. Shepherd isn't a bastard. The situation is a bastard, but Mr. Shepherd . . . he's a good boss, Wolfie, he really is. It's been a privilege to serve him these twenty-three years, and the only thing I want in the world is to serve him for another twenty-three."

"Well, yeah, take your point," said Wolf. "But I mean, come on, man—one mistake, you'd think he could live with that, wouldn't you? Bloke that rich, what does it matter?"

The pub, in Covent Garden, was empty. Full of people, so packed it'd take a bomb scare to clear a space at the bar, but as far as Sultan and Wolf were concerned it was empty: full of nothing people, tourists, office workers. Zombies. No one they knew ever drank here, no one from Sultan's arena in North London, or Wolf's south of the river. They could talk as loud as they liked, no one who mattered a damn would hear a damn.

"Three hundred thousand pounds, Wolfie, that's what I cost Mr. Shepherd last Saturday."

"It happens," said Wolf with a shrug. He was in the same line of work: sheepdogging people, merchandise. Ten years younger than Sultan, nowhere near as experienced, but still basically off the same shelf. He knew you couldn't get it right every time.

"Never happened to me," said Sultan. "Never happened to Mr. Shepherd, neither, not since I been with him. And I been with him pretty much since the start."

And another difference between the two of them: Wolf didn't take the stubborn pride in his work that Sultan did, didn't go for all this old-shit loyalty stuff. It was a living, that's all. If you're big, you don't lose your bottle, and you can keep your mouth shut— yeah, a good living. But just a living, not some sort of bleedin' *religion*.

"You got a number of choices," said Wolf, getting down to business, growing mildly irritated by his friend's company. Hell—*friend.* Professional acquaintance would be more like it. If poor old Sultan wanted to do something about all this, fine, Wolf could see a way. But if he was just looking for someone to whine to, let him buy a woman with big ears.

"Choice number one," he said, hoping the big fool was listening, because he wasn't going to say this twenty times. "You get him before he gets you."

"No," said Sultan, and that was the end of that.

"Okay, choice number two. You do a runner."

"Where to?" said Sultan, and Wolf realized, with another flicker of annoyance, that the question wasn't rhetorical.

"Hell, *wherever,* man! You got family somewhere, yeah? Friends, whatever. Or, better yet, somewhere where nobody knows you, start again. Spain, America, Eastern Europe."

"I don't want to go," said Sultan, and that, too, was that.

"Right," said Wolf, leaning in, getting serious now. "You want to keep your job, yeah? Okay then, there's only one way we can fix that."

"He says it's because I'm too old," said Sultan.

"I know, man, you told me. Too old to do the business anymore. That's crap, man, and you're going to prove it."

"I heard him talking about it with that poofter son of his. Too old, getting past it, got to go."

"Yes," said Wolf. "Now listen to me: the poofter son, Tony—am I right in thinking you don't have the same feelings of loyalty to Tony as you do to his father, yeah?"

"I don't give a toss about Tony," said Sultan. So, hell, he *had* been listening. Well, well, you just never could tell.

"Good," said Wolf. "In that case, go get us a couple of pints and I'll make a couple of phone calls, and pretty soon all your troubles will be behind you."

For a further hour, they discussed details. At no point in the conversation did Sultan say "Thanks" to Wolf, for all the trouble he was going to on Sultan's behalf.

Loyalty: You were loyal to your boss, your friends, family if you'd got one, and that was that. Thanks didn't come into it.

"Okay, Tony—get in the car."

"Who the hell are you?" said Tony, in that second-generation-money accent to which Wolf, himself, aspired in vain.

"You don't ask, you don't find out," said Wolf. "And if you don't find out, you don't get killed. All right?" It was pretty dark here, and pretty deserted, but even so—a thing like this, you don't want to hang about, take your time over it. If the guy has time to think, to work it out, to say to himself *He's not going to kill me,* and just walk away . . .

"This *is* a gun in my hand, by the way," Wolf added. "Just in case you thought it was something else, and the crime under way here was, maybe, indecent exposure. It isn't, Tony, it's kidnapping. Now get in the bloody car!"

Tony got in. What the hell, his dad would sort it out.

"You know who's got him?" Geoff Shepherd's voice was frankly incredulous.

"Not exactly *know,* Mr. Shepherd," said Sultan. "But I am sure I can find out. I am sure I can get him back for you. There's no one knows North London like I know it, Mr. Shepherd, you know yourself that's true."

Provided they're keeping my son in a pub, thought Shepherd. But then, none of his other people seemed to have a clue about this. It had come from nowhere—who the hell would snatch Geoff Shepherd's son? Who could possibly be that crazy? "All right, Sultan, listen." He'd had plans for Sultan—plans for that very day, in fact—but they could wait. The old dog wasn't going anywhere, too stupid to run. He'd let him do this, sniff around, come up with nothing, and then he'd take care of him.

No hurry.

"Yes, Mr. Shepherd?" said Sultan eagerly.

"You do what you can. And if you find him . . . well, obviously, if you do find him, Sultan, I'll be very grateful. Most grateful indeed." Which was true. A son is a son, after all, no matter how big a waste of space he might be.

Three nights later, Sultan watched from across the road as Wolf deposited a heavily doped Tony Shepherd in the disused beer cellar of a gay club in Soho. After a while Wolf came out of the cellar and gave Sultan the thumbs up.

Sultan waited five, ten minutes. Made love to the shadows, smoked a cigarette. Kept watch.

Nothing moved; nobody on the plot.

He ground out his cigarette and set to work with the bolt cutters. Easy job, didn't even sweat, but it'd look like he'd had a struggle, should anyone ever come checking. Which he doubted: The club was an independent, its security guy just happened to be unlucky enough to owe Wolf a favor. There was nothing here to lead Mr. Shepherd to his son's kidnappers.

"Tony! Tony, you there, son?" Sultan shouted into the mildewed darkness. "Tony, it's okay, mate, it's me—Sultan."

A groan. Sultan took out his penlight, called again, received another answering groan, navigated toward a far corner.

There—lying on the stone floor, his ankles cuffed to his wrists: "London's most ineligible bachelor," as Mr Shepherd sometimes referred to his son. The heir to one of the capital's most successful, and fastest-growing, and most rapidly modernizing business empires.

"Tony? You alive, mate? It's me, Sultan. You're all right now, I've come to take you home."

Still blindfolded, still groggy, the heir cocked his head toward his savior's voice. "Who the hell are you?" he asked with a croak.

"Sultan," said Sultan.

"Who the holy shit is Sultan?" asked Tony, sounding deeply unimpressed.

Who am I? thought Sultan. *Who am I? Not only am I the man who's just saved your life, you little prat, I have also been one of your father's most loyal employees since before you were born!* He felt blood burning in his ears. *You want to learn to take a bit more interest in your inheritance, boy!*

And then—because, after all, his loyalty was to the father, not the son—Sultan drew back his booted foot and let it fly, nice and hard, into Tony's stomach.

"Oi, you!" cried Sultan. "Get out of it!" He stumbled about the cellar, banging into walls, grunting and groaning, wrestling with an invisible opponent. The fight ended in the slamming of the door, and Sultan leaned down to place a solicitous hand on Tony's shoulder. "Christ, you all right, son? One of the bastards must've been still hanging around—he got that kick in before I could stop him. You all right?"

"Now I know who Sultan is," Tony said, as if to himself. "He's the fat, stupid one."

Sultan's foot was halfway back through its swing when he stopped it—with an effort, and with the thought that, No, one kick was free, but two and the little sod'd be sure to rumble him, dope or no dope.

Instead, he picked the boy up, threw him over his shoulders, and carried him out to the backseat of the car. A mile or so later, he pulled in to an empty pub parking lot and removed Tony's blindfold.

The heir opened his eyes, one by one, blinked, gobbed up a blatant lump of blood-smeared phlegm, and raised his eyes to see the face of the man who'd come to deliver him to his father's wrath.

"Took your time, didn't you," he said, sneering. "And I don't suppose you thought to bring a flask with you, huh? *Sultan?*"

Sultan stared at him. Hating him. *The things I do for my boss,* he thought.

"Tell you what, lad," he said. "You behave yourself and I won't tell your dad where I found you."

That had the little bastard white-faced all the way home.

Sultan enjoyed the moment. Another thing his job, his life, had taught him: Enjoy the moment. You get up in the morning and you've still got your face, you're ahead of the game.

For three weeks, Sultan enjoyed the moment.

And then Wolf turned up one night, smiling and licking his lips.

Sultan, back in his master's good books—in better books, if the truth be told, than he'd been in for some years—was baby-sitting one of Mr. Shepherd's young executives taking delivery of a consignment of merchandise at a road café near Heathrow International Airport.

The deal made, the young executive slapped Sultan on the back, said, "Won't be a mo, Granddad, just nipping to the gents," and left Sultan, and the merchandise, sitting in the firm's BMW in the café parking lot.

Which was when Wolf rapped on the passenger-side window.

Sultan didn't jump out of his skin. You did that in his line of work, and you were dead. But as he leaned over to crack the window open, keeping his right hand carefully out of view, he did have to concentrate on his breathing just a bit. Especially when he saw who was there.

"Hell did you spring from?" he said, trying to imagine the kind of innocent coincidence that might have brought Wolf to this same parking lot on this same night.

Wolf, long tongue running over dry lips, got straight down to business. "There's ten separately wrapped units in that package, Sultan," he said. "I only need one of them."

Ah, right, thought Sultan. He nodded to himself: There's no such thing as coincidence, Mr. Shepherd often said, and as usual, Mr. Shepherd had been proved right.

"Come on, Sultan," Wolf wheedled, his over-the-shoulder glances increasingly edgy. "You owe me, don't you? You don't deny that?"

"All right," said Sultan, unlocking the passenger-side door, sliding over to get out on that side. This time he didn't bother hiding the gun as he slipped it into his waistband.

"Good man!" Wolf crowed, and then gasped as his fat, stupid, sometime pal stepped out of the car, and, seemingly in the same motion, picked him up by his hair and his balls.

"In case you was wondering," Sultan said, carrying Wolf over to a bank of metal mesh litter bins at the far side of the parking lot, "it's muscle, not fat. Just in case you was wondering."

While Wolf lay, winded in body and spirit, amid the burger

boxes and the hardened blobs of chewing gum, they both heard a car squeal off into the night.

"Looks like you lost your lift," said Sultan. "You got money for a cab?"

Wolf nodded.

"Okay, then," said Sultan, walking briskly back to the BMW. He turned once, to say, in a quiet but carrying voice: "I do owe you, Wolfie, that's right. And one day I will repay you. But I'll tell you when, all right?"

The junior executive got back in the car moments after Sultan. "All cool on the Western Front?" he chirped.

"Yeah," said Sultan, foot on the pedal.

It shocked Sultan that Wolf didn't give up after that. Really shocked him. "Know when to go for it, know when to call it a day"—how often had he heard Mr. Shepherd say that? That was the trouble with blokes like Wolfie—no mentors, no education. Different generation.

Wolf's second approach was, by his standards, a little more subtle.

In a pub full of Greek Cypriots in Crouch End, Sultan sat one Saturday at lunchtime, more than a month after his daring rescue of Tony Shepherd from the still unidentified hands of his kidnappers. He was watching the dart players, enjoying a quiet pint and that particular restfulness he sometimes found in the company of people he didn't know, when the bench he was sitting on sagged under the weight of a bodybuilder's buttocks.

"Listen," said Wolf without preliminaries, "sorry about that crap the other night."

"Forget it," said Sultan, and the way he said it—firm rather than dismissive—made it clear that he was not employing a mere cliché.

"No, look," said Wolf, leaning his mousse-scented lion's mane into Sultan's neck, putting his mouth next to Sultan's ear, "I went about it all wrong. You had every right to slap me. I was being crude, I wasn't thinking. All right? Apology accepted?"

Sultan said nothing beyond a murmured "Good arrows, son,"

addressed to a player who'd just stuck in a three-dart finish while his opponent was still warming up.

"Thing is, Sultan, I know what you were thinking, and you're totally correct—doing it that way, you're just going to get yourself into trouble. And I don't want that. Do I? After all the trouble I went to before, getting you out of trouble. Hey?"

No response.

"Point is, though," Wolf continued, because he'd come here to say his piece, and no dumb act was going to stop him, "point is, man, a favor deserves a favor. Yeah? So this time I got a plan, a proper plan, and I just need you to help me out."

Sultan hadn't looked at Wolf since he sat down. He didn't now, as he said, quietly, "I'll help you out that fucking window, you don't do as I say and forget it."

Wolf stood up. "All I need," he said, "is for you to go blind and deaf for about thirty seconds. That's all. And then we're quits. I'll be in touch."

And he was. Two more chance meetings, a phone call—even, for God's sake, a letter, sent to Sultan's home address! Sultan couldn't remember the last time he'd had a letter. Nobody wrote to Sultan, not even the government. Not even American Express.

This had to stop.

"Thanks for agreeing to a meet, man. I mean it," said Wolf, buckling his belt in the passenger seat of the BMW. "I truly appreciate this. And listen, before you say anything, I just want to say this, right? This can work for us. You and me, we're two of a kind, Sultan, and this thing can work *big* for us. And the beauty of it is, no one need ever know. Because I've worked it out, yeah? What I figure is—"

Sultan hadn't buckled his seat belt. He leaned down, produced the gun from under the driver's seat.

"This is what *I've* worked out, Wolfie," he said.

"Oh God," whispered Wolf. "You're not . . ."

He said nothing more, just stared at the gun, and Sultan felt sure there wasn't going to be any fighting here. Just in case, though, he looked right into Wolf's eyes and said, "Muscle, remember? Not fat."

Wolf hardly resisted at all as Sultan locked him in the trunk of the car.

Sultan got back in, lit a cigarette, fastened his seat belt. Pulled out into the weekend traffic, and made for the highway.

He only stopped once on the long drive, at a service station three hours into the journey.

He got out, walked around the car, and banged on the lid of the trunk. "You alive?" he said.

"*Listen, Sultan—*"

"Right," said Sultan. He got back in, buckled up, and drove on.

Looking at Wolf now, naked, sitting on his bare bottom on the damp soil, Sultan could see he was nothing special.

Younger? Yeah, sure, he was younger and prettier than Sultan. But then, so was a newborn baby. You can get a body from a gym, Sultan thought, but you can't get an education. You can't learn the rules. Only experience teaches those kind of lessons.

At least the man was smart enough not to run. Unless he wasn't being smart, just tough. Either way, here in what must be pretty damn close to the exact geographical middle of nowhere, Wolf had stripped at Sultan's command, had sat at Sultan's command, had remained still at Sultan's command.

Still except for the shivering, and Sultan could hardly blame him for that. Dusk had fallen long since, and they didn't go in for warm nights in deepest, unspoiled Scotland.

"I thought you helped me because that was what friends did," Sultan told Wolf, speaking slowly, speaking loudly, trying to make this foolish, vain apprentice understand the way things worked. "I thought you was being loyal to me, because we were mates. I didn't know that you was doing it so that I would have to do something for you."

Wolf said nothing. He knew there was nothing worth saying now, in this place and time. He just wished it was over. He just wished he had something to drink: cold always made him thirsty. Cold and fear both.

"But okay," Sultan continued, scratching his spiky chin with the hand that wasn't holding the gun. "You thought you were doing me a favor, you thought I owed you one, you don't know what loyalty means. All right then, we'll play by your rules. I *do* owe you one, and now I'm going to pay it back."

Wolf managed a wispy laugh. "Some favor, fat man."

Sultan didn't reply. Just stuck the gun in his jacket pocket, began walking back to the car, parked uninhabited miles away.

"What—where are you—what are you doing, man?" For the first time in hours, Wolf didn't feel that he was minutes away from death; and—it was weird, but he kind of felt like he'd been stood up on a date.

Sultan turned, walked slowly backward as he said: "You stay there until I'm out of sight. Then it's up to you. You and I have no further business."

Wolf stumbled to his feet, fell to earth again as his cramped legs collapsed. "I'll die out here, man! No clothes, no water—I'll bloody die out here, you fat bastard!" And then, more reasonably, he added: "At least give me my contact lenses back!"

"If I ever see you again," said Sultan, "in London or anywhere else, I will kill you dead. No discussion, just *blam.* Got that?"

Sultan *was* almost out of sight before it struck him that he was leaving unfinished business behind him. Had he really taught Wolfie the lesson he so badly wanted him to learn? Unsure, he retraced his steps.

There was Wolfie, still sitting there. He looked a mess. Stinking, from his long imprisonment in the car. Wretched, from his predicament. His face filthy with tear tracks. His hair still looked good, though, you had to give him that.

He looked up at Sultan's approach and started crying again. "I knew you'd be back, you fat bastard."

"I wanted to make sure you understood. If I ever see you again, I *will* kill you. Not to punish you, or to shut you up, or because I'm scared of you, or any of that crap. But because it would mean that you'd been disloyal to me. It would mean that you'd done me a favor, I'd done you one by return, and then you'd turned around and flung it back in my face."

Satisfied now, he turned and walked away again. This time he didn't look back.

He was busy thinking: Loyalty—it works both ways, and in all directions. If you don't know that, then what's the point of getting out of bed in the morning?

Now to go home and work out a way of teaching the same lesson to Mr. Shepherd.

Elizabeth Engstrom is best known for her dark suspense stories. The late Theodore Sturgeon, one of science fiction's greatest talents, felt that she was one of the best writers of her generation. In the following story, "Hansel and Gretel" encounter a very nasty witch indeed.

ELIZABETH ENGSTROM

Harvest Home

By the time Roman had hauled himself out of bed, dressed, slogged down a cup of coffee while shaving, grabbed his lunch box, and made it slowly, tiredly out the door for work, Cindy was agitated to the point of dizziness.

The minute the door slammed behind him, she roused the children. "Get up! Get up! C'mon, we have an adventure today. Five minutes. C'mon, we have to leave here in five minutes." She pulled the covers off each of the kids and shook their shoulders. "C'mon, Freddie. C'mon, Kewpie. We're going for a ride."

Freddie's eyes opened and he rubbed them, but Kewpie just screwed up her face and reached for her teddy bear.

"Get her up, Freddie," Cindy said. "I've got to dress."

She ran a brush through her hair and smeared on some eye shadow. She didn't need to be beautiful for this transaction. She just needed to be present. And on time.

She pulled on a pair of slacks and a sweater, spritzed some perfume to mask the scent of sleeping next to Roman all night, brushed her teeth, and pulled the suitcase from the back of the closet, where it was packed and ready to go. Roman never even noticed that her side of the closet was empty.

"Get up!" she said to Kewpie, grabbing the little girl by the ankle and pulling her to the bottom of the bed.

"Don't pull her," Freddie said.

"Then you get her up," Cindy countered, checking her watch. "And get dressed. We have a plane to catch."

"An airplane?"

Even Kewpie's eyes opened at that, and she sat up.

"Yep," Cindy said, now realizing how to motivate them. "We're going on a trip."

"What about Daddy?" Kewpie asked.

"He'll meet us later," Cindy lied.

"Where are we going?"

"Florida."

The children's eyes widened. "On an airplane?" Freddie asked again.

"Yes, but only if you hurry. Get up now, get your backpacks and pack two pairs of fresh underwear and a change of clothes. Don't forget socks."

Freddie got their backpacks from the closet.

"Freddie, you can help Kewpie. Two changes of underwear and one change of clothes. And you can each bring one toy." Cindy walked out of their bedroom and into the kitchen, but she had no taste for breakfast. She'd had no internal battle over this situation until just now, just this moment, when the children looked at her with such trust in their eyes.

Too bad. Too late. The wheels—whatever they were—had been put into motion.

The children were dressed and ready to go in record time. Cindy handed each of them a bagel, checked again to make sure she had the tickets, and hustled them out of the apartment and into the frigid car.

"How come Daddy never mentioned going to Florida?" Freddie asked.

"Know how you can never sleep on Christmas Eve?" Cindy said. "We didn't want you to get so excited you couldn't sleep. Today is going to be a big day; you needed your rest."

"Mickey Mouse lives in Florida," Freddie said to Kewpie, and Cindy's heart gave a squeeze.

She parked the car and hustled the kids through the airport, and they made the gate just as the flight to Miami was boarding. The children were wide-eyed and excited, and they made sure the flight attendant knew they were going to Florida. The pretty girl smiled at Cindy with an "aren't you a lucky mom" smile. Cindy scowled back. If she liked the children so much, *she* could entertain them. Cindy plugged in the headphones and turned up the music.

The idea of having a family was a good one at first. Roman was big, handsome, and a hard worker. Cindy was heartbroken and damaged and saw no future for herself. Roman needed a mom for his kids, Cindy needed something to cling to, so they married and Cindy moved in.

Within a month, she knew it had been a bad move.

Freddie at seven and Kewpie at five were incredibly high maintenance projects. Cindy didn't have enough energy to care for herself, much less two little kids. Roman worked two jobs just to pay the bills, so she never saw him and had to do all the work by herself. And there wasn't even enough money left over for any of the sweet things. Like jewelry. Or trips. Or a winter coat, like a husband ought to buy his wife. Life for Cindy became a steaming pit of resentment.

When Roman went to his night job, Cindy put the kids to bed, locked their bedroom door, and went to hang out at the Cyber-Café. A cute guy had shown her how to log on and chat with a variety of interesting people, people she felt she had more in common with than her husband. Soon she was hooked.

And that's where she met Della. On-line.

Della seemed to understand everything Cindy was going through. She understood how frustrating stepchildren could be, she understood an inattentive husband, she understood having not enough money to buy a fresh lipstick. She became Cindy's best friend. Cindy poured out her heart and soul to Della, who responded with sympathy and empathy and love.

Over a period of time, Della convinced Cindy that she ought to bring the kids to Miami for a visit. There were investment opportunities. There were things Cindy could do to climb out of that pit. Go stay with Della and let her take over the kids for a couple of days. Cindy had made an investment in Roman and his family, a hasty, unwise investment, and perhaps it was time for her to consider her own needs. Cut her losses, liquidate her assets, and get on to the next adventure.

Everybody would be better off. Everybody except perhaps Roman, but he'd survive. Someday he'd thank her for helping him shed a little baggage.

Della talked softly and sweetly about it to Cindy, and before Cindy knew it, a packet of airline tickets showed up in the mailbox. A round trip for Cindy and two one-way tickets for the kids.

Must be a mistake, Cindy told herself, rationalizing that she didn't know what she was getting into. She hid the tickets, and from that moment on, everything Roman or either one of the children did made her want to scream. Everything, every little thing, reinforced her decision to go spend some time with Della.

The plane touched down at Miami International, and Cindy felt her heart pounding in her chest.

It's not too late, she told herself. *I can turn right around and put the three of us on the next plane to LaGuardia and be home by the time Roman gets off work.*

But she knew she wouldn't.

Della met her at the gate.

She looked like someone's well-tended grandmother, not at all the good-times soul sister that Cindy expected. They hugged like old friends, then Della squatted and hugged each one of the children and gave them Disney toys. She carried a briefcase.

"We'll walk you to your gate," Della said.

Cindy looked at her ticket, then up at the wall clock and realized with a taste of panic that her return flight left in forty minutes.

Della engaged the kids in spirited conversation about their flight. Della knew exactly how to talk to kids. Cindy had never acquired that enviable skill.

They got to Cindy's departure gate as the plane was boarding. "I'm going to take the children to the rest room while you board," Della said softly. "No good-byes." And she handed Cindy the briefcase. Then she turned with the children and walked down the concourse, leaving Cindy lonelier than she had ever felt in her life.

She dully handed her ticket to the agent and boarded the plane. In the tiny airplane rest room, she opened the briefcase and found it full of packets of twenty-dollar bills. It was more money than she had ever seen before. It was more money than she could ever have imagined having.

It didn't help. Somehow it didn't help, and tears leaked out of her eyes, ran down her cheeks, and fell onto the cash.

"Where's Cindy?" Freddie asked Della when he came out of the men's room.

"She's gone back to fetch your daddy," Della said. "You're going to come home with me and they'll meet us later."

Kewpie wrapped her arm around her bear's neck, stuck her thumb in her mouth, and grabbed Della's hand with her other. It was clear to Freddie that Kewpie preferred Della to Cindy, and, in fact, so did he.

They rode in a blue van and looked at palm trees and blue sky with soft clouds. They'd never seen palm trees before. Freddie had a feeling that something wasn't right, but Della kept talking to him, and the longer they talked, the more he liked her.

She took them to a big house and gave them their own bedroom. It had twin beds with matching blue bedspreads and curtains. There were games and puzzles and toys in the closet, and clothes in the drawers. "When do we get to see Mickey Mouse?" he asked Della.

"Soon," she promised. "Now get into your jammies."

"Why?"

"Because a doctor is going to come and talk to you in a little while, and he wants to see you in your jammies."

Kewpie did as she was told, and Freddie reluctantly followed her example. Something wasn't right about this. He wanted to see his dad.

Somebody was crying. Somebody in the house. Some little kid.

Freddie got out of bed and went to the door, but it was locked.

A little while later a doctor and a nurse came in and told them that every person's fingerprint was different, and he inked up each of their forefingers and pressed it to a card to show them. Then he put a rubber band around Kewpie's arm, stuck a needle in her vein, and filled up tubes with her blood. Kewpie screamed, and when it was Freddie's turn, he tried not to cry, but it hurt and he was scared. "It's called tissue matching," the doctor tried to explain, "it's just like a fingerprint," but Freddie wanted to see his dad, and he wanted to see him *now.*

The nurse gave both of them something cherry-flavored to drink out of a tiny plastic cup. Kewpie settled down with a baby doll and a red sucker, and soon Freddie had a hard time keeping his eyes open. Kewpie slumped sideways over her new doll, a spit bubble blowing in and out of little lips still red from the liquid she drank.

Freddie closed his eyes. In spite of himself, he liked the feeling of this new bed, new sheets, new pajamas, but he still hoped that when he woke up, he'd be back at home, hating Cindy all the way to hell.

Cindy's plane touched down in New York about the time Roman would be getting off work. Her stomach was in an uproar. She could no longer deny the fact that she had foreseen this outcome— a briefcase full of cash and no more kids—and she found out that she didn't have a plan to take from here. If she had been smart, she would have just taken off for Rio or somewhere, right from Miami. Why did she use her round-trip ticket? It didn't make sense. Some kind of a homing device, she thought. Her suitcase full of clothes was in the trunk of the car.

She got off the plane in the stream of passengers and looked around the airport full of people with purpose. She was too antsy, too agitated to get on another plane. Maybe it was good this way. She could drive. She could drive across country. She could drive to Canada. She could put the pedal to the metal and get out of town under her own power. She could drive fast and hard and sing loud along with the radio. Somewhere along the way she'd ditch the car. Maybe she'd just drive down to D.C. and leave it in the airport parking lot there. Maybe she'd fly to Paris or Zurich and make a fresh start.

She squealed tires in Roman's old beater and headed south.

With hands shaking from cold and guilt, and trying not to think about the nausea that was building like a volcano, she fiddled with a recalcitrant heater and a shorted out AM radio as two lanes merged. While her attention was desperately elsewhere, a Volvo sideswiped her rattletrap car going seventy-five miles an hour.

The car spun across four lanes of traffic, hitting everything and everyone in its rush-hour path. Nightmare Bumper Cars. Ultra Pinball.

Cindy screamed with what breath was in her as terror squeezed her throat. She was bashed, rolled, flipped, and tossed.

Roman's car ended up slowly spinning on its crushed top, the steering wheel embedded in Cindy's chest, packets of twenty-dollar bills littered all around her.

The phone began to ring as Roman stared blankly, unseeing, uncomprehending, at Cindy's empty closet. Somewhere in the back of his mind he knew what had happened; it had been inevitable, really. She'd been too young, too much of a free spirit for him to tie down with kids that weren't hers and who resented her. But that didn't mean that the sight of tangled, empty hangers didn't sear his soul.

Oh, well. Kiss marriage good-bye. This was his third-time-charm effort. He'd be disinclined to try again. Not until the children were grown and gone. He didn't want to put himself through this again, but he *really* couldn't put the kids through it again. They'd never learn how to trust.

Hookers and day care. His life would be reduced to hookers and day care and working his ass off. What a charming thought.

Speaking of day care . . . Cindy must have left a note telling him where to pick up the kids.

He walked out of the bedroom and into the kitchen, where logic told him a note would be. There was no note. He picked up the ringing telephone more to quell its relentless noise than to talk to anyone, but habit made him put the receiver to his ear and say, "Hello?"

"Mr. Daniloff? Mr. Roman Daniloff?"

"Yes?"

"New York police, Mr. Daniloff. Your wife has been in an accident. She's at Good Samaritan Hospital."

Life clicked into focus and Roman could count the microseconds float by. "Is she hurt?"

"You better come down right away."

"The children?"

"Children?"

"Were the kids with her?"

"No, sir."

Thank God.

Twenty minutes later he was sitting beside Cindy's empty bed while she was in surgery. On his lap rested a paper sack full of money.

When he first arrived at the hospital, he began going through the things the police brought in from the twisted wreck that had been his car. The suitcase, full of her cheap, floozy clothes. Her purse. Her passport. Her address book.

And a big paper bag full of twenty-dollar bills.

He went through her purse, but there was nothing extraordinary in there, either. No clues to where the kids might be. Nothing.

He dumped the cash out onto the hospital room floor and picked up each blood-soaked packet of twenties, fanned through it, and put it back into the paper bag. One hundred thousand dollars.

Good God, what had she done?

Hours later, they wheeled her bed in.

Cindy was pale, cut, bruised, and hooked up to a variety of machines, one of which was keeping her heart going. Her rib cage had been crushed, they'd removed one lung, and her heart was damaged beyond repair. Her only hope of survival was a new heart. The doctor told Roman she'd been bumped to the top of the priority list. She could be saved if she remained stable long enough. If a heart could be found.

Roman didn't know about all that stuff. He only knew that something had happened to his kids, and this faithless bitch and this bag of money were all part of it.

When a nurse came in to check on Cindy, Roman asked if she could be awakened.

The nurse looked at him pityingly as if he were an idiot and shook her head. Then she left the room.

Roman thought he was going to lose his mind.

He opened the closet to put the cash and the suitcase in there, and saw a plastic bag with Cindy's torn, cut, and bloodied clothes. He emptied that out and went through it. Nothing.

But her stained coat hung in the closet, and in its pocket, he found a paperback romance with two airline ticket stubs stuck in as bookmarks. LaGuardia to Miami, Miami to LaGuardia. Today.

Roman looked over at her—small, pale, every breath initiated by a hissing machine in the corner. *Wake up, you evil bitch,* he thought. He wanted to jump up and down on her ravaged chest and have her spit out the information with her dying breath.

He talked to the police, but they were only mildly interested. They had too many things to take care of right there in New York. They didn't have the time or the resources to track down a couple of kids who may or may not be missing. And without any further information, it would be futile for Roman to fly to Miami.

His only hope was for Cindy to get her new heart. Hopefully, they'd replace the hard lump of stone she had in her chest for a real flesh-and-blood heart. Then she would wake up and tell him what she'd done for one hundred thousand dollars.

He'd go to Florida, return the money, and pick up his kids.

Roman set his jaw and sat down on a plastic chair, listening to Cindy's various monitors and ventilator. He was prepared to wait.

When Freddie woke up, Kewpie was gone. A lady brought him a tray of breakfast, but he wasn't hungry. He was homesick and worried about his baby sister.

"I want my daddy," he said and started to cry.

"I know you do, honey," the lady said and sat down on the bed. She had a nice face, and Freddie knew she would help him. She held him and rocked him and cooed to him until he was all out of tears and only hiccups were left. Then she gave him another drink of that cherry syrup and Freddie fell asleep.

*　　*　　*

"We have a heart," the doctor said. "It's young, very young, but we are optimistic that it will continue to grow, and will serve your wife well for many years. It's an unusually good tissue match, and the timing is amazingly fortuitous. But your wife's movement will be restricted for a length of time—she'll probably be confined to a wheelchair for as much as two years, while everything adjusts. And, of course, there are the antirejection drugs, which take their toll." He leaned forward. "This is outrageous good fortune," he said. "Unheard of, actually. Five years ago, your wife would have died. But with today's technology—"

"Just wake her up," Roman said.

The doctor handed him the consent forms, and Roman signed.

"The heart will be here tomorrow," the doctor said. "I'll notify the team."

When Freddie awoke, he didn't know what day it was. It seemed to be dawn, and Kewpie still wasn't in her bed.

He pulled the covers up over his head and tented his knees so he could see around in his dark little bed cave and tried not to cry. He tried not to be afraid. He tried to figure out what he could do. He wanted to get dressed, and when they came in to bring his breakfast, he could just push the lady over and run out the door. He had his own clothes. He even had fresh underwear.

He thought about what was in his backpack.

A cell phone.

The cell phone! He always kept it in his backpack in case he needed his dad. It was so small and light, and it was kind of fun. Best of all, he could beep his dad anytime, day or night, if he had a nightmare, or if he missed the school bus, or whatever. He never had, but he knew he could.

He snuck out of bed, opened the closet, unzipped his backpack, and grabbed the phone, then zipped up the backpack, closed the closet door, and dove back under the covers.

He didn't want to screw this up.

He opened the phone and turned it on. Then he pressed Memory 1 and heard the phone dial. Just as the beeper operator came on, there was a soft knock on his door, and it opened.

Heart pounding, he clicked off the phone, hoped nobody heard the beep, folded the phone, and peeked out of the covers.

"Good morning," the doctor said. "How are you?"

"Where's Kewpie?" Freddie asked, sliding the phone under his legs.

"She's helping someone right now," he said.

"How long are we going to be here?" Freddie asked. "I want to go home."

A nurse came in with a tray full of tubes and packages and sat on Freddie's bed. "We need to take some more samples," the doctor said, and Freddie began to cry.

"I hate this," he said.

"I know, sweetie," the nurse said. She was so nice, and so pretty that Freddie wanted to trust her, he wanted to trust her so bad, but he just couldn't.

He got out of bed, leaving the cell phone under the covers, and peed into their jar. Then he got back into bed and grit his teeth while they took a tube of his blood, thinking not of the needle, but of the cell phone underneath him. It would be terrible if his dad remembered the phone about now and gave him a call.

"Someone's going to come and help you take a shower," the nurse told him.

"I can take my own shower," Freddie said. "I'm no baby."

"Of course you're not," the nurse cooed. She gave him a Tootsie Roll pop for bravery, and while Freddie was unwrapping it, the doctor stuck another needle in his arm and gave him a shot.

The doctor left, and the nurse stayed, smoothing his hair and talking quietly to him, and Freddie felt woozy and sleepy. He wanted her to go, because he needed to call his dad. He didn't want to close his eyes, but she kept telling him to close his eyes, and so he thought that maybe if he did, she'd leave.

He closed his eyes and began to have little dreams about his room at home.

He opened them again, and she was still there, speaking softly, her fingers cool on his hot cheek.

He closed his eyes, afraid, and little dreams of Kewpie played about in his head.

He felt the nurse get up off the bed, and when he heard his door open and close, he reached for the phone under his covers.

But his eyes weren't working quite right, and the dreams kept imposing themselves upon him with his eyes wide open. His fingers felt thick and stupid.

He opened the phone and dialed the Memory number again, and this time when the beeper lady answered, he pressed 5555, or thought he did, or hoped he did, and then he hung up, just exactly the way he and his dad had practiced. That was their signal.

Freddie clicked off and held the phone to his chest, his eyes closing. *Please call right now,* he prayed. *Please call me before they come in with breakfast. Please call me before . . .*

Roman's beeper went off as he was dozing in the plastic chair in Cindy's room. First he cursed it, then he looked at it, and then he jumped out of his chair so fast that he almost tore down the flimsy curtain that surrounded her bed. He went directly to the pay phone in the hallway and dialed Freddie's cell phone number.

God, he had completely forgotten about the cell phone.

After Roman's second wife abandoned them, Freddie, then five and fearful, was terrified that Roman would go to work and not come back. So Roman had got one of those cheap cell phones for $9.95, had the airtime activated, and they practiced a signal. Whenever Freddie was feeling lonesome or scared, he could dial Roman's beeper, and Roman would call him back.

Freddie kept it in his backpack all the time, but never used it. Roman paid the minimum charge on the damned thing every month, it was a security blanket for the kid—and for him, too, he supposed—and he never considered canceling. Now he was grateful he hadn't.

The phone rang once, then clicked on. In a whisper, he heard his son say, "Dad?"

Relief flushed through Roman like a tidal wave. "Freddie, where are you?"

"Um. Florida," but there was something wrong with his voice. It was slow and low, not like Freddie at all.

"Hold it together, Freddie. Are you all right? Do you know where you are? Is Kewpie with you?"

"They took Kewpie."

He sounded as if he'd been drugged. "Okay, son, don't hang up. Just put this phone somewhere where the people won't find it and I'll get the police to trace the signal. Are you okay?"

Freddie nodded, remembered that his dad couldn't hear a nod, then croaked out a "Yeah."

"Don't be afraid, boy, I'm coming for you."

"Yeah."

"You have a place to put the phone?"

"Yeah."

"Good. Do that now, and I'll see you soon."

"Um. Hurry."

"I will. I'll come get you and The Kewp. Okay?"

Freddie nodded. Roman knew he was nodding. He could see his brave little boy, and the thought tore his heart out. "Put the phone away now, and I'll see you soon." He listened as rustling sounds came over the phone. "Freddie?"

"Mmm?"

"I love you, boy."

"Me, too," Freddie said, his voice fading.

Roman's throat filled up with hot emotion as he lay that receiver on the ledge and picked up the receiver from the pay phone next to it. He dialed 911 and hoped to God the NYPD or the FBI or somebody knew how to handle something like this. And handle it before the cell phone battery went dead.

Within an hour, the hospital corridor was filled with police.

Freddie looked at the closet. He should get up and put the cell phone back in his backpack, zip it up, and they'd never find it.

Or in between the mattresses.

But his legs wouldn't work, and his fingers just twitched when he wanted them to do something. The cell phone sat on his chest, in full view of whoever might come in, and the dreams he kept having were interfering with the task he knew he was supposed to perform.

Gotta do it for Kewpie, he said to himself, but it didn't help.

Against his will, his eyes closed, and the dreams played about on the inside of his eyelids.

When he woke up, the maid was cleaning his bathroom, he was dressed in fresh pajamas, and his sheets had been changed.

"Buenos días," she said when she saw that his eyes were open.

It took Freddie a minute or two to remember just exactly what was going on. He couldn't seem to keep track of everything.

The phone!

He rummaged in his bed, still feeling like his head was out of focus.

"Your toy is on the nightstand," the maid said, and pointed at it with her elbow as she wrung out a cloth into a soapy bucket.

Toy?

The phone.

"It fell out of your bed when I changed your sheets," she said.

Freddie grabbed it—it seemed as though his arm stretched out a mile. It was still on. The red light still glowed. He almost put it to his ear, but he didn't want the maid to know it was a phone. How could she not know it was a telephone?

He pulled it under the covers, hugged it to his chest, rolled over onto his side, and closed his eyes.

The next thing he knew, someone was yelling. Somebody ran past his door, then what sounded like a whole bunch of people ran by. He heard whispering just outside his door, then more yelling downstairs.

Then people walked up and down the hallway, up and down, up and down, and he heard that kid crying again. He wrapped his arms around his knees and prayed that nobody was going to bust through his door, but if somebody did, he hoped it would be his dad.

"Mr. Daniloff? FBI. We have your son."

A sob broke out of Roman's chest. "Is he all right?"

"He's fine. He's eating ice cream here in the lounge with thirteen other kids."

"And my daughter?"

There was a pause so deep Roman could have fallen through it. "No word on the girl yet."

That took away most of the relief. "Who are these people, anyway? What were they doing with my kids?"

"Let us get back to you as soon as we find out about your daughter, Mr. Daniloff."

"Tell my son I'll be down to pick him up."

"I'll do that, sir. He's a smart and very brave boy."

With a trembling hand, Roman clicked off the cellular phone the police had given him and looked over at Cindy, whose ventilator continued to aspirate in a maddening rhythm.

Special Agent Monroe had a five-year-old daughter himself, a precious little blue-eyed blonde who was the essence of his late mother. He believed it was no accident that he was involved in this disgusting case. He made it his personal mission to find that boy's little sister and rescue her from these monsters.

It had to be done soon. They certainly wasted no time processing these children—he couldn't afford to waste any time, either.

He mustered the city and county uniformed police and had them canvass every hospital, every clinic, every veterinarian. He wanted them to inspect every inch of any place where surgery could be competently performed. And he wanted it done within an hour.

They caught his urgency. They caught his desperation. He told them about five-year-old Kewpie Daniloff, whose name alone was enough to strum their heartstrings. Most of those uniformed cops were in the right age bracket to have five-year-old daughters themselves.

He had a ray of hope. A slim, solitary ray, but it was better than absolute darkness.

Roman watched a crew of scrub nurses wheel Cindy's bed out of the room. Apparently her new heart had arrived.

"Would you like to walk along with us?" one nice nurse asked.

Roman shook his head, respectfully declining. The thought of it made him sick. The thought of Cindy made him sick.

They wheeled her out and down the hall, and the room was uncomfortably quiet. He wanted to go get a cup of coffee, but he didn't want to move. He just wanted to sit, solid, until he heard that his baby girl was safe.

His phone rang.

He picked it up, clicked it on, pulled up the antenna. "Yes?"

"Daddy?"

It was Kewpie. Roman started to cry. "Hi, baby," he said. "You okay?"

"My back hurts . . ." He heard her voice fade out.

"Special Agent Monroe here, Mr. Daniloff. She's fine, or as well as can be expected. It appears as though she has donated a kidney, but otherwise she's just fine."

Donated a kidney?

"Tell her I'll be down to pick her up tonight," Roman said, then without waiting for the FBI guy's reply, he hung up. He had something to do.

Surging with energy, he got up out of that damned plastic chair, ran down the hallway, pushed through doors, followed signs to the operating rooms, and finally caught up with Cindy. He grabbed the metal-jacketed chart from the end of her bed, flipped it open, and ripped out the consent forms. "No consent," he said to the assembled people in green masks and gowns. "I *forbid* you to operate."

"Mr. Daniloff," some masked doctor said, "we have her heart. We have the team. We *have* to operate."

"No operation," Roman said, tossed the chart onto Cindy's blanketed legs, and ripped the consent forms into little pieces.

The speechless medical staff watched them flutter to the floor. "She'll die," someone said.

"Fine," Roman replied, and walked away. He had a plane to catch. Then he and his kids had some money to spend. First stop: Disney World.

The late William L. DeAndrea won three Edgar Awards and drawersful of great reviews for his fair-play mysteries, brilliant espionage novels, and Western mysteries. Bill was not only a first-rate writer, he was also a first-rate human being. He will be missed. This story, one of his last, isn't based on a particular fairy tale, but examines several tropes of the genre, contrasting them brilliantly against harsh reality.

WILLIAM L. DeANDREA

Prince Charming

PART ONE

She opened her eyes to semidarkness, cuffed by one wrist to a pipe by the wall opposite the stairs. She could slide the other cuff up the pipe and stand up if she wanted to, or needed to use the bucket they'd provided for her. She had about six or seven feet of radial reach out from the pipe. Not much, but enough to keep from going totally insane in the week and a half or so she'd been in captivity.

She hoped. In this kind of situation, how could you really tell the state of your mind?

She never saw her captors. They never tortured her or anything. They changed her bucket and her food tray while she slept, a sleep so sound that she was sure on occasion they drugged the food. She had a kid's sleeping bag, occasional clean clothes, and as many towelettes as she needed to keep her body decently clean.

Nobody ever spoke to her.

In a way, that might have been the absolute worst of it. Rachel Hanver had a decent measure of both intelligence and imagination, and her father, Leo Hanver, could have been a lot less rich and powerful than he was and still have the Society press feel justified in saying that Rachel was "stunning" or "beautiful."

Rachel had grown more sophisticated than that in her nineteen years. In the real world, she would have been classed "Okay-pretty." Expert makeup and hairwork. Perhaps a little surgery for the fleshy bumps on the nose or jawline.

Rachel also realized she was rich enough not to have to worry about any surgery, and she was definitely not interested in any surgery.

She was, however, interested in being rich. So many of the girls from school never even seemed to give it a thought. Maybe it was because Leo Hanver had made the money during Rachel's own lifetime, and she had seen it grow, seen the kind of difference it made in her life, and in the last few (restful, at last) years of her mother's life.

So she thought about it, and she had come to realize that yes, there was a downside to it.

Leo Hanver had seen fit to refer to his daughter frequently as "my princess"—he was persistent rather than original—and that word undoubtedly helped her make the fairy tale connection. The beautiful, rich princess could frequently wind up as the focus of a diabolical plot of some wicked warlock or modern-day equivalent, someone against whom she could focus her own hatred and defiance. A person to match wits against. Something to fight, even if only emotionally, until she was rescued. Here, she saw and spoke to no one. There was nothing to focus on.

Of course, the person she was angry with right now was herself. There was no reason for her to be in this "dungeon," just as there had been no reason for her to have gone to the party they'd kidnapped her from.

She couldn't now even remember what had decided her to go along instead of staying home and reading a book. You can toss a book aside if it doesn't please you. If you went to one of Jennifer Clarke's impromptu parties, even knowing in advance that Jen was one was of the most boring people who had ever lived, and kept a coterie of similar personalities around for constant comparison, it wasn't that easy.

She sincerely hoped she hadn't gone because Daddy had nagged her about spending time with "more people of her own age." People of her own age seemed to be stodgier than practically anybody she knew, and besides, her father had promised to let the subject drop a long time ago.

In any case, all she remembered was that she had wanted to

think and she wanted a cigarette. She didn't want anyone to tell her it would be bad for her health. She didn't want to be commended as a champion of libertarian rights. She just wanted to get away from the hive-society mind and enjoy what she considered a minor vice, to think for a couple of minutes, then decide how soon she could make her excuses and get the hell out of there.

She walked over the small rise among the oak saplings, a nice walk on a warm spring night.

It also provided a lot of cover for whatever person or group was waiting in ambush for her with the pungent-smelling rag that was clapped over her nose and mouth without Rachel's ever having had a chance to see a thing. She didn't remember being dragged to a car. She didn't even remember losing her feet.

She just remembered waking up with a headache who-knows-how-long-ago, chained to the same pipe she was chained to now.

And then came the crashing.

After her week of comparative silence, the sound came like an exploding bomb. All it was really was the prying open of the bolt outside the cellar door at the top of the stairs.

Suddenly, Rachel was speechless; she couldn't have made a sound if her life depended on it. She had room in her brain only to watch that doorway and to see what came through it.

It was a young man in jeans and a short-sleeved shirt. In one hand he had a crowbar; in the other, a remarkable bunch of keys, what looked to Rachel's inexpert eye like handcuff keys.

It was darker now than when she'd first woken, but there was enough dim light coming through the high window for her to form the impression that he was handsome.

He stopped on a platform and scouted the basement. "Rachel?" he said.

She tried to talk, but managed only to make a weak grunt. Still, that was enough for him to find her. He ran to the bottom of the cellar stairs, and across the concrete floor toward her.

"It's good, he said, you're being quiet like this—"

He rolled her over to try to shine the small plastic flashlight he'd put in his mouth on the handcuffs, when the week of fear, of silence, of doubt broke inside Rachel, and she started to scream. She didn't want to; she just couldn't help it.

"Look," the young man said, "this isn't a good idea. They're not back yet, but they're never gone long, and if they hear us—"

Rachel screamed again.

"Oh, to hell with it," he said. A little awkwardly, he took the flashlight into the hand that held the crowbar.

Then he leaned forward and kissed her, firm but not rough. She stopped screaming.

When he finished, Rachel looked at him. He *was* handsome. She moved toward him, and they kissed again. It was—reassuring. Rachel let him get the handcuffs off. It didn't take long at all. He helped her up the stairs, helping her weakened legs fight gravity. The house, she could see now, was one of those cottages they'd managed to fit in on the north shore before people like her father had decided that *any* real estate lapped by any clean bit of ocean had to be worth incredible amounts of money. She could hear the gentle waves not too far off.

Little by little he hurried her faster through the small house.

"There're three or four of them," the young man said. "I've already scared myself to death doing this much, so I'd really like to have you safely back to your father before I have to fight them or anything."

She was too breathless to speak at the moment. As soon as he strapped her in the passenger seat of the dusty little Nissan wagon, and ensconced himself safely into the driver's side, she said, "Don't be ridiculous." She looked at him. He really was handsome, small but strong, regular features under curly brown hair, and bright, tender eyes.

"You're a hero," she said.

PART TWO

"Your father's out at the country place," he told her. "I guess he wanted to be closer to the action."

"You guess? Don't you know?"

"Huh? Why would I know?"

"Didn't my father hire you? Aren't you a private eye or something?"

He laughed. There was a trace of bitterness in it that didn't suit him.

"I've been accused of that all week, of trying to profit in some way from your disappearance. I'm not. I'm just . . . not, that's all.

"Okay, now I'm sure they've got a doctor inside for you, but believe me, when he's done they're going to have a lot of questions for you."

"I'll tell them whatever I know," she said.

"That's exactly the way to do it," he told her.

Rachel pointed up a private drive.

"There it is," she said.

"I know," he said. "Look, things are going to get confusing around—"

She cut him off. "*Get* confusing! I don't—"

Now she was cut off as the car suddenly stopped just inside the first row of hedges. A group of security men, some uniformed, some not, all of them armed, ran out to meet the car.

"What's going *on*?" Rachel demanded. She was beginning to think she was less terrified back in the dungeon.

"Just routine," her rescuer said. "You'll even appreciate it once you understand why they're doing it."

"But I—"

The young man was already opening the car and stepping out very slowly with his hands up.

"Me again!" he called to the guards.

"It's the pest," said a gruff voice from among the guards.

"Better check and see who I've got with me this time," the young man suggested.

Rachel reached over and took a tight grasp on his wrist. "I don't even know your *name*!"

That brought a chuckle from Prince Charming.

"Richard," he said, "Richard Keating. Don't worry about it, you've never heard of me, either."

"I will," she promised.

"I'd like that," he said.

They brought Keating to a sitting room, a room he'd been in before, if only long enough to be threatened with the police and then thrown out of. This had led to a longer session down at the local station, which lasted until they'd convinced themselves that he was just a social-climbing crank who wanted to get his name in the papers.

It ended with a warning not to bother them anymore.

He suspected that what he had done tonight, delivering the victim alive and well (so far as a cursory examination would show) to her father's doorstep, would not be considered a bother.

The evidence of the sitting room seemed to bear him out on this. For one thing, they invited him actually to sit, in a very nice chair, at that. Jenkins, the houseman, who had shown the ability to make the syllables "Richard Keating" sound completely interchangeable with those in the phrase "pariah dog," had offered him a drink. Keating had just taken orange juice, but he was sitting in the chair.

They had even left him alone.

Keating was sure he was under surveillance, so he was very careful simply to sip his juice and enjoy his chair until Leo Hanver came back.

Keating rose to take the old man's hand, which enveloped his, and gave a squeeze of real appreciation.

"I owe you an apology, Mr. Keating," he said.

Actually, by Keating's rendering, it was more like six or seven apologies, but he let it go.

"You were distraught, sir," he said. "I can't imagine anything worse than having a child disappear."

Hanver took a seat of his own and called for Jenkins, who brought him something light brown on ice. Hanver took a sip, then let out a breath he seemed to have been holding for a long time. He leaned back with his eyes closed and nodded.

"Of course," Keating went on, "I had one great advantage."

"What was that?"

"I was the one person who was absolutely certain that Rachel had, in fact, been kidnapped."

Hanver began to get huffy. "I never for a second doubted that my daughter had been kidnapped!"

"I'm sure you didn't, sir. But you must have gotten an earful of Patty Hearst from the local police and from the FBI."

"The FBI," Hanver grumbled, and Keating expected there'd be some intense questioning for potential congressmen in this district from at least one powerful citizen before the next election.

"It had to have been a distraction. Sergeant Meggessy hit me pretty hard with it, did a pretty good job of implying I was in on it with Rachel somehow, even though I had never laid eyes on her before Jennifer's ridiculous party the night of the kidnapping."

"Yes," Hanver said. "Yes, you must tell me everything that happened."

Keating spoke quietly.

"I tried to, sir."

Hanver grimaced. "I know, I know I should have listened to you at the time. I'm ready now, if you're ready to tell me."

Keating grinned apologetically and began to tell his story.

He'd only been at Jennifer's party in the first place because he was a part of the huge family to which they both belonged—very distant cousins, something like that.

Keating's role was something between hereditary black sheep (he was the third generation of his branch who had been tragically denied the gift for making money) and stray dog (he was insufficiently guilty about this).

The idea had been to ship him off to this part of the country for a while and see "if he would fit anywhere into Jen's circle."

He'd been there about two weeks before the party, and he'd already known he'd never fit into that circle.

"They're perfectly fine young people," Hanver insisted.

"I know they are, sir," Keating said. "But none of them has made or found his or her own place. The way you have, for instance. And I'm having a hell of a time finding mine. Maybe I don't have one."

Hanver leaned forward and ticked points off on his fingers.

"Nonsense, boy. What are you? Twenty-two years old? Considering what you did tonight . . . and we didn't make it any easier for you, either. That kind of determination and guts is bound to make a place for itself. And for a total stranger, too."

"Well," Keating said, leaning back in his chair, "that's part of it. I didn't *feel* like a total stranger to Rachel, I felt like I knew her quite well."

Keating explained how standing near the bar, he'd been startled to hear someone else order straight orange juice. Usually at a gathering like this, the young folks made a game of drinking the stiffest (or in the case of the girls) most bizarre concoctions they could cajole the bartender into making.

He looked up to study his fellow juice-drinker and found himself looking into Rachel's eyes.

"It was the strangest experience," Keating said. "There was nothing you could call a physical resemblance, but it was like looking into my own eyes." Eyes that were looking for the same things, but finding them devilishly hard to find. Eyes that were much older than they ought to have been, and a lot less happy.

"I don't like," Hanver said, "the implication that my daughter is living a miserable life."

Keating shrugged. "You've asked me to explain what I did and why I did it. Well, part of the reason is that I felt—and still feel— as if your daughter and I are kindred spirits. She'd really be the one to talk to about this. I could be wrong."

Hanver rubbed his chin. "You're twenty-two?"

"Just."

"And Rachel's nineteen, almost twenty. Maybe you are kindred spirits. Go on. Want more juice?"

Keating said yes; refills were sent for.

"Anyway," Keating said when Jenkins was gone, "I decided I had to make an opportunity to talk to her, just to see if I was right. But I never managed to do it. Jen would ask me for a drink, or someone would want to know if I had played hockey for Dartmouth, and so on, and then when I got a moment I could never manage to find her."

Then Keating had seen her heading out a side door. This, he

thought, was a great opportunity to catch up with her, and in the best circumstances to have an actual conversation as well, so he took off after her.

He didn't call out her name. They hadn't met, after all, and he didn't want to frighten her away. He got a little nervous when she passed in and out of the shrubbery—she seemed to know every twist and turn; he'd lived there for a couple of weeks but he hadn't made a point of exploring the place.

Anyway, he had a clear view of her when the man popped out from behind his own bush, grasped her around the neck, and clapped a rag over her face.

Rachel had a big head start on him. He knew there was no use in yelling; he saved his breath to run, and wound up chasing the man down the slope without, he was sure, the kidnappers' being even slightly aware of it.

Keating saw two other men hop out of a white panel truck (no writing on it that he could see) and stuff Rachel inside. They clambered in themselves, then drove off.

Keating, puffing by now, had run to the place where the truck had been parked. He tried to get the license-plate number, but distance and dim light kept it from him.

There was nothing to do now but to go back to the house and get some action started.

PART THREE

"They all thought you were crazy," Hanver said.

Keating shook his head with just a trace of bitterness. "They sure acted as if they thought I was crazy. I remember Jennifer pretending to be offended. 'I never thought I'd throw a party so dull that people would want to get themselves kidnapped away from it.'"

The rest of the guests seemed to think that was remarkably amusing, and they achieved even more hilarity when Keating insisted he'd seen a real kidnapping.

"Come off it, Richard," they'd say.

"What's this, your initiation?"

Keating, genuinely bewildered, demanded to know what they were talking about.

He learned that there were two primary theories. One: that Rachel was playing a joke on all of them, and two: that Rachel had somehow prevailed upon him to help with the hoax.

"Don't be ridiculous!" Keating said. "I never laid eyes on her before tonight. We've never said a word to each other."

A voice came around the rim of a Scotch glass. "So *you* say."

For a split second, Keating flirted with the notion of punching the glass down past the speaker's teeth, but he managed to control himself.

"So I say," he said grimly, "and so I'm going to tell the cops. Where's a phone?"

"The cops? Ha! Good luck."

Then they tried to keep him away from the phone. Finally, Keating had said to hell with it; he'd drive to the police station himself.

Jennifer looked up and surprised him. "That's probably the best idea. If you insist on going ahead with this."

"I insist, all right."

"Then the cops will probably need you there for descriptions and stuff."

She got to her feet. "All right, I'll drive you."

The Scotch drinker said, "Jen, you can't be serious."

"Oh, you people will think of something to do to keep the party going until I get back."

Another thirty seconds of verbal scuffling and they were out there on the road in Jen's Mercedes. When Keating tried to thank her, she said, "Don't. The cops will probably think you're just as crazy as I do. They've got a Sergeant Meggessy down there who thinks we're a bunch of spoiled nuisances. You might even be asking for a whole lot of trouble."

Leo Hanver snorted. "Think of something to keep the party going," he murmured. "I take it back, about their being fine young people. The little bastards were *arranging* for you to have trouble."

Keating frowned. "You mean they called Meggessy and told him some kind of drunken crank was on the way to tell them a wild story?"

"I wouldn't be at all surprised; you can bet I'm going to find out."

"But why would they do that? Rachel's friends?"

Hanver sighed.

"Because I've been selling my daughter's observations short all her life—haven't wanted to believe it, you know? It's like having worked myself and my family into this particular social status, I wanted everything to be perfect about it.

"But I wasn't fair to Rachel. There's more *to* her than to these other kids, a need to know things more deeply, and to get things done. I'd say like me, if it wouldn't sound so egotistical."

He leaned back with a rueful sigh. "I don't feel as if I have a lot to be egotistical about tonight, that's for sure.

"Anyway, Rachel says sometimes—'Beware the mutant.' I'm not entirely sure what that means, but I think a big part of it is that everybody senses Rachel's being different somehow, and they all resent it. Rachel herself most of all, I think."

Keating sifted through his own list of rueful memories and could come up with only agreement.

"So I apologize, Keating."

"For what?"

"For my part in your difficulties. Rachel's so-called friends poisoned the police's minds; I allowed them to poison mine. I was so worried about her—and, since it seems to be the night for admitting things, so afraid she *might* have run away from me, I was not a thinking man.

"*You*, however, seem to have been thinking all week. What have you been doing while the rest of us have been sucking our thumbs?"

Keating shrugged. "I did whatever I could think of. I went to the library, through the old newspapers, finding out everything I could about Rachel. Why she should be picked for kidnapping, that sort of thing.

"The key thing I found out was that she couldn't have been. Picked for kidnapping, I mean. Just couldn't. Unless she'd been in on it herself, which I totally rejected from what I'd learned of her character." And, he admitted to himself, what he wanted to believe. "This led me to think there was no personal element in this."

The kidnappers, Keating told the old man, had found out that a bunch of rich kids were having a party at Jen's house. Surely nothing too hard to find out, what with catering and liquor orders and the like.

All they'd done is drive their white van on the grounds, then post a lookout to see if one of them came outside for a minute. Then they could snatch him—or her—confident in the knowledge that anyone they did grab would have healthy ransom potential.

It was like kids setting themselves up besides the outfield bleachers at the ballpark, hoping someone hits a home run out. A lot less wholesome, though.

"The next thing to do was to wait and see if you *got* a ransom demand. The cops seemed to have the town pretty well sewn up, but I figured *that* ought to make it to the newspaper."

"It's pretty well sewn up," Hanver agreed. "There were a couple of messages—stand by for ransom instructions, no interference from me personally. The cops and FBI to lie low. None of that got out."

"No, I've been following the paper."

"But a ransom demand came in today. Just the amount, no pickup instructions."

"How much?" Keating asked.

"A hundred thousand dollars."

"Mmmm," Keating said. "If anything absolutely clears Rachel—I mean, if she needed anything further—that does it."

"How?" Hanver demanded. "Where do you get all this expertise?"

"It's not expertise, it's just a lifetime of reading and a lot of concentration and . . ." and, Keating couldn't force himself to say, the start of the quenching of a lifelong thirst for adventure.

"Anyway, the amount of money is wrong if Rachel is the one who is asking for it. For someone like her to do something so totally out of character (we agree on that, don't we?), she'd have to ask for at least five times as much to justify it to herself."

"On the other hand, a hundred thousand is the perfect amount for potluck kidnappers to ask for. You could pay it relatively painlessly, and after a week of anxiety—that's probably why they made you wait so long—it would seem a cheaper price with every day that went by. It also makes a convenient split for three or four men."

Keating shrugged. "The main thing I tried to do during the wait for the ransom demand was to learn things and to remember things." He had tried motor vehicles, but when all you can say is "medium-sized white van" you don't stand a chance of learning much. He visited the caterer and the liquor store, even applied for jobs, just to see if he could get hold of delivery records and learn something that way.

He did learn that the liquor store had a medium-sized van in pale, pale green that could well look white under a sodium vapor lamp.

That just depressed him.

One cheering note, though, was that even with the reaming out and dressing down Sergeant Meggessy had given him the night of the kidnapping, the cops seemed to pay no attention to him at all. He even got so brazen as to wander into headquarters and ask to look at mug shots, on the theory that he might see *something*.

Well, okay, that hadn't gotten him very far, except for a minor tongue-lashing from Meggessy to the effect that some people don't know when they're well off.

Keating had shrugged and left. It had been the longest of long shots, anyway.

Perhaps not quite.

"Because the other day," he told Rachel's father, "something occurred to me."

"You remembered something?"

"Let's say I *noticed* something. So I made a couple of unwarranted assumptions, linked them together, checked them out, and found out they worked. They led me to the little house on the shore and gave me a timetable for getting her out of there."

"Then you know who did this," Hanver said.

"I know who I followed," Keating said.

"Well?" the old man demanded.

Keating was silent.

"Don't get coy on me now."

"I've got to talk to Rachel about this."

"Why?"

"She was the one who was kidnapped. This is still about Rachel. I have to talk to her before I can talk to anyone else."

The old man chortled.

"I don't think you'll need to talk as long as you might have thought."

"Why's that?"

"Because if I know my daughter, she's found her way to the nearest intercom, and she's been listening to practically everything we say."

Keating smiled. "Now that you mention it, I'd be surprised if she weren't."

Rachel apparently knew a cue when she heard one. She scampered into the room, shot her father an exasperated look, took a few more quick steps toward Keating, and . . .

And stood there, suddenly shy.

Leo Hanver got to his feet.

"All right, all right," he said. "Take my seat, Rachel. I'll go check with the doctor to see exactly how you are."

"I'm a little wobbly, but I'll be all right."

She was more than a little wobbly. She plunked into her father's chair with real gratitude.

"I'll still go check with the doctor," the old man said. "And I'll stay away from intercoms. But don't try to keep me in the dark too long on this."

"Of course not, Daddy. You're a dear."

"I'm something," her father conceded. "Keating, I owe you more than I can say."

With that, he left.

There was a long, awkward silence, the stuff of absolute cliché. They'd both start talking at once, or they'd insist the other go first until nobody went at all.

Finally (for the first of many times) Rachel settled it.

"Well," she said, "according to you, you've been wanting to talk to me for a week and a half. Start talking."

PART FOUR

Four days and a couple of good nights' sleep later, Keating and Rachel were driving toward town in a car somewhat bigger, cleaner, and more impressive than Keating's Nissan.

"I love you, Richard," Rachel said. Obviously the days had been filled with some intensive talking as well.

"You know how I feel," Keating told her. "At first sight. I never believed in it."

"I do. I always have. I saw you drinking orange juice, too, you know."

He smiled.

"So why do you seem worried?" Rachel demanded. "Everything is under control. We're in love, my dad is crazy about you, and you and I are about to find that place in the world we've always been looking for."

Keating smiled disbelievingly and shook his head. "Private eyes, for God's sake."

"*Not* private eyes, if you please. We will head up the Leo Hanver Foundation, and we will help crime victims and their families of whatever social or economic level as soon and as suitably as we can. The amount of personal involvement is up to us."

"Sounds ideal," Keating admitted. "The only thing is, we haven't wrapped up our first case yet, remember?"

"Oh, but that can be wrapped up any number of ways," Rachel said. "I insisted we do it this way for the personal satisfaction."

"You insisted?"

She looked at him. There was no banter in her eyes now, or fear. Just pure, righteous anger.

"I was chained to a pipe for a week and a half, and I'll never forget it. So let's finally go explain to Sergeant Meggessy how you found me, and get some arrests made."

The sun was bright on Main Street, and it seemed to follow them through the front door and past the venetian-blinded doors of police headquarters. They reminded the receptionist they had an appointment with Sergeant Meggessy, and were shown right in.

Meggessy's smile was something more than embarrassed as he rose to shake hands. At that, Keating thought, it was an improvement. The only other smiles he'd ever seen on that face were cold and mean.

He gestured them to seats. "Well, Keating, I guess I owe you an apology, to say the least."

"Forget me," Keating said. "What about Miss Hanver? She's the one with the bruised wrists."

"Of course, of course. I'm so sorry. We—I—took the wrong attitude. Police work isn't an exact science—well, Keating, you must realize that. Without luck, you could never have found Miss Hanver with a needle-in-a-haystack search the way you did."

Keating smiled.

"I won't deny I had luck," he said. "But it wasn't exactly that kind of search. I was following up a notion I had, and it paid off."

"Oh? What kind of notion?"

"That's what I've come here to tell you. You see, when I first came here with the news that Miss Hanver had been kidnapped, you were full of dire threats about what would happen to me if I 'kept sticking my nose in police business.'

"Now, I went ahead and did, anyway. I didn't even bother much to keep a low profile after the first day or so.

"Nothing happened. No boom got lowered. No additional warnings listed. I was left to go my way."

Keating leaned forward in his chair. "In fact, I didn't hear from you again until I put myself right in your face, asking to see mug shots. Even then it was hardly the wrath I'd been promised."

"What the hell, kid, I could see you were having a tough time with this. . . ."

"So you *were* keeping track of me. And you knew I was working my tail off trying to get something like proof. But that wasn't enough to get you to listen to me, or to throw me out of town.

"You could have done either one of those two things, except for the fact that they *might* have gotten somebody to pay attention to me.

"So it seemed to be enough for you simply to know I wasn't making any progress—and to keep bad-mouthing me to Mr. Hanver and the local media.

"I began to ask myself questions about that."

Meggessy wasn't trying to look tough anymore, or friendly, or any particular way, and now, for the first time, he seemed frightening. "Go on," he said.

"At first, I started with useless questions like Who'd know better how to stage a crime than a cop? Or, Do they pay cops enough in this town that a quick, tax-free twenty-five or thirty grand in cash wouldn't be a help?"

Keating got to his feet and walked around behind his chair. "Then I asked myself something intelligent, like Did Meggessy have access to the right kind of van? You did.

"One night I followed you—you weren't in the van—and saw you bring some things out to the house near the shore. I knew you didn't live there. I staked out the place at random intervals and saw you go back a few times. So the other night, I made some preparations and went and got her."

Now Meggessy leaned back in his chair and laced his fingers behind his head.

"Yep," he said. "You've got her. But you don't have much else. It'd be your word against mine, and no one ever even sent any ransom instructions. So why don't you just call yourself a winner, and get on home and enjoy the rest of your life?"

"Yes, sir," Keating said. "As soon as we get the pro private eye in here to talk to Rachel's friends. So-called friends."

"Her friends?"

"Sure. The ones at the party. One of them had to be a lookout for you, to tell you if something'd gone wrong, if you'd been spotted. How long do you think it will take to break one of those wimps and get him or her to talk?"

Meggessy sighed. "I knew it." He drew his gun. "You're too smart for your own good, Keating. Come on, I've got a bag packed. We'll take your car. You're coming, too, Miss Hanver."

"No, we're not, Sergeant," Rachel said firmly.

Just then, the first-floor window behind him shattered. Rachel and Keating hit the floor as dark-uniformed state troopers climbed through the glass.

"Didn't you think, Sergeant," Rachel said, "that when we made the appointment to see you, my daddy helped us make the appointment for you to see the State Police, too?"

Keating went to her and kissed her as the troopers led Meggessy away.

EPILOGUE

Autumn leaves burned red and gold in the trellis as Richard Keating and Rachel Hanver were declared husband and wife. They couldn't have looked happier.

Nearby, Leo Hanver (who had personally chosen the guest list, making sure to leave the right names out) was talking to a business associate named Breen.

"Beautiful day, Leo," Breen said. "Beautiful day. Beautiful bride."

Leo Hanver beamed. "My princess," he said.

"But look," Breen said. "This foundation thing. It's great for publicity, and it's a good cause, but isn't it a handful for a couple of kids?"

"Don't you worry about those kids," Hanver pronounced. "The kids will be fine."

Actually, they did a lot better than that.

They lived happily—and adventurously—ever after.

Jane Haddam writes mysteries about retired FBI agent Gregor Demarkian. Each novel is set around a holiday, and each one gives us a palpable sense of the Armenian-American community in Philadelphia. Haddam is a superior stylist and a truly diabolical wit. She is also capable of rendering an already dark fairy tale, "Rapunzel," into a modern-day version that is just as chilling.

JANE HADDAM

Rapunzel

There were not supposed to be advertisements for prostitution in the *Waterbury Republican,* but there were advertisements for the Carnival there every day, in the bottom right-hand corner of the page with the television news on it. Daniel Markham had never paid much attention to them until the summer he was fifteen. He lived with his mother out on the edge of Thomaston Road, in a trailer in a cluster of half a dozen other trailers. When he got up in the morning, he could look through the window in his bathroom at the Waterbury Division of the Connecticut Department of Social Services. At night he could sit on the trailer's steps and watch the lights of the Carnival itself. The Carnival had rides as well as girls for sale. In the middle of the summer, men came with bottles of whiskey in plastic flasks and paper bags. Women came in metallic Spandex stretch pants and plastic hair clips. There was a rumor you could get tattooed right on the Carnival's main drag—but most of the people Daniel knew who had tattoos had gotten them at the parlor next to the adult bookstore on East Main Street. The parlor had a big billboard right next to it that said: *Real Men Don't Use Porn.*

Actually, Daniel Markham hadn't done much of anything until the summer he was fifteen. There didn't seem to be anyplace where he could fit. He was small and very thin. He wore his hair down to his shoulders and his jeans carefully torn across the knees. He wasn't strong enough to be a biker or smart enough to be elevated to the heights of Honors III. He had tried a marijuana cigarette only once. It had made him throw up in a garbage can at the edge of the athletic field. Real drugs scared him. Guns scared him even worse. When he tried to imagine what he would be like in five years' time, he came up totally blank.

That was the summer his mother was coming up totally blank, too—the summer she started drinking "for real," as Daniel put it to himself. He spent a lot of his time sitting outside, smoking cigarettes and throwing rocks into circles drawn in the ground. He had never really had any friends and long ago stopped wanting them, but he was bored and depressed and lonely, and he kept thinking that if he had more courage he could hitchhike out to the Naugatuck Valley Mall to hang around. Mostly he thought about the guys at school that the guys he knew called rich fags, even though they probably weren't homosexuals. They had fathers who were doctors and lawyers and new cars they could drive to school in. They spent lunch sitting next to girls with straight blond hair and pastel cashmere sweaters. They talked all the time about whether they really wanted to go to Princeton or Yale. It had started to seem to Daniel as if this game were rigged. Something had happened back there somewhere, at the very moment of his conception, that had decided everything for ever after. He thought it might have something to do with the stars, because they ran horoscopes in the newspaper every day. He was sure it had something to do with drinking, because he had paid attention in health citizenship class on the day the teacher had gone over the particulars of fetal alcohol syndrome. Whatever it was had left him sitting here, throwing rocks at dirt, while everybody else in the world drove by on their way to God-knew-what.

When it got late enough, he would stretch out on the ground with his back against the cinderblocks that held the trailer up, and listen to his mother getting sick in the kitchen sink.

It was early July the first time Daniel talked to Bobby Donovan—talked with him and laughed with him and smoked one of his father's expensive English cigarettes. The cigarettes made Daniel's lungs ache and his body long for money. The talk with Bobby Donovan just bewildered him. Bobby Donovan was definitely one of the rich fags. His father owned a whole string of car dealerships in Bristol, and he had a brand-new Mustang convertible every year. He was big and good-looking and smart, too—although Daniel thought maybe not as smart as the rest of them. For as long as Daniel could remember, Bobby Donovan had always been in trouble for one thing or another. It was just that the trouble never seemed to have the same sort of consequences it would have had for anybody else. Even this summer, when Bobby was "on probation" for shoplifting a gold Dunhill lighter from Kay's Jewelry Store in Danbury, all probation seemed to mean was that he wasn't being allowed to go away to soccer camp. Bobby Donovan was seventeen and headed into his senior year in high school. He wore thick LaCoste shirts and no socks under his loafers. He had never in his life met a social worker.

"Listen," Bobby said that first night, when he had pulled up his Mustang in front of Daniel's trailer, "it's like you see it there all the time and you think you know where it is, and then when you try to get to it, you can't."

"I know how to get to it," Daniel said.

They were both looking off into the distance, at the lights from the Carnival. Bobby kept squinting into the sharp smoke spiraling up from his cigarette.

"You ever been there?" he asked. "I've been telling myself I'd go for every summer since I was twelve, but I could never find anybody to go with me."

"I'll go with you," Daniel said. It seemed like a good idea not to say that he hadn't been there himself yet. Bobby wasn't looking at him anyway. He was just staring and staring at the lights, especially at the lights of the Ferris wheel going around.

"Everybody says they've got girls out there in cages," Bobby said. "Just like in Hamburg, Germany. They've got girls in cages and you pick one and you can have her."

"It's like a game," Daniel said. He knew this, because Steve Carpenter in the next trailer over went out to the Carnival all the time and talked about it. "It's like shooting ducks and that kind of thing, a different game for every girl, and if you win the game you get the girl."

"For a quarter?"

"It's twenty dollars," Daniel said.

Bobby dropped his cigarette on the ground and put it out under the heel of his shoe. There was something twisted in his face that Daniel didn't like—but he didn't understand it, either. He thought it might be just the way the rich fags were, a different culture, the way Mrs. Hamilton always talked about in civics class. He was sure it couldn't be as ugly as it looked.

"Listen," Bobby said, getting another cigarette out of the pack and handing the pack to Daniel, "most girls are shits. Did you know that? Most girls are absolute shits."

"Mmm," Daniel said.

"Most girls think they've got Fort Knox between their legs. They really do. And then if you call them on it, they scream bloody murder."

"Mmm," Daniel said again.

"If anything made any sense anymore, you'd be able to teach them all a lesson without ending up with your own ass in the sling. You know what I mean? You get it?"

"Sure."

"You'd just be able to ram it in and ram it in and ram it in until they bled. You'd just be able to ram it in until they died."

"I don't think you can do that," Daniel said judiciously. "I don't think you can—you know—somebody until they died. I don't think it's physically possible. You know?"

Bobby had his new cigarette lit. His head was wreathed in smoke. "They've got a girl up there called Rapunzel," he said, pointing at the lights again. "I heard all about it. She's the best girl in the best cage at the very top, and you only get to have her if you're rich."

"Right," Daniel said.

Bobby dropped the more than half-full box of cigarettes into Daniel's lap. "You keep these. I've got another box. I've got to be going."

"I thought you wanted to go out to the Carnival," Daniel said.

"I've got to be going. I've got to be in tonight. I have to be in every night. I've got summer school."

"Summer school," Daniel repeated—and now he felt really stupid, stupid beyond belief, because he couldn't think of anything to say. He thought the nicotine in these cigarettes was stronger than what he was used to. They seemed to be making him stoned.

"I've got to go," Bobby said again, vaulting over the side of the mustang and more or less into the driver's seat. It wasn't the way it looked in the movies, flawless and graceful. Daniel thought Bobby was going to break a leg.

"I'll be back," Bobby said, turning the Mustang's engine on and revving it. "I'll be back every night this week. We'll go up to the Carnival and get laid. Right?"

"Right," Daniel said.

"I'll be back," Bobby said.

The Mustang made a tight little backward turn in the flattened grass that stretched out between the trailers. Then it bumped out onto Thomaston Road and was gone.

"Shit," Daniel said into the air. His head ached. His body felt poked through with needles. He hated everything about these expensive English cigarettes.

"Shit, shit, shit," he said, and wished like hell that Bobby had never gone.

It was a week before Bobby Donovan came back. By then, Daniel had decided he was never going to show, which was not surprising. Every guy Daniel had ever known had wanted to go up to the Carnival or had gone. There were probably loads of guys in Bobby's own neighborhood, with their own cars and their own weird foreign cigarettes, who would be more than willing to check out Rapunzel and all the rest of them. It was too bad, though, because it seemed as if Bobby had opened something in Daniel that Daniel had never expected to find in himself: an obsession about sex, a lust that had no object. Ever since Bobby's Mustang had disappeared in the dark on Thomaston Road, Daniel had been thinking about the Carnival and the cages there, about bright round breasts straining against the coiled cotton straps of a string bra. They would be breasts just like the ones he saw on the *Playboy* Channel, over at Steve's trailer. They would be perky and high, and the women they belonged to would be held with ropes and leather straps to the bars of the cages that contained them. It all got mixed up in his mind: the bars and the ropes and the straps; the money and the helplessness. He would drift off to sleep, thinking there was no way they could refuse him, and he would wake up to find himself pumping off into his own white sheets. It was a pain in the ass in a way. His mother never washed anything anymore. He had to take the sheets down to the Laundromat himself, and sit on a molded green chair for an hour waiting for them to be clean.

When Bobby showed up, he was wearing a pair of chinos so white, they made Daniel blink. He got out of the Mustang and threw a small plastic bag of white powder into the dirt at Daniel's feet. There was no one around to see them, but Daniel flinched anyway. He had never tried cocaine and didn't want to. The very idea of heroin made him sick.

"I've got some grass in the trailer," he told Bobby. "If you want to get high. I don't like much of anything except grass." The grass belonged to his mother. There was no need to tell Bobby about any of that.

Bobby jabbed a toe into the side of the plastic bag. "It's fake," he said. "Can you believe that? I got taken."

"Oh," Daniel said.

"I paid three hundred dollars for it and it's frigging nothing," Bobby said. "It's like everything else, you know what I mean? It's like this whole damned year."

"Oh," Daniel said again. He had a pack of cigarettes of his own tonight, Marlboros he had bought after he'd found a five-dollar bill on the ground near the Taco Bell at the Colonial Plaza Shopping Center. He sucked away at it and wished that he liked to get high.

"The thing is," Bobby said, "the way life is going, you know, they're going to end up owning everything, you know what I mean? They're going to end up owning all the balls in the world and the crime is going to be that we let them do it, we just let them come right in here and castrate the hell out of us, and then what? Then what?"

"I think you're stoned," Daniel said. "Isn't that it? You're stoned."

"They all get bought and sold no matter what else they do," Bobby said. "Isn't that the truth? They all get bought and sold and then they want us to pretend like it doesn't matter."

"They make it into a game," Daniel said. "You shoot ducks or throw baseballs at a hole in a piece of wood. Like a midway, you see what I mean. Then they hand them out like prizes from a board."

"You know what I'm going to do someday?" Bobby said. "I'm going to get one of them in the back of my car and I'm going to nail her good and then I'm going to throw her out. Right over the side of the car. I'm going to get that car going a hundred miles an hour and when it can't go any faster, I'm going to throw her out, and then I'm going to watch her skull split all over the highway."

Daniel took another long, slow drag on his cigarette. When he was around Bobby, his head always seemed to be swimming. It was as if Bobby carried a drug in the air around him, like a miasma. Daniel thought of a skull smashing on the asphalt, but it didn't feel good. It felt awful. He got rid of the image and started thinking about the cages again.

"I don't think they let them out to go in cars," he told Bobby, but Bobby wasn't listening.

Out in the dark and the distance the lights of the Carnival were glowing. The Ferris wheel went around and around. The multicolored strips looked like beads in the blackening night. When Daniel closed his eyes, he thought he could hear the music from the carousel and the sounds of the barkers' voices. If he had had the faintest idea how to drive, he would have climbed into the Mustang and taken off by himself.

"Let's go," he told Bobby. "Let's get in your car and go on up there, right now. Let's make a night of it."

"I wonder what they let you do to them once you get them in the dark," Bobby said. "You ever think about that?"

"They let you nail them," Daniel said. "That's the point."

"I bet you could do anything at all if you were able to pay for it. Anything at all. Have you ever met a pimp?"

"Mmm," Daniel said.

"Pimps are supposed to be in it for the money. That's the point of pimps. So they'd probably sell you anything if you had the money."

"Let's *go,*" Daniel said. "What are we waiting for? You've got a car. We can just take off."

"When her head was good and smashed I'd come back and throw her goddamned sweater into it."

"Bobby, look—"

Bobby had been leaning against the Mustang. Now he stood up and got in behind the wheel, the ordinary way with an open door and everything. He looked deflated.

"I got to go," he said. "I've got to be in, for Christ's sake. I'll be back tomorrow."

"Yeah," Daniel said.

This time he never really saw the Mustang leave. He was looking at the lights of the Carnival and thinking about Rapunzel.

By August, when Bobby was finally ready to go, Daniel had started smoking marijuana. He had started by sneaking it out of his mother's stash when she was drunk. She would disappear behind the trailer, and he would sit out in full few of Thomaston Road, sucking hard on loosely packed joints that made his fingers burn. After a while he took it whenever he wanted to. She never seemed to be aware of anything. When she was aware, she never seemed to care. The last night Bobby showed up, Daniel had five joints rolled and laid out next to him on a piece of concrete block. He had already smoked two.

Bobby pulled the Mustang into the roundabout in front of the trailers very slowly this time. He cut the engine and sat at the wheel, drumming his fingers against the dashboard. Daniel wanted to get up and go over to him. He at least wanted to call out. He had too much smoke in him. He suddenly wondered what it would be like to do something really serious, such as amphetamines or cocaine, that sped you up instead of slowed you down.

Bobby got out of the car and walked over to where Daniel was lying on the ground. He was wearing the same old alligator shirt and chinos, Daniel saw. Back at home, he had to have a bureau with nothing but alligator shirts in it. He leaned over and took one of the joints off the concrete block and stuck it in his mouth.

"Mind?" he said.

"No," Daniel said.

Bobby took his lighter out of his pocket and let it flame. "My parents are in the Bahamas," he said. "On a *cruise*. You ever been on a *cruise?*"

"No," Daniel said.

Bobby sucked on the joint until it seemed as if he were sucking all the air out of the universe. He let go of it too fast, wasting it. "I don't get to go because I'm on probation. That's what my mother said. I'm on probation, so they're finally going to go away and leave me alone."

"Oh," Daniel said.

"I want to go on up to the Carnival," Bobby said. "Why the hell not? I want to go up to the Carnival and not come back till Tuesday."

"Right," Daniel said.

Bobby propped open the door of the Mustang and stood back. Daniel made himself get up off the ground and stand straight. He was dizzy as hell, and a little sick. No matter how often he got high, he still got sick. He took the joints off the concrete block and stuffed them into his pockets. He walked carefully around the Mustang's trunk and made his way to the passenger seat. Up close, the car frightened him in a way he hadn't expected it to. It was too new and too warm and too full of money.

Daniel opened the door on the passenger side and stared in at the leather bucket seat. Bobby came around behind him and pushed him in.

"Let's go," Bobby said. "For Christ's sake."

"Shit," Daniel said.

Then he was sitting down on the bucket and the door was closed next to him. Bobby was climbing into the driver's seat and revving the engine.

"Girls are all cunts, did you know that?" Bobby said—and Daniel thought that he had heard this before. This was Bobby's song.

"Girls are all cunts," Bobby said again as they bounced out onto Thomaston Road. "Someday I'm going to put every single one of those holes in a row and plug them up. Plug them up. Plug them to pieces and let them rip."

The entrance to the Carnival looked like the entrance to any Carnival anywhere, except that all the signs were anchored into the ground for permanence and there was a small sign—*Adults ONLY Entertainment*—right under the window on the front ticket booth. The girl in the ticket booth was like girls in Carnivals everywhere. She sagged in too many places even though she was very young. Bobby parked the Mustang on the choked grass of what looked like an impromptu lot. There was no paved-over place made ready for cars, although there were plenty of cars. There were even more motorcycles. The girl in the ticket booth was chewing gum. Her nails were much too long and much too blue and had far too many sparkles in them.

"You ought to lock up the car," Daniel told Bobby. "You can't leave the top down like this. Somebody will come along and steal it."

"Fuck the car," Bobby said.

Daniel got out onto the grass and looked around. The Ferris wheel was turning and turning. It didn't look as big up here as it had from down below. Bobby was standing at the ticket booth, taking money from the wallet he kept in his hip pocket. Daniel had forgotten all about money.

"Hey," Daniel said. "Hey, man, listen—"

"Never mind," Bobby said. "I've got your ticket. Are you coming?"

"Sure."

"It's all adult entertainment in here," the girl in the ticket booth said. "All we ever do is adult entertainment. You two don't look like adults."

Bobby grabbed Daniel by the wrist and pulled him through the gate. "Shithole cunt," Bobby said.

Daniel stumbled down a short, dark path. There seemed to be a long way to go without lights. There seemed to be too much music, too, tinny and hard, not the kind of thing Daniel was used to hearing. Bobby was pulling him and pulling him along the path, into the dark, behind a long line of big canvas tents that smelled sour.

"Listen," Bobby said. "We want to be ready for it, right? We want to be ready to go and ready to rip them apart."

"Right," Daniel said.

"Look at this," Bobby said.

Bobby pulled what looked like a cigarette case out of his front chino pocket. Daniel had only ever seen one like it in a black-and-white movie his mother had watched once. Inside the case, instead of cigarettes, there was what Daniel knew had to be cocaine. People like Bobby Donovan didn't use heroin, and that was the only other thing Daniel could think of that looked like that.

"Oh, shit," Daniel said. "Oh, shit. All that stuff makes me sick."

"This won't make you sick," Bobby said. "Trust me. It's expensive. My father left a roll of bills as thick as a fist in his sock drawer. When he went to the Bahamas."

"Oh, shit shit shit," Daniel said.

"You know anything about the Menendez brothers?" Bobby said. "They walked in their house one day and just offed their parents with a shotgun. Just boom boom boom. Blood all over the place. Heads in shreds. I love the Menendez brothers. I love everything they do. They get the point."

There was a long line of powder lined up on the shiny side of the open case. Bobby had a little silver straw to suck it up with.

"Heads in shreds," Bobby said. His nose and eyes were running. His face was very red. He seemed to be laughing, but there was something about it that wasn't quite a laugh, that didn't make sense. "Heads in shreds," he said again. "Blood on the wallpaper."

When it was his turn, Daniel leaned over and only pretended to snort up coke.

It took them nearly half an hour to find the part of the Carnival they wanted. They had to go through the midway and the rides and the food booths first, as if this were nothing but an outing to the annual Lions' fundraiser, as if they were both still ten years old and cared about cotton candy. Bobby stopped twice more behind the tents to spike his cocaine high. Daniel managed twice more to fake it and walk away clear. He was actually clearer all the time, because the marijuana he had smoked back at the trailer had started to wear off. He was also bored to tears. There were girls staffing all the ticket booths and food stalls. They had very little on, but they were nothing at all like the girls on the *Playboy* Channel. They were wrinkly and tired and saggy and dull. They all looked like they hated what they were doing. Daniel saw men tucking five-dollar bills into the girls' bikini bottoms and reaching out to grab a handful of breast. Daniel didn't have five dollars and he didn't want to grab these particular breasts. He wanted to be home, in front of the television, where the girls were all fresh and beautiful and new and tied down tight.

Bobby took a turn to the right between a pair of souvenir stands and then another turn to the right, into the dark for more cocaine, and then there it was, the arch with the lights on it, the place where the cages started. It happened so fast, Daniel thought it had appeared by magic. *Poof,* somebody had said, and there it was, rising out of nowhere, with a dragon waiting at the portal to keep them out. Actually, it wasn't a dragon, but a woman. She was well over fifty. Her hair was too long for her age and too dark to be real. Her lips and her cheeks were too red with lipstick and rouge. Daniel looked past her and saw the cages stacked one on top of the other and lined with lights. He saw the girls in their thong bikinis, swaying and bumping to no music he could hear. A couple of the cages were empty. A little knot of men on the ground were throwing dice down a long wooden chute. To Daniel, it all looked awful.

"Shit," Daniel said, grabbing Bobby by the sleeve. "This is terrible. Let's get out of here."

"Don't you want to get laid?" Bobby said.

Daniel had never been laid. He thought about himself lying on top of some woman, sticking himself into her, and never being able to get out.

"Let's get out of here," Daniel said again.

"Look," Bobby said, pointing upward.

Daniel looked. He hadn't seen the cage at the top before. It had been so far beyond him and everything in between had been so awful, he hadn't seen any reason to bother. Now he realized that the girl up there was truly different. She was blond and bright, very much like the girls on the *Playboy* Channel but maybe even better. Nothing about her sagged. She didn't look as if she hated where she was. She wasn't bothering to dance. She had a perch up there, like a long swing made out of a plumbing pipe. She was sitting on that and swaying back and forth.

The men around the wooden chute had started to chant. One of them was spitting on the dice and raising his hand over his head to throw them. He was a thick man with a beer gut and two days' growth of beard. The men watching him weren't much different, except that one or two of them were skinny in that way people got when they drank too much and didn't eat. The watching men were drawing away from the man who was rolling dice. The man who was rolling dice was dead still only when he let the dice go into the chute. The rest of the time he was rocking and huffing.

The dice hit the end of the chute. "Fifty-six!" the men in the crowd yelled.

Daniel had no idea what that meant. Dice added up to twelve, not fifty-six. The men turned to look up at the cages. The girl in the cage at the top stopped her rocking and came to stand in front of the bars. She put her hands behind her back and unhooked the bra top of her bikini.

"Fifty-six!" the men in the crowd yelled. "Fifty-six, fifty-six, fifty-six!"

The girl dropped her bra top into the air above the crowd. One of the biker boys caught it and tied it around his neck.

"Hell," Bobby said. "She's perfect. Do you see that? She's absolutely perfect."

"Right," Daniel said.

The man with the beer belly was rolling dice again. The men who were watching were standing back again. The man with the beer belly held the dice above his head, wound his arm up like a baseball pitcher, and let the dice go into the chute.

"Sixty-five!" the men said. "Sixty-five, sixty-five!"

"I don't get it," Daniel said.

"I do," Bobby said. "It's how many points you can get without rolling a seven or an eleven. That's what it is."

Daniel wanted to know how Bobby knew that. He didn't ask because he knew it would turn out to be something stupid, like it was written on the side of the entry booth and he hadn't noticed it. He looked up at the top cage again. The girl there had unhooked one side of her bikini bottoms. She was bumping and grinding like a stripper, but she didn't seem like a stripper, somehow. Her breasts were firm and high and elastic. Her nipples were pink and round. She got the other side of her bikini bottoms unhooked and pulled them off. She hadn't shaved herself. Daniel could see the neat triangle of blond hair. She took the bikini bottoms and dropped them down, this time right on the head of the man with the dice.

Bobby Donovan was sweating. He was hot and agitated, far more wired than the cocaine had made him. Daniel hadn't noticed when it started. Bobby didn't seem to remember that Daniel was here. The man with the dice was winding up for another shot. The girl in the top cage was spinning and dancing, doing a kind of hula, graceful and unhurried. The girls in the other cages were looking bored. Bobby grabbed one of the men in the watching crowd and spun him around. It was one of the biker boys, a big man with six holes in his left ear. Daniel thought for sure there was going to be trouble. Instead, the biker boy spun around, saw who had hold of him, and just relaxed.

"Listen," Bobby said. "How much does it take? To get her. How much does it take?"

"A hundred points," the biker boy said. "With no sevens and no elevens."

"How much do you have to pay to get a throw?"

"Twenty-five bucks. Get the hell out of here."

"Seventy-three!" the other men started chanting. "Seventy-three!"

Now the dark-haired woman from the gate came over to watch. She looked up at the girl in the top cage for a long moment, then got a pack of cigarettes out of the pocket of her smock and lit up.

"It's not just getting the hundred points," she said—to Bobby, Daniel was sure. There wasn't anyone else she could be talking to, although she didn't seem to be talking to much of anybody. "You can't just get a hundred points and take her home."

"She's got to let down her hair," the biker boy said.

"She's got treasures in her hair," the woman said.

"What kind of treasures?" Bobby said. "What happens when she lets down her hair?"

"Eighty-three!" the men who were watching said. "Eighty-three, eighty-three, eighty-three!"

Up at the cage at the top, the girl was naked and moving. Daniel thought of her bound to the bars and only able to sway. He thought of her helpless and raw and silent. He looked at Bobby and almost stopped breathing. Bobby had lost it completely now. Bobby was nuts.

"Hey," Daniel said, grabbing Bobby by the sleeve again.

Bobby's eyes looked too big. All his muscles were twitching. The bad in him—the thing that Daniel had always picked up and never really liked—was all over the surface.

"Ninety-one!" the men said.

Bobby hopped back and forth from one foot to the other. He was shaking too hard to stand still.

"Ram it up her, ram it up her," he kept saying under his breath. "Tear her apart. Tear her apart."

"Ninety-nine!" the men said.

Suddenly everything got very quiet. Even Bobby got quiet. The woman with the dark hair put her cigarette out on the ground and folded her arms across her chest. The girls in the cages stopped moving. Even the girl in the top cage stopped moving. She came all the way to the front and pressed against the bars. The metal seemed to make stripes against her skin.

"Ninety-nine!" someone in the crowd said.

Somebody else giggled.

The man with the dice put his hand in the air again, and wound his arm like a baseball pitcher again, and let the dice go. Daniel pushed as far forward as he could get, right up against the wood of the chute. He saw the dice come down the worn felt surface and strike the bottom board. He saw the outcome before he knew what it meant: a one and a two, three altogether, not seven or eleven, not bad luck to kill the play. It took a moment for anybody else to realize what had happened, too. Then Bobby was jumping up and down, hitting Daniel on the back hard enough to crack his spine.

"A hundred and two! A hundred and two!" Bobby said, sounding delirious, sounding crazy. "A hundred and two!"

It was like being in a movie, in a way. Everybody was doing things that made no sense to him, but they were doing them together, as if this were a dance number, as if he were the only one present who didn't know the drill. The men were all backing up, leaving the man who had rolled a hundred points on the dice on his own in front of the cages. Daniel went back with the crowd, not wanting to make himself conspicuous. Bobby never got all the way back. He was out in front on his own, just behind the man who had thrown the dice. *Rip them apart,* Daniel thought, finding himself wanting to giggle uncontrollably. He didn't want to rip her apart. He wanted to tie her down until she couldn't move and then— what?

The girl in the top cage was no longer swaying. She was standing at the very front of the cage with her feet wide apart, looking down on them. The woman with the dark hair was standing off to the side, so tense she seemed to vibrate. The man who had thrown the dice threw his head back and called out,

"Rapunzel, Rapunzel, let down your long hair."

Now Daniel knew there was a drill here, some ritual he didn't get. Did this happen every night? He couldn't imagine that someone threw a hundred points without getting a seven or eleven every night. What did they do when someone did it who had never been here before? Did they give instructions?

The man who had thrown the dice was still standing where he had been, taking big breaths now. The snickers in the crowd sounded like bubbles.

"Rapunzel, Rapunzel," the man said again, "let down your long hair. That I may climb the golden stair."

The girl in the top cage sat down on her floor. She put her hand to her head and took some pins out of her hair. Her hair was coiled around and around her head in a braid. Until she unwrapped it, there was no way of telling how long it was. Once she got it loose, though, Daniel could see it was long beyond belief. It was as blond as sunlight. It reminded him of that woman who was supposed to have ridden through town stark naked, covering herself up with her hair.

This girl's hair was full of little silver balls. She lay down on her back in the cage and lowered her hair through the bars. It fell in front of the bars to the other cages and shivered in the wind. The silver balls tinkled and jumped.

The man who had thrown the dice stepped forward. The hair wasn't really long enough for him to climb up. It wasn't strong enough, either. Daniel was glad to see he wasn't going to try. Instead, he reached up and took one of the silver balls for himself.

As soon as the man had the ball in his hand, the girl was moving. She wound her hair up into a coil and settled it in her lap. The silver balls shimmered as she stroked the hair around them. The man who had rolled the dice looked at the silver ball in his hand. Then he closed it in his fist and crushed it.

"Rapunzel, Rapunzel," somebody said.

The man opened his hand and looked inside it. In among the shards of broken silver ball he had a little Christmas-ornament-sized rocking chair, like a piece of furniture for a very miniaturized dollhouse. A sigh of disappointment went up from the other men. In the cage at the top, Rapunzel put her hand to her head and came down with another silver ball. When she crushed this one, it had a little golden ladder in it, that she held up so everyone on the ground could see.

So that's how it works, Daniel thought—and then Bobby was standing beside him, hot and angry, wired.

"Listen," Bobby said, "it's a gyp. It was fixed. It's a gyp."

"What?" Daniel said.

"She didn't have that ball in her hair," Bobby said. He was whispering now. The woman with the dark hair was staring at the two of them. Daniel knew that look. She would love to throw them both out. Daniel didn't want to get thrown out. He wanted to stand here all night and look at Rapunzel, in the flesh, even if he couldn't get close enough to touch. He had the feeling he was never going to see a woman like this again, except in photographs.

"It's a gyp," Bobby said again, grabbing Daniel around the wrist. "You could waste your money here all night and it wouldn't matter. You'd never get her."

"But—" Daniel said.

Bobby was pulling him, past the woman with the dark hair, past the gateway booth. There was somebody else throwing dice at the wooden chute now. The man who had broken the silver ball was still looking at his miniature rocking chair. Bobby forced Daniel back onto the dark path and then into the bushes. Everything was wet and hot and rancid.

"It's a scam," Bobby said calmly when he'd stopped pulling. "It's a way to take the suckers for their money. She never had that ball in her hair. I saw her. She took it off the floor of the cage."

"I thought you wanted to have a girl," Daniel said, bewildered. "I thought you wanted to go in and play the game and get a girl—"

"Not *any* girl," Bobby said. "*That* girl."

Daniel was about to say he didn't see what difference it made, but he did see. "Even if it wasn't a gyp it would be nearly impossible," he said. "It would be like winning the lottery."

"I don't like to gamble," Bobby said. "I like to be sure."

"But you can't be sure. How can you be sure?"

"I don't like people to treat me like an idiot, either. That calls for retaliation, don't you think?"

Daniel didn't know what "retaliation" meant. He rubbed sweat off his bare arms. "I wish I had enough money," he said. "I'd go back there and get a girl. Any girl. I'd be happy just to get laid."

"You're going to get laid."

"How? You going to lend me fifty bucks?"

"You're going to lay Rapunzel. Just like me. Just you wait. You're going to lay Rapunzel and it's not going to cost you a dime."

"You're crazy," Daniel said, but Bobby had hold of him again. Bobby was pulling him again.

That was when it occurred to Daniel that this was not the first time Bobby had been at the Carnival. Bobby knew his way around far too well.

There were bushes and shrubs, back alleys and big patches of dirt. The Carnival was built into the side of one of those dirt cliffs that had been made by highway construction, and in the places where people weren't supposed to go it hadn't been decorated or even kept up. Daniel saw wires bare of rubber coating and big pieces of equipment left to rust. In one place there were three carousel ponies clustered together, as if they were part of a herd that had gotten lost and petrified. Everywhere there was garbage rotting in the open, stagnant pools that seemed to collect mosquitoes like dust. Daniel's marijuana buzz was more than just completely gone. He was as conscious as he ever wanted to get. Everything was awful.

Bobby pulled him until they could see lights again, and the sounds of men, and Daniel finally understood where they were— out in the back behind the cages, almost as close to Rapunzel as they had been on the other side.

"See?" Bobby said. "All you have to do is wait. There aren't any walls. There're just those canvas flaps."

"Right," Daniel said.

"We'll just climb right up there and go in," Bobby said.

"There's a door, do you see? There're doors in all the cages. That's how the girls get out to do their business."

"People will see us," Daniel said. "We'll be right there in front of everybody."

"We won't do it now. We'll wait until the Carnival closes."

"Then she'll go home. She must go home, Bobby. She can't live up there in that cage."

"She doesn't go home right away. The other girls do, but she doesn't. She waits for that woman with the cigarette to finish closing up."

"Then that woman will see us. This is crazy, Bobby. This is nuts."

"Look up there," Bobby said. "To the right of the cage. That's the changing room. It's just a room, like a treehouse. All the girls use it. We're going to use it. We're going to nail Rapunzel."

"Crap," Daniel said.

Bobby spun him around and grabbed him by both his arms. "They all deserve to be nailed, don't you know that? They all deserve to be nailed. And you're going to help me. We're going to get it done while my fucking parents are down in the fucking Bahamas."

Daniel wished he knew where the Bahamas were so he could go there, too.

It took a long time for the Carnival to close, hours and hours. Daniel kept thinking that he ought to do something for himself, like get up and leave. Instead, he just drifted, lying in the dirt as if he were at home, keeping his eyes shut under the heat. Every once in a while, girls would come out the backs of the cages and go into the dressing room Bobby had pointed out to him. They would come out again in long, shiny robes and run down the metal steps to meet the men who were waiting for them. Then they seemed to disappear under the stage, or more or less in that direction. Daniel expected Bobby to give him another lecture about how all women were really just selling it one way or another, but Bobby didn't. Bobby just sat hunched in the dirt, singing to himself.

By the time the Carnival actually began to shut down—one

o'clock in the morning, Daniel thought, or two; whenever last call was—Daniel was half asleep and beyond caring. He heard the grinding squeal of machinery going off as if it were just another accident on Thomaston Road. Then Bobby was shaking him by the shoulders, making him move.

"Wake up," Bobby said. "Look at this. Here they come."

Daniel opened his eyes and saw a small stream of girls leaving the cages and going into the changing room. There were some men waiting at the bottom of the pyramid.

"Those are the all-nighters," Bobby said. "You can get one if you've got the money and know how to approach it right."

"Yeah," Daniel said.

They were whispering. With so much of the machinery off, their voices sounded loud anyway. Nobody at the pyramid seemed to hear them.

The girls came out of the changing rooms one by one. The men who were waiting for them hitched and hawed and spat on the ground and then went, too. A moment later the woman with the black hair came around back and seemed to check some things near the base of the stage. Then she walked away in the direction of the main Carnival.

"See?" Bobby said. "And Rapunzel's still in her cage."

"Why?" Daniel said.

"We've got forty-five minutes," Bobby said. "I've timed it twice. She always takes forty-five minutes. She's probably counting up her money."

"Why?" Daniel said again, because it suddenly seemed very important. Bobby was moving forward again, though, so he moved forward again, too. There were almost no lights anywhere in this part of the Carnival now, just one bare bulb over the door to the dressing room. *This is the part where the aliens come and abduct us,* Daniel thought.

When they got to the stage, there were a series of ladders, like fire escape ladders but flimsier. The canvas flap that covered the back of Rapunzel's cage was all the way down. Bobby hopped around on the ground, unable to contain himself.

"She doesn't come out, see?" he said. "She just sits up there while the old lady goes and does the money stuff. You think the old lady is a dyke?"

"I don't know," Daniel said.

"Rapunzel, Rapunzel," Bobby said.

Daniel was about to say something about turning around and going home. This was crazy. Then Bobby started climbing the ladders, humming a little under his breath. Daniel thought about girls with ropes around their wrists, and tapes, and slender lines of leather. He started to climb the ladders behind Bobby, moving carefully so he wouldn't fall.

"Rip her up," Bobby said, just loud enough, Daniel was sure, to be heard even by Rapunzel. Rapunzel did not pull back the canvas flap at the back of her cage. Bobby got to the top of the last ladder and waited for Daniel to catch up with him.

"Here we go," Bobby said.

Bobby pulled back the canvas flap and looked inside. Daniel looked, too. There was another canvas flap covering the bars at the front of the cage, now. The cage itself was black.

"She isn't here," Daniel said. "Bobby, listen, she got away somehow. She isn't here."

"Shhh," Bobby said.

Then Daniel saw her, standing in a corner near the cage's front. She was wearing her little bikini, but her hair was down, blond and braided and impossibly long. Bobby had started to hop and giggle again.

"Rapunzel, Rapunzel," he said, "let down your long hair."

Rapunzel looked at her hair. It was down. She looked back at Bobby and cocked her head. Daniel thought that if he were a girl in this situation, he would be afraid. He was afraid of Bobby as it was. Rapunzel just stood there, looking at them.

"Rapunzel, Rapunzel," Bobby said again, moving into the cage even farther now.

Rapunzel turned her back to them and shook her hair out. Bobby went a few more steps toward her. There seemed to be no light anyway, just a glow in the air.

"Let's go," Daniel said, suddenly cold. "Bobby, let's—"

It happened so fast, Daniel didn't know what to think. Bobby sprang forward, his arms outstretched, reaching for her. Daniel thought he was going to land right on her head and crush her neck. Bobby was still in the air when she began to turn back to them again. Her hair flowed in the slight breeze. Her body was fluid. *She's so perfect,* Daniel thought.

What he saw was Bobby landing at Rapunzel's feet. It was like a scene from the fairy tale. He was kneeling in front of her, doing homage. Then Rapunzel leaned over to him, the way princesses do when they are about to kiss frogs. Bobby put a hand up to touch her face.

"Rapunzel, Rapunzel," he said.

Rapunzel's hands reached out and got Bobby around the neck and started to squeeze.

It shouldn't have been possible. Bobby was only seventeen and out of shape, but he was a young and naturally strong man. He should have been able to throw Rapunzel off him with ease. It didn't happen. She had her hands around his throat and a good aim on his windpipe. Bobby thrashed and struggled, but she only straddled him. Once she kicked him, hard, where it would hurt. Bobby cried out, but it didn't sound like much. It didn't sound like anything at all. Rapunzel sat down on his side and began to pound his head on the floor of the cage, over and over again, the way children did when they were trying to crack nuts.

I should help him, Daniel thought. *I should do something.*

He couldn't make himself move. He couldn't make himself do anything. Rapunzel was pounding and pounding Bobby's head against the floor. Bobby seemed to be unconscious, or worse. Daniel didn't see how it could have happened. Rapunzel was a girl. The floor of the cage was not strong.

Then Rapunzel stopped pounding and took her hands off Bobby. Daniel could see Bobby's head and neck. His neck looked all bloody, as if Rapunzel had broken something in there and it had poked through the skin. Daniel could feel the sweat rolling down his back and soaking into his shirt. He could feel his sphincter begin to spasm. He was losing all kinds of control.

Rapunzel looked up and smiled at him. Her smile made him bone cold. *She's crazy as a loon,* he thought. *She's worse than crazy.*

Rapunzel started to come toward him. Daniel's sphincter let go. He had started to cry. He couldn't remember the last time he had cried.

"Rapunzel, Rapunzel," Rapunzel said pleasantly.

Daniel whirled around and headed for the ladder. His own shit was rolling down his legs. He stank and he thought it was going to get worse. He was going to end up dead, and if he didn't end up dead he was going to end up in the middle of a million policemen with shit running down his legs. He got to the ladder and swung himself over. She would follow him, he was sure of it. His hands were sweating so badly, he couldn't get a grip on the ladder's edge. He was going to fall to the ground and she was going to fall on top of him. She was humming under her breath, just the way Bobby used to do. It wasn't a song Daniel recognized.

"Rapunzel, Rapunzel," Rapunzel said.

Daniel thought of Bobby's car parked in the grass. He thought of the way home and the miles and miles of back roads he would have to use to get there, soiled as he was, stinking and raw. The ladder was so slippery and he was shaking so hard.

"Rapunzel, Rapunzel," Rapunzel said.

Daniel let go of the sides of the ladder without even thinking about it. He fell and fell through the air, endlessly. His sphincter let loose again. *I want to be dead,* he told himself. *I want to be dead I want to be dead I don't want to die.*

When he hit the ground, it knocked the breath out of him. He lay in the dirt and tried to breathe. He could see Rapunzel above him, with the canvas back flap of her cage pulled up, leaning out into the air and looking for him. He tried to make himself breathe slowly, but he couldn't make himself breathe at all.

"Rapunzel, Rapunzel," Rapunzel said.

"What's going on?" somebody said.

Daniel lay very still. The old lady was coming back. She was waddling along the path with a big pocketbook stuck under her arm and a cigarette stuck in her mouth.

"Rapunzel?" the old lady said.

Rapunzel swung her hair into the wind and laughed.

"Jesus Christ," the old lady said. "She did it again. She did it again."

Daniel lay as still as he could. The old lady was right next to him now. She had to be able to smell him. It was a miracle she wasn't coming after him.

She kept going along the path and then to the ladders. She put the strap of her pocketbook around her neck and started to climb up.

"Rapunzel, Rapunzel," Rapunzel said, laughing and laughing now, the only sound in the night. The whole world seemed to be full of dark.

"Jesus Christ," the old lady said, disappearing into Rapunzel's cage.

Daniel started to roll, full body length, just the way he was. He rolled and rolled and rolled across the sparse patches of grass and the rock-studded patches of dirt. He rolled until he got to the edges of the trees and dared himself to stand up.

He thought of girls with their hands tethered to the sides of beds and their legs spread out. He thought of girls with gags in their mouths so they couldn't laugh. He thought of Bobby saying: Rip them up, rip them up, rip them up. It was just what he wanted to do.

In a little while, he would stand up and start walking. He would find a stream—they didn't call it Waterbury for nothing, there were streams everywhere in this part of the state—and wash himself off. He could get himself naked and sit in the grass. He would walk home stark naked if he had to.

What he wouldn't do was tell anybody what he had just seen. They wouldn't believe him, and they would never believe he had come here with Bobby Donovan, who was a wheel when he was nothing at all.

He would go home and he would lie down in the dirt in front

of his mother's trailer and he would smoke marijuana until his throat was bleeding, but he would never come back here again and he would never tell anybody and he would never think of Bobby Donovan except when he heard people talking about him.

When he finally had himself a girl, though, he was going to make sure she was tied down good and that she had a gag in her mouth. He wasn't going to want to hear her laugh.

Gary Braunbeck is a young writer just now beginning to appear in many major mystery anthologies. He has a style all his own, and a very different slant on some of the more familiar conventions of the mystery writer's art. His story combines elements from two different fairy tales, "The Poor Boy in the Grave" and "The Old Beggar-Woman," into something that is uniquely his own.

GARY A. BRAUNBECK

Resurrection Joe

When strolling one night midst the chill midnight long,
I met a poor boy who was singing a song;
Although he was singing, he wanted for bread,
Although he was smiling, he wished himself dead.
—nursery rhyme

My given name is Joseph Allan Conners, and my job is tending the graves. It's a responsibility I don't take lightly. As I see it, when a person's loved ones come to pay their respects, they should find a final resting place that's neat and tidy. I think it helps them feel better about still being alive.

It started at the old County Home Cemetery. It's kind of a pathetic place, but I do for it what I can. Until 1967 it was used to bury the residents of the home or homeless folks and transients. The home was shut down in '67, and the residents moved to a newer building closer to town. About a year later the original home caught fire and burned to the ground. Rumor has it that all the records are buried in the subbasement, locked away in fire-proof file cabinets.

Over the decades the cemetery fell to neglect and decay. The elements set to work, rain and snow smoothing away the head-stone inscriptions, so now the folks buried here are known only by sloppily engraved numbers: 107, 122, 135, and so on. It makes me sad, knowing there's not a soul on Earth besides me who cares, who wonders who these people were, what they might have dreamed about, if they died feeling they'd had rich, full lives or crossed over with a sick, lonely heart, believing the world would only be an emptier place for their leaving it and not a poorer one.

I suppose I feel a kinship with this place because I was a foundling, county-raised, county-trained, and, except for a tour of duty in Vietnam thirty years ago, county-employed all my life. When I die, though, I've got enough money set aside for a nice spot in Cedar Hill Cemetery, so at least the county won't have to bury me here. I just can't help thinking that, had things been different, I could be one of the nameless dead folk who rest here.

Every once in a while we still have a homeless person die, and the county has me come out and dig a fresh grave. I throw in the numbered marker for free.

I'd gotten a call telling me that I needed to make room for a John Doe taking up space at the morgue. I finished about seven-thirty, a bleak and cold November night, and had just packed the last of the equipment in the back of my truck when I realized I'd left one of my shovels back by the grave. Cussing my absentmindedness, I turned my lantern back on and went to get it.

I heard the sound just as I reached for the shovel.

A sigh, full of pain and weariness.

From inside the grave.

For a second, old horror movie images flashed through my head, starring Karloff and Lugosi and Lorre.

I knelt down, lifting the lantern over my head.

In the grave lay a pale, thin child, seven or eight years old. He was barefoot and shivering, dressed in clothes too old, dirty, and small; he was clutching some kind of package.

At the sight of his face something inside me cracked and splintered.

It wasn't just the bruises and cuts covering his skin, it was the history etched into his features. It was the face of a child unloved, who had seen only the fearsome, ugly, brutal side of life and had come to expect no tenderness or affection. In that face I saw starvation and abuse, no memory of summer days in a park, no picnics or kite flying, building a snowman after the first big snow. There was only loneliness and pain, desperation and want.

I set down the lantern, jumped into the grave, and took off my coat, wrapping it around the child's shoulders.

He was so thin, little more than a skeleton covered in skin.

"Please . . . *don't* . . . don't hurt me . . ." he whispered.

"Shhh, son, c'mon, don't talk. I'm not gonna hurt you, I swear. We gotta get you to a hospital." I wondered where he'd come from, how he'd gotten down in—

Then I heard movement from above.

I poked my head out of the grave just as the first shot came, blowing the lantern to pieces and sending hot sections of glass into my cheek. I dropped, clutching the searing left side of my face and feeling blood trickle through my fingers.

Waiting for the pain to ebb, I felt the child's foot tap against my leg. Through the darkness, I saw him pull open my coat and try to yank up his shirt, but he was too weak.

I leaned close and whispered, "What is it?"

"Shirt . . ." was all he could get out.

I reached down to pull up his shirt and saw something glimmer.

He had a pistol of some kind stuffed into his pants.

Good Christ, I thought. *What kind of a life have you endured?*

Another sound: footsteps, quick, getting closer.

I ran my hands over the gun to get the feel: a 9mm, the clip securely in place. I hadn't shot at anyone since Vietnam; I didn't much care for it then and didn't want to do it now, but I had to get this boy to the hospital.

For a clear shot I'd need some light. I reached over to the little boy and unsnapped one of the pockets of my coat, pulling out the flare. Spend as much time traveling back roads as I do, you find that having a flare on your person comes in handy.

I chambered a round, touched the boy's face—"Don't move, son, okay? It'll be all right"—then ignited the flare and rose to my feet, throwing it as high and as hard as I could.

As I'd hoped, it took the shooter a couple of seconds to react.

I saw him clearly as he watched the bright flare arc overhead.

I didn't see a gun, though. I wasn't about to fire until I was positive he'd been—

He whipped his head around and saw me, then lifted his pistol.

My first shot went wild—I wasn't ready for the force of the recoil—but the second one got him square in the knee and he went down, screaming and firing. I fell back into the grave as the bullets winged and ricocheted against the headstones.

I had no idea how many shots he fired, or how many remained in his clip.

The little boy shuddered. I adjusted the coat and touched his face, then checked his pulse. God, it was so weak.

"What's your name, son?"

". . . ert . . ."

"What?"

". . . R-R-Robert . . ."

"Good name, like the actor Robert Ryan. Strong name. You a strong boy, Robert?"

". . . kids . . ." He pulled in a deep breath, then lifted his head; it seemed to take everything out of him, and it broke my heart. "You gotta go back and get the other kids before they finish."

"Who? Finish what?"

He started to cry, quiet, tight little tears streaking his unloved face. "They're gonna kill 'em tonight, I . . . I h-h-heard 'em say so. Oh, *please?* I tried to get them to stop but they . . . my sister, Sandy, she's—" He spasmed in pain, and I wondered about internal bleeding.

"Some of 'em are too little to fight back," he croaked. "If you don't . . . *promise* you'll go get them?"

Damn if I didn't have tears in my own eyes as well. "I promise, Robert. I'm a man of my word. You a man of your word, Robert?"

". . . yeah . . ."

"Then you got to promise me you'll stay still, don't move or speak. I'm gonna go out there—"

"No, don't go, don't leave me—"

"Not going to leave you, son, I just need to make sure that guy out there isn't going to shoot at us again, okay? Then I'll come right back here and you and me'll get in my truck and everything will be just fine.

"I won't leave you, Robert, I swear it. I'll be *right back,* okay?"

He tried to smile at me but looked like he wasn't used to it.

I hugged him to me as gently as I could. "Just a minute or two, then you won't ever be left alone again. I promise."

". . . 'kay," he whispered, then tried to hug me back but didn't quite make it. I wondered if he'd ever been hugged before or even knew what I was doing.

I crawled out of the grave and, holding the pistol out, did a crouch-run toward the guy.

He was still down, his gun about a foot away from him. I kicked it aside, then knelt beside him.

"Sorry," I said.

Then froze, recognizing him.

Judge Arthur Buchanan, better known around Cedar Hill as "Adoption Artie." If a couple wanted to adopt a child and found themselves getting drowned in red tape, they went to Buchanan and he took care of it in a hurry. He'd earned the respect of a lot of Cedar Hill folks.

"Judge, what the hell are you—"

"You're . . . you're not—*O God*—"

"I'm not who?"

He rose up on his elbows, grimacing in pain. "I thought you were one of his goons! I'm sorry. I was only trying to . . . to—" He started to pass out.

I grabbed the collar of his coat and pulled him, slapping his face. "What were you trying to do, Judge?"

"I couldn't . . . couldn't live with it anymore. It wasn't supposed to be this way. The k-k-k-kids weren't supposed to be . . . be—"

"Where are they, Judge? Where're the other kids?"

I'm still ashamed about what I did next, but I was scared and angry.

I pressed the gun barrel into the pulp of his kneecap. He screamed and thrashed.

"Where?" I said.

He gave me an address, then passed out.

I grabbed his pistol. The only other thing he had on him was a card key. If the address was where I thought it was, this was probably for the security gates.

I went to get Robert.

As soon as I lifted him in my arms I knew he was dead.

I knelt there in that cold, dank grave, cradling his head against my shoulder, rocking back and forth, crying, whispering over and over again how sorry I was that he'd died alone and lonely.

"I kept my word," I whispered to him. "I came back. I said I would, Robert. I came back."

I put him in the front seat of my truck and covered him with a piece of tarp, then put the engine in gear and drove out, trying to clear my eyes and breathe steadily.

C'mon, c'mon, I thought. *You got to hang on.*

The address Buchanan had given me was about eight miles down the road, almost as isolated as the cemetery. The nearest telephone was at a gas station fourteen miles in the other direction.

I looked at the body of the little boy on the seat next to me.

They're gonna kill 'em tonight, he'd said. Promise *you'll go get them?*

I'd left him alone in that grave. He'd begged me not to, but I had, and he'd died alone and lonely, in misery and sadness, never knowing tenderness or summer days, picnics or flying kites.

I am a man of my word. I would not insult the dignity of this dead child by wasting time.

And I wanted to see his murderers' faces for myself.

Damned if I wasn't right; the address was Wesley Rodgers's estate.

Wesley Rodgers, one of the richest and most powerful men in the state. A businessman with "diversified international interests." Rumor had it he and his wife had more political pull than the governor himself (not surprising, considering they probably funded most of his reelection campaign).

I killed the headlights and pulled over, staring at the massive, seemingly endless wrought-iron fence that surrounded the grounds. The mansion itself sat high up on a hill in the distance. I saw a couple of lights on and wondered what old Wes and his young wife were up to: *A little more coffee with your dessert, dear? Why, yes, thank you, and a little extra raspberry sauce for the chocolate mousse.*

I followed Buchanan's directions to the delivery entrance and used the card key to open the gate.

I sat there staring at that great house up on the grand hill and grew angrier.

Finally, I opened the package that had cost Robert his life.

Dozens, maybe hundreds of little plastic packets fell out.

Drugs. It figured.

There were also several papers. I pulled my flashlight from the glove compartment, turned it on, then hunkered down in the seat and read a few.

You know, it's enough to make you puke sometimes, realizing that there isn't anything in this world a person can't buy if he or she has enough money.

Including children.

A lot of the forms were, as far as I could figure out, receipts for the sale of children (the papers called it something like ". . . additional costs for expediency and simplification of acquisition process"), usually one to two years of age. Each one was signed by Buchanan and whichever woman was selling her kid at the time.

That was sickening enough. Then I read one of the other papers:

Mix 100 g of anhydrous ethylamine and 220 g of cyclohexanone. Keep 16 hours, shaken with solid KOH. Remove oil layer by decantation. Distill the oil layer in vacuo to get the intermediate N-cyclohexylidenethylamine, then—

I stopped reading. It didn't matter that I had no idea what crap this was the formula for, only that someone thought it was worth killing a child over—maybe several children.

Then I saw the little girl.

She was clutching a package just like the one Robert had and was heading toward what looked like a tool shed. Behind her was

Mrs. Rodgers, pushing the girl none too gently along. They went inside the shed and closed the door behind them.

I got out and stumbled over to the shed, then slowly pulled open the door and looked inside.

One bare bulb hung from the ceiling, revealing nothing but empty space.

I stepped inside, so scared and dizzy I almost didn't see the handle under my feet.

A trapdoor.

I rearranged the pistols in my pockets and belt, then knelt down, lifted the door, and saw a cement staircase.

Bomb shelter, I thought. A lot of older homes in Cedar Hill have them.

I stepped onto the first stair, closing the door as quietly as I could, and started down.

At the bottom of the steps stood a second door, this one thick steel.

It wasn't closed all the way.

I nudged my foot in and began to open it.

Wesley Rodgers and his wife were at the far end of the room, stepping through another door and closing it behind them.

Along one of the side walls of the incredibly large shelter stood rows and rows of laboratory tables and equipment—beakers, burners, tubes, vials, and I don't know what all. Toward the back of the room, near the doorway where Wes and his wife had gone, were tall shelves filled with crates.

The other sidewall held bunk beds—and not the type you see parents buying for the little ones, either; these reminded me of those pictures of the Auschwitz barracks.

The worst of it, though, was the kids.

There must have been fifteen or twenty of them, dressed in the oldest, filthiest clothes you ever saw. A lot of them looked foreign. They sat on stools along the length of the lab tables, each one performing a different task.

It took a second before any of them noticed I was in the room, and in that time it all came clear to me.

The Rodgers, supposedly childless, had been buying children through the black market to use as slave labor in this goddamned drug lab, and Judge Buchanan must have arranged it for them.

There are times when I am ashamed to be a member of the human race.

One by one, the children stopped their labors and turned to look at me, and I felt a chill that I have felt only one other time in my life.

In Vietnam I was shot by a sniper outside Qui Nhon and wound up sharing a hospital room with a small, smoke-skinned Montagnard girl whose chest was being held together by large gold pins. The nurses told me that she was the only survivor of a Viet Cong attack on her village.

She never spoke. She never smiled. She never looked up.

I tried to get her to smile, but she didn't seem aware that I was even in the room.

One night, around two in the morning, she turned her head and looked at me.

I had never seen such total loneliness and fear in anyone's eyes before. One corner of her mouth twitched slightly upward, as if she were trying to smile but didn't quite know how to do it, and she stared at me like she wasn't sure if I was going to save her or slaughter her.

I gave her a smile. She died a few moments later.

Some nights I still weep for her.

Before me now were fifteen or twenty children whose faces wore the exact same expression as that little girl.

"It's all right," I whispered to them. "I'm gonna take you away from here."

"What about Bobby?" said a thin, strawberry-haired girl to my left.

Keeping my eyes on the door in the back of the room, I went over to her and said, "Are you Sandy?"

"Uh-huh. Bobby, he ran away. He said he was gonna"—her lower lip twitched and tears formed in her eyes—"he said he was gonna go somewhere so he could die. They beat him up *real bad*." She wiped some snot away. "Where's Bobby?"

I couldn't tell her, not then. The thought of that boy walking fourteen miles to the cemetery, in unspeakable pain, just so he could lie down and die in peace filled me with too much rage. "He's outside, in my truck. That's where I want all of you to go, right now. You get out of here. You'll see my truck over by that big oak tree when you get outside. Go on. *Now.*"

They moved slowly, like zombies, climbing off their stools and shuffling out the door.

As the last few of them were heading out, Wes and his wife came out.

"What the hell is . . . ? Who the fuck are *you?*" shouted Wes.

"Kids're coming with me," I said, pointing both pistols at him. "You try and stop me and I'll kill you where you stand, you worthless piece of shit."

He smiled a damned ugly smile, like I wasn't man enough to carry through on my threat.

"Where's Artie?" he said.

"Doesn't really matter, does it?"

He sighed. "I suppose not." He shrugged. "All right, then, Mr.—?"

"Conners."

"Mr. Conners. I gather that the good judge told you everything?"

"He told me some. I figured out the rest for myself."

"Ah—so you found Robert?"

"Yes."

"And how is little Bobby?"

It was everything I could do not to blow a hole in his chest. "Dead."

"Hmm. Too bad. He was a good worker."

"I'm sure he was."

"I don't suppose there's any chance we could come to some sort of an arrangement?"

His wife stood behind him.

I heard a child cry out and turned to see if they were all right.

One of the smaller kids had slipped, skinning his knee on the steps.

I turned back around just as Rodgers fired his pistol, hitting me in the shoulder. I dropped to one knee and fired, opening up his chest. His wife screamed and fell to the ground, scrambling for his pistol. I threw myself behind one of the lab tables just as she shot at me, hitting one of the beakers. I don't know what was in the thing, but as soon as the liquid hit the burner beneath it, most everything nearby blew up in a cloud of flame and glass and smoke.

I rolled out from behind the table and plowed off another shot, hitting some of the vials at the far end of the lab.

The explosion was unbelievable. Looking back, I suppose it wasn't all that big, but down there in that room, with no windows, it was like a small-scale version of Hiroshima.

I scrambled out for the steps and barely made it outside before the fireball followed me.

A few seconds later Mrs. Rodgers came running out, every inch of her body aflame.

She dropped to the ground, and the children surrounded her.

Not one of them made a move to help.

A couple of them—Sandy included—held out their hands, warming them in the heat.

I sat on the cold ground, bleeding from my shoulder and face, wondering what kind of nightmares these poor kids were going to suffer for the rest of their lives.

Judge Buchanan told the authorities everything, and took his punishment like a man.

The kids were turned over to Children's Services, and all of them were eventually placed in good homes, thanks to a lot of national news coverage.

My face is kind of scarred on the left side, but folks around here don't treat me any different; in fact, most of them are a lot friendlier now.

Robert was buried at the old County Home Cemetery. I dug his grave myself. He's got a real nice headstone. No number for him: I paid for it myself, and it bears his name.

The folks who adopted Sandy are a real nice couple. They let me visit her. She tells me stories about Robert, the things he wanted to do, how he protected her. Sometimes she tells me about her nightmares. Sometimes she cries, sometimes we both do. Every few months I take her out to visit her brother's grave and we plant fresh flowers. She helps me spread out the new topsoil and seeds so we can make the old cemetery a nicer place.

Sometimes, in summer, we even fly a kite so Robert can enjoy it.

Folks around here have taken to calling me "Resurrection Joe" because I talked the City Council into having the ruins of the County Home cleared away so I can get to the cabinets in the subbasement. Somewhere down there is a file drawer that has the names of all the folks buried here, and a chart showing who's where. I'm gonna make damn sure that these folks are given back their names so maybe someone else besides me will remember them. Maybe it'll give them a dignity in death they didn't enjoy in life. I don't know.

Most nights I think about Robert and the little Montagnard girl. I imagine they know now what was in my heart, that I cared, that I tried to help.

It makes me feel better about still being alive.

Besides, my job, after all, is tending the graves.

Brendan DuBois has written some of the most memorable short fiction of the past five years. His novels are just as excellent. He is one of the few writers who seem at home in both the city and the country. His story, a very different look at "Rapunzel," is one of his best.

BRENDAN DUBOIS

RAPUNZEL'S REVENGE

Beside her, Clem Tyson said in a low voice, "Well, it doesn't look like a castle."

Marie Celluci tried not to sigh in frustration. She stood with Clem in Québec City on a wide and long boardwalk called Terrasse Dufferin, and before them was an enormous building made of red brick, with dull copper green roofs and turrets and skylights and ramparts. It dominated this point of land that overlooked the St. Lawrence River, and at this moment, one room in that building to her was the most important room in the world. Unlike many of the people on the boardwalk this early summer evening, they stood still. Around them, tourists moved about them, laughing and smiling and holding hands and taking photographs and watching the street performers juggle and perform tricks. She ignored them all. She looked at the quiet windows. Hundreds of windows, it seemed. Just one, she thought. Just one.

She said, "It's called a *château*. In French, *château* means castle. Believe me, Clem, it's a castle."

He shrugged. He was a few years younger than she and a bit shorter, and he favored tight, short-sleeved shirts that highlighted his hours in the gym. His thick hair was combed back with some sort of petroleum-based product, and he had a tiny mustache that he preened whenever he thought she wasn't looking.

Clem said, "Hell, I've seen the movies and television shows, you know? Castles got drawbridges. This one ain't got a drawbridge. So how come they call it a castle?"

Around her the tourists flowed and ebbed, like a slow-moving river of people. Everyone looked happy. She could not remember the last time she could have said that word about herself. Many of the visitors stopped to look at the street performers, mimes and clowns and tricksters who performed feats of magic for the applauding crowds. Tricksters, she thought, looking over at Clem. I need a trickster, and this is what I get.

And what do you expect, on a cop's salary?

"They call it a castle because they want to," she said gently. "If they wanted to call it a superdome, I really wouldn't care. All I know is that Greg is in one of those rooms and we've got to get him out, and I want to know what ideas you have."

He smiled, showing teeth that hadn't been to a dentist lately. "Hon, I've got some ideas, don't you worry." He laughed. "Some of them even involve springing your husband. So don't fret yourself, we'll get him out."

A joke, she thought. He thinks this whole mess is a joke, or an adventure, or, God help us, a quest. That's right. A quest, to rescue the one I love from a castle guarded by the forces of evil. Despite all of it, she laughed, and Clem looked at her, smiling himself though a bit puzzled, she could see, at what possibly was so funny.

"Let's go eat," she said. "And then you'll tell me what you've got planned."

"For the rescue or for later?" he said, leering.

"Rescue first," she said, resisting an urge to use one of the three takedown holds she knew to toss him to the ground and knee him in the groin. "We get Greg out and everything else is negotiable."

What struck Greg Celluci so much—despite the moments of sheer terror every now and then—was how blessedly polite the three men could be whenever they wanted. Eventually he learned their names—Tony was the skinny one, Carlos was the pudgy one who could move so fast when he wanted to, and Paulie was the older one, and the leader. Tony and Carlos would lounge around in Polo shirts and designer jeans, but Paulie would wear a suit and tie.

Paulie also reported directly every day to Mr. Carmichael, and while in the past couple of weeks, both Tony and Carlos had caused him pain—his left forefinger and knee throbbed in memory of those dreadful few seconds—Paulie was the one who scared him the most. It was the eyes. Looking into those eyes was like looking into the rooms of an empty house.

He was in a luxurious room on the third floor of the Château Frontenac, and his room had a window overlooking a park—Governor's Park, it was called—and beside his bed there was a make-shift work area, with computers, terminals, keyboards, cables, modems, and phone lines. He was never left alone, except for sleeping at night. Right now, Tony was stretched out on the bed, working a crossword puzzle from a crossword puzzle digest. Greg could nap, watch television—and see *Baywatch* dubbed in French, which, despite his circumstances, was kind of amusing—and order every type of meal from room service. In some way, for a confirmed gearhead like himself, it was bliss. All the computer time, long-distance time, and free room service food he could want. It was heaven. Save for two things, of course. One was Marie.

The other was the ability to walk out the door.

He had pleaded and had argued and had even threatened a strike, all for just the privilege of getting outside for a walk around the city and some fresh air, and Paulie had sat him down in another one of the suite's rooms and had gently explained the facts of life for him. He, Greg, was to stay in this room until his task for Mr. Carmichael was complete; then, and only then, would the situation change. And, to ensure that Greg never forgot this, Paulie had stood up and looked at him and had said, "You're right-handed, are you not?"

"You know I am," he had said, his chest growing heavier with each passing second, knowing, this is not good, this is definitely not good.

Paulie had nodded. "I just wanted to make sure." And he said to Carlos, sitting on the other side of the room, "A finger on his left hand, if you please, Carlos. But nothing broken. Understood?"

And Carlos had put down his magazine and had walked across,

and in fifteen seconds, Greg had been face down on the couch, sobbing in pain, while Carlos had quietly gone back to his magazine.

Greg shivered again from the memory, looking out the window from his hundreds-of-dollars-per-day cell. He should have listened to Marie. Should never have gone to Mr. Carmichael. Should have never done a lot of things.

He looked out the window, gazed down at the hundreds of tourists walking along the boardwalk. Are you down there? he thought. Are you?

The door to his room opened. Tony put down his crossword puzzle book. Paulie came in and said, "You're not at your terminal. Is something wrong?"

Greg's throat was dry. "No, nothing wrong. I'm just running a test program, and it should be done in a few minutes. Then I'll be back."

Paulie nodded, made an attempt at what passed for a smile on that face. "Fine. It makes me feel good to see you work."

After the door shut, Tony picked up his crossword puzzle book and said, "Kid, them's the best kind of words you can hope for, to make that guy happy. You do that, and everything will be just fine."

"I already know that," he said, suddenly angry. "You don't have to tell me."

"Maybe so," he said. "But I get the feeling every now and then you need a reminder."

He turned and looked out the window again. Where are you?

She had never been to Québec City before and was still amazed that this place even existed, less than a day's drive from home. It was odd enough, crossing over the border and seeing the speed-limit signs in kilometers per hour and the billboard signs in French, but when she drove into Québec City, it was like being transported to an old section of French Europe. The streets were narrow—some even with cobblestones!—the buildings had steep roofs and bright shutters, and there were scores of horse-drawn carriages clop-clopping along the twisty lanes. She felt like they had gone back in time.

She had made the mistake of mentioning this to Clem as she drove around, and he had said, "Yeah, well, history is great but I can't make out this freakin' map. What in hell is a *rue,* anyway?"

Tonight they were in one of the many hole-in-the-wall restaurants that thrived along the narrow streets, and she was forcing herself to eat. For the past week she hadn't much of an appetite, but she knew she had to force herself to stay fit for what lay ahead. Greg needed her, and he didn't need her faint from hunger or groggy from lack of sleep.

Clem slurped at his wine and said, "I still can't believe this whole mess started over a computer game."

"Not just any game," she said. "*The* game. How to win horse races, all the time."

He shrugged. "I know half a dozen guys from where I hang out who could give you good odds on the ponies. And probably cheaper, too."

She hid her impatience by jabbing at her veal with knife and fork. "You still don't get it, do you. After he was laid off from Digital, Greg worked full-time on a computer project he had been noodling with off and on the past couple of years. He found a way of predicting horse races, seven out of ten times. Consistently."

Clem chewed with his mouth open, swallowed. "So?"

She leaned forward. "Consistently, Clem. Do you understand all the variables that have to be considered in designing a program that can be relied on? There's the weather, track conditions, history of the jockey, history of the horse, the time of day, and about half a dozen other factors. Greg found a way of tying that all together and making it work. Seven times out of ten."

"So he did. And what happened?"

She grimaced. "We . . . we had a disagreement. I wanted him to just use it quietly every now and then, so we could pay off our bills and start getting a good nest egg. Greg had other ideas. He wanted to go to a relative, a distant cousin of his in the family.

Someone with . . . lots of disposable income and a healthy interest in gambling."

Clem grinned. "Connected, right? Somebody in the mob. That's hilarious, you being a cop and all."

"Sure," she said dryly. "Hilarious. You see, Greg wanted a deal. The program in exchange for a set yearly fee, a percentage of the profits."

Clem almost seemed to choke on his steak. "Was he out of his mind? That's the stupidest damn thing I've ever heard of."

She felt defensive toward Greg. "He's very smart, especially about computers and how to make them work. Sometimes he doesn't know people that well. I tried to tell him otherwise, but he had his own idea. He went and talked to a distant cousin, a Mr. Carmichael, and he made a counteroffer." She paused. "I'm sure you've heard the phrase. An offer he couldn't refuse. If Greg set up the program and got rid of the last-minute bugs and proved it could work, then Mr. Carmichael would let him live. That's what Greg told me a week ago, and I haven't heard from him since."

"So how do you know he's in that *château* up there?"

She put her knife and fork down, suddenly not hungry anymore. "A phrase here, a word there. I'll show you later."

Now Carlos was stretched out on his bed, reading a comic book in Spanish. Greg sat before one of the terminals in the room, feeling a bit of comfort in being in front of his machines, in being in his own element. Small comfort indeed, but he would take whatever comforts he could. He went through some screens, checking on a few things, and then glanced over at Carlos. He was intent in his comic book. His lips moved as he read.

Greg went back to the terminal, slapped a few keys. A page of what looked like code appeared, random numbers and letters. Which is what it should look like if Carlos or Tony or Paulie were looking over his shoulders, which was often. But there was something hidden there in the code, thanks to an inspired piece of programming he had figured out in his mind while being smuggled across the border, hands and feet duct-taped together, mouth gagged. There. A message, which was only a message if you read down:

m
a
c
a
r
t
h
u
r

4
4

MacArthur 44. In 1944, what did Douglas MacArthur do? He returned. She was here. She had come for him.

He tried not to let anything get away from him. Time not to hope, time not to gloat. Just send a quick reply, which he did.

Then, as he backed out of the program, the door opened. Paulie was there, waiting.

"Progress?"

"Some," he said. "Just a bug I have to chase down. Two days, three days max, and then everything will be fine."

"I'm sure," Paulie said, and after he walked out the door Carlos said something in Spanish and laughed fiercely, and Greg said nothing and looked at the screen, the little boxes of files and numbers, cute little icons that were about to get him killed.

She had insisted on being within walking distance of the Château Frontenac, which meant renting a room in one of the scores of little B&Bs and rooming houses in the area. But since it was tourist season and she hadn't made a reservation—hell, getting the time off from the cop shop in Boston and driving here was a chore in and of itself—she had taken what she could. Which meant a fourth-floor room in a little hotel on Rue Geneviève, within view of the Château, and which had the distinct advantage of having separate beds. Clem's face had fallen when he had seen the rooming arrangements, but she had no sympathy for him. Good God, what did he expect?

When they had come back from dinner she opened up her laptop and dialed up her on-line service, which luckily had a Canadian subsidiary. Her heart raced a bit with joy when she saw the blinking mailbox icon that meant she had mail. Clem was standing over her shoulder as she typed, and while part of her thought he was trying to scope out the view from her open-neck sweater, he did seem interested in what she was doing.

"What you got there, Marie?" he asked.

"A message from Greg," she said, double-clicking on the icon. "Right after he was kidnapped, he managed to send me messages. Just a few words here and there, but enough to tell me he's alive."

And sure enough, a few words is all she got:

Pillow place half number beast minus four.

Clem said, "What in hell is that? That's not a message. That's crap."

Marie felt herself smiling. "No, that's Greg, and he's being very careful. He must be under some sort of surveillance all the time, so we've been sending each other little riddles and puzzles that only we can know about."

Clem said nothing and she looked up at him and said, "Haven't you ever had a girlfriend, Clem? And didn't you have like little sayings or messages that would mean something only to your girlfriend?"

Another of his patented leers. "Most of my messages have been more direct, if you know what I mean."

She frowned up at that little face. "No, I don't know, thankfully. Look." She opened up another computer file, which had a row of one-sentence messages. "Here's what I've gotten from Greg. First message was very direct: 'Bruised but breathing.' That told me he was alive, though maybe not entirely in good shape. So

I sent him back another message, saying, 'Loud and clear.' That way he knew I was reading his messages. Then he wrote back 'Where Montcalm and Wolfe met.' "

"Who?" Clem asked.

"Wolfe and Montcalm. They fought in the Battle of Québec back in 1759. One of the most decisive military battles in North America, which led to the British conquering all of French America."

He looked suspicious. "And you know this, being a cop?"

She glared at him. "Besides watching the occasional TV game show with Greg, I read a lot. You should try it sometime. Then I sent Greg a reply: 'Marion Morrison rides.' That was John Wayne's real name, and I wanted to tell him that the cavalry was on its way. And last night he sent me this one: 'QC's Gibraltar.' Winston Churchill once called Québec City the Gibraltar of North America, and Churchill said that while visiting the Château Frontenac."

"And that message," he said, pointing to the latest line. "And what does that mean?"

"Come on, Clem," she said. "What does pillow place mean?"

"His room, right?"

"Right. And did you ever get Bible schooling, anything like that?"

He almost looked embarrassed. "Nope."

"Well, in Revelation, the Number of the Beast is six-six-six. Half of that number is three-three-three, and if you minus four, that equals three twenty-nine. Greg is in room three twenty-nine. Now, are you ready to tell me what you've got planned?"

A confident smile. "You bet."

Greg paced around the room, stretching his back muscles. Funny, isn't it. A guest in one of the most luxurious hotels in the world, and trapped. Like a maiden in a castle. And he didn't know what Marie had planned, but he had faith in her. Had to, for what she did in her life. A cop, out on the dark and sometimes mean streets of Boston. She went out to work and there was always that little voice inside of him that said, be nice, this could be the last time you see her. Hah. Now the joke was on him. He went into the bathroom and washed his face and looked up in the mirror. Married to a cop, and knowing all of the macho and swaggering co-workers she encountered every day, he always wondered what she saw in him. He looked at his tired face. Kind of bland, nothing that stands out in the crowd, and definitely balding, like his father and two older brothers. He had talked to her about it, after they had been going out for almost a year, and Marie's answer had been direct. "You're smart. And you make me laugh. That puts you miles ahead of everyone else I know, Greg."

He washed his face again. He knew he should be humiliated at what was going on. Kidnapped and depending on his woman to rescue him. How funny. But in their relationship, it made a kind of odd sense. She depended on him for ideas and thinking things through. He depended on her for her tough, street cop way of looking at things. And damn it, he should have listened to her when he talked about going to Carmichael with this horse racing program. Then he wouldn't be here, wouldn't be dependent on her.

Damn, damn, damn. He dried off his face and went out into the bedroom. Tony was back again, working his crossword puzzle. Still, trapped in here and not being able to do much of anything besides his project, he had learned some things. Like the last names of Tony, Carlos, and Paulie. That had taken a little work, but it gave him a small advantage, one he intended to use.

Tony said, "Back to work, brainiac?"

"Yep, that I am," he said, settling back into the chair before the terminal.

"Glad to see it," Tony said. "Hey, do you know the name of the biggest volcano in the solar system? Two words, seven and four letters apiece."

Olympus Mons, he thought. Aloud he said, "Sorry, can't help you," and went back to work.

Clem, God help us all, was in the bathroom, preparing his demonstration for what he had planned. Clem wasn't her first, second, or even third choice, but after that desperate phone call from Greg that said he was being taken away, she didn't have many choices to work with. She knew she couldn't do this job by herself, and she needed help. And since this whole adventure was going to be somewhat illegal, she knew she couldn't count on any of her cop friends. So she asked around and Clem's name came up, and after some negotiations, here he was, in her hotel room in Québec City, ready to do her bidding.

The bathroom door opened up and he came out. "Ta da," he said. "What do you think?"

She stared. He was dressed in a hotel uniform, with dark pants and green jacket and a nametag that said Raoul. "Is that—"

He was smiling with triumph. "Yep. Uniform from that castle place. Got it while you were taking a nap yesterday."

"How in the world did you get it?" she said, still staring. The damn thing even fit him.

He shrugged, trying to be nonchalant. "Hey, people are the same around the world, no matter what language they speak. I went over there and rummaged around in the service areas, and made some guy an offer with that funny-looking money they got, and here it is."

"And what do you intend to do?"

"Thing I first learned, doing some deals when I was younger, is to keep it simple," Clem said. "I get over there tomorrow morning, grab a service cart, and knock on the door. Guy answers the door, and then I get to work with these. . . ." Clem put his hands into his pants pockets and each hand came out with something different. The left hand had a small Mace canister, while the other one had a small automatic pistol. Marie was horrified.

"What the hell are you going to do with those things?" she asked.

Clem proudly said, "First guy that opens the door gets sprayed in the face. I kick my way in and wave this baby around"—he motioned with the small pistol—"and spray anybody else within range. I yell to Greg that it's time to go, we beat our way out of there, down an elevator, and out on the street. You're there with the car running and we make tracks. Simple and to the point, right?"

Crazy. Reckless, stupid, and insane, she thought. And so stupid, it just might work. She told him that and he grinned like a dog who's proud that he's been housetrained. But there was one more thing she wanted to know.

"The pistol and the Mace," Marie said. "Where did you get it?"

He shrugged. "I brought it with me. I hid it in my luggage."

"You did what?" she demanded. "Are you an idiot? They could have searched us at Customs and we wouldn't have even gotten here! How come you didn't tell me you had those weapons with you?"

Now Clem looked hurt.

"You didn't ask me," he said.

Before going to bed that night, Greg checked his stealth e-mail system and saw a message that sent him to bed with a smile for the first time in a week:

Train leaves tomorrow half past waking time.

As a self-professed gearhead, Greg was punctual in many aspects of his life, and every morning he got up at the same time: 7:00 A.M.

Tomorrow would be no different, except for one thing: He was getting out of here at seven-thirty.

Driving her rental car, she pulled up by the rear service entrance to the Château Frontenac, which was near an underground parking garage. At one side was the small Governor's Park. It was seven-fifteen in the morning and she wished she smoked, for she needed something to occupy her mind and to pass the time. Clem was in the passenger seat and looked over, grinning. "Hey, come on, it's gonna be a piece of cake. You'll see."

She tapped her fingers on the steering wheel. "You'll see, Clem. Get in there, will you?" She paused, her voice almost breaking. "And you come back with my husband. Understood?"

He patted her leg, which she allowed. "Get your kissing lips ready, 'cause he'll be right at my side."

He got dressed early and put a floppy disk in his shirt pocket. On the disk was a copy of the horse racing program and a few other gems. He wiped his hands on a bathroom towel and went out to the sitting room of the suite, where Tony and Carlos were watching television. Paulie was reading a day-old Toronto *Globe and Mail* newspaper. On the television was the black-and-white version of *I Love Lucy,* and as a dubbed Desi Arnaz said, *"Lucy, tu as besoin de t'expliquer!,"* he went to the small kitchenette and pretended to look into the refrigerator.

There was a knock at the door. His head suddenly felt light. Paulie's eyes snapped up and looked over and said, "Greg. Back into your room."

"Hunh?" he said, trying to keep his voice level. "Why?"

Those damn eyes. "Because I said so."

He turned without a word and went into his room. He left the door ajar. He sat on the bed.

Voices. Some voices. He rubbed his moist hands on his pants and waited.

A louder voice. A thudding sound, and others too quick to identify, and then a loud *bang!* as the door to the room slammed shut.

He tried to swallow. He couldn't.

The door to his room opened wider. Paulie was there, a wry, deadly smile on his face.

"You can come out now," he said.

She had driven around the park five times, each time seeing the American flag flying from the U.S. consulate, at the corner of Rue St. Geneviève and Rue de Classe. She remembered the odd movie or novel, where an American overseas runs to an embassy or a consulate for help. Not in this little action film, she thought, as she rounded yet another corner. The call from Greg had been quite explicit: Any outside agencies brought in, any at all, and Greg would be dead. Period.

So, pretty clear. But she was under no illusions. There were no illusions in cop work. She knew that once Greg could prove that he had that program up and running, he would disappear. As simple as that.

And she would not allow that.

There!

Clem was running out of a service door, running across the street. . . .

Something was wrong, something was wrong, something was wrong.

Clem was by himself, he had a handkerchief to his face, and his face was quite bloody.

When he got out into the suite, he was motioned to a chair by Paulie. Greg sat down and Paulie sat across from him, his thin hands folded in his lap. "We had something happen here, something I hope you can clear up," he said, his voice low and even, which Greg recognized as a danger sign, like those red-and-black hurricane warning flags flown at portside when the clouds came and the wind rose.

"Sure," Greg said, not knowing what in hell he was going to do.

"A man came to the door," Paulie said. "He was dressed as a hotel employee, and was definitely not a hotel employee. So he was here for a purpose, obviously. And I think we both know what the purpose is, Greg. So. Why would he be here? Your wife, perhaps?"

He thought furiously for what seemed to be long seconds, and then cleared his throat and said, "Maybe it was Mr. Garfonti."

Both Tony and Carlos turned away from the television, and Paulie sat up, taking in a breath. "Why would he be from Garfonti's organization?"

Greg tried to shrug, like he had not a care in the world. "I went to see him before I went to see Mr. Carmichael. He said no. Maybe he's changed his mind."

Paulie's eyes narrowed. "How much longer before you're done?"

"Two days," Greg said.

Paulie stood up. "You have one."

When Clem stumbled into the car he was moaning and he said, " 'rive, 'rive, God, it 'urts, it 'urts!"

In the short drive back to the hotel he managed to stem most of the bleeding with a handkerchief and she got him upstairs without seeing any of the other guests or help. He laid out on the bed and she got to work with wet towels and ice from an ice machine, and after a few minutes he was able to talk more clearly and answer her questions.

"They made me, they flippin' made me the minute I knocked on the door," he said, tears running down his eyes, mixing in with the bloodstains on his skin. "I don't believe the luck. . . ."

"What happened?" she said, furious and scared and upset, everything jumbled in as she got another set of towels ready for his face. Lord, what will the maid think. . . . "I thought you were going to get to work the moment someone answered the door."

"That's the problem!" he protested. "Two of the guys answered the door, not one. And you know what one of 'em did? He asked me something in French! I don't know any French! And when he asked me again and when I tried to say something is when they popped me, but good. . . . God, it hurts. . . ."

She looked down at Clem, the man looking pathetic, sobbing into a soiled white towel, wearing a service uniform for a hotel, white socks and black shoes. What in hell had she been thinking? A joke. This whole thing was a joke. She tossed a clean towel at him and said, "I'm going out."

"To do what?"

"To think," she said, and as she slammed the door behind her, she listened to his groans of pain.

Greg sat before his computer, listlessly tapping on the keyboard. If he ever got out of this . . . well, he wondered what deals he could make with the Big Guy upstairs that would work. The Big Guy was no doubt very busy, and he doubted he'd be too much concerned with one Greg Celluci this evening. No, the only person who cared, the only person he trusted, was Marie, and he knew that she was behind the little rescue mission this morning that had turned into a fiasco.

It seemed like a fist-sized piece of ice was in the middle of his chest. Nope, didn't work, not at all.

And he had one more day.

He looked through his stealth e-mail system. Nothing.

The television was on in the next room, Tony was snoring on the bed, and hundreds of thousands of people were living satisfactory lives outside of these hotel windows, yet never had he felt so alone.

Think, she thought, standing back on Terrasse Dufferin. Think real well or your husband is going to be among the missing, and soon.

She shivered and rubbed at her arms. Music echoed along the boardwalk, and nearby some people were clapping for a group of jugglers. Too many happy people, and she couldn't stand looking at their beaming faces. Instead she looked up at the blank windows of the Château Frontenac. A castle, she thought. How true. A castle that she couldn't get into to get her man out. A strange type of fairy tale, a princess rescuing a prince. It would be funny if it weren't so deadly.

So. A castle. How does one get into a castle? A variety of ways, of course. Siege tower, a Trojan horse, a tunnel under the ramparts, set up a blockade, get the catapults ready, everything from history or books that had anything to do with castles, she thought. How to break in, how to gain entrance, how to . . .

Marie froze. She stared up at the windows.

"Fool," she murmured.

The question was wrong. She wasn't trying to get into the castle, she was trying to get someone out. . . .

She turned and ran back to the hotel.

Clem stared glumly at the television set as she set up her laptop and furiously started typing, a half smile tickling at her face.

"What's so funny?" he said, his voice sounding strange, since a towel with ice was still pressed against his jaw.

"You want to go home tomorrow?" she asked, staring at the screen.

"That's a stupid question," he said. "Of course I want to go home tomorrow, but what about—"

"Then it's settled," she said, pressing the key that sent her e-mail message out. "And I hope you don't mind sitting in the back, because Greg is going to be riding up front next to me."

And she refused to answer any of Clem's questions for the rest of the night.

Before he went to bed Greg checked his system one more time, and saw the flashing letters that meant he had a mail message. He worked his way through the screens and then sat back.

Impossible. The message made no sense.

He tried to read it from different angles, tried to see if there was another message, but there wasn't. There was just the single, crazy line:

Same time tomorrow. Rapunzel, Rapunzel, let down your hair.

Greg rubbed at his bald forehead. Was she nuts? What hair, what did she—

Then he smiled, looked at his computer, and understood.

His reply was quick:

See you there, fairy princess.

The next morning she was back in her rental car, and this time Clem was in the rear seat, his face swollen and yellow and green with bruises. Their luggage was packed and in the trunk of the car, and she felt something joyous and terrifying racing through her arms and legs as she realized this was it, this was the last chance. Greg had gotten her message last night, and on this morning, it would work.

It would have to.

She drove slowly around the park, straining her eyes to look up at the window, to see if there was any movement.

"Almost time," Clem said from the rear seat.

"I know, I know," she said, braking as a couple of tourists, burdened under cameras and suitcases, walked across the narrow, tree-lined street.

"You sure it's gonna work?"

"It's got to," she said, "so it will."

Greg awoke early and went to his computers, on his hands and knees, rummaging around underneath the work desks. The door opened, and Paulie poked in his head.

"Problems?" he asked in that quiet, deadly voice.

"Just a power surge problem," he said, lying easily. "I'll have it done in a couple of minutes."

"Good," Paulie said, leaving the room. "Just remember this is your last day."

It sure is, he thought, and as Paulie closed the door, Greg got up. He was dressed and that disk was in his pocket, just like yesterday, but today was going to be different, thank you, and he went into the small bathroom. He grabbed a can of shaving cream, put it into his pants pocket, and then went out into the suite. Carlos and Tony were not even dressed yet, yawning and wearing terrycloth robes, arguing about what to watch on TV. Paulie was in his shirt and tie, reading a copy of *Maclean's* magazine. None of them paid him any attention as he went into the small kitchen area, opened up the microwave, and put in the shaving cream can.

He closed the door. He was still being ignored.

He went to the refrigerator, grabbed a carton of orange juice, and as he passed the microwave on his way back to his room, he turned it on for a half hour on the highest possible setting.

Clem said in a disbelieving voice, "He's comin' out today because of a fairy tale message? Are you nuts?"

"No, not at all," she said, trying hard to drive without hitting anything while keeping watch on a certain third-floor window. "He knows what I mean."

"But Rapunzel . . . hell, I know what your husband looks like. He's bald!"

"No, he's not!" she said. "His hair's just thinning, that's all. . . . But he's got enough hair, don't you worry."

There. Motion at the third-floor window. She sped up and parked illegally, heart thumping and car's engine racing.

He opened the window after he had finished his morning task, his hands shaking. Could this be it, after these days of confinement and misery? He looked down at the park and streets and saw a car brake and pull into a no-parking zone. It was driven by a woman and there was a man in the back, it could be Marie, but he wasn't sure. He stepped carefully, not wanting to disturb what he had done, wondering if he could go through with it, wondering if he could be brave enough to step through that window, brave enough to—

BANG!

And when the shaving cream can exploded in the microwave, he bent down, grabbed a handful of his work, took a deep breath, and jumped out the window.

She got out of the car and was running across the street, when she saw him, and she yelled at Clem, "There he is! Here he comes!"

And it was Greg, and everything was moving so fast and oddly that part of her couldn't even believe it, but there he was, falling down the side of the old *château,* clothes fluttering, his hands holding on to something, something very strange indeed, and then he jerked to a halt, slid some more, and in a few seconds he was there, falling into her arms, her Greg, her husband, her love. She knew people on the sidewalk were yelling and pointing, but she didn't care, didn't care at all.

A quick kiss, that's all she would allow, and when he started talking to her in great gulping breaths she said, "Shut up, Rapunzel, and let's get a move on!"

She ran back across the street again, this time with the joyous and warm feeling of his hand in hers, and she spared a quick glance back at the brick wall and open window and the hair that allowed him to escape: a braided, thick strand of power cords, cable connectors, and surge suppressors.

Later they were on a secondary road, preparing for a long drive west and then back over the border into the United States, and Marie agreed to let Clem off at the first good-sized American city, but she wouldn't let on to Clem where they were going. That was secret, but she was sure she and Greg could make a quiet go of it someplace out West. Someplace quiet, peaceful, and near a couple of horse tracks. . . .

Though they had been gone from Québec City for a while, Clem was still confused and said, "This was a private joke, that saying?"

"Sure," Marie said, driving with only one hand and refusing to let go of Greg with her other. He was sweaty and his clothes were ripped and he had a bunch of bruises and scratches, but he looked wonderful.

"Tell me again, 'cause I don't believe it," Clem said.

Again, a smile at the memory. "Once Greg was setting up a new computer, and the floor in his office was a mess of cables. He was right in the middle of it, rooting around on his hands and knees, and I teased him that the black cables looked like the color of his hair. And if he ever decided to get a toupee, he should just make one out of his cable collection."

Greg grinned back at her. "And I did that, one Halloween. Made a wig out of cables."

Clem shook his head. "You guys are nuts."

She squeezed his hand. "No, we're married. And we're going far away, and we'll never have anything to do with those thugs, ever again. Right, hon?"

Silence.

She looked over. Greg was trying hard to hide a smile. "Greg . . ." she started, her voice starting to get a bit forced. "Greg, what in hell are you saying?"

"Well," he said, pulling a disk out, "there is one thing I want to do, minute I get to a computer. And soon."

"And what's that?"

"This," he said, holding up the disk. "My program's here, and it works, but I also had some extra room. So I decided to do something for the three guys who were holding me."

"And what's that?"

He winked. "When they get to the border, U.S. Customs will be waiting. And they'll be searched. Including body cavity searches. And I'm sure the border cops will find something to keep them in prison for a long, long time."

Behind them, Clem laughed. "Oh, that's beautiful, that's real beautiful."

She tried not to laugh and failed, squeezing her husband's hand one more time. "A perfect end to a perfect day, love."

Greg squeezed her back. "Let's see if we can start living happily ever after. Deal?"

"Deal," she said.

Edward D. Hoch is probably the only person in the world making his living from writing short stories. Hoch excels at everything—funny, sad, clever, biting, his skills are virtually without boundaries. His story, based on "Snow White," illustrates this perfectly.

Snow White and the
Eleven Dwarfs

On one of those glorious late June nights when the sun seems never to set and the warm breeze blows endlessly off the sound, Amy Bradley decided to run away. It was not a difficult decision. She knew something terrible could happen if she stayed another night under Mason Bradley's roof.

He was her father yet not her father, the friend and business partner who'd adopted her when a plane carrying her own parents plunged into the Indian Ocean and left her an orphan at age eleven. That was nine years ago. Mason Bradley was a kindly man, a widower and real-estate developer who'd tried his best to be a real father to her. During those first years he'd succeeded, until he met and married Sibyl Carlin, a beauty queen turned fashion model who excelled at everything except being a mother to Amy. She wanted the wealth and prestige of being Mason Bradley's wife without any of the responsibilities that went with it. She seemed especially to resent any comments by friends that compared Amy's raven-haired beauty to her own.

Amy had heard them talking one evening when she'd returned from a date earlier than expected. "Isn't she old enough to be out on her own now?" Sibyl was asking. "Give her some money for an apartment."

Mason Bradley sighed, a sound that Amy heard too frequently of late. "I think she should stay with us a while longer, Sibyl, at least till she finishes college. That's only two more years."

Amy had been living on campus during her college years, coming home weekends and summers, but even this was too much for Sibyl. Sometimes Amy imagined she was caught up in a frightening fairy tale, except that the cruel stepmother was only ten years older and was rarely cruel to her face. Hearing them argue about her like this, she wished that she could simply disappear out of both their lives. Instead she took to staying away more often on weekends, accepting invitations to classmates' homes or even just spending the time by herself in New York City. Once during spring break she even went off to Florida with a boy she'd met at a fraternity party, but that had been a disaster. The following weekend she was back at home.

Amy and Sybil managed to stay out of each other's way for the next couple of months, but it was that summer when things finally came to a head. Amy had posed with some of the other girls for a campus calendar that was sold at the college bookstore. She was tall and long-legged, as her mother had been, without the superslender look of a model but with an attractive face and smile the photographer had liked. This long after the first of the year, she'd forgotten all about the calendar until someone called from a Manhattan modeling agency.

That night she told her father about it, asking his advice. "We'll ask Sibyl," he said at once. "Modeling is her business."

Amy's heart sank. "I hate to bring her into it."

"Nonsense!" His bushy eyebrows seemed to emphasize the word. "Maybe this is just what we need to bring you two closer together."

"Father—"

"Please, Amy." His face had the sad expression she'd seen so much since his remarriage. "Do it for me."

Amy told her about the modeling offer, and knew from the first instant it was a terrible mistake. "You, a model?" Sibyl snorted. "Maybe if you lose twenty pounds!"

"I'm not fat," Amy protested. "Besides, it wouldn't be fashion modeling. Most shots would just use my face. They say I have a pretty face."

"Believe me, you're wasting your time, child."

"I'm not a child! I'm twenty years old."

Sibyl's face contorted with pent-up fury. "And still seeing yourself as my rival, aren't you? It's been like this ever since I married your father!"

"Sibyl, I don't know what you're talking about!"

She reached out and grabbed Amy's shoulders, shaking her violently. "Then suppose I tell you. Suppose I put it in plain English. You try to outdo me in everything, and now you want to prove you're more beautiful than I am. I could end that in a hurry, you know. I have friends who'd throw acid in that pretty face for less than the cost of a steak dinner."

"Sibyl!"

"You want to sleep with him, don't you? You won't be satisfied till you get your father in the sack!"

That was the night Amy decided to run away.

She left a note for her father, begging that she not be judged too harshly. Then she packed her bag, took almost two hundred dollars and her credit cards, and left in the car he'd given her as a high-school graduation gift. She drove through the night, heading into the Pennsylvania hills, trying to put as many miles as possible between her and that woman.

As the sun rose she pulled over to the side of a country road, next to a bean field, exhausted from driving and in need of sleep. She had no idea where she was, except that it was northern Pennsylvania, not far from the New York border. Squinting through the windshield, she made out a building at the top of a distant hill. It could have been a motel, and that was what she needed right now. She started the motor and headed toward it. As she drew closer she saw it was indeed a motel, though it seemed to be closed and abandoned. The neon sign, identifying a popular discount hotel chain, had been partially removed. Only a rusting pickup truck stood in the parking lot.

Amy pulled in next to the truck and got out. Surprisingly, the front door was unlocked—perhaps because there was nothing worth stealing inside. She entered cautiously, remembering the rusty truck in the parking lot. "Hello? Is anyone here?"

There was no answer, and she ventured farther inside, past the remains of a small registration desk. The building was all on one floor, with a corridor leading straight back to the rooms. She pushed open one of the unlocked doors and was surprised to see a pair of cots, with mattresses and bedding. A few personal belongings—a thermos, a portable radio, and a knapsack—stood on a wooden crate nearby. A hot plate was plugged into a wall socket. It appeared that someone was living here, but she was too tired to care just then.

She explored a few other rooms until she found a cot with the mattress folded up and apparently unused. She unfolded it, pulling it down over the exposed springs of the cot, and fell on it with a sense of relief. Just a few minutes' rest was all she'd need. . . .

It was the voices that awakened Amy. People were speaking softly, quite close to her, yet she couldn't understand a word that was being said. She rolled over and tried to open her eyes, but she was too tired.

Where was she? Not at home, certainly, but not at college, either.

Then she remembered. The abandoned motel, and these voices speaking in a strange language.

Spanish! They were speaking Spanish!

Her eyes came open and she saw the men grouped around her cot. "Who are you?" one of them asked.

She shook her head to clear it. "Amy. My name is Amy. What are you doing here?"

"We live here," the speaker said. He was short and dark-haired, with strong, tanned arms, and probably in his twenties. And he spoke English quite well. "Where did you come from?"

Amy slid off the cot and got to her feet, feeling vaguely threatened by these strange men standing around her. Now she caught the odor of their sweat and guessed they had been working in the fields. "I'm just driving through from Connecticut. I drove all night and I was exhausted this morning." She looked around at their faces. They were all Latins and, surprisingly, all seemed shorter than her own five-foot, nine-inch height. "You're migrant workers, aren't you?"

"Yes," the man answered. "My name is García. We are all from Cuba. We live in Florida during the winter and come North for the fruit harvest."

"Do you bring your families?"

"Those with families live elsewhere," García explained. He grinned and added, "We are the bachelors." Some of the other men laughed.

Amy glanced around at the dusty, almost bare room. "You didn't have to tell me that. I can see no woman's been in here."

"Where are you going?" one of the other men asked, his English not quite as good as García's.

"I don't know," she answered, surprising even herself. "Just away. I have family problems."

There were a few snickers and she came to realize that all of them spoke and understood at least some English. García told her, "We know of family problems. You can stay here if you wish, for a few days."

"I—"

"No one will bother you," he assured her.

"Someone must own this place."

"The farmer we work for owns the property, but he never comes here. We stay free and provide our own food, until it is time to move on."

She considered her options. "I have some money. I could buy food, maybe clean the place a bit." She giggled at a sudden thought, standing there peering at the tops of their heads. "Something like Snow White and the Seven Dwarfs."

"Eleven."

"What?"

"There are eleven of us," he corrected. He started to introduce them. "This is José, and Miguel, and Jesús—"

"Wait, wait! I'll never remember all those names. Suppose I just name you after the dwarfs in the Disney film." As she pointed to each of them she spoke his name, starting with García. "You'll be Doc, because you're the leader. Then there's Happy, Sneezy, Grumpy—sorry about that—Bashful, Sleepy, and Dopey. Oh, my! I'm sorry about that one, too!"

"There are four left over," García pointed out.

Amy thought about it for several seconds. "How about Dasher, Dancer, Prancer, and Vixen?"

"These are dwarfs?"

"Well, tiny reindeer."

She could tell that García thought her a little goofy, but they liked each other from the outset. He assigned her to one of the empty rooms and made sure she had sheets and pillows for the cot. There was no kitchen in the place, but Amy immediately took over one of the rooms and collected some of the food and hot plates. In one room she found an ancient toaster that seemed to work pretty well. That belonged to Dasher, but he said she could use it.

"Tomorrow I'll buy us a frying pan," Amy decided. "At least I'll give you guys a decent breakfast before you go off to work in the morning."

The following day, after they'd driven out to the field in one of their trucks, she searched through the place until she found a mop, bucket, and broom for cleaning. Then she drove into the nearest town and spent almost a hundred dollars on an electric frying pan, food, and a few decorations for the motel. She bought some colorful artificial flowers in little vases to place in every room, and curtains for the front windows that looked out onto the road. By the time the eleven dwarfs returned from the field that evening she had the place looking halfway livable.

"You've done a fine job," García told her. She still thought of him as García rather than Doc, perhaps because he was the first one she'd spoken to.

"I liked doing it."

Grumpy, who wasn't really grumpy at all, had brought a nine-inch color television with him from Florida. After dinner several of them gathered in his room, drinking beer and commenting on the movie they were watching. Amy stayed with them for a half hour and then went to her own room to read a New York newspaper she'd picked up in town.

It was on page two of the metropolitan section that she came upon her picture, next to an old one of her father. The headline sent a chill through her body: Daughter Sought in Killing of Real-Estate Developer.

Her hands trembled as she read the story. Mason Bradley had been found shot to death in the living room of his Connecticut home by his wife, Sibyl. Police were seeking his twenty-year-old daughter Amy, who disappeared with her car and some clothing. Sources said she'd left a handwritten note at the scene asking not to be judged too harshly for what she'd done.

She felt a chill reading the words. Someone had killed her father and cut off the top of her note addressed to him, leaving it to look like a message intended for the world, asking not to be judged too harshly for killing him. Only one person could have done that: Sibyl.

And that meant it was Sibyl who'd killed him.

She'd found the note and realized it was her perfect opportunity to rid herself of both Mason and his daughter, collecting the bulk of his estate in the process.

When García found her a few minutes later she was seated on her cot, quietly sobbing. For her father and for herself.

It took a long time for her to tell him about it, this man who'd been a stranger to her only the previous day. He held her and comforted her for a long time, and when Sneezy came in to ask if he was going into town with them, he declined. When they were alone again Amy found herself telling him about her life, about Sibyl and college and even the death of her real father and mother. She ended with Sibyl's threats and her certainty that the woman had killed Mason Bradley.

"Somehow we must clear your name," he said, cradling her in his arms.

"But I have no one to turn to! My parents are dead—"

"I know how hard it can be," he said quietly. "My own parents were killed in a storm, fleeing Cuba on a raft when I was only five. These men"—he gestured toward the other rooms—"these dwarfs, as you call them, are the only family I have."

"I suppose they'll be my family, too. I have nowhere else to go with the police hunting me."

He gazed at her sadly. "It is only till the end of the fruit season here. Then we must move on."

"Maybe I could pick fruit along with you."

He laughed at the thought. "No, no! You stay back here and clean and cook for us. It is more than enough."

A few days later she did ride out on the truck with them, to see what they did. She watched them harvesting a field of strawberries, stooping to strip the bushes and deposit the berries in baskets. She could see it was hard work, and after watching for a time she understood their weariness at the end of the day. This could not be her life, and walking back to the old motel, seeing its stark outline against the summer sky, she realized that all of this was but an interlude. In the fall she would be back in college.

Then she remembered Mason.

He was dead, and the police were looking for her. Sibyl had effectively blocked the road back, now and forever.

That evening García did not return with the others, and Amy asked Happy where he was.

"He goes into town for something, *señorita*," Happy replied, smiling broadly. Since she'd named him that, he'd tried to live up to it.

It was nearly seven before García returned, driving one of the trucks and looking pleased with himself. "Where've you been?" Amy asked. "Everyone else has eaten already."

"I have something for you," he said. He took out a small box and handed it to her. "I bought it with part of my week's wages."

The gift surprised her, especially when she saw what it was. García had not brought her flowers but rather a small tape recorder. "What—what is this for?" she managed to ask.

"I see how it is done on the TV," he confided. "You will go back and meet with your stepmother and get her to admit to the killing. You will secretly record her confession with this and give it to the police."

She touched his cheek in gratitude. "García, this is lovely. To think that you care that much for me and my troubles!"

"You can hide it under your shirt, tape it to your skin."

She hated to dampen his enthusiasm. "I'm afraid Sibyl would

never agree to meet me alone. She'd have the police there to arrest me. But it's a wonderful gift anyway."

He pondered that problem while she prepared some of the leftover food for his supper. "All right," he decided finally, sitting down to eat. "We will get her to come here."

"How could we do that?"

"I will think of a way," he said, and kept on eating.

Amy had been at the motel for more than a week, cleaning the place and fixing meals for them, trying to make it a little more like home. García said to her one night, "We will tell Sibyl you are dying."

Amy replied with a snort. "That bitch would probably send me a poisoned comb."

"A what?"

She laughed. "Never mind. It's a reference to Snow White."

"Really, what do you think of the idea?"

"Let me sleep on it."

When she awakened in the morning she said to García, "I think I know how it could work. You phone her and tell her I'm dying, and that I've given you two sealed envelopes—one addressed to the police and one addressed to her. Tell her you thought she should know I couldn't last more than a day or two."

"What are you dying of?" he wanted to know.

"Blood poisoning. Tell her I'm afraid to go to a hospital because the police are looking for me."

"What do you think she'll do about it?"

Amy smiled. "Tell you to hang on to both letters until she gets here."

García was uneasy. "She may send the police instead."

"I don't think so. She'd be afraid of what I might tell them if I'm still alive."

He tried calling the Bradley house and got only an answering machine. Following her instructions, he left an urgent message, saying it was about Amy and giving their number to call. He stayed at the motel that day when the others went off for the harvest, and they waited for the call together. It was not until midafternoon that Sibyl returned the call. Amy leaned close to García so she could hear her voice in the receiver.

"You left a message for me to call?" Sibyl asked suspiciously. "About my stepdaughter Amy Bradley?"

"That's right, Mrs. Bradley. She's had a bad accident."

"Where are you calling from? The area code—"

"It's Harken, Pennsylvania, right by the New York State border. She accidentally jabbed herself with a rusty nail and developed blood poisoning. That was several days ago, and now she's running a fever. I tried to get her to the hospital, but she's afraid to go. She says the police are looking for her. She's given me two letters, one addressed to you and the other for the police. She wants me to mail them if she dies. I got your address from that and thought I should phone you."

Amy heard Sibyl take a deep breath on the other end of the line. "Look, don't do anything till I get there. I have to see my lawyer in the morning but I'll be on the road before noon and drive straight through. How long should it take me?"

Amy held up five fingers. "About five hours," García told her, and gave directions for reaching the place. "I don't know if Amy will last that long, though."

Sibyl's voice crackled through the telephone. "We'll hope for the best. Remember, don't do anything with those letters until I get there, even if she dies."

García hung up and sat looking at Amy. "Now what?"

Amy had already thought about that. "Tonight I'll speak with the others."

Sibyl Bradley arrived at the motel at about four-thirty the following afternoon. García saw her driving down the road and warned Amy to get into bed. "Here comes the wicked stepmother," he called to her. "I recognize the car from your description."

García met her at the door, and Amy could hear the conversation. "Has she died?" Sibyl asked.

"Not yet. She's clinging to life."

"And the letters?"

"I have them here."

Sibyl entered the room where Amy lay beneath a heavy blanket, her face moist and pasty. "You should be in a hospital," she told her stepdaughter.

"Sibyl, what happened to my father?"

"You shot him, Amy. Don't you remember?"

"I don't—I would never kill him. I loved him."

"You left a note. The police found it."

García was standing at the door, a bit behind her. "Leave us alone," Amy told him. "I'll be all right."

When he'd gone, she lifted herself on one elbow. "You killed him, Sibyl. You couldn't wait for his money. You saw a chance to frame me for it with that note I left, so you killed him."

She took a step toward the cot, close enough to reach out and touch Amy. "Do you think anyone would believe that?"

"You shot him, Sibyl. After I'm dead the police will get a letter."

"We'll see about that."

"If it meant seeing you behind bars, I'd rise up off my deathbed."

Sibyl's face twisted into an animal fury as Amy started out from under the blankets. "I killed one Bradley and I can kill another!" Her hand appeared with a hypodermic needle, jabbing out toward Amy's bare leg.

"García!" she yelled, and he was there in an instant, wrapping his strong arms around the woman. He shook her until she dropped the needle.

"Did you get it on tape?" he asked.

Amy produced the little tape recorder from under her blanket. "Every word. This tape is the finish for you, Sibyl."

"We'll see whose word they believe."

The others were coming back. Dancer had kept watch from the field and summoned them when he saw the car arrive. They trooped in, one by one, until they filled the small room, blocking any escape for Sibyl. And Amy called each one by name as he entered.

"This is Bashful, and Happy, and Dasher . . . Sneezy, Dopey, Dancer, Vixen, Grumpy . . . Prancer . . . and Sleepy, of course."

SNOW WHITE AND THE ELEVEN DWARFS   209

She was out of the bed now, reaching out her hand to García's. "Let her go, Doc. She can't do anything now."

"Dwarfs!" Sibyl snorted. "Eleven damned dwarfs!"

Amy stepped over to join them. "And I make twelve. I'm going to play the tape for us."

Sibyl seemed frightened for the first time. "I thought you wanted it for the police and the courts."

"We don't need them."

"What do you mean? What are you going to do to me?"

Amy stepped closer to her, no longer afraid of this woman. "That's for the jury to decide."

"Jury? What jury?"

"Us. Snow White and the Eleven Dwarfs."

In the past few years, critics have started to appreciate John Lutz and the wide diversity of his talents. While his novels center on the dour Fred Carver or the dogged Alo Nudger, his short fiction spans a range of story forms and types. Here is another unexpected tale from the author of SWF Seeks Same, *the basis for the hit movie* Single White Female. *In his story he turns the Grimms' Seven Swans into seven country and western singers and weaves a masterful plot along with them.*

Swan Song

"**P**hotographs don't mean a thing," Tony King said, with the casualness of a man who'd had three drinks for lunch. "Everybody knows they can be faked and often are, especially photos like the one you described. I'll just deny I ever knew the young lady, and since she's dead, nobody will be able to prove otherwise."

They were sitting in the Deco Lounge in Nashville, in a booth where they might see and be seen. Tony was sure Willa Witcher wanted it that way, wanted him to feel embarrassment over what was no more than a long-ago sexual peccadillo with a woman he had no idea at the time was not only married but also the wife of a powerful southern governor. And, of course, it would do no good to tell Willa he'd actually loved the woman and had plans for their future together.

Willa was one of the most feared and relentlessly scheming agents in the country music industry. Part of it was her appearance. She was a tall, gaunt woman with a hatchet face and intense dark eyes that could melt cheese. The other reason for the fear was that she was clever and ruthless almost beyond belief.

But Tony wasn't worried. The photo of him *in flagrante* with the woman, who'd since died of a drug overdose, would do little harm to his reputation or career in the sorts of places it would be published, the publications that also featured photos of aliens, Elvis apparitions, and children born with the heads of animals. So despite his three Dixie beers—he'd switched from martinis when he'd decided to give up crooning and go country and western—

Tony didn't see why Willa was bringing up this tragic matter she'd somehow learned about. Tony stretched out his jeaned legs beneath the table, crossed his ostrich-skin cowboy boots at the ankles, and smiled confidently at her.

She smiled confidently back. "I'm offering you the negative," she said.

Tony felt his heart dive into dark water. A photo was one thing; a negative was something much more damaging and dangerous. "The developer has the negative," he said, hearing the fear in his voice, as if he were trying to convince himself of what he was saying.

"Not anymore. I have it."

He knew it wasn't in her character to bluff. "What do you want, Willa?"

"To be your agent. To represent the great Tony King. You're past your prime and half pickled in alcohol, but still believable as a handsome Italian cowboy—if there ever was such a thing."

"Dean Martin sang country and western."

"Very briefly," Willa said. "Stop stalling and give me your answer, Tony. Yes, and you're in my stable. No, and the negative goes to my favorite supermarket tabloid."

"That's all there is to it?" Tony asked. "You want to represent me?" This might not be so bad. He wasn't that pleased with his present agent, anyway.

"There is one other thing," Willa said. "At this late stage of your career, I think you need a young partner. Somebody who'll gain instant credibility because of her appearances with you."

"Her?"

"My daughter Greta. Only she'll perform under the name Lorna Lonesome."

This was much worse than he'd thought. "Willa, I don't—"

"—want that photograph made public along with the negative," she finished for him. "You've got a choice between hope and nothing, Tony. And you're not a fool."

"You *are* a witch!"

Willa smiled. "That's what they say about me around town. After I've cut the best deals for my clients."

Tony's alcohol-hazed mind darted this way and that, seeking an escape from his predicament, but the sober part of him knew he had no choice. "Can Gre—— Lorna sing?"

Willa shrugged. "Does it matter?"

It should matter, Tony thought as he drove from the Witcher Agency parking lot and headed toward his apartment to think things through. What Willa didn't know was that *he* knew his career was in its dying stages, and he was about to forge a new career as a talent agent. He was going to be Willa's competition.

His first client was to be his daughter Anne, who *could* sing. His only other clients were also people with rare talent, the Okeechobee Brothers. They weren't really brothers, of course, but they sang as if they'd been harmonizing all their lives and played every instrument from banjo to mouth harp. Tony could tolerate having to sing duets with Lorna Lonesome as long as Willa didn't find out about Anne or the Okeechobee Brothers. Once she knew about them, she would want them, then she would own them. Then Tony . . . well, he didn't know exactly what he'd do, but it would be *something,* and it might get out of hand and people would be destroyed.

Of course, he couldn't say that, or much else about the dilemma he was in, when he called a meeting in his office and gave his clients their instructions.

"I don't get it, Daddy," Anne said, shaking her lustrous, dark hair. Not only could she sing, but she also was as beautiful as her mother, Tony's second wife. "You want me to stay out of sight in a furnished apartment, and the Okeechobee Brothers to go stay at this cabin in the woods and sharpen their act, and you won't tell us why?"

"I'm sorry, honey, but I can't. Just trust me, please!"

"The dude's made the right calls so far," said Crawly Evans, an Okeechobee Brother recently of the heavy metal band Sludge. "Let's play it like he says."

"Anne can come and go as a liaison and so she can use the recording equipment in the cabin," Tony said, "but I'd like for you guys to stay there out of sight till I get things settled on this end."

"You don't want anyone to know we exist, right?" asked handsome Larry Gunner, who'd struggled in gospel before finding his niche as an Okeechobee Brother. All the brothers other than Crawly wore full beards, so few of their fans would associate them with their former groups. With Sludge, Crawly had worn a beard and long hair that concealed most of his face, so he was reasonably unrecognizable clean-shaven. Bearded or clean-shaven, Crawly didn't remotely resemble anyone other than Crawly. The other five Okeechobee Brothers—Curt, Clint, Chris, Clyde, and Carl—really did look like brothers. They were blond and fair, with blue eyes, hawk noses, and receding hairlines.

"There are a few people I don't want to know you exist," Tony said. "Believe me, I have good reasons for this, but I can't tell you about them."

"That's good enough for me, boss," earnest Chris said.

"You know best," the others agreed, almost in unison.

"I hope so," Tony said.

"Give us the directions, man, and we'll drive there in my old Volkswagen bus." Crawly seemed eager to go now.

"We're like going to a retreat to get our heads straight," not-too-bright Clint proclaimed happily. "Like them middle-evil monks."

Tony assured everyone that was a good way to look at it.

"Let's go to this cabin and practice and party," Crawly said. "I'll show you guys how to grow different kinds of plants."

Handsome Larry winked at Tony, letting him know he'd keep the group under control. Tony hoped so. Hoped Larry hadn't actually been winking at Anne.

The next day Tony quit his agent and signed on with Willa's agency. She demanded 25 percent of his earnings, and Tony didn't argue. Smiling triumphantly, she tore up the potentially disastrous negative in front of him and burned its pieces in an ashtray. Watching the flames devour the old celluloid, he felt immense relief along with trepidation.

While Anne acted as liaison between Tony and the Okeechobee Brothers, Tony and Lorna Lonesome worked out a routine where Tony was the romantic cowboy and Lorna the disinterested

State Fair Queen. Lorna was a younger, somehow prettier version of her mother, and within a limited range she had an almost passable singing voice. Spurred by familial interest, Willa managed to get them gigs at some of the better C&W lounges and even a TV spot. In less than a month, Lorna's career was about to take off even as Tony's was settling to earth.

Tony stayed away from alcohol most of that time, but one night he did succumb to temptation. When he overslept the next morning, Lorna went to his apartment to rouse him.

She was just stepping out of the elevator when she saw a young, attractive woman use a key to enter Tony's apartment.

Lorna smiled. Men! They were such dogs. It was in the genes. Lorna understood knowledge as leverage, and she knew her mother would approve if she waited until the woman emerged from the apartment and followed her, found out who she was.

She retreated to her parked car and waited, forgetting all about rehearsal that morning. This might advance her career much faster and farther than learning to hit a high note.

Lorna was surprised when Tony and not the woman emerged from the apartment. This was curious. The woman was either still inside or had left by a back door. Tony was carrying a large leather suitcase and what appeared to be a sack of groceries. After placing sack and suitcase in the trunk, he climbed into his aged Mercedes. Lorna decided to follow him and not wait for the woman.

Tony drove not to the rehearsal room at her mother's agency but out of the city and into hilly, wooded country to the north. With difficulty, Lorna followed him in her low-slung sports car along increasingly narrow and roughly paved roads, until she saw him brake the Mercedes and turn left into a gravel driveway.

She parked her car out of sight in the woods, changed into the expensive jogging shoes she kept in the trunk for impromptu workouts to improve her abs, and approached the driveway on foot.

It led to a crude but large cabin with a cedar-shingled roof and a long plank porch. Lorna stayed concealed among the trees flanking the gravel drive, then advanced to where she could crouch down behind Tony's Mercedes and observe the cabin's windows up close.

But the curtains were closed. She could see nothing inside.

She was about to move so she could see if the curtains on the west side of the cabin were also closed, when she stopped and listened, puzzled.

From the cabin drifted perfect harmony, a country and western tune that had *hit* in every note, and rich lyrics describing how a good girl gone to the big city had turned bad and died of heartbreak. But what interested Lorna most was that she knew she wasn't listening to a recording. The music she heard was live!

It took her only a moment to realize what this meant: Sly Tony had another act he was working with. One he didn't want Willa to know about.

Lorna returned to her car, confident that any sound she made would be covered by the music from inside the cabin. She returned with the recorder she always carried in the glove compartment so she could practice or write music while driving. With the recorder running, she crept back to the house, to a side window whose curtains she was glad to see were parted about four inches.

Leaving the recorder on, she raised herself on her toes and peeked inside.

The first thing she saw was a portable sound setup that had turned the cabin's sparsely furnished interior into a makeshift studio. The leather suitcase sat in a corner. On a sink counter along the far wall sat the grocery sack Tony had just delivered.

Then she saw Tony standing with his arms crossed, smiling as he watched six men, all but one of them bearded, playing instruments and singing the heart-throbbing melody and tragic lyrics that made Lorna see platinum records and dollar signs.

When the song was ended, Tony applauded and grinned widely.

"We can't miss!" he said. "The Okeechobee Brothers will be the biggest thing to hit the country music scene since Dolly or Hank!"

"Only there's more of us," one of the Okeechobee Brothers said, grinning wider than Tony.

"I don't think the second verse is exactly where we want it," said the brother with the longest beard.

"Then work on it," Tony said. "You guys aren't getting stir-crazy out here, are you?"

"We can stand it," said long beard.

"As long as you or Anne keep bringing us food and the latest gossip," said another brother.

"It won't be much longer," Tony said. "I want you to be more than ready so when I part company with that witch Willa and become a full-time agent, we can take off like a rocket to the top ten."

My, my, my, Lorna thought as she switched off the recorder and backed silently away from the window. She did enjoy a juicy secret, so much so that she was compelled to share it. Wouldn't Mother be interested in *this* development!

She hoped her recorder had picked up the conversation as well as the music.

Tony arrived at Willa's agency an hour after Lorna, with a story about oversleeping, then discovering his car had a flat tire. They ran through rehearsal as if nothing had changed, while Lorna and Willa traded sly glances. Willa seemed angry, but at the same time appeared to be enjoying this.

After rehearsal, she invited Tony to join her in her office. Staring at her face, sensing the sudden emotion and drawing away of Lorna, Tony suspected something was wrong.

He sat in the black leather chair before Willa's desk, hearing the seat cushion hiss at him like a snake as his weight sank into it. She closed the office door and stood looming over him for a moment, then settled her gaunt body down into the oversized chair behind her wide desk. He didn't know that as she sat, she unobtrusively touched the button that switched on the office recording system. Willa recorded every conversation that occurred in her office, so she could check later for anything she might have missed, any weakness that might allow her an advantage in negotiations. At the end of each week, since the tapes might prove embarrassing to her or incriminating, she destroyed them. She often wondered why Nixon hadn't done the same.

"Know what a competition clause is?" she asked Tony, smiling and toying with a sharp pencil.

"Vaguely."

"It's a clause that says if you leave your employer, for a certain amount of time you can't work for a competitor. Or *be* a competitor."

"Meaning?" Tony asked, knowing full well what it meant. She'd somehow found out about his fledgling agency.

"There's such a clause in our contract, Tony." Willa reached into a desk drawer then tossed a copy of the contract into Tony's lap. One of the pages was paper-clipped. He turned to it.

There was the clause, circled in ink.

"What that clause means," Willa said, "is that if you leave here, you can't work for another agency or become an agent for the next five years."

Or become an agent . . . Tony felt rage burn in the pit of his stomach as he stared at the clause. Rage and helplessness. "How did you find out?"

Willa smiled wickedly. For the first time, he noticed the smallness and sharpness of her teeth. Piranhas must have teeth like that. "Witchcraft, Tony. I'm a witch; you said so yourself to your exiled, would-be clients."

So she knew about the cabin, everything!

Tony stood up.

"Sit back down!" Willa commanded.

He wavered for a few seconds, then sat.

"This morning was your swan song as an agent," Willa told him. "I'm taking over your contracts. That means the Okeechobee Brothers are now the Swan Brothers, and they belong to me."

Tony nodded, standing up from the black chair again, but slowly this time. His legs felt weak, his knees rubbery.

"Don't leave the building yet," Willa told him. "I'm not finished with you. Rehearse some more with Lorna. You can do it even if you don't like it. You're a trooper, Tony."

She must have been right. Tony sang with Lorna and not only didn't like it, he hated it and hated Lorna.

But most of all, he hated Willa.

Since the lease on the remote cabin ran for another three months, the newly renamed Swan Brothers continued to polish their act there, but with more powerful sound equipment supplied by their new agent, Willa. Tony visited the cabin from time to time, but it made his heart ache to hear the Swan Brothers sing their tragic lyrics, revised and neutered now to reach the mass market. Willa had insisted on adding an advanced electronic synthesizer to the mix, and Tony had to admit that while it gave the Swan Brothers' music an irritating, shrill quality, it also made it more likely to cross over into the lucrative rock market, with its millions of fans.

Tony feared now more than ever that Willa would learn about his talented daughter Anne, and he knew that Anne sometimes came to the cabin to hear the Swan Brothers and to share their remorse over being controlled by Willa. In Anne's presence, they would forgo the synthesizer and sing their old songs, and for short stretches of time be the smooth and mellow Okeechobee Brothers again.

The situation so pained Anne that she went to a man she knew loved her, a powerful and unethical superagent named Benny Reulor. She offered to leave her father's agency for Reulor's if he could think of a way to free the Okeechobee Brothers from Willa's contractual trap.

Reulor was a darkly handsome man with a warm smile that he utilized to mask his deviousness. But he did have a soft spot for Anne, and he did want to represent her in her future and undoubtedly lucrative career. It didn't hurt her chances that she was Tony King's daughter.

"I know Willa and her daughter Greta-Lorna," he said, leaning back in his desk chair and almost salivating at the thought of the millions this young woman before him was going to earn. "I think I know a way to get you—er, help you. It will be tricky, but I think we can free the Okeechobee Brothers."

"There will be nothing personal in our relationship," Anne told him. "You'll simply be my agent."

"Of course." Reulor smiled.

Within days he summoned Anne back to his office in downtown Nashville and showed her the contract his lawyers had drawn up.

She read it carefully, then signed.

"You'll be happy with my agency," Reulor told her. "We'll both be happy—and rich." Then through his glowing smile he said, "You really should have waited until after I freed the Okeechobee Brothers before signing the contract, though."

She drew a sharp breath. "But you promised—"

He raised a hand. This lovely young woman certainly didn't understand the show business world or the predators who inhabited it. "And I'll keep my promise. I only want to demonstrate to you that you're special to me. *You* can trust me."

"And other people can't?"

"Of course not. I'm an agent." He got up and walked to a mahogany credenza in a corner, opened it, and revealed a small combination safe. With his back to Anne, Reulor opened the safe. But instead of placing her contract inside it, he drew from it a second contract and handed it to her.

"What's this?" she asked.

"It's a contract my agency signed with Willa's daughter Greta, a.k.a. Lorna Lonesome. Read the second page."

Anne did, and her eyes widened. "You can't think Lorna's worth this kind of money! Why, without my father she's nothing but a modestly talented lounge singer!"

"True," Reulor said, "but *she* doesn't know it. The mistake Willa made was locking up your father contractually so he had to sing with Greta. That gave Willa control over him, but she didn't have a contract with her own daughter. She didn't think she needed one; she'd always easily controlled Greta. She never counted on anyone offering Greta that kind of money to lure her away from her own mother's agency." He smiled. "But someone has. Me. And Greta's accepted the offer. This is a harsh world; family means nothing."

"But how does this affect the Okeechobee Brothers?"

Reulor moved close to her and rested his right hand on her left. She was too intrigued by what he was saying to notice. "Without Greta, Willa's contract with Tony is meaningless. He's worthless to her."

"That's wonderful. But doesn't Willa still have the Okeechobee Brothers under contract?"

"Oh, yes. They're still tied up tight."

"Then I don't see how you've changed anything where they're concerned."

"Come to the cabin tomorrow evening," Reulor said. "I've arranged a meeting there where everything will be made clear."

Anne rose from her chair, frowning. "Are you sure? I mean, it seems so impossible!"

"Trust me," Reulor said.

Anne couldn't help herself. She did trust him. It wasn't as if she had a choice. And she didn't think show business was as hard and cruel as he seemed to think. Or as her father had come to think since signing his contract with Willa.

At seven o'clock the next evening, Anne and Tony arrived together at the cabin and found most of the others already there. Reulor had talked to Tony, but like Anne, Tony had no idea what Reulor was going to spring. Tony looked around. The Swan Brothers were lounging on the floor, leaning with their backs against the wall. Crawly was staring into space, humming. The others were silent. Willa was seated in a corner of the sofa, sipping a glass of ice water. At the sound of a car driving up and parking in the gravel driveway, everyone stared at the door.

Benny Reulor entered. He was wearing a silky blue suit with a white shirt and a paisley tie. Ready for business.

"Crunch time," he said.

"We should wait for Greta," Tony said.

Reulor smiled at him. "We can fill her in later." He began to pace, still with the smile. "Willa and I go back a long way, know a lot about each other." He looked at Willa, who glared hard at him from the sofa.

"We were lovers years ago," he admitted, still with his gaze fixed on her.

Willa gave no indication that this was true.

Reulor glanced over at Anne, then continued. "I know about the hidden recorder in Willa's office, how she uses the tapes as business reminders, and occasionally as sources for blackmail. Her dealings with Tony are no exception."

Willa stared coldly at Reulor. Tony noticed that a corner of her thin lips was twitching.

"After getting Greta's name on a contract," Reulor said, "I sent her to show a copy to her mother. In fact, after she left my office, I followed her to make sure she drove directly to Willa's agency."

"You cold, cold bastard!" Willa said.

Reulor smiled. "You don't know the half of it, Willa, but you're about to learn it all." He turned his attention back to the others. "Half an hour after Greta entered Willa's agency, I saw Willa drive away in her black Cadillac."

"You followed me!"

"No, Willa, I simply entered your agency after you left."

She seemed to become smaller, as if she were melting.

"Willa reacted exactly as I thought she might when I sent Greta to her with the contract copy."

"Greta will contradict you," Willa said, but without conviction. "She's with relatives in Costa Rica and will come back and prove you a liar."

"This will prove otherwise," Reulor said, and tossed an audio-cassette into Willa's lap. "It's a copy, of course."

Realizing where Reulor was going with this, Tony sat down. He was having difficulty breathing.

"Greta's body was in the trunk of Willa's Cadillac when she drove away from the agency," Reulor said. "Willa flew into a rage and murdered her for what she'd done, then hid the body."

"It's a lie!" Willa squeaked.

Reulor smiled. "It's on the tape I removed from your office recorder before you returned from your urgent errand and had a chance to destroy it. You screaming about Greta's betrayal. Even Greta pleading for her life before the sound of the shot. By the way, I also took the murder weapon from your desk drawer. It still has your fingerprints on it."

Willa suddenly leaped up and threw the tape cassette, then a heavy ashtray, at Reulor. Both missed him, but the ashtray struck Crawly in the arm. Willa broke for the door. The Swan Brothers stopped her, and after a brief struggle and some foot shuffling and hard breathing, subdued her and held her arms pinned to her sides.

"Don't worry," Reulor told her. "We'll see that everything stays in the family, Willa. I'll keep the original tape well hidden, and I'm sure you'll destroy your copy. And, of course, the gun is in a safe place. All you have to do to remain free from a murder charge is to sign this paper releasing the Swan Brothers from your employ and any further obligations."

He smiled.

She signed.

Then she scooped up the audiocassette and stormed out. They heard her Cadillac's tires kick up gravel as she sped away.

"Everybody okay?" Tony asked, glancing around the room.

The resurrected Okeechobee Brothers all nodded. "I think I got a busted wing from that ashtray hitting it," Crawly said, pointing to his left arm, "but I'll be able to play the guitar again and I bet it won't even hurt."

"She killed her own daughter!" Anne said breathlessly. "I can't believe it!"

Reulor drew a second audiocassette from beneath his suitcoat. "Now that we've got Willa's signature on paper," he said, "there's no point in not sending this and the murder weapon anonymously to the police."

Anne stared at him.

He shrugged and smiled warmly at her. "Showbiz, baby."

John Helfers is another relatively new writer. His natural gifts are considerable, and his craft grows with each new story. He has a nice ear for the way people talk, and a forgiving eye for the way they occasionally screw up their lives. Using elements from "Little Red Riding Hood," he proves that wolves aren't the only danger in the forest.

THE BETTER TO
EAT YOU WITH

Henry watched as the wolf stopped halfway into the clearing, not more than twenty feet away from him. Its golden eyes searched the surrounding forest, looking for any possible threat. He tried to remain as still as possible, his stiff legs and cold feet forgotten. His breath caught in his throat as he examined every detail of the animal before him. He could easily count the wolf's ribs as it stood there, sniffing the air for other danger. After one last look at the copse of pine trees Henry was hidden in, the wolf turned around and loped off.

Sighing, Henry stood up, feeling his joints pop in relief. Looking down, he saw his unused camera resting in his hand.

"Great, just great. Best opportunity since fall, and I blow it. Unbelievable." Stretching, Henry felt his spine crack. Shaking his head, he stepped out of his blind and started putting on his snowshoes. *No use staying here any longer,* he thought, knowing the wolf had caught his scent and gotten spooked. *The scout'll warn the pack away for the rest of the day. Looks like it's been a rough winter for them.* He shook his head, remembering how pitifully thin the wolf had looked.

After he finished tightening the nylon straps around his boots, Henry rose and felt his back twinge, a not-so-subtle reminder about staying out in the forest too late.

"Definitely not a young pup anymore," he said, feeling every one of his sixty-six years catch up to him. *Good thing Clara's not here to see me,* he thought, *she'd box my ears for staying out so long.* Henry put his camera away and checked his compass to verify his location, more out of habit than any real need to know. After four years of exploring the Minnesota forest, he knew the terrain surrounding his cabin like the back of his hand. Right now he was about a mile away from his front door, give or take a hundred yards. *And that's a few steps too many,* he thought, taking one last deep breath of the crisp winter air before heading back. Making sure his sunglasses were secure on his nose, Henry started circling around the clearing, not wanting to leave any tracks out in the open.

He had just reached his own trail back to the cabin when he heard something out of place in the forest: the high-pitched whine of an aircraft. Looking up, he saw the shape of a small plane block out the sun for just an instant as it shot past above him. Henry ducked as it flew overhead, its landing gear barely clearing the treetops. A few seconds later, the forest was filled with the sound of a crash landing.

After the noise had stopped, Henry started walking in the direction the plane had been headed. After threading his way through the forest for several minutes, Henry came upon the trail of broken branches and destroyed saplings the plane had left in its wake. One wing had broken off and was lying near a large pine, a clear sign that nature had won that contest. Now Henry could see the single-engine plane, half buried in a large snowdrift. Greasy smoke was still drifting from under the left engine cowling, which had crumpled like a crushed tin can. From where he was, Henry couldn't see anything through the plane's windows.

"Hello?" Henry called out as he approached the plane. "Is anybody in there?" There was no answer. Taking a deep breath, he trudged to the pilot's door and opened it.

A man sat limply in the pilot's seat, a pair of aviator headphones half covering his face. He wasn't breathing, and his face and flannel shirt were both covered with blood. There was a red spatter on the cracked windshield as well. Without having to check him, Henry knew he was dead. He had seen enough bodies in Korea to know that.

Looking past the body, he saw that the passenger door was

hanging open. Walking around to the other side of the wreck, Henry noticed footprints leading away from the plane, ending at another parka-clad body a few yards away. Hurrying over to the still form, Henry knelt down and rolled the body over.

The face framed in the red hood was that of an attractive young woman, about twenty-five years old. Her features were marred only by a large bruise on her forehead. Unlike the pilot, a ragged plume of breath drifted slowly from her mouth. Looking more closely at her, Henry saw her cheeks and nose were turning red from exposure. Pulling his scarf out of his pocket, he wrapped it around her face. *She must not be too badly injured if she was able to get out of the plane,* he thought. *The most important thing now is to get her to shelter.* Rising, he thought about how he was going to get her back to the cabin.

Twenty-five years ago I could have just slung her over my shoulders and carried her back, he thought. *Carrying more than a hundred pounds of deadweight now, however—that's out of the question.* Henry slowly walked back to the plane, trying to figure out what he was going to do. Under the wing he saw a small hatch in the fuselage. Opening it revealed tools and a few spare parts for repair, along with a grease-stained plastic tarp and a coil of nylon line. Henry took the folded tarp and shook it out, noticing the brass eyeholes along the edges.

A sensation that he was being watched made Henry spin around. It took him a moment to spot the wolf scout in the tree line. For a minute, all he could do was watch the animal watch him. Henry had never seen the wolves more than once a day. Now, however, he didn't have time to indulge his hobby. Shaking his head at his jitters, he grabbed the rope from the storage area and walked back to the woman.

A sneeze made him look up. The scout had been joined by two of his comrades, a small black female Henry had seen before and a gray and brown wolf he called Pancho, since it always appeared with other wolves as their sidekick. The three looked expectant, as if they were waiting for something to happen. The female stepped forward, the expression on her face a carnivore's smile.

They followed me, Henry thought. *They must think I'm leaving them food. Well, not this time.* He wasn't worried about them attacking him. *After all, there's never been an unprovoked wolf attack on a human being. At least, according to the books, there hasn't been. Still, they look pretty anxious, and I don't want to become the first.* Opening the covered holster at his belt, Henry drew his .22 pistol and fired it into the air. The trio of wolves disappeared into the forest, the scout looking back one last time, as if memorizing Henry for future reference. Henry took a deep breath, then returned his attention to the woman.

Laying the tarp on the ground next to her, Henry rolled her over onto it, then wrapped it around her. Tucking the edges around her body, he tied the drawstrings of her parka to the eyeholes. Measuring out what he guessed was a ten-foot length of the cord, he cut it and tied each end to an eyehole. Resting for a minute, he surveyed his handiwork, then looked at the sun and realized he'd better get moving.

Making sure everything was secure, he stepped into the loop he had created. Snugging the line around his waist, Henry held the cord in place and stepped forward. The plastic tarp slid smoothly along the snow. It wouldn't be an easy walk back, but he could manage. Adjusting the rope one last time, he set off.

As he walked, Henry thought about the close call she might have had if the wolves had gotten there first. *She might have been safe enough for a while, since the smell of the crash site would probably keep them away. At least, until she died of hypothermia,* he thought. It had been a lean winter, and Henry had noticed the pack had thinned a bit. The small caches of food he left in the woods for them were always gone the next day. *I know they'll never accept me as a part of the forest, but after all this time, it's hard to believe I don't have some sort of kinship with them.* Whether this was true, he didn't know. *Well, if the pack ever got hungry enough to try anything,* he thought, *I'm not worried.* The walls of his cabin were solid enough to withstand anything they might try. And there was always his Winchester. But Henry hoped it never came down to that. He didn't know if he'd have the heart to shoot one of them, even to save himself.

It was strange, though, seeing them at that plane crash so soon after I had gotten there, he thought. *I don't think I've ever left anything there for them before. Maybe they do associate my presence with food nearby.* "Well, I'm not a scientist, so I guess I'll never know," he muttered.

The tarp caught on a fallen tree branch, and Henry wrestled it free. By now he was panting from the exertion and sweating freely. Stopping for a moment, he looked at his compass and corrected his course. He guessed he was a little less than halfway home. The tarp and its cargo already seemed twice as heavy as it had when he had started out. His heart slammed against his ribs as he struggled to keep moving. Setting his eyes on a large tree about a hundred feet ahead, he promised himself a rest when he got there.

At the tree, he flexed his fingers to restore some circulation back into them. The rope was cutting into his fingers, even with the sheepskin-lined leather gloves he wore. Checking on the woman, he was relieved to see that she was still breathing, although the red-tipped patches on her nose and cheeks looked larger. Glancing at the sky, he guessed he had about an hour of daylight left. He didn't want to be out here when night fell. Settling the rope around his waist again, Henry set out again, determined not to stop until he had reached home.

He wasn't successful, having to rest twice more, but finally he climbed the small rise leading to his one-room cabin and plodded to the door. Dropping the rope, he bent over, feeling light-headed from the exertion. When he had recovered enough, he took off his snowshoes and stuck them in a drift next to the cabin. The woman was unmoving. Henry wondered if he had hauled her all this way only to discover he might be too tired to carry her in.

Taking a few deep breaths to clear his head, he opened the door and half carried, half dragged the tarp and its cargo inside. He was already bathed in a light film of sweat, and the warmth of the cabin made it worse. Closing the door, he wrestled the tarp nearer to the potbellied stove. Opening the stove door, he threw in a couple of logs and made sure the fire caught, then shut it.

Shucking off his heavy parka, he hung it on a wooden rack

next to the door as he went to the kitchen half of the large room. Opening a large cooler in the corner, he took out a plastic jug of water, poured some in a small pan, and set it on top of the stove. Then he went over to the tarp and unwrapped the woman, untying her jacket from the tarp's eyeholes. He saw her face was returning to a normal color already. Unzipping her coat, he got her out of it and took the heavy coat to the rack, where he hung it next to his.

Walking to his bed, he took a fleece blanket and gently wrapped it around the woman. By now she seemed to be coming around and, with his assistance, she was able to walk over to the reclining chair next to the stove. She sank down into the chair, wrapping the blanket more tightly around her, even though the stove was three feet away. Henry shrugged out of his sweatshirt, leaving him in a flannel shirt, and sat on the bed for a moment, resting again.

The hiss of boiling water drew his attention to the pot on the stove. Rising, he walked over, then took it off the heat and over to the counter next to his dry sink. Taking a mug down from a shelf, he poured some water into it. Adding some sugar from a coffee can on the counter, he took it back to the woman, who was flushed and beginning to sweat. She watched him from the chair in silence as he approached. Holding out the cup, Henry said, "Here. Be careful, it's hot."

Her hand tentatively reached out, then took the mug as she felt its warmth. Looking at the liquid inside, she looked up at him with a frown.

"It's just hot sugar water. Your body needs to replace the fluids you lost while out in the cold."

"N-no brandy or rum, huh?" Her voice was still a little rough-sounding from her ordeal, but quiet and guarded.

Henry shook his head. "That'd be worse for you."

She smiled and nodded, then took a sip of the water, huddling over the mug. Henry just let her sit for a few minutes. He got one of the wooden chairs from the kitchen table and set it down by the stove, sitting down with a sigh.

"How do you feel?" he asked.

"Like I was in a plane crash," she answered with a wry smile.

Henry smiled back. "I meant is anything broken?"

She thought about it, then wiggled her arms and legs. "No, just sore from the impact."

Henry nodded, relieved.

"Where am I?" she asked.

"In my cabin," he said.

"Still in Minnesota?"

Henry nodded.

"How far from the border?" she asked.

Henry assumed she meant Canada. "About forty miles."

"Oh." She looked away from him and seemed to be lost in thought for a minute. Then, looking around, she said, "You have a nice place out here."

"Thank you." Henry sensed she was as nervous as he was. He put out his hand. "Henry Bishop."

She smiled as she tried to disentangle her hands from the mug handle. "Alison, Alison Blair. Sorry, I guess plane crashes don't help me remember my manners."

"That's understandable. You took quite a knock on the head. What do you remember?"

She hunched forward again, leaning over the steaming mug. "We had taken off from northern Iowa and been flying for about three hours when we just . . . lost power. I don't know what happened. Jack, that's the pilot, was trying to turn toward somewhere called Bemidji to try to land. The last thing I remember is him yelling at me to put my head down." She looked up as the same thought occurred to them both. Henry shook his head.

"He didn't make it. I'm sorry."

"Oh. I am, too. I mean, I didn't know him or anything, just hired him to fly the plane, nothing more." She leaned back, sighing. "What a fucked-up mess this is."

Henry blinked as he thought about what she had said. It shouldn't have surprised him when she swore like that, but somehow it did. As did her casual reference to the pilot. He returned to the conversation. "Anything I can do to help?"

"You've done more than your share already. Saving me and

all that, I mean." She looked at a slim watch on her wrist, shook it, and held it to her ear. "Do you know what time it is?"

Henry looked at the clock on the far wall, pleased that he didn't have to squint to read it. "Exactly four forty-seven P.M.," he said.

"And how far to the nearest town?" she asked.

"Waskish's about five or six miles from here. No airport, I'm afraid; the town's way too small for that," Henry said.

She nodded. "Please don't think I'm not grateful or anything, but there's an important meeting I have to get to tonight. So if you'll just let me collect my things and run me into town, I'll be happy to get out of your hair."

"Things? What did you need?"

"Well, my backpack, for starters . . ." she trailed off as she leaned forward and looked around, then slowly got up and walked the length of the cabin, searching for something. "You didn't bring it, did you? A blue backpack; it would have been in the rear of the plane."

Henry frowned. "Miss, I had enough problems getting you here. I wasn't going to haul any more than I had to."

Now her expression matched his. "Haul? Don't you have a snowmobile or an ATV or something out here?"

He nodded. "Snowmobile. But the gas line's frozen. I'm too old to be tinkering with it in this weather. Besides, I usually don't go into town much."

She just looked at him. "How far away was the crash?"

" 'Bout a mile," Henry replied.

She drifted over to the small window next to the door and looked outside at the darkness. Henry got up and turned on his electric lantern, the glow lighting the entire room. The young woman still stared out the window. Finally she spoke. "That's quite a thing you did."

Henry looked down at the table and realized he was hungry. "Would you like something to eat?"

"Yes, I'm starving. Thank you," she said.

Henry turned and went to the cooler, where he removed a

large plastic bowl of stew and took it over to the stove. When he turned back to her again, the cabin was empty. Then he saw the curtain that partitioned the toilet from the rest of the cabin was swinging slightly, and knew where she had gone. Another movement caught his eye, and he realized that her coat was also swinging on its peg.

Pouring the rest of the sugar water into another mug for later, Henry dumped the stew into the pot and let it warm on the stove. The toilet made its peculiar flushing noise, and Alison stepped back out. Shaking her head, she ran her fingers through her hair, combing it as best as she could. Henry just watched, the stew on the stove forgotten for the moment.

"Smells good. What's in it?" she asked as she walked over to the stove.

"Rabbit, carrots, potatoes, wild onions, that sort of thing. I have a garden out back, at least in the summer, where I grow my vegetables. I also run traps around the house, and the rabbits provide me with plenty of meals." He realized he was rambling, and stopped, feeling a little idiotic.

She hadn't seemed to notice, and was watching the stew, which was bubbling by now. "Henry?"

"Yes?"

"Are you going to take that off the stove?" Alison asked, pointing to the pot.

"Oh, right." He took the pot over to the table and set it on a wooden holder. Going to the kitchen, he pulled out two well-used plastic bowls and spoons from under the counter. Walking back, he sat down across from Alison and spooned the stew into both bowls. They ate in relative silence, each one concentrating on the food and his or her own thoughts.

Whatever her thoughts were, they didn't affect Alison's appetite much. After the second bowlful, she leaned back in the chair and sighed. "Henry, you'll make someone a good husband someday."

He smiled back. "Already have."

"That picture on the wall?" she asked.

Henry nodded.

"She's very pretty," she said.

"Yes, she was," Henry replied without a moment's thought.

"I'm sorry. I probably shouldn't be dredging this up for you," she said, looking back at him.

"That's all right. She's buried, my memories of her aren't," Henry said.

Alison took both bowls to the sink and washed them. Then she walked to the small window beside the door and looked out again. Turning back, she asked, "When can we leave?"

"Leave? By now it's thirty below out there. We can't make it to town until tomorrow morning," Henry replied. "I'm sorry, but it would be crazy to go out there now."

"I can make it worth your while. I'll pay you a thousand dollars to get me to town tonight," she replied as if she hadn't heard him.

Henry put his elbows on the table. "It's not a matter of money, it's matter of staying alive. With a temperature of thirty below, plus a wind of, say, twenty miles an hour, you're looking at a wind-chill factor of about eighty below. That'll freeze bare flesh in about twenty seconds."

"It doesn't look like it's very windy out there now," she said, peering out the window again.

"It could be perfectly calm and I still wouldn't go. I'm sorry, but we're not going. When morning comes, we can head to town and get you taken care of." Henry shook his head at her determination.

"There's nothing I can say to make you change your mind? I'll pay you two thousand dollars," she said.

She's in a big hurry to get somewhere, Henry thought. *Typical city folk, they think money will solve everything.* "No."

It was silent in the cabin for several seconds. Then Alison spoke quietly. "All right, all right."

Henry decided to change the subject. "How about some music?" he asked, turning on the radio. *The news should still be on,* he thought.

It was, the announcer just finishing up a local summary. "In other news, a small plane was just reported missing somewhere over the Minnesota north woods today. The plane was headed for International Falls when it disappeared off radar this afternoon. Rescue teams will be searching through the night for it, to increase the chance of finding survivors before the approaching storm. Coming up, the—"

Wow, that was fast. Of course, in Waskish, a piece of news like that can be milked for three days, Henry thought, turning down the volume. He looked over at her. "Looks like the cavalry is on the way."

Instead of appearing pleased by the news, she looked worried. Shaking her head, she said, "Goddammit, Henry, I didn't want it to happen this way."

Henry was going to ask her what she was talking about, but then she turned, and the sudden gun in her hand made him pause in disbelief. Then he stood up, the gun tracking him as he moved.

"Don't. Take the pistol from the holster with two fingers and lay it on the table. Do the same with the knife, then step away from the table."

Slowly Henry complied, not saying anything. The shock of the gun in her hand made him automatically obey. Looking into her eyes, he was surprised at the change he saw in them. Instead of the bright green they had been, now her stare was flat and cold. It was the same kind of look the female wolf had given him earlier, like she was sizing up a potential meal.

Henry stepped away from the table, wondering if he could talk to her without getting shot. He wondered what was so important at the plane that she had to take him hostage to get it. Now that the initial shock had faded away, he was evaluating his chances of survival. Trying to surprise her now would be impossible. *Better to wait for an opportunity to present itself later,* he thought. For now, he would have to play along.

"Get your coat on. We're going to take that walk now." Henry took his sweater and wriggled into it, then followed with his coat. He reached in his pocket for his face mask, and heard the distinctive click of a pistol hammer being cocked. Henry looked up again, staring down the barrel at her. He nodded, acknowledging what he had accidentally done.

"I just wanted to get my face mask out. I'm going to need it out there."

She nodded and uncocked the gun, its barrel never wavering from his chest. "Where are your extras?"

Henry pointed to the rack behind him. She motioned him away, then took a ski mask off the hook. "From now on, you do exactly as I tell you. Turn around and walk to the wall."

He did so, then heard the rustle of fabric. *Pretty smart,* he thought. *There's no way I can get to her from this far away.*

"Okay," she said.

Turning back around, he saw no sign of a gun. Then he noticed the odd bulge in her pocket. While he knew it was still pointed at him, the very fact that it was out of sight made him feel a little better. "It was in there all the time, wasn't it?"

She shrugged and said, "Let's go." Henry realized there wasn't going to be much more conversation than on the first trip with her.

"May I put my mask on?" he asked. She nodded. He did so, then started to turn toward the door, but was stopped by a single head shake from her.

"Open the door, step out, and walk straight out from the cabin, three steps away. Understand?"

Henry nodded. "What about snowshoes?"

"Where's your wife's pair?"

For a second, Henry thought about lying to her, but realized that he'd be the one walking without them. "In the storage shed."

"All right. You're going to go outside like I told you, and wait there."

Henry stepped outside, gasping for breath as the freezing night air hit his mouth as if his face mask wasn't even there. It was calm outside, the kind of night that could trick a person into thinking it wasn't as cold as it really was. Because everything was so still, you didn't notice the cold gradually stealing your body heat away. You just went numb little by little. He looked back at Alison, who was sitting in the doorway, adjusting the snowshoe straps to her feet. She worked steadily, not looking up, but Henry was sure she knew exactly where he was.

After a few minutes, she had the shoes on and the gun back

in her pocket. She motioned him forward, and they started heading behind the cabin to the small storage shed. When they got there, Henry slapped his head. "Forgot the flashlight."

A yellow beam of light hit him in the chest. "That's all right, I've got my own," Alison said. "Open the door and take three steps to the side."

Henry did so, fumbling with the stiff latch. After a minute, he got the door open.

"Where are the snowshoes?" she said.

"They're just inside the door, on the left side," Henry said. In a moment, she took them out and tossed them at his feet. Henry resized them for his feet and strapped them on.

"Where's the snowmobile?" Alison asked.

"Behind the shed," Henry replied.

"Take me to it," she said, pointing the way with the light. She followed him around the shed to where the snowmobile sat under a tarp. "Try it."

The snowmobile was an older model. Henry grabbed the starter cord and yanked it a dozen times, each pull producing the same hollow cough from the machine. "Satisfied?" he asked, more than a little angry now. His shoulder throbbed, unused to the sudden exercise. She nodded.

"You have a compass?" Alison said, more a statement than a question. Henry nodded. "Give it to me," she said.

"How will I find my way back?" he asked, holding it out to her.

"I wouldn't worry about it. We'll leave enough of a trail for you to follow," she said. Henry wasn't sure whether to be heartened by that statement or not. After all, she could have just said it to placate him and kill him once they were back at the plane. Still, it was a chance for survival, and until Henry could do something about the situation, it was the only hope he had.

They went back to the front of the cabin and headed into the forest. Henry was about five feet ahead of her, following the patch of light she shone past him. He walked slowly, pacing himself. She didn't hurry him. After a moment, Henry realized that it was because of the snowshoes. It takes a certain rhythm to walk comfortably in them, which he had developed after years of practice. He thought about waiting for her to stumble and then jumping her. But he dismissed the idea as more dangerous than it sounded. Snowshoes also weren't the easiest things to turn around in. *Besides,* he thought after they had been walking for about ten minutes, *I haven't heard her stumble once.*

By now Henry was panting from the exertion. He wasn't surprised, although this was easier than the trip back to the cabin. Again he thought about the futility of struggling on when he was probably going to get shot. *Given a choice, I'd rather die of hypothermia than a bullet,* he rationalized. *If you freeze to death, at least you have the illusion of being warm for a while.*

The trip went quicker this time, and at the halfway point Henry held up his hand.

"What?" came Alison's voice behind him.

"I've got to rest," Henry said.

"All right, five minutes," she said. Henry didn't doubt that his allotted time would be exactly that. He put his hands on his knees and tried to catch his breath. He was surprised she gave in so easily. *In the grand scheme of things, she probably figures she can wait five minutes to get whatever she needs at the plane rather than having me keel over and never get there,* he thought.

Straightening, Henry looked at Alison. She was about five feet away, the gun still on him. A sudden movement behind her caught his eye. Without moving his head, Henry shifted his gaze. There was a wolf behind them, trotting silently over the snow.

"We'd better get going, I suppose," Henry said, glancing at Alison's face for a second. When he looked behind her again, the wolf was gone. She didn't say anything, just motioned him forward with the gun. *Are her fingers as stiff as mine right now?* he thought. *If she were only a couple of steps closer, I'd be able to get my hands on that gun. I wonder who would win.* So far, she had been handling the hike with ease. Of course, this was the first time she had walked it. Henry remembered an article he had read in one of Clara's health journals about how a seventy-year-old man was supposed to have the equivalent strength of an eighteen-year-old. *I wish that was true right now. I sure don't feel as strong now as I did when I was eighteen.*

The moon came out from behind a cloud, bathing the forest in silver. As he walked, Henry noticed dark shadows flitting in and out of the trees around them. The wolves were pacing them. He had never read about wolves behaving this way before. Usually they avoided humans as much as possible. *Unless they're hunting us. Then they're just following standard pack behavior. Run the prey to exhaustion and attack the sick, injured, or old.* Henry wasn't sure if that's what he was seeing, but so far it matched everything he had read about pack hunting behavior. He knew that only madness or starvation would lead the wolves to attack humans. Either of those didn't sound very good to him.

He heard the click of a hammer being cocked and half turned to look back at her. Alison was looking around them, the gun still on him.

"We're being followed," she said.

"For the past couple hundred yards," Henry said.

"Wolves are afraid of people," she said.

Henry thought he heard doubt in her voice. He decided to keep on being helpful. "Usually. It's been a long winter, though. Game's scarce," he said.

She didn't say anything, just motioned him forward with the light.

Henry thought about what she had said. *That's true, wolves have never attacked a human being . . . no, that's not it.* Then he thought of a phrase he had read in several books about wolves: *" 'There hasn't been an unprovoked wolf attack on a human being in the past century.' "* The odd phrasing of the quote struck him. *I bet there have been plenty of attacks, unprovoked or not, before then. They were probably never reported because the victim never lived to tell the tale.* He wondered if they would become two more "unverified" victims. He was still inclined to dismiss the possibility. *But it has been a really hard winter,* he thought. *Now I have three choices: death by gun, death by freezing, or death by wolf.*

As they approached the hill where the crash site was, Henry thought that maybe rescuers had found the plane by now, and would be there investigating. But his first look at the site dispelled that hope. The plane was just as they had left it, crumpled and alone.

"Stop here," she said. Henry did so. Alison walked around him to the plane, her eyes flicking from him to the trees all the while. She put the flashlight away, propped open the passenger door, and reached in behind her seat. A few seconds later she hauled out a large blue backpack, the kind with a metal frame that was used for mountain climbing or extended backpacking trips. Keeping her gun on him, she unzipped one of the compartments and took out a small bundle of paper and examined it. As he watched her, Henry saw that bundle was made up of large-denomination bills. Everything suddenly fell into place.

Henry had been following the news reports of a group of bank robbers who had been moving through the Midwest in the past few months. They robbed as they traveled, just like Bonnie and Clyde back in the 1930s. The most recent report three days ago had placed the gang in Dubuque, where they had shot their way out of a police trap. Alison must have been part of them. Now she was on the run, fleeing the country.

Alison had slung the backpack over her shoulders and shut the plane's door. Henry didn't say a word; he just kept watching her.

"Which way to town?" she asked, holding the compass in her other hand.

Again Henry thought about lying, and again he dismissed the idea. He didn't want her accidentally finding her way back to the cabin. He pointed back over his shoulder. "Just go due east for about four miles; you can't miss the highway. Town's another two miles north."

She nodded and motioned for him to step back. He did so. She started to move around him.

The loud wolf howl nearby startled them both. For a second, Alison's gun wavered away from Henry, pointing toward the forest. In that second, he moved, taking one giant step forward and putting all his remaining strength into swinging his fist at her head. She had just started to bring the gun back when the blow landed. It knocked her sideways, her snowshoes tangling together as she stumbled. She reeled against the plane and went down, the pistol spinning from her hand.

Henry's first move was for the gun. By the time he found it, Alison had sat up and was leaning against the plane, holding her oddly bent knee. Henry realized she must have twisted it as she fell. He stared at her for a while. She stared back, both of them silent. In the forest, Henry could hear the movement of the wolves.

"If you make it into the plane, you might survive the night. I'm sure help will come eventually. Here," Henry said, picking up the bundle of dropped bills and tossing it to her. "Maybe you'll have better luck buying them off."

With that he turned and started back toward the cabin. Within minutes he was back in the forest. He tried working the slide on the pistol and wasn't surprised when it didn't move, frozen solid. He shook his head and continued walking. It was then he remembered that he had left the pilot door open. He could hear the wolves' excited barks mixing with her screams. Then the screams faded, replaced by the sounds of the pack, still snarling and yapping. Henry thought about the wolves as he continued home. He had been counting on the fact that, given a choice, the pack would attack a sick or injured target rather than a healthy-looking one. "Still, I was damn lucky they didn't decide to go after me as well," he muttered.

That phrase from the books came back to him as he walked. *There has never been a report of an unprovoked wolf attacking a human,* he thought, *and as far as I'm concerned, that statement is still true.*

Ed Gorman has written virtually every type of crime novel. Called "one of the world's great storytellers" by Britain's Million *magazine, he is at his best when he is at his most ironic, as in the following dark fable based on "Gossip Wolf and the Fox," about mistaken identities and the power of truth.*

ED GORMAN

Of the Fog

David Huggins was pushing radio buttons to find a decent song when he looked up and saw, there on the edge of the interstate, there in the fog and light drizzle, there against a backdrop of deep green Iowa countryside, one of the most beautiful young women his thirty-four-year-old eyes had ever seen.

She was maybe a hundred yards away. She wore a man's red windbreaker, jeans, hiking boots. Her short blond hair made her classically beautiful face seem even younger. Her blue eyes were possessed of a radiance that was almost alarming, even at this distance.

Only the mouth troubled him, and he instantly knew why. It was Lavonne's mouth, full and insolent. He'd gone with Lavonne for the first three years of college. It took him all the way to his senior year to learn just how unfaithful she was. He'd walked in on her one day. She was in bed with one of his fraternity brothers. Huggins had literally gotten sick, gone in the john, and thrown up. She'd treated him scornfully. It wasn't any big deal, she'd said. Being somebody's girlfriend wasn't like being his wife. All the time she'd talked, he just kept looking at her mouth. How much pleasure those erotic lips had given him over the past three years. But now they smirked at him.

This girl had the same mouth.

She held up her lone suitcase for him to see. GRINNELL, read a large Magic Marker sign on the front side of the suitcase. Huggins was on his way to Des Moines. He made the trip three times a month. He was a hospital supply salesman and covered this whole section of Iowa.

His right foot hovered three inches above the brake. A drizzle like this, a cold morning like this, he should be a gentleman and stop to pick her up. Though he didn't pick up hitchhikers as a rule, she didn't seem dangerous. A beautiful girl like her, she had more to fear than he did.

His black oxford descended another inch.

If he was going to stop, he'd better stop now.

This close, she was even better-looking. She leaned her face toward the car. She broke into a nice, girlish midwestern grin, all freckles and innocence.

His black oxford eased down the final inch, until it came in contact with the brake.

All he had to do was step down a little harder now, and the new Buick, for which the company paid half, would come to an easy stop.

She was still smiling at him. Anticipation gleamed in her startling blue eyes. Just another minute or so and she'd be out of this fog and drizzle.

All he had to do was stop.

She smiled, then, the young woman. Smiled, her full lips suddenly insolent, as if she had just appraised him and found him wanting somehow. All he could see was Lavonne smiling, that practiced, empty, deceitful smile.

He slammed his right foot on the gas pedal and started to fishtail away.

The young woman went into combat mode. She leaned even farther toward Huggins' car and then flipped him the finger. She called him several names, each of which challenged his right to call himself a man.

He watched her in his rearview. She kept her middle finger up straight and proud for him to see.

Her name was Marcia Quinn, and she was a Drake University junior from Chicago, and sixty miles ago she'd been pushed out of the car when she'd finally answered her boyfriend's question about whether she'd been faithful while he'd been studying in Rome this summer.

"You couldn't be goddamned faithful for two goddamned months?"

"It didn't mean anything, Todd. I mean, it was only a couple of nights. And I didn't fall in love with him or anything. I guess I was just bored or something."

Slam went the brakes. Open went the door.

Todd Bellamy, who was also a Drake junior, then pitched her suitcase out of the car and took off down the interstate, traveling fast and angry.

This was about an hour ago, just when the drizzle started.

If it hadn't been for the rain, she might have enjoyed hitchhiking. All her life she'd been told how dangerous this was. Especially now that the Highway Killer had taken the lives of four young women. Which just made the experience all the more exciting. Who knew what lay ahead—maybe later on, she'd take candy from a stranger. Or maybe she'd be picked up by the man who'd killed three young women on this interstate over the past fourteen months. He used a heavily serrated blade to kill his victims. Even after all this time, the police had no real clues. None they were admitting to, anyway.

Her mood started to be good again until the guy in the Buick came along.

If there was one thing Marcia Quinn wasn't used to it was being treated shabbily by men.

Men, most men, treated her with almost embarrassing deference. They wanted to go to bed with her. A young woman with her looks . . . men, most men, were trophy hunters. And she was indeed a trophy. Years from now, the men she'd shared a bed with would look back and recall how beautiful she was, and her beauty, in memory, would be even more astonishing.

Or so she'd been told by a professor she'd slept with last spring term. Todd'd really be pissed if he found out about *him.*

All of which was why she was so angry about the guy in the Buick.

Where the hell did he get off pretending that he was going to give her a ride . . . a girl so many men would have been happy to have in their cars . . . and then speeding off like she was some kind of leper or something?

She continued to hitchhike.

The fog was what made it so difficult.

Drivers couldn't see her until they were right upon her . . . and then it was unsafe to stop. A car in the fog behind them might slam right into their rear end. Happened all the time in conditions like these.

The longer she walked, the sorrier she felt for Todd. She shouldn't have slept with that guy this summer. All the temptations Todd had likely had in Rome . . . and he'd passed them all up because he loved her. The only reason she slept around was so she could say she'd cheated first. Her first few boyfriends had cheated on her . . . and she never wanted to go through that humiliation again. It became a point of honor to sleep around before your lover did. But Todd wasn't into sick love games like that. Todd was a decent guy. And she felt terrible now that she'd betrayed him. She was going to apologize to him as soon as she got a chance.

Todd was a keeper.

She didn't want to end up like her gorgeous older sister . . . three failed marriages by age thirty-two . . . her good looks a curse rather than a blessing.

She really did need to work things out with Todd.

Drizzle became rain now . . . hard, cold winter rain in late August . . . rain that hissed, rain that stung, rain that soaked.

She started thinking about the Buick again, and how much she hated the driver. Somehow he became symbolic of all her troubles.

She trudged on through the gray, foggy downpour.

Huggins wished he wasn't hungry. Though he worked out twice a week at a gym, he had put on twenty pounds over the past few years, pounds that resolutely refused to come off. For the first time in his life Huggins, who had been one of the skinniest kids in his high-school graduating class, began to think of himself as "overweight."

The café was up on a hill just east of where the off-ramp

ended. He'd stopped there a few times before. The place was basically a greasy spoon where the people of the nearby small town came for breakfast and lunch. Truckers tended to use the truck stop thirty miles due west of there.

The café covered the ground floor of a two-story concrete block building that had the look and feel of the kind of construction done right after World War II, fast and cheap. This year, the place was painted pea green. There were three pickups and a few cars in the parking lot.

The moment Huggins opened the café's door, he heard a country and western singer whine plaintively, "You got custody of the kids, but who gets custody of my heart?"

The smells of cooking grease, cigarette smoke, and coffee mugged his olfactory nerves.

He regretted coming in here, but he was too self-conscious a person to turn around and walk out.

Three men in green John Deere caps sat at the counter, watching him. They didn't look impressed. Huggins wasn't an impressive guy. He'd always done moderately well with women but not with men. Men tended to ignore him. He wasn't tough or clever or even particularly interesting. He didn't even care much for sports. Men seemed to sense all these lackings instantly, and they avoided him.

The restaurant was laid out simply. The counter and the kitchen took up the west wall. Booths took up the east wall. The red vinyl was patched in many places with tan masking tape. The walls were hung with framed photographs of country and western singers. The photographs were signed.

Huggins was still getting used to the harsh and sour smells of the place.

He went to the counter and sat down on the last available stool. He'd just have a cup of coffee and get out of this place.

"You're wearin' that bra again, aren't you, Ellie?" said one of the men at the counter. The other men at the counter all smiled and laughed like schoolboys, filling their eyes with the considerable sight of Ellie.

Ellie was a big bottle–blond woman—big but not fat, just big—dressed in a pink polyester waitress's outfit. The pink allowed the black push-up bra beneath the polyester to be on full display. Huggins studied her a moment. She had a panther tattoo on her left forearm and she wore a teeny-tiny nose ring. The tattoo might be one of those press-on dealies. She couldn't be much more than twenty or so. Huggins filled her bio in with ruthless prejudice—high-school dropout, denizen of a trailer park. Cruel but probably true.

"I bought it with a gift certificate Charlene gave me," she said. Immediately Huggins saw the faces of the men change into hard, harsh masks.

Whoever Charlene was, she meant a lot not only to Ellie but also to these three men.

"That sonofabitch," Roy said. He had a white scar running down his right cheek.

"I just hope I'm the one to catch him," said the second man. He had a badly broken nose.

"I hope you're the one who catches him, too, Phil," Ellie said, her eyes and voice overbrimming with sudden tears. "What he did to Charlene and all."

Roy put out a quick, strong hand and touched Ellie's arm. "They'll find him. Don't worry about that, Ellie."

"She was like my own sister," Ellie said, tears still strong in her eyes and voice. "My own sister."

The third man, the one closest to Huggins, leaned over and said, "Girl who used to work here, Charlene Tuttle, she was Ellie's best friend. That Highway Killer, they call him."

Ellie sniffled and said, "Sorry, mister, I forgot to wait on you."

"That's fine," Huggins said. "No hurry."

"You want coffee?"

Huggins nodded. And added, "You have any breakfast rolls left?"

"I think so."

"Good. I'll take one."

He hadn't been going to eat here, but now that he was actually sitting at the counter he felt a bit drowsy, tired. He liked the warmth of this place, and the man next to him seemed friendly enough. Wouldn't hurt to stay out of the downpour, either. He hadn't been in any major car accidents in his life. He didn't want to start now.

Ellie popped Huggins's breakfast roll in the microwave, then melted two pats of butter on top of it. Then she brought it over to him.

Huggins thanked her and started in on the roll. It was delicious.

Marcia Quinn's ride took her to the same café where Huggins's blue Buick sat in the parking lot.

The young farmer behind the wheel of the Chevrolet pickup pulled up to the edge of the lot and stopped.

"My farm's about ten miles from here," he said. "I've got to go home and see how the calving's going. Vet's been out there since early this morning." He nodded to the café. "There may be somebody inside there going to Des Moines. I'll probably be back myself. I usually pick up a sack of burgers here and bring them home for the wife and me."

Marcia thanked him for the ride, jumped down from the cab, and then yanked her suitcase to the ground.

The young farmer touched his hand to the bill of his Cubs cap in a kind of salute and then took off.

The parking lot was eerie with rolling fog and a slimy, cold mist. Marcia felt disoriented and vaguely frightened.

Maybe this'd be like a horror movie. She'd walk through the fog and get into the café, only to find it inhabited by ghouls and monsters. She envisioned Dracula and Frankenstein and the Wolf Man all sitting at the counter—Todd loved the Universal horror films from the forties, and by now she loved them, too—watching for her. Waiting for her.

Then she saw the blue Buick and got pissed all over again. She recalled the driver's angry face, the slight sneer of his lips as he floored his car and sped away from her.

Been intimidated by her looks. A lot of guys were like that. So they had to hurt her in some way. Some petty little sting just to prove to her—and to themselves—that they weren't under her lovely sway.

She thought about writing some obscenity on the trunk of his car in lipstick. Then she thought about giving him a flat tire.

But they both sounded pretty juvenile. And, for that matter, not really much in the way of retaliation.

She started to walk toward the door of the café. Even lost in the fog, she could faintly hear the whine of the country and western music and smell the hot, tart scent of steaming lard.

Then she stopped and smiled.

And glanced back over her shoulder.

There in the fog she could see the outlines of the blue Buick.

Oh, he was going to pay, the bastard who'd sneered at her and passed her by.

He was going to pay real good.

Huggins had just returned from the rest room, had just seated himself at the counter again, when the front door of the café slammed open and the woman staggered inside.

Her jacket had been torn, her face was scuffed with dirt, her hair was a wild, soaked mess.

She made sounds that were half sobs, half moans.

"Oh, my Lord," Ellie said.

She hurried over to the young woman and caught her just as the woman was about to pitch face-first to the floor.

Everything in the little café came to a halt. The two other waitresses, who had been serving people in the booths, stopped what they were doing. The cook came out from the kitchen, wiping his hands on a grease-spattered white apron. A man who'd been about to deposit money for a phone call suddenly hung up the receiver.

Ellie half carried the young woman over to the only empty booth.

"Get me a clean towel and some hot water," she said to one of the other waitresses.

The woman hurried to the kitchen.

Ellie propped the young woman up against the wall, then set her legs up on the seat.

By now the three men at the counter had drifted over to the booth to inspect the young woman more carefully.

"What happened, hon?" Ellie said, sounding maternal, even though she was a couple of years younger than the woman she was caring for.

"He . . . he tried to rape me," the young woman said in a monotone. "And then he tried to kill me with his knife. But I . . . I jumped out of the car."

She looked up at Ellie with sorrowful eyes. "I don't remember much about . . . running. I guess I just . . . just ended up here."

Then she started crying.

She made almost no sound at all. Her shoulders trembled and her head shook back and forth but you could barely hear her. It was very moving.

The only thing that bothered Huggins was . . . how had all this happened to her in the time since he'd passed her on the highway?

This was definitely the same young woman who'd flipped him the bird. Not more than twenty, twenty-five minutes could have passed since that time. So how could all this have happened to her?

But maybe he was rationalizing, he realized.

Maybe by challenging the time frame of her story he was simply trying to put the blame on her instead of where it properly belonged.

On him.

Given the condition of her clothes and face, something had clearly happened to her.

And it *wouldn't* have happened to her if he'd picked her up and given her a ride.

He felt guilt and shame, sitting there so isolated at the counter, the other men gathered helpfully around the booth where the young woman was propped up.

He'd probably best get out of here. She was probably going to recognize him and probably going to tell everybody here what he'd done to her.

Passing up a woman in a downpour wasn't exactly a gentlemanly thing to do. The people in this little café, no matter how long he explained, were never going to understand about Lavonne and how she'd betrayed him back in college and how *this* young woman reminded him of Lavonne, which was why he'd passed her by. . . .

"What's your name, sweetheart?" Ellie said.

"M-Marcia Q-Quinn," she said, fighting more tears.

"Where you from, hon?"

"C-Chicago. I g-go to D-Drake."

No, they'd never understand why he hadn't given her a ride. . . .

Better to make his quiet way up to the cash register and leave money for his bill (plus enough for a nice tip) and get back in his Buick and finish the drive to Des Moines.

He didn't want these people to dislike him—all his life he'd desperately wanted people to like him—which they'd certainly not do if the woman recognized him.

He took out his wallet.

The bill was $1.87, bkfst rll and cff as Ellie's scribbling read on the green ticket.

He took three ones from his wallet, nice green crisp ones, and then stood up.

Nobody was even looking in his direction. They were all too concerned about the woman.

They were asking questions about when it happened, where it happened, what her assailant looked like.

Huggins was certain now that she'd get around to telling them about him. About the man who'd refused to give her a ride. About the man who had thus inadvertently caused her to be in this terrible situation.

He was just a few feet from the cash register when he heard the young woman say, "My God."

"What's wrong, hon?" Ellie said.

"That's him. Over there. By the cash register."

Now *everybody* was looking at him.

"Him? That guy?" Roy said, nodding to Huggins.

"H-He's the one, all right!" Marcia Quinn said.

"Hey!" Roy shouted. "You just freeze right where you are, mister."

"Damned right," said Phil-of-the-broken-nose.

They started walking toward him, moving slowly and carefully, as if he were a wild and dangerous animal who might attack them at any moment.

He tried to speak. But his throat was so dry he couldn't.

"Spread 'em, mister," Roy said.

Before Huggins could understand what was about to happen, Roy grabbed him and turned him around and hurled him so hard against the cash register that it wobbled the entire stand.

"You search him, Phil," Roy said. "I'll make sure the sumbitch don't try anything."

"Maybe introduce myself to him first," Phil said, "before I go feelin' him up 'n' all."

Huggins didn't know what he was talking about. Not until Phil drove a hard fist deep into Huggins' kidney was Phil's message clear.

Huggins felt all the strength go out of his knees . . . and indescribable pain radiate from his kidney all the way up under his armpit.

Now he knew how Phil had gotten his nose broken so many times. This was a guy who loved to fight. And who was good at it, too. He used his fists with fury and precision.

The punches sapped Huggins of all strength. He could do little more than cling to the checkout counter. He was afraid he was going to fall down.

As Phil started to pat him down—wasn't that what the cops always called it on TV cop shows?—a sense of unreality overcame Huggins.

A small, hick café in the middle of a vast ocean of rolling fog . . . perhaps this was a nightmare.

Had to be.

He hadn't done anything to the woman . . . and yet they were so eager to believe her.

Another punch slammed into his kidney.

This time he heard himself moan. Felt his knees start to weaken.

No, this was real. The fog . . . the café. So isolated and *unreal* . . . yet real.

Phil patted him down.

When he came to Huggins' crotch, he rapped him with his knuckles, sending shock and pain through Huggins' entire lower body.

"Nothin'," Phil said as he reached Huggins' ankle.

"Throw me his wallet," Roy said.

"Who died and made you fucking pope, huh, Roy?"

"Just throw me his goddamned wallet."

Huggins felt his wallet leave its familiar, warm place riding next to his right buttock.

"You're David Huggins?" Roy said as he went through the wallet.

"Yes."

"I can't hear you, asshole."

"Give it to him, Roy," Ellie said. "Give it to him real good."

"She's lying," Huggins said. "I didn't even let her in my car. I saw her but I passed her by."

"A real gentleman," Roy said.

"She never even got in my car, do you understand?"

"I asked you a question, asshole. Your name is David Huggins?"

"Call the law if you think I'm guilty. Get one of your deputies over here."

"We'll worry about the law, jerk-off," Roy said. "For now, I want you to answer my questions. Or Phil'll start in on your kidney again, you understand?"

"Do the bastard like he done them," Ellie said.

"You're David Huggins?"

"Yes."

"And you live at 393 Maple Lane in Cedar Rapids?"

"Yes."

Pause. "There're a couple of photographs in here. A good-looking woman and a little boy."

"My wife and son."

"What's your wife's name?"

"Cindy."

"How old is she?"

"Twenty-eight."

"What's your boy's name?"

"Brian."

"How old's he?"

"Four."

"Where's Cindy work?"

"I want you to call the law," Huggins said. "Right now. You don't have any right to do this."

Ellie snorted. "You just happen to be talking to an auxiliary policeman, asshole. And you're too dumb to even know it."

"Ask the woman there."

"Ask her what?" Roy said.

"Ask her if she's telling the truth."

"You seen her same as I did. All busted up that way," Roy said. "She sure as hell *is* telling the truth."

"Ask her."

"You're lyin', mister," Ellie said.

"Go on. Ask her."

"Hit the bastard, Phil."

Phil hit the bastard.

Apparently Phil had tired of hitting the bastard in the kidney. This time he hit the bastard in the side of the head.

Darkness was instant. Darkness and more pain.

Huggins felt his knees start to give way. His thighs were trembling the way they did when he and Cindy made love standing up. But now the trembling was not from pleasure.

"This could be fake ID," Roy said.

"With my picture on it?"

"Hell, yes. You can buy any kind of fake ID you want."

"Why would I have fake ID?"

"So nobody could trace you to where you really live."

"Why the hell would I do that?"

"So people wouldn't find out you're the one been killin' all those poor girls out on the highway."

"I'm really David Huggins."

"What's your phone number?" Roy said.

"In Cedar Rapids?"

"Yes."

"I really want you to call the law," Huggins said. His voice sounded funny to him now. Part of Phil's punch had landed on Huggins' ear. There was a kind of tinny, distant quality to his voice now.

"You want Phil to hit you again?" Roy said.

"No."

"Then tell me your phone number."

Huggins told him his phone number.

"I'm going to call that number right now. She be home?"

"She should be. Tell her to call the law."

Roy laughed. "Right. That's just what I'll do. I'll tell her to call the law."

Then Roy and his voice started to move. Huggins could hear the voice toward the back of the café now.

"If you're making up this number, I'm going to let Phil have himself a field day, mister."

"Kick his ass, Roy," Ellie said. "I just keep thinkin' about what he did to Charlene."

She had started to cry again.

"Ma'am, I'm not the man you're looking for," Huggins said. "I'm sorry what happened to your friend. But I didn't do it. I really didn't. Ask that woman if she's telling the truth. She was just pissed that I didn't give her a ride."

"She isn't makin' anythin' up," Ellie said. "If anybody's makin' anythin' up, it's you."

"Quiet now," Roy said.

Huggins angled his head toward the back of the café where Roy stood next to the pay phone.

The three kitchen men stood near the kitchen door, smoking cigarettes and watching everything without a word.

The coins were loud as they dropped down the pay phone.

Roy dialed, then glanced at Huggins. "You better not be makin' this up."

Huggins said nothing. What was there to say?

For the first time, he let his eyes drift to the front door. It was no more than ten, twelve feet away.

There was at least a chance of reaching the door, then running out into the fog. Weather like this, they'd have a hell of a time finding him. They'd probably have hunting dogs around to help them look . . . but by that time he'd have made his own contact with the law and told them what was going on . . . how the blonde had lied about him . . . about how Roy and Phil had become judge and jury and jailer.

Roy said, "Mrs. Huggins? Mrs. David Huggins?"

Silence.

"Is David home, ma'am?"

Silence.

"I see. On his way to Des Moines, then."

Silence.

"No, no, thank you, ma'am. No message. I'll just try him a little later tonight."

He didn't even think about it. He just did it.

One moment he was still spread-eagled in front of the cash register.

The next he was running toward the back, toward the pay phone, shouting, "I'm at the Bluebird Café, Cindy! Call the cops! Call the cops!"

But he wasn't fast enough.

He'd been able to blurt out only one or two words . . . when Roy hung up.

Huggins was sure that Cindy hadn't heard him at all.

He sensed—then heard—Phil coming up behind him.

Though he'd never been much of a fighter, Huggins spun around and went into a crouch just as Phil delivered a roundhouse right hand.

The punch missed by several inches.

Instinctively, Huggins took the moment and brought his knee straight up between Phil's legs.

Phil's scream had an alien, animal-like quality to it as he crumpled to the floor, grasping his crotch.

Huggins ran straight to the booth where Marcia Quinn sat. He pushed Ellie aside so he could get to Marcia better.

Marcia started to work herself backward in the booth, as if she might try to scale the wall. Her eyes showed her fear.

"Stop him! Stop him!" she screamed.

"Tell them the truth," Huggins said. "Tell them that I didn't even stop to pick you up."

But Marcia, never one to miss a dramatic moment, picked up her butter knife and waved it in front of Huggins as he leaned in to shout in her face.

"Stay back!" she said.

By now Ellie had regained her flat-footed strength and grabbed Huggins around the neck, getting him in a very effective choke hold.

She was big enough and strong enough to kill him. And nobody seemed inclined to stop her.

He didn't have any choice. She was a woman, true, but she was also one of his chief persecutors. There was only one way to stop her.

He knifed an elbow deep into her ribs and the side of her stomach.

Her grip didn't lessen at all.

He felt himself gasping for air, his entire body beginning to writhe as oxygen was being cut off.

He slammed his elbow into her ribs a second time, much harder.

He could instantly feel her arms loosen a bit as her brain registered the shock of his elbow.

She cursed him.

And redoubled her effort.

"Tole you that was one gal who could take care of herself," Phil said.

Roy laughed. "Guess you were right."

For them, this was professional wrestling, and the best sort of all—a big farm woman kicking the hell out of a small city fella.

This time, he gave her the double whammy: His elbow again

found her ribs and stomach. And this time the heel of his shoe also found the center of her lower leg.

She cried out when the kick came.

Her grip loosened enough that he was able to wrench himself away from her and grab Marcia Quinn by the front of her red windbreaker.

"Tell them the truth!" he shouted. "The joke's over! You've paid me back enough!"

But Marcia just sat there staring at him. She said, very quietly, "You were going to rape me. You told me you were."

He sensed them coming up behind him again, Roy and Phil, and this time he decided *he'd* be the aggressor.

He turned around and smashed Phil in the face. Phil wasn't the one who cried out. Huggins was. From years of watching TV, he'd gotten the impression that slugging somebody else was pretty easy. All you did was take a swing and let go. What nobody had told him about was how your knuckles hurt—hell, your whole hand—when it came in contact with the solid bone of jaw.

Phil smiled. "You candy-ass."

Phil was a lot more used to be being hit than Huggins was to hitting.

Roy came for him now, too. "Just relax, Huggins. You're starting to get hysterical."

"I want you to call the law right now."

Roy said, "That's probably a good idea."

Phil looked sharply at his partner, as if Roy had just suggested something exceedingly stupid.

"We can take care of him," Phil said.

"Go call Rick Shay," Roy said.

Phil didn't look happy. But he walked to the back and made the call.

"I want her to give a sworn statement," Huggins said, "that I tried to hurt her in any way."

"Hard to prove," Roy said, sounding skeptical. "Your word against hers. And, friend, I'd take her word any day."

"If she was really in my car," Huggins said, "they'll be able to find footprints from her hiking boots and pieces of her hair and strands from her red jacket."

As he finished talking, he glanced at Marcia Quinn. "And she'll have to lie to an officer of the law. Then she'll be in a lot of trouble."

She just stared at him. Said nothing.

"I'd also advise you and your geek friend back there to keep your hands off me." He nodded to Ellie. "Same with you. You don't have any legal right to hurt me in any way. When your lawman gets here, you're all going to be in trouble."

"The fact is," Ellie said, "you're still the Highway Killer. Still the guy who stabbed Charlene and them other girls."

"No, I'm not," Huggins said. "I'm a salesman driving to Des Moines. I probably wasn't much of a gentleman to turn Marcia down for a ride. But that's all I'm guilty of."

One of the kitchen men said, "Maybe he's tellin' the truth, Roy."

"My ass he's tellin' the truth," Phil said. "And we got this young college gal here to prove it."

Pain still radiated up from Huggins' punch-damaged kidney. The sense of unreality was back again, too. This still had the dimensions and feel of a nightmare. Or of a terrible and cosmic practical joke.

The dark gods were working overtime today.

"You just go over there and sit down," Roy said, pointing to the counter. "And keep your mouth shut."

There was no point in arguing. Huggins did what he was told. The law would be here soon and this would all be over. He'd be on his way to Des Moines again.

He went over and sat down.

"Do you think I could use your bathroom?" Marcia Quinn said, really playing up her helpless-female routine.

"Sure, hon," Ellie said. "You think you can walk back there by yourself?"

"I think so," Marcia said.

Academy Award performance, Huggins thought bitterly.

The performance got even better when she stood up and walked to the rest room in the back.

She walked as if she'd been shot six or seven times. Or maybe eight.

"You don't think she's faking it at least a little?" Huggins said.

"Shut up," Phil said.

"Damn right shut up," Ellie said. "Or I'll get you in that choke hold again, you sonofabitch."

Marcia Quinn wasn't about to let down her fans.

When she reached the jukebox, she suddenly lurched to the right, clinging to the glass of the big music machine.

"Aw, hon," Ellie said, hurrying to the back to help her new friend.

"You sumbitch," Phil said. "Look what you done to that gal."

"Same thing he done to Charlene," Ellie said, " 'cept he didn't stab her."

"He would've," Phil said, "if she hadn't jumped out of his car."

Ellie got Marcia into the rest room. The poor dear was probably going to need surgery, the way she was carrying on.

"I thought you called the police," Huggins said to Phil.

"You just stand there and shut up."

Huggins looked toward the small man who worked in the kitchen, the one who'd suggested that maybe Marcia Quinn wasn't telling the truth. He appeared to be Mexican. There were a lot of illegals in this part of the state because of the coming harvest.

"She's lying," Huggins said, knowing he sounded desperate. "She really is."

The kitchen man looked away. He obviously didn't want to be associated with Huggins. He probably regretted speaking up in the first place. Everybody in the café seemed absolutely certain that Marcia Quinn was telling the truth. Only a fool wanted to stand up against everybody that way.

"She really is lying," Huggins said.

"You get back in the kitchen, Juan."

"Yes, Miss Ellie."

This time Huggins heard the accent in the man's voice. A Mexican in this part of the country, he'd probably sympathized with Huggins' situation. Mexicans still didn't have many liberties out here. And right now, Huggins didn't either.

Juan disappeared into the kitchen.

Inside the rest room, the toilet flushed explosively. Then the sound of water pipes engaging could be heard.

Roy and Phil still stared hard at Huggins.

Where the hell was the local law? What was keeping them so long? They were Huggins' last hope. A good law officer would have a lot of questions for Marcia Quinn.

The rest room door opened. Marcia Quinn reappeared, and Ellie rushed to help her. Marcia was forgetting her acting continuity. This time she was limping on her left foot. She hadn't been limping before. Not that anybody seemed to notice. They were too busy glowering at Huggins.

Ellie and Quinn were just reseating themselves in the booth when Huggins heard the sound of a car in the parking lot.

The fog was so heavy, he couldn't see anything. Just hear a car door opening and chunking shut. New car. Had to be, the way the door closed so nice and tight.

Now everybody was looking at the front door.

A man in a khaki uniform filled it. Literally. He had to run six-three, six-four and weigh two-fifty.

He opened the door and came inside. He walked that kind of slant-walk, body at a slight angle, that most people associated with John Wayne. The rest of him suggested the Old West, too, the burning blue eyes beneath the heavy shelf of brow; the taut, hard line of mouth; and the large, wide jaw.

From his waist hung a Sam Browne belt packed tight with a large, holstered Magnum; a night stick that looked vicious enough to bring a deadly animal to heel; a small walkie-talkie; and enough fine, new shiny bullets to start a war.

He walked over to Roy and Phil and said, "I sure hope this was important, boys. You dragged me out of a town council meeting."

"Oh, it's important, all right, Rick," Phil said. Then nodded to Huggins.

Huggins said, "I want to bring charges against these men."

He knew how desperate and weak he sounded—almost hysterical—but he didn't care.

"Who's this?" Rick Shay said.

"Name's Huggins," Roy said. "Least that's what it says on his license."

"He tried to kill her," Ellie blurted from the booth. "Same as he killed Charlene."

With the mention of Charlene, Rick Shay's face got even tighter and he looked at Huggins with even harsher scrutiny.

"That true?" Shay said.

"No, it isn't true," Huggins said, still sounding desperate. "She's just mad because I wouldn't give her a ride. That's why she made all this up. To get back at me."

"A ride?"

"She was hitchhiking, officer."

This kind of guy, Huggins figured he'd wanted to be called "officer."

"But you didn't give her one?"

"No, I didn't."

"Why not?"

Huggins averted his eyes a moment. "This is going to sound stupid."

"Let me decide that."

Rick Shay sounded a lot smarter than he looked, thank God.

"Well, I'd usually give a woman a ride, especially on a nasty day like this one."

"So why didn't you?"

"Because she reminded me of Lavonne."

"Who's Lavonne?"

"My old college girlfriend."

"I see."

"Lavonne and I didn't end up on real friendly terms."

"She dump you?"

Huggins shrugged. "I guess you could say that."

"So you didn't pick her up, this girl Roy and Phil are talking about?"

"She's right here, Rick," Ellie said, nodding to Marcia, next to her in the booth.

"No, I didn't."

"She never got in your car?"

Thank God. These were the kinds of law-enforcement questions that Huggins had been wanting to hear.

"No, sir, officer, she didn't."

"All right, sir. You just wait right there."

"I want to say something else," Huggins said.

"Oh?"

"Roy and Phil. They hit me several times."

"Roy and Phil. These two?"

"Right," Huggins said, knowing he sounded more like wuss-of-the-year than ever. "Well, I mean technically, it was Phil who hit me."

"Technically?"

"Roy was giving the orders. Phil was carrying them out."

"He was trying to escape, Rick," Roy said.

"He sure was," Phil said.

"We were all afraid he was going to get violent," Ellie said.

"I'll get back to this later," Rick said. "Right now I want to talk to the girl. Ellie, how about you getting me a cup of coffee?"

Nice, cool, professional.

Huggins knew this wasn't over yet for sure. But he felt better now that a competent lawman was on the scene.

Rick slid into the booth across from Marcia Quinn.

"Morning, ma'am."

"Morning," she said. "I'm real sorry for all this trouble."

Now she was playing the innocent schoolmarm in an old-fashioned Western.

He took out a small notebook he carried in the pocket behind his badge.

He then took out an expensive ballpoint and snicked it into action.

"Your name?"

"Marcia Quinn."

"Middle name?"

"Anne."

"Age?"

"Twenty-two."

"Occupation?"

"I'm a junior at Drake."

"In Des Moines?"

"Yes."

"And you were on your way back to school?"

"Yes."

"Do you normally hitchhike?"

"No. I was driving back with my boyfriend."

"And where is your boyfriend now?"

"Probably in Des Moines. We had an argument in the car."

"And he left you on the road?"

"It was as much my fault as his."

"I see."

"He's actually a very nice guy."

"I'm sure he is." He wrote something in his notebook, then looked up at Marcia. "Now I'll have to ask you some questions that'll probably make you uncomfortable."

"That's all right."

"You heard what he said. He said you didn't get in his car."

"That's not true. He pulled over to the side of the highway and"—she gulped, cast her eyes down to the table, as if it was all simply too-too much to remember—"I started to get in the car and he whipped out his knife and grabbed me and—"

"Just a moment, ma'am." Rick Shay looked over at Roy and Phil. "Did anybody search Mr. Huggins?"

"I did," Phil said proudly.

"You find anything?"

"No, I sure didn't, Rick."

"You search him carefully?"

"He did, Rick," Roy said. "I taught him how to search people the way I learned in the auxiliary police."

"And you didn't find anything, Phil?"

"Nothin'."

Ellie brought Rick Shay his coffee. Rick thanked her and then picked up the white cup in one massive hand.

"So he didn't let you get in the car?"

"No, because when I looked in and saw him, I decided not to take a ride after all."

"So you didn't get in the car?"

"Well, I think I started to sit down. I mean, I may've sat down on the seat but—"

Marcia teared up.

Huggins had to give it to her. She belonged in Hollywood.

No doubt about it.

"I don't remember exactly."

"But you do remember that he had a knife?"

"Yes."

"Do you know what kind of knife it was?"

"What kind?"

"The style, I mean."

"I'm not sure what you're talking about."

"Was it long?"

"I think so."

"Did it have a white handle or a black handle?"

"White, I think."

"Did he try and pull you in the car?"

"No, he didn't," Marcia Quinn said. "He jumped out at me. I guess he felt safe because of the fog."

"So he jumped out of the car and then what?"

"He got me on the ground."

"Was he hitting you?"

"Not really. But he was holding the knife to my throat."

"Was he touching you sexually?"

"Oh, yes. All over."

"Did he try to unzip your Levi's?"

"Yes."

"Were you fighting him?"

"As hard as I could. The knife really scared me."

"But you managed to get away from him?"

"Yes, sir," she said, shuddering. "Yes, sir, I did."

"Did he come after you?"

"I don't remember."

"Where did you go?"

"Just ran. I'm not sure where. I kept falling down. Every time I did, I figured he'd catch up with me."

"But he didn't?"

"No. I didn't see him again after I ran away. Not until I got in here."

"In the café?"

"Yes."

He wrote a few more things in his notebook and said, "Anything you want to add?"

"I'd just like to get going."

"To Des Moines?"

"Yes."

"I don't blame you."

He looked over at Huggins. "Sounds like you've been a very busy boy, Mr. Huggins."

"She's lying."

"And you can prove that?"

"Yes, I can. You won't find any evidence of her being in my car. No fibers, no hairs."

"I see. Scientific evidence, you mean."

"Yes."

Huggins watched curiously as the lawman pushed himself to his feet, adjusted his Sam Browne, glanced back at Ellie, and said, "Good coffee, missy."

"Thanks, Rick."

"And I enjoyed meeting you, ma'am."

"Thank you."

He turned and faced Huggins fully. Then he took five very large steps, until he stood about two feet away.

"I guess they didn't tell you, huh?" he said.

"Tell me what?"

"They mention a little gal named Charlene?"

"Yeah, Ellie did. I guess that Highway Killer got her."

"Yeah," Rick said. "The Highway Killer."

He stared directly into Huggins' eyes as he spoke. "The Highway Killer. About the most chicken-shit creature I've ever heard about, you ask my opinion. Snatchin' gals that way, then cuttin' them up the way he does."

Huggins felt himself start to tremble. His bowels were doing cold and slithery and distasteful things. "I'm not the man you want, officer. I'm really not."

He felt claustrophobic again. Closed in by the fog. The café. The people who hated him so much.

"Guess they didn't tell you anything about me and Charlene, huh?" Rick Shay said.

"No; no, they didn't."

"We were going to be married three weeks after she died."

"Oh, God."

"I been waiting to meet you for a long time, you bastard."

With that, he pulled out his nightstick. It seemed to shine like Excalibur in the dusty light of the café.

"A long time," Rick Shay said.

He knew just how to do it, Rick Shay did. Just how to hit.

First the left knee, Huggins crying out and starting to sink to the floor. Then the elbow, right on the very tip of it, Huggins blind now with pain, grabbing at his elbow as he started to collapse. Then the shoulder. Right on the corner of it.

"Give it to him, Rick!" Ellie shouted. "Give it to him good!"

"Damn right," Phil said.

Rick Shay went to the right knee this time, cracking the stick downward, at an expert angle, so the kneecap felt as if it was exploding.

Huggins screamed. He no longer cared about looking like a wuss.

"No! Don't hit him anymore!"

Huggins was too busy with his pain to notice what was happening. He grabbed the edge of a chair and let himself sink downward.

"I made it all up!" Marcia Quinn said. "Honest to God, Officer Shay, this is all my fault."

Huggins looked up now, saw Marcia push herself out of the booth and past the formidable Ellie.

She came over to him and put her small white hand on his bruiser of an arm. The arm that yielded the nightstick.

"I was just mad that he wouldn't give me a ride," she said. "I just wanted to make him sweat a little. But it got out of hand so fast—"

She walked over to Huggins now. "I'm really sorry, Mr. Huggins. I really am. I don't blame you for being mad."

"Just get the hell out of my sight."

"I really don't blame you for hating me. I'd hate me, too."

"Just get the hell away from me."

"I really do apologize, Mr. Huggins. I really do."

Huggins, still very much in pain, said, "Every one of you in this café is going to be in a lot of trouble with the law. Including you, Shay. If you thought I was guilty, you should've taken me in. I wasn't resisting arrest at all. There wasn't any need to hit me."

"She was my fiancée," Rick Shay said. "What the hell did you expect me to do?"

Ellie came up and stood next to Marcia Quinn. "I can't believe you lied to us this way. And about somethin' so important."

She didn't wait for Marcia to apologize or explain, Ellie didn't. She cocked her right hand back and drove a punch deep into the fetching face of the young woman. Blood burst from Marcia's nose. She immediately began sobbing.

"Little bitch," Phil said. "Kick her ass, Ellie. She's got it coming."

The irony wasn't lost on Huggins. They didn't much care who they pushed around. They were just as happy to start working Marcia Quinn over . . . and forget all about Huggins.

Much as he didn't want to, Huggins saw that he would have to help Marcia.

No way he was going to leave her here with these violent hayseeds.

"Leave her alone," Huggins said to Ellie.

"Punch her face in," Phil said.

"You're in one hell of a lot of trouble, young lady," Rick Shay said. "I'll tell you that much for sure."

Marcia Quinn was angry, humiliated, terrified. "Aren't you going to arrest her?" she demanded, putting napkins to her nose to stop the bleeding.

"I'll tell you who I *am* going to arrest," Rick Shay said. "And that's you."

"The hell you are," Huggins said, getting wearily to his feet.

His entire body ached. Every step was torture.

He walked over to Marcia Quinn and put his hand on her arm in a clearly possessive way.

"I'm going to make a deal with you folks," Huggins said, "and you'd damned well better take it." He didn't give them a chance to say anything. "I could bring serious charges against every one of you—just the way you could bring charges against Marcia. So we'll call it a draw. I'm going to forget about everything, and so are you. And right now Marcia and I are going to walk out that front door. Does everybody understand that?"

"I'm the law here," Rick Shay said.

"Not right now you're not," Huggins said. "I've got a friend in the state attorney's office. Once he hears about your little example of hillbilly justice, you and all your 'auxiliary deputies' are going to be out of a job."

"Maybe he's right, Rick," Roy said. "Plus you've still got those brutality charges against you and—"

"Shut up," Rick said.

"So you won't bring any charges against anybody here?" Rick said.

"Not if you let Marcia and me walk out that door."

"She deserves to get her ass kicked," Ellie said.

"Yes, she does," Huggins said. "But not by you or Rick. Or Roy or Phil."

He nodded to the door. "Now we're going to walk out of here and nobody's going to try to stop us."

"I've got your word about not bringing any charges?" Rick Shay said.

"You've got my word," Huggins said. "Now I want to walk the hell out of here. And right now."

Rick Shay said, "You go right ahead, Mr. Huggins."

Shay glanced at the others. "Nobody's going to try to stop you, isn't that right, folks?"

They all nodded silently, sullenly.

All their fun was walking out the door.

Now they'd only have townspeople to beat up on.

Huggins gripped Monica's arm, urging her to the door.

"You didn't have any right to hit me," Monica said to Ellie.

"Slut," Ellie said.

Huggins pushed her forward.

Marcia finally got the message and started walking quickly to the front door.

Huggins grabbed the handle, yanked the door back, and half pushed her out to the parking lot.

"Hurry, dammit," he said.

"She didn't have any right to hit me," Monica said.

"Just keep quiet."

The fog was thicker than before. Damp, slimy, wrapping and roiling around them.

"I can't even see your car," Monica said.

Huggins led the way.

He found his car by running into its back fender.

He got the door open and pushed her inside.

"What the hell's the hurry?" she said.

"Before they change their minds," Huggins said. "Unless you want to spend some more time with them."

"I guess you're right."

Huggins slammed the passenger door then walked around and got in the driver's side.

She looked over at him and gave him a little smile. Not even a bloody nose could take the shine from her good looks. "I guess you ended up giving me a ride anyway."

"Yeah," he said. "I guess I did."

He started the engine.

"Will you be able to drive all right in this fog?"

"I'll just have to keep my headlights on and drive very slowly," Huggins said. "I just want to get the hell away from here."

He started his foggy trek, moving at ten miles per hour. As they reached the road, the fog started to thin enough so that he could see the center line down the asphalt that led to the interstate.

"I don't blame you for hating me."

"You said that already."

"I just thought it'd be funny."

"Yeah. Hilarious."

"I didn't have any idea it'd get that far out of hand. Then I got afraid to speak up. Afraid they'd turn on me, you know?"

"Yeah," he said. "I know all about being afraid."

"I really am sorry."

"Right."

"Just imagine," she said, laughing just a little bit, obviously trying to calm herself down. "Just imagine if you'd really been carrying some kind of knife when Phil was searching you."

He leaned down so that his right hand could reach his shoe. People who searched you never thought to look in your shoes.

"You mean like this one?" Huggins said, bringing up the pearl-handled switchblade with the eight-inch blade.

"Oh, my God," she said. "The blade is serrated. Then you really are—"

"—the Highway Killer," he finished for her.

"Oh, my God," she said.

"Yes," Huggins said, at last finding some humor in this whole situation. "Oh, my God."

Les Roberts is both a critic and an author. His books are invariably praised for their perceptive and seriocomic social observations, and for their smoothly rolling plots. Here he is with an exceptionally good story, a wry retelling of "The Brave Little Tailor."

LES ROBERTS

The Brave Little
Costume Designer

Oliver Jardiniere left his job in the wardrobe room of the Martin
Beck Theatre at ten-thirty that evening with a spring in his step
that was almost a skip. It may be argued that Oliver walked that
way all the time, but tonight was special. Having agonized over
suitable outfits for the seven dancing chorus boys in the new
Broadway musical he was costuming, tonight he had come up with
a single design, varying only in color and fabric, that would do for
all of them. It would save him long hours making sketches and
sewing and doing trial-and-error fittings, and perhaps most important, it would stop the seven of them from buzzing all over his
costume shop like rapacious flies, begging and entreating and
demanding.

He'd now completed all the designs for the show, and the creative part of the job was done. He felt a little sad and let down on
top of his elation. Finishing a show was almost like leaving home
for the first time.

He turned toward the river on West Fifty-third Street toward
the little spaghetti joint where he'd arranged to meet his current
companion, Lot, for a late supper. Thinking of Lot, Oliver's walk
slowed just a tad; the relationship wasn't going well. It wasn't going
well at all. It wasn't Lot's fault, really—it was simply that the magic
was gone.

Once inside the restaurant, with dinner and wine ordered, Oliver breathlessly told Lot, who had suffered through the past

week's aborted designs and discarded ideas with him, the happy news.

"I did it! I actually did it! I took care of all seven of them at one time," he said. "Bing-bing-bing-bing-bing!" And he made a pistol of his thumb and forefinger.

At the booth against the wall, Guglielmo "Little Guggie" Mazzarino, a loyal soldier in the army of Big Caesar Annunziato from Red Hook, tore his attention from the well-displayed cleavage of his dinner companion, one Debbie Marie Positano of West Forty-eighth Street in the neighborhood that was once called, for good reason, Hell's Kitchen, and took note of Oliver Jardiniere and what he was saying. Oliver was speaking so loudly and enthusiastically that Little Guggie couldn't help overhearing, and since he was uniquely familiar with the 'bing-bing-bing'' concept—and he didn't use his forefinger, either—he eavesdropped with undisguised interest.

Lot was excited for his roommate. "I don't believe it!" he said in a hushed tone.

"It wasn't that hard. I just kind of—sneaked up on them and—"

"My God, you have the guts of a burglar!" Lot enthused.

Little Guggie Mazzarino, straining to listen, leaned sideways toward the two men like a listing ship just before it sinks beneath the waves.

"It didn't take any guts," Oliver said. "The way to do it came to me all of a sudden, and I just went ahead and did it without worrying over it. Now those bastards won't ever bother me again!" He and Lot tinked glasses as the stuffed-shells-with-pesto arrived.

At the next table Little Guggie frowned. Had something gone down tonight that he didn't know about? If so, his employer, Big Caesar Annunziato, would be righteously pissed. And that was a consummation devoutly to be avoided. Little Guggie removed Ms. Positano's stockinged foot from where it rested in his crotch, went to the pay phone in the back of the restaurant, not being high enough up in the food chain to rate his own cellular, and called Big Caesar.

He was told that, indeed, on that very evening seven members of the rival DiGiralamo family had met with some misadventure in a warehouse down on the docks, involving a good deal of semi-automatic weapons fire engineered by a person or persons unknown, and when he informed Big Caesar that he believed the person or persons was at this moment slurping pesto sauce at Mama Angelina's, he was assured that if he knew what was good for him, he would bring said person forthwith to the Annunziato compound in Red Hook, Brooklyn.

And so it was that Oliver Jardiniere, Broadway costume maven, was entreated and coerced into leaving Lot in the middle of his tiramasu and accompanying Little Guggie from Mama Angelina's restaurant, his napkin still tucked under his chin like a bib. He was hustled into Little Guggie's black Oldsmobile Sierra and escorted to the home of Big Caesar Annunziato, where he was presented to the mob boss like a gift to the Christ Child.

Big Caesar was unimpressed at first, and suspicious of strangers. "I never seen you before," he gargled.

"We probably travel in different circles," Oliver explained.

"Where you come from?"

Since Oliver was always loath to tell people he hailed from Pierre, South Dakota—especially since when he pronounced it correctly, "Peer," nobody knew what in hell he was talking about—he named the place he'd lived for three years, working at the Flamingo Hotel, before coming to New York and cracking the big time.

"I'm from Las Vegas," he said.

"Vegas? What's your name?"

He wasn't about to admit that his name was really Albert Gardner—he had left that one behind in the dust of Pierre. Instead he said, "My friends call me Ollie."

Big Caesar sat up a little bit straighter in his chair. This must be the infamous Ollie the Ox—in the somewhat narrow world of gangdom a legend, a creature of nightmare, who was likely to turn up in Chicago one week, Miami the next, then Cleveland or Detroit—do his appointed deeds with discretion and dispatch, and disappear before anyone left standing knew he'd been there. And no one in any of the New York five families had ever seen him before.

Big Caesar could taste the canary feathers in his mouth.

But he couldn't let on; he had to play it tough, cool, careful, as though he didn't know he was talking to one of the foremost freelance enforcers in mobdom. "Vegas, huh? And you think you can just come walkin' in here on my turf and be the big shot, the big swingin' dick?"

Oliver pulled modestly at a forelock. "I've never had any complaints before," he offered.

Big Caesar and Little Guggie exchanged significant looks. An unknown shooter from Vegas could come in mighty handy for what Big Caesar had been turning over in his mind for months.

"You want to do a job for me?" he said, straightening his black bow tie. Big Caesar loved tuxedos—it was his wont to wear them on a nightly basis, even when he was staying home. And on this particular evening he was surrounded by four extremely attractive chorus girls, as was also his wont, late of the dancing ensemble of the most recent Broadway revival of *Guys and Dolls,* in which Big Caesar was a substantial, albeit silent investor. So Oliver can be forgiven for thinking he was a producer.

"Well—I just finished with my last job tonight. Why not?"

Oliver's very matter-of-factness about dispatching seven souls to the Big Trattoria in the sky sent chills up Big Caesar's hairy back. He was a cool one, Big Caesar'd give him that. Absolutely calm, almost condescending in his attitude. And he talked funny. Walked funny, too. Like no one Big Caesar had ever known. He shuddered again. But with the dispatch of seven major players in the DiGiralamo family, a unique opportunity was presenting itself—and Caesar had survived and prospered by taking advantage of such unique opportunities.

If he could somehow eliminate the heads of the the DiGiralamo and Pingitore families without becoming implicated himself, he, Big Caesar, could step in and fill the leadership vacuum.

"You come back here tomorrow night, nine o'clock, and I'll tell you all about it," he said. "And to show you my heart's in the right place . . ." He peeled ten bills off a roll and handed them to Oliver, who didn't realize they were hundreds until he got home and put them in a place Lot would never dream of looking, at the back of the vanity drawer where Oliver kept his daintiest underthings.

At nine o'clock the next night he presented himself to Big Caesar once more.

"Vinnie 'the Fox' DiGiralamo and Pasquale 'the Bull' Pingitore," Big Caesar intoned.

"Yes?"

"I want you should take care of them. You know—like you did those seven guys last night."

Oliver didn't know how Big Caesar had found out about his brilliant seven-for-one costume coup, but his own producer, Irving Shlepkowitz, had been thrilled not only with the concept but also with the substantial savings it entailed, and Oliver supposed that all producers had some sort of network through which they shared information, and that Irving had probably bragged to his producing colleague, Big Caesar, of the skill and cunning of his costume designer.

"Can I see a script?" he said. "I need a script, don't I? I can't just work in the dark."

"Improvise," Big Caesar suggested.

"All right, but that just makes it harder. Where can I find them?"

"They'll be at the Ristorante Palermo on MacDougal Street."

"Oh, God, the *Village!*" Oliver protested. "It's so tacky anymore, so unsoigné." When Big Caesar seemed unmoved, Oliver sighed a deep sigh. "Well, if I must, then. What kind of a budget are we talking about?"

"That's good," said Big Caesar. "A man like you wants to talk business first. I respect that." He went to his safe and pulled out three thick packets of bills bound in rubber bands. "There's thirty large here," he said, handing them over. "Do a good job. Nice and clean. And fast."

Oliver rolled his eyes ceilingward; producers were all the same. "Do you want it *fast?*" he said in the time-honored whine of creative artists everywhere, "or do you want it *good?*"

THE BRAVE LITTLE COSTUME DESIGNER

He didn't wait for an answer—the questions were rhetorical.

He took a cab from Red Hook to the Village, oblivious to the conversation his taxi driver attempted to engage him in about something mysteriously called the Nix. As in, "How 'bout the Nix?" or "You think the Nix got a chance this year?" Oliver had heard other New Yorkers speak of the Nix, but since he didn't know what it was, he declined to discuss it. He was too busy thinking about his most recent commission.

If Big Caesar was willing to spend thirty thousand dollars on just two costumes for Vinnie the Fox and Pasquale the Bull, what must the budget be for the entire show? Visions of tulle and ostrich plumes and shimmering metallic Mylar danced in Oliver's head.

He arrived at the Ristorante Palermo to find Vinnie the Fox and Pasquale the Bull in deep conversation in a back booth. Several large, uncouth-looking men rose to deny him access to them, but when he mentioned Big Caesar's name, like a magic password in a fairy tale, all resistance melted away. Big Caesar, Oliver thought, must be a very important producer, and he wondered idly why he'd never heard of him before.

One look told him that Pasquale the Bull, whose napkin, tucked under his chin, was stained with marinara sauce and a Valpolicella of an indifferent vintage, was going to be impossible. He was short and squat and must have weighed more than three hundred pounds, all of it gut, and he had a shiny bald pate to boot. He would look positively horrendous onstage, like a hippo in rut. Hopeless, Oliver thought. Unless . . .

Think black, Oliver said to himself, something long and flowing like a caftan or a djellaba in billowing silk. Think vertical stripes. Think platform heels.

Vinnie the Fox, however, was another story entirely—and it was a love story, at that. Vinnie the Fox was aptly named—tall, possessing the chiseled features of a young Tyrone Power, black wavy hair with an errant curl that fell across his forehead and made him appear vulnerable and in need of protection. Oliver was swept off his feet at first look, into a magical world full of glitter and soft-focus clouds and show tunes playing softly in the background.

This was it. The One. Big casino. Thoughts of Lot, and of his former soulmate, William, who had dumped him for a performance-art choreographer, were banished. Oliver was smitten, truly smitten, for the first time in his life.

Almost ignoring Pasquale the Bull Pingitore, he locked gazes with Vinnie the Fox, his own blue eyes sending laser messages into the soulful brown ones of his object of desire. He swooped, he fluttered, he flirted shamelessly, he flattered Vinnie on his breadth of shoulder, slimness of waist, depth of chest, his coloring, the way he carried his head, despite Vinnie's glossy Italian suit that made him look like a refugee from a Martin Scorcese film, and his too-thin and undistinguished gray tie. In his head he envisioned Vinnie in a suit of ecru linen, nipped at the waist and flared at the hips to emphasize the gladiatorlike physique, worn over a creamy lemon silk shirt, a solid mocha tie that would bring out Vinnie the Fox's eyes, a chocolate-brown Borsalino worn at a rakish angle over the forehead with ostrich-leather shoes dyed to match—Oliver would begin haunting fabric shops and specialty men's stores first thing in the morning. And then he fantasized the two of them in a large, exquisitely furnished penthouse with huge, slanted windows overlooking the lights of the East River, picturing himself slowly removing each item to eventually reveal the Olympian god beneath.

Vinnie DiGiralamo was a little overwhelmed. The scion of one of the five-state area's oldest crime families and one of the most dedicated womanizers on the Eastern Seaboard, he was more than used to being fussed over. But Oliver Jardiniere's attentions were new to him, and while they made him more than a little uncomfortable, the fulsome praise worked its way with him, and he found himself beaming in the sunshine of Oliver's adoration.

Pasquale the Bull, on the other hand, felt his irritation mounting, until he could taste for the second time the highly spiced sauce that had covered the fettuccine noodles of his recently eaten dinner. It wasn't as if he had any illusions about himself; his mirror told him every morning that he was a squat, ugly toad of a man. He simply resented having the fact pointed out to him, especially in front of his rival Vinnie the Fox, and soldiers from both their families. It was humiliating, and showed a lack of respect, and while Pasquale the Bull was noted for his habitual perspicacity, discretion, and even temper, the one thing he could not and would not abide was any disrespect to his person, his position, or his family. He signaled the waiter to bring another bottle of the Valpolicella, and when it arrived, he sent it back to the kitchen in a fit of pique, pronouncing it cat piss.

Oliver extracted a promise from Vinnie to meet him at noon the next day for luncheon and a fitting in his small West Side studio. He would have to move slowly, he thought, and carefully. This was no fling to Oliver, it was the beginning of a lifetime commitment of caring and sharing, and he didn't want to spoil things by coming on too strong. And there was the matter of Lot, of course, and of extricating himself from what had become a most unsatisfying liaison.

Then, remembering his commission from his producer, Big Caesar, he offhandedly assured Pasquale the Bull that he would be calling him for a fitting as well, and flowed out the door of the Ristorante Palermo into the night, his senses reeling happily, his libido simmering, his heart a veritable dancer inside his slim, frail chest.

"Big Caesar has some strange friends all of a sudden," Pasquale observed when the door had closed behind Oliver. He spoke quietly, but a flush of anger suffused his simian features.

"I thought he was very nice," Vinnie answered.

"He thought you were nice, too. I think he wants to do you."

"Excuse me?"

"He wants to do the job on you."

"Meaning no disrespect, Pasquale the Bull, but I think you're probably full of shit."

"All I'm saying is, the guy was coming on to you, and you were eating it up like it was your mother's *salsiccia.*"

"I hope, Pasquale, that you are meaning no disrespect to my mother, who, as you know, passed on three years ago. I hope, too, that what you are saying is not that I am the type of person which walks a little light in his loafers."

"All what I am saying, Vinnie, meaning no disrespect, is that you were certainly acting like a person which believes in fairies."

"I think, Pasquale, that you are meaning a lot of disrespect,"

Vinnie said, and upon the word he rose from his seat, pulled out his Sig-Sauer automatic, and blew a large hole right where Pasquale the Bull's eyebrows came together over the bridge of his nose.

At another table, Pasquale's twin cousins, Mongo and Mario, and his nephew Severio, upon observing Vinnie the Fox's ill-considered action, rose as one and cut Vinnie almost in half with fire from their .357 Magnums. This caused several members of the DiGiralamo contingent in a booth across the restaurant, already nervous and on edge because of the slaughter of seven of their compadres in a waterfront warehouse the previous evening, to stand up and fire their weapons as well.

The guns roared like thunder, a total of fifty-three times, and when it was all over, eight men lay dead on the floor of the Ristorante Palermo, leaving the establishment's proprietor-chef, Paolo Bacciagalupe, wringing his hands and wondering (a) who was going to clean up the mess, (b) who would pay for the broken dishes and the repair of the bullet holes in the walls, and (c) what in hell he was going to tell the cops when they arrived.

Noon of the following day arrived and departed, leaving Oliver heartsick and disillusioned. The cucumber-and-watercress sandwiches he had prepared so lovingly, even cutting the crusts off himself, the Earl Grey tea, the one red rose in a slender bud vase on the tray had all gone for naught. It became obvious that Vinnie the Fox had stood him up.

He could at least have called, Oliver sniffed. And after he'd gone home from the Ristorante Palermo the previous evening and told Lot that he'd have to move out by the end of the week, too.

With slumping shoulders and heavy heart, he was clearing away what would have been a romantic luncheon, when the door to his studio was flung open and Big Caesar Annunziato came bursting in, followed by Little Guggie Mazzarino and two chorus girls whom Oliver had actually seen before but didn't recognize without their stage makeup and cat drag.

"What a guy!" Big Caesar enthused, taking Oliver's face between his two meaty hands and kissing him on the mouth. "What a guy! Not only Vinnie and Pasquale, but their soldiers, too. A genius!" he said, kissing Oliver again. Then he lowered his voice to a more respectful tone. "No. Not a genius. *An artist!* Didn't I say that this morning as soon as I heard, Guggie? What'd I say?"

"You said 'an artist,' Big Caesar," Little Guggie parroted.

"But I didn't even do anything yet," Oliver protested.

"Listen to this guy, will you? Modest on top of it. Lemme tell you a little secret, Ollie. In this world, you gotta toot your own flute, otherwise nobody's gonna toot it for you."

As Oliver pondered the physical improbability of tooting his own flute and the depressing possibility that no one would do it for him, Big Caesar took his face between his mitts again and squeezed his cheeks, causing his lips to pucker like Tweety Pie's in the cartoons.

"Whatsa matter? You look like you lost your best friend."

Oliver considered telling him, but decided Big Caesar might not be the person who would give him the most sympathetic hearing. "I'm depressed," he said. "It's a—a relationship thing."

"Hey, hey, hey! Shine it! There's a million more where that one came from, especially for a guy like you."

At that moment a brilliant thought fired the synapses in Big Caesar's brain, lighting them up like one of the pinball machines the profits from which in all the five boroughs and Connecticut found their way into Big Caesar's pockets. It was even a better idea than the one he'd had to wipe out Vinnie the Fox and Pasquale the Bull in one fell swoop.

As with most men who share Big Caesar's ethnicity, the idea of family, of royal succession, was vitally important to him. And yet the good Lord had never seen fit to bless him and his wife with a male child, or even a nephew, to whom he could someday pass on the mantle of *capo di tutti capi,* boss of bosses. All he had in the way of issue was one daughter, Benita, who was named for Big Caesar's own personal hero, Il Duce, the former dictator of Italy, and who, being something of a nymphomaniac, was singularly ill-suited to run the Annunziato family when Big Caesar finally met his reward.

And yet there was this empire he had created—dope and policy and gambling and prostitution, to say nothing of the seafood importing company that laundered all the money he made off the rest—that would surely pass out of the Annunziato family for lack of male succession, just as the throne of England had slipped through the fingers of the Tudors upon the death of Henry VIII.

Big Caesar's idea, which had begun as a tiny speck, grew bigger and bigger inside his head until it threatened to explode.

"Ollie," he said, almost unable to contain his glee, "I want you should come to the house tonight for dinner. Seven o'clock."

"Sharp," Little Guggie added. When Big Caesar was around, Little Guggie always tried to act the tough guy.

So it was that at seven o'clock sharp, Oliver Jardiniere stepped out of a taxi in front of the Annunziato house in Red Hook. He was admitted through the wrought-iron gate and subjected to a full-body frisk by two of Big Caesar's employees, a process he rather enjoyed, and was then ushered into the dining room, where he found Big Caesar with a proud arm around his daughter, Benita.

Benita didn't want to be there at all—for two reasons. The first was that she would have much preferred spending her evening with Sean Malone, a young dockworker who had a shock of red hair and a face that might have come right out of the Book of Kells, and who was the latest in a long line of inappropriate young men whose brains Benita was boffing out. The second was, her father had informed her with undue emphasis, that this night she was to meet the man he wanted her to marry.

Oliver wasn't bad-looking at all, Benita decided—if you like the effete, willowy type, which she did not. But like everyone else in Brooklyn, and most of Manhattan and Queens as well, she knew better than to cross Big Caesar once he'd set his mind to something.

The dinner was a work of art, the centerpiece of which was a seafood risotto cooked by Paolo Bacciagalupe, who was working as Big Caesar's personal chef while his own restaurant in the Village was shut down for repairs and a thorough cleaning. The wine flowed as freely as Big Caesar's praise of Oliver; he was trying hard to "sell" Benita on the idea of marrying the young man and keeping the family business within the family.

When the plate of biscotti and pastilles was down to mere crumbs, Big Caesar expansively suggested that the two young people "go for a nice walk or something" to get better acquainted. Oliver, who was feeling stuffed, thought a walk would settle his dinner, and agreed.

So he and Benita, followed at a discreet distance by Little Guggie and two more of Big Caesar's handpicked janissaries, strolled the streets of Red Hook in the orange gloaming. Since the warmth of the day had faded along with the sunshine, Benita had donned a cape she'd bought at Bloomie's and a gray snap-brim fedora that had once belonged to her father. She thought she looked pretty sharp.

"You're awfully quiet," she finally said after they'd walked a few blocks. "Is anything wrong?"

"I hate who does your hats," Oliver told her.

"What's wrong with my hat?"

"It looks like something Humphrey Bogart left behind on the set after they'd finished principal photography on *The Maltese Falcon*," he replied. "I see you in something softer, something that will bring out the symmetry of your pretty face and highlight your hair. A beret, perhaps, for casual wear, and one of those little Peter Pan hats with a feather for when you go out in the evening. And the cape—the cape has to go. Why hide that beautiful figure under a shapeless cape? Tell you what—first thing in the morning I'll do some sketches for you, and we can look at them and you can decide."

Benita's heart melted. Growing up motherless in the Annunziato family, surrounded by Big Caesar's hitters and shooters and button men, she had never before met a male who had a lick of fashion sense. She decided then and there to put herself in Oliver's capable hands for a total makeover. From then on, the two were inseparable. Oliver realized that, for reasons he knew not of, he had fallen into some high, fragrant clover.

Three months later they were married before the altar at St.

Rocco's Church in Red Hook, with Benita resplendent in a bridal gown Oliver had designed and sewed especially for her. Everyone from the Annunziato side of the family agreed they'd never seen a more beautiful—or more tastefully dressed—bride.

Immediately after the ceremony and the reception, which yielded more cash-stuffed envelopes than Oliver had ever seen before, the happy couple flew to St. Bart's for their honeymoon, a wedding gift from Benita's father.

On the bridal night, Benita emerged demurely from the bathroom of their hotel suite clad in a black bustier, matching garter belt and hose, and a pair of crotchless panties, an ensemble that, in her single days, had never failed to make Sean Malone go ballistic. But to her astonishment, her bridegroom remained unimpressed.

To move things along a bit, Benita stretched out on the bed next to him and told him in no uncertain terms exactly what she wanted him to do to her. He reacted in a fashion that was, to her, very surprising.

"Who'd want to do *that?*" Oliver said, crinkling his nose in distaste, and rolled over and went to sleep.

After two solid weeks of this, it finally dawned on Mrs. Benita Annunziato Jardiniere exactly what was wrong. Upon their return to New York, where they took up residence in a penthouse in an upper Fifth Avenue co-op that normally refused to admit theater people, Catholics, or anyone whose surname ended in a vowel until Big Caesar made the screening committee an offer they couldn't refuse, Benita took a taxi all the way out to Red Hook and told her father of her disappointment.

Big Caesar raged. He stormed. He bellowed. He shouted and stomped and put his fist through the glass of a faux Louis Quatorze breakfront he'd ordered from Macy's several years earlier for the dining room. Not knowing where to direct his anger and mortification at having been fooled, having lost face, having been disrespected by a man to whom he'd not only deeded his hard-won empire but also to whom he'd given his only child, a man who apparently regularly committed that sin we dare not name, he fired his housekeeper, old Mrs. Sidotti, who had been with the family for thirty-six years. He had his cat, Serafina, put to sleep. It was only after Little Guggie begged and entreated and invoked the name of the Blessed Mother herself that he was dissuaded from having the legs of Monsignor LaRussa, who had performed the wedding ceremony, broken in several places.

He bade Benita go upstairs to her old room, which still had several dolls and stuffed animals on the bed and a poster of Billy Idol affixed to the wall with Scotch tape. Then Caesar, raging for revenge with Ate by his side come hot from hell, took the BMT to Manhattan by himself—the first time in twenty-four years he had gone out of his house alone. He transferred to an uptown subway, got off at Columbus Circle, and hailed a cab, which took him across Central Park to the co-op where Oliver awaited him, all innocence.

"Dad!" Oliver said when he answered the door, and threw open his arms for an embrace. Instead, Big Caesar punched him right in the mouth, sending him stumbling backward across the Aubusson rug, banging into a Queen Anne end table, and sending a Tiffany lamp crashing to the floor in pieces.

As Oliver sat there, his back against the sofa, gently fingering his bloody lip, Big Caesar proceeded to tell him exactly what he thought of him, calling him every bad name in the book and a few that weren't even in there.

"You made a monkey outta me, Nancy-boy," he rumbled. "And nobody makes a monkey outa Big Caesar Annunziato."

Upon the word, Big Caesar slowly put his hand inside his jacket for the automatic pistol with which he'd vowed to send Oliver to hell. His movements were tantalizingly deliberate and precise, because he wanted Oliver to feel the fear, to sweat and plead and beg before he blew him away.

But Oliver was faster. Reaching under his silk caftan, which he'd made for himself with some material left over from a production of *La Cage aux Folles* he'd costumed at a dinner theater in New Jersey, he pulled out his own .22 pistol, which he had carried ever since three gay-bashing hooligans beat him up coming out of a leather bar in TriBeCa several months before. With it, he shot

Big Caesar in the throat, some eight inches lower than he'd hoped. Big Caesar staggered, fell, and died gurgling.

Then Oliver stanched the bleeding of his lip, dressed himself in one of the twelve Armani suits he'd purchased with the bounty paid him for Vinnie the Fox and Pasquale the Bull, called down for the doorman to summon him a taxi, and went out to Red Hook to reclaim his bride and to announce to the soldiers and underbosses and *capos* of the Annunziato family that, like Alexander Haig when Ronald Reagan was shot, he was in charge.

The marriage, I am happy to report, worked. Benita, who had never held much fondness for her father anyway, became known in gangland circles as the best-dressed mob wife in history, and since her husband didn't care one way or the other, resumed her affair with Sean Malone, and subsequently with a string of Sean Malone clones.

Oliver ran Big Caesar's crime family with a firm but gentle hand. He outlawed jeweled stickpins and pinkie rings for all his employees, and insisted rather forcefully that from now on they buy their clothes at Brooks Brothers. Instead of sleazy nightclubs in Brooklyn that featured pomaded Italian boy singers warbling "Chena Luna," once a week he took his most trusted lieutenants, foremost of whom was Little Guggie Mazzarino, to dinner at someplace elegant such as Le Cirque or Twenty One, and thence to the theater, usually to see a musical. After two years, Little Guggie knew all the lyrics to every song Stephen Sondheim ever wrote.

Since he had quickly gotten over the loss of Vinnie DiGiralamo, Oliver had no qualms about constructing a discreet relationship with one Sonny Donofrio, the beautiful young man who had served as the undertaker's assistant at Big Caesar's funeral. They remained together for seventeen years.

And since he'd never really been Ollie the Ox in the first place, Oliver became known throughout the underworld—and at One Police Plaza as well—as Ollie the Gent.

And so the little designer lived like a king all his lifetime.

Simon Brett's Charles Paris books have always sold well, but have never been taken as seriously as they deserve. For all their humor, they are the serious chronicling of a rather sad man's life in the crumbling theater world of contemporary London. It's foolish to try to predict which writer will last and which of their creations will last, but one secretly suspects that Charles Paris, for all of the humor and pathos he encounters, will outlive some of his more famous contemporaries. He takes a look at a most unusual type of mobster in an updated version of "The Emperor's New Clothes."

SIMON BRETT

THE EMPEROR'S
NEW CLOTHES

Some say he's called "Emp," like short for "Emperor"; others, 'cause it's the kind of rope he should wind up dangling at the end of. Me, I don't express an opinion. I live longer that way. The Santa Rosita graveyard's full of ginks who expressed opinions in Emp's earshot.

I try to keep out of his earshot. And his eyeshot. And, in particular, his gunshot. That's another way I live longer.

Sometimes I have to go up to his rudd and see him, though. He's my employer. We do business. I'm down at the lower end of Emp's setup, mind you. Not management, more shop floor. At least shop floors are what I nail store managers to, when they're a bit behind with their payments. Then the real heavy boys, the drodgers, come in. They do the thumping, the slabbering, and the stomping. I don't do that.

Early on, I had aspirations, thought I might graduate to the thumping, the slabbering, and the stomping. Now I'm content to stay where I am. It may not be challenging, but it's regular work, and I can do it. Also if you're a thumper, slabberer, and stomper, you have to report back to Emp at his rudd after each job. And Emp's the kind of blunto whose temper's so unpredictable, reporting back can be a risky operation. Few more cavities down Santa Rosita's are filled with ginks who reported back on the wrong day.

I admire Emp, though. And I'm not just saying that 'cause I'm afraid he might read this. I don't know that he can read, actually.

Least I've never seen him with a book. . . . No, I tell a lie—I did once see him knock an old froop's teeth out with a family Bible. But point I'm making is that Emp's favorite spare-time activity ain't literature. He favors more cosmetic pastimes—body-piercing, razor-shaping, doing the old manicure with the pliers. Not literature, anyway.

But I admire him because he's straight. Wrong word in one way . . . I mean he's as bent as a bamboo watch spring. He's as crooked as the soil pipe in a Turkish hotel. But in another way, Emp is straight. No messing. You always know where you're going to end up with him.

Lying down in Santa Rosita's. Or in very real danger of lying down in Santa Rosita's.

'Nother good quality he has—we are, you understand, using "good" in the widest possible sense here—is Emp listens to advice. May not always take it, but he does listen to it. Me, I don't give him advice. That's even riskier than expressing opinions.

Can pay off big, though, if you get it right. Choose the wrong day and you're displacing yet more earth down Santa Rosita's. Choose the right day and you're a rich man for life.

Let me give you an example. Few months back I had to go up to the rudd to see Emp two days on the trot. Not, as you've gathered, something I'd go out of my way to do. I value my digestion too much for that kind of kamikaze stuff. But needs must, certainly when Emp's grabbed hold of the steering wheel. He'd summoned me, and in those circumstances "no" is a word used only by the terminally tired of life.

So I was there the first day in the rudd's main room, doing my well-known impression of the wallpaper, hoping nobody could distinguish me from the vinyl chrysanthemums, and Emp's discussing with some of his drodgers what they're going to do to some old froop who's been pocketing the ding from his molasses jar.

So Emp—who, give him his due, always favors at least the illusion of consultation—sits there toying with his steeler and says, "I'm bored with all the old stuff. I need new nerve-tweakers. Anyone got any ideas?"

And this young scribber, who fancies himself going places,

pipes up, "Why don't you make him swallow a gasoline cocktail and light a cigarette?"

"Well, do you know," says Emp, slow as a snail with a limp, "that's the worst idea I've heard since the self-adhesive golf tee."

Up comes the steeler—boom, boom—and the scribber's doing a passable impersonation of a lead pencil.

Next day, I'm at the rudd again. Yesterday's old froop has been dealt with by one of the traditional methods—basic shish kebab without the peppers and onions—but there's a new old froop been pulling the same pirk, so we get like a replay.

Emp sits there once again toying with his steeler and says, "I'm bored with all the old stuff. I need new nerve-tweakers. Anyone got any ideas?"

And there's another young scribber there, and he also fancies himself as going places. I don't have to tell you he hadn't been there the day before, because he pipes up, "Why don't you make him swallow a gasoline cocktail and light a cigarette?"

Me and the drodgers—well, you can imagine—we make like we're ice cubes and wait to call in the ginks with the shovels.

"Well, do you know," says Emp, slow as a snail waiting for a hip replacement, "that's one of the best ideas I heard since the two-ended baseball bat. You two drodgers—go give the old froop his cocktail!"

And the young scribber, he gets given a Ferrari, four chorus girls, and a steeler disguised as a mobile phone.

Like I said, get the right day for expressing an opinion to Emp and you're a rich man for life.

Not actually that "life" was too long in the case of that particular scribber. Week later Emp tornadoes him for wanting two sugars in his coffee, but that detail doesn't change the point I'm making. Emp does sometimes take advice.

In fact, nearly everything he does, he does on advice. Sounds odd to say it of a frapper like Emp, but it's almost like he's unsure of himself. Like he daren't make a major decision without the authority of someone else having suggested it.

Alternative view, of course, is that, if the decision proves to be a wrong one, Emp's got someone to blame. He tornadoes the gink who gave him the idea, and he can get back to business with like a clean drawing board.

So I knew all about Emp and taking advice, but this occasional habit of his hadn't prepared me—nor none of the other drodgers—for what happened when he met Virgin Oil Vicario.

Now, they say the leopard can't change his spots, but Virgin Oil had sure done an effective paint job. Two years before, he'd been a major frapper—not up there with Emp, of course, but big. Good network of drodgers. Had tornadoed enough ginks to earn a degree of respect around town. And had pots of ding in his molasses jar.

Then suddenly he done this paint job on his spots. Like overnight. Virgin Oil claimed it was a St. Paul–style conversion, but, if so, most ginks reckoned it was closer to Minnesota than Damascus. He said he'd been "born again," but I figure it'd be easier to get toothpaste back in a tube than Virgin Oil back into a womb, however metaphorical.

My view, it was a pirk. Virgin Oil'd looked around, seen there were too many bluntos chasing too little ding in his current business, and made a career move. Reckoned if he set himself up on the chat-show and lecture-hall circuit, he'd clean up.

And he did. Number of times you'd see his caption flash up on the TV—"Born-Again Criminal Who Has Seen the Evil of His Ways"—tell you, it was more a frequent sight than that Nordic exercise machine.

He done the books, too. *Police Yourself; Good Self, Bad Self; Arrest the Criminal Inside Yourself; Forty-Eight Hours to a Reformed Character; The See-the-Light Diet.* And they sold. Sold and sold. Self-improvement's always gone down well, but few authors before had improved from such a low starting point as Virgin Oil Vicario.

Now, before Virgin Oil done his Damascus Road makeover, he and Emp coexisted in a kind of mutual respect situation. They were both big frappers, but most of their operations were in different parts of town, so there wasn't too much direct rivalry. They knew each other by reputation, but that was all. If they had met, obviously honor would have demanded they whip out their steelers and try to tornado each other. But that moment never arose while Virgin Oil was still a frapper.

So you could have described his decision to visit Emp—and carrying not even the tiniest foldaway steeler—as "brave." Other adjectives that might spring to mind could be "rash," "foolhardy," "brain-test-deserving," "imbecilic," or "suicidal."

But, in one way, Virgin Oil knew what he was doing. It was a career move. Although his media profile had developed very promisingly, you can never relax in that kind of world. Very unsettling, I imagine it must be. At least, if you're a frapper, or a drodger, or a gink, you know there's always going to be work for you. There're going to be old froops out there with plenty of ding, so you're always going to have opportunities to relieve them of it.

Showbiz, though, that's different. Makes my world look like an extremely safe one. You see, out there in the media your career is controlled by the interest of the general public, and they're fickle like you wouldn't believe. Lose concentration for a moment, slip out of the public eye for as long as it takes them to blink, and you're forgotten. Yesterday's news, last week's regular fries.

So a media career needs constant nurturing. Not just nurturing, but also building up. In my world the work's pretty regular—boring, even. You do a bit of nerve-tweaking, you slabber the odd gink, maybe you tornado a few rival drodgers . . . it all runs along pretty smooth and predictable.

In the media, on the other hand, you always have to be doing something bigger and better. The public are well impressed by whatever it is that first brings you to their attention, but soon they get bored with that and want something new.

Which was what Virgin Oil was finding. First few times the TV audience saw this reformed slabber with his "Born-Again Criminal Who Has Seen the Evil of His Ways" caption, their attention was held. And he controlled the flow of barbarity well, feeding out a little bit more, letting slip some new disgusting detail, in each chat show he appeared on.

But like continuing to nerve-tweak a gink after he's passed out, that kind of approach is going to have diminishing returns. You soon get to the point when you've described the most destructive act you've ever perpetrated. Okay, you can keep going a bit longer by making stuff up, but it doesn't take long before your atrocity tank's running on "empty." At that moment, either you're going to lose your audience, or you have to think of something new that's going to nail them back to the screen.

That was the stage Virgin Oil Vicario's media career had got to. He'd done well as a novelty guest, he'd chilled his viewers' hearts with tales of mayhem, nerve-tweaking, and slabbering. But he was coming to the end of his body count, and he needed something new.

What he thought of new was becoming a missionary. Not just being a born-again frapper who's gone straight, but also persuading other frappers to go through the rebirth process.

Which was obviously a kind of risky business. But good for Virgin Oil's ailing career. Because the way he done it was not going to see the frappers on his own, but making his visits with a camera crew in tow.

The viewing audience liked this. Seeing major bluntos, heavily armed with steelers, surrounded by equally heavily armed drodgers, seeing them confronted live on television was good news. Like watching motor racing, that kind of scenario offered the appealing prospect of somebody getting tornadoed. The viewing public's always gone a bundle on that kind of thing.

And, though risky from Virgin Oil's point of view, the setup wasn't entirely stupid. The television camera has a strange power. Even the most hardened rapper tends to play up to it. Ginks who've gone through their lives slabbering everyone in sight without a twitch of remorse suddenly start wanting to be liked. They smile for the camera, they make reassuring noises, they become positively ingratiating. Even serious psychopaths turn pussycat with the camera on them.

And so it proved when Virgin Oil and his crew cornered Emp. Shouldn't have been a good moment. Emp'd been on the verge of going out with his drodgers to tornado a couple of old froops who'd been holding back on the ding they owed, and at such moments he makes the average tiger with its tail on fire look docile.

But soon as the camera crew arrive and Virgin Oil explains his mission, a ghastly transformation comes over Emp's face. The general view of those present at the time was that it was a smile, though no one could be sure because they'd never seen one there before. Emp's face, up until that point, had been a strictly smile-free zone.

Still, whatever it was, the facial phenomenon was reflected in a total change in Emp's manner. "Woe is me!" he cried. "I done seen the error of my ways. From this moment forth, I will make it my life's work to undo the wrongs what I have visited upon various harmless ginks. It shall be my earnest endeavor to make reparation for my past misdeeds."

Well, okay, we were all impressed at the time—by his command of vocabulary, apart from anything else. And it undoubtedly made good television.

But what really shook us was that Emp kept the routine up after the camera had been switched off.

It was like he actually meant it.

First indication we had was straight after the transmission finished. Virgin Oil came up real close and, with a finger wagging virtually up Emp's nostril, said, "One thing we need to make clear is, if you do go in for this turning-over-a-new-leaf crap in a big way, you don't queer my pitch—right? You start trying to muscle in on the chat-show circuit—or the publishing—and, born-again or not born-again, I'll tornado you. Got that?"

As he said the "Got that?," Virgin Oil's finger stopped wagging and started to poke. It actually poked Emp's cheek.

Well, everyone in the room—camera crew, drodgers, the lot—went into the freeze-frame. Those of us familiar with Emp's little ways knew that he didn't like being touched, and the ones unfamiliar with his little ways seemed to get the message without too much problem.

When I say Emp didn't like being touched, that is by way of an understatement. He hated being touched. He had a pathological horror of being touched. Being touched set off a positive Hiroshima in what, at its most passive, was a pretty explosive personality.

So, after Virgin Oil poked his face, the air in that room didn't move. We all had our minds on things other than breathing.

The silence and the freeze-frame extended themselves. Then, very slowly, Emp moved. Just moved his head. Very, very slowly he moved it around.

And you know what he did?

He turned the other cheek.

And Virgin Oil poked him in that cheek, too.

Then slowly Emp moved his face back, inviting a repeat treatment to the first cheek.

Virgin Oil duly obliged.

It went on for about five minutes, Emp's cheeks being poked alternately. None of us in that room could believe what we were seeing.

And for the next few weeks our disbelief got pushed to the limits. It's been said that anyone who breaks a habit generally frames the pieces, and it was certainly true of Emp. Talk about the zeal of the convert . . . he'd got zeal coming out his ears.

Trouble was, though, Emp's rebirth wasn't like a private thing between him and God. He dragged the rest of us along with him. If Emp himself was going to turn over a new leaf, there was no way any member of his organization—drodger, gink, or even scribber—was going to escape with his personal leaf unturned.

The things he made us do . . . it's a few years back, but I still shudder with embarrassment at the memory. I mean, have you ever heard twenty grown men, whose main expertise lies in slabbering people, sing hymns? And hymns Emp had chosen, hymns with titles such as "Jesus Puts the Sugar in My Coffee Cup of Life" or "God Has Chosen Me to Play Defense in His Great Team." Words like that being sung by twenty drodgers is not a noise you'd even wish on someone who'd taken a chain saw to your mother.

And seeing the same twenty men helping old ladies cross streets and carrying their shopping wasn't a pretty sight, either. Nor was seeing them back at Emp's rudd, dishing out soup to the homeless. And even uglier was watching Emp flagellate himself—literally—on network television.

'Cause, in spite of Virgin Oil's warning, Emp had gone in for the media. Or perhaps it would be truer to say the media had gone in for him. His live television conversion had gone down well with Mr. and Mrs. Average Viewer, and they were keen for more.

Emp was the new media sensation. Because he'd been a bigger blunto and frapper than Virgin Oil ever was, he'd got that much more to confess. He could pour out an endless litany of slabberings and tornadoings, and the audience lapped it up. Emp's chat-show caption—"Mass Murderer Who Has Seen the Error of His Ways and Found God"—was up there as regular as a forecast on the Weather Channel.

And lecture agents fell over themselves to book him.

And publishers flapped million-dollar contracts at him, and he wrote the books. *Murder No More; Penance Made Easy; Twenty-eight Days to an Honest You; Be Your Own Penitentiary; The New Leaf Cookbook;* they all came pouring out.

You might be forgiven for thinking that this was all good news on the career front. Like Virgin Oil, Emp had moved from a lucrative illegal business to an equally lucrative legal business. Which he had, potentially . . . except for one thing:

Emp gave away all the ding.

It's so unbelievable, I'll have to say it again to convince myself.

Emp gave away all the ding.

He took his conversion so seriously that he didn't want to profit from his former life. So now, when he could have had his molasses jar spilling over with ding from the television companies, from the lecture-fixers and the publishers, he didn't touch any of it.

I tell you, that ding didn't touch the sides. Check came in, check went out. And you wouldn't credit the places it went to. Children's homes, drug rehabilitation centers, hospitals, poverty action groups, hostels for the homeless—you could weep at the sheer waste of it all.

Well, needless to say, there was a growing groundswell of discontent among the drodgers about everything that was going on. They hadn't joined Emp's setup to spend time singing hymns and helping old ladies with their shopping. Apart from anything else, they missed the slabbering and the tornadoing.

And yet . . . and yet . . . nobody liked to say anything.

It was like insane. You got these twenty heavy-built drodgers and ginks, whose combined efforts had probably filled Santa Rosita's twice over, and they've now got a frapper who doesn't even carry a steeler, and who, when his cheek gets poked, turns the other one . . . and they're still afraid to say a word to him about the situation.

They've lost any respect they might have had around the town, they're reduced to doing good works, they haven't got any ding . . . and still not a single one of them dares say anything.

I mean, I was as guilty as the rest, but then, as I said, I've always kept such a low profile that I've been nicknamed "Floor Tile." I'd've thought one of the others would've dared say something, though. I'd've thought one of the others might even have made a bid to take over Emp's operation, set himself up as a rival frapper.

But no. Nothing. Even now he's been made over from blunto to pussycat, Emp's hold over them hasn't altered a bit. Even though they're all suffering, even though they can all see how wrong it is for Emp to behave like he's behaving, not one of them dares to point out the obvious.

And that's how I guess the situation might've continued until we all starved to death, if it hadn't been for one little scribber.

He was a pushy kid, reckoned he was going places, and he arrived at the rudd acting on out-of-date information. He didn't know about Emp's conversion, he thought he was coming to meet a major blunto, and it was his ambition to work for a major blunto. Not just any major blunto, but specifically Emp.

Well, soon as the scribber got into the rudd, he could see there was something funny. There's all these homeless lying around for a start, and drodgers dolloping out soup to them. Not a single steeler in sight. It wasn't what he expected in the rudd of a top frapper.

Next thing, Emp comes in and starts leading us all in singing hymns. "Jesus, Bleach My Stains Out, in the Washing Machine of Life," that's what he started with. Always was one of Emp's favorites.

And all the drodgers immediately join in, growling away like postvindaloo stomachs. Well, they're only like two lines into the first verse when the scribber claps his hands and says, "Stop this! Stop this!"

We're all so amazed that anyone dares to go against what Emp wants us to do, that we do stop. The hymn kind of grinds down into silence.

And, quiet as a cobra, Emp looks at the scribber and says, "What?"

And the scribber says, "It's rubbish you carrying on like this. It doesn't suit you. You look ridiculous."

"I look ridiculous?" Emp echoes, still quiet as a trigger finger.

"Yes," says the scribber. "Bloody ridiculous. You should do what you're good at. You're good as a frapper, you're good as a blunto. At doing good, you're no good at all. You're bloody useless!"

"What?" says Emp again, and even though everyone in the rudd had been longing for months to say what the scribber's just said, nobody speaks, nobody moves.

"You heard what I said." And, as he repeated his words, the scribber poked his finger into Emp's cheek. "You're—bloody—useless!"

"Really?" drawls Emp, slow as a snail in a coma.

Then, suddenly, he moves. He reaches toward the nearest drodger, pulls a hidden steeler out of the guy's waistband, and—boom, boom. Once again the worms are going to have to make space at Santa Rosita's.

Pity about the scribber. In a good cause, though. 'Cause it is kind of comforting to have Emp back the way he was. At least now you know where you are.

Seriously at risk.

Peter Crowther is an Englishman who recently turned to full-time writing after spending many years in P.R. and advertising. His talent bloomed suddenly and full-born. In a single year a dozen of his stories, each one a gem, appeared in magazines. Peter has published a collaborative novel and edited several anthologies, with more on the way. In between those he has continued to turn out first-rate pieces like this one, based on "The Musicians of Bremen."

THE MUSICIAN OF
BREMEN, GA

I guess the whole thing started—as far as you can ever *credit* things starting—when Cal Williston was born. Maybe it started when Lester Durphy was born, but Cal being a couple years older than him, we'll blame it on Cal.

Truth to tell, events got set in motion even before Cal set foot on the planet, with him being spoon-fed jazz while he was still all curled up in his mommy Dansy's tummy, listening to all the great musicians and singers even before most folks got to recognizing they was great.

And when he finally did come out—prob'ly to hear what all the noise was about—he got to hear even more of it. Sitting in a bouncy chair rigged up by his daddy, Ben Williston, Cal got to hear all the latest sounds on Ben's Motorola while, at night, tucked up alongside him in bed, Dansy would sing to him in a voice that would have made either of the Holiday girls weep with envy.

Even when he wasn't *playing* it—from old record albums that felt and looked like they'd been molded out of cement instead of plastic—Ben *talked* jazz to his son. And later, much later, after Dansy's accident, Ben would hum around the house, strange, wistful tunes that echoed the sadness in his heart and the restlessness in his soul.

All this I got from him, in those late-night, early-morning conversations when it seems like everyone in the whole world is asleep and with someone . . . everyone excepting musicians and maybe the occasional sleepy-eyed waitress shuffling ketchup bottles around well-worn truck-stop counters while they grab a quick smoke and check the *Enquirer.*

I seen a lot of those counters in my time. Cal, too, though he started late into the game.

When Cal—it was short for Calvin, though his daddy always joked with folks and told them his son's name was Calliope . . . after the reedy organs that played around the carousel rides in the fairgrounds. You should've seen their faces! Anyways, when Cal was turning the corner into his teenage years and the air was filled with reversed tapes, feedback, and the sweet-smoke smell of youthful rebellion, Chet Baker's trumpet was the order of the day.

Yes, sir, rain or shine, day or night, Cal would listen to Baker's plaintive horn drifting from the hideaway speakers in Ben's old Williston Motorola hi-fi, one of those fine-looking Drexel-designed cabinets in walnut veneer. My, but those must've been good days . . . the kind of days too few people ever have.

One song that Baker made his own was "Moonlight in Vermont," a song on an album from the Gerry Mulligan Quartet put out sometime in 1953, the same year Baker was arrested for drug possession and held in custody all the way to Christmas.

The song's beauty contradicted the stormy relationship in the band. There was bad blood among the players, and no denying, and the following year, 1954, the year Cal Williston was born, saw Baker replaced by Bob Brookmeyer, a talented valve trombonist. The quartet did some more good things but nothing matched the heights of "Moonlight." Dansy, Cal's mommy, had the song on a Percy Faith album called *American Serenade* but it was the Baker-Mulligan version that held Cal in thrall. His daddy, too.

In 1964, when Cal was all of ten years old, Ben Williston bought his son a secondhand trumpet for $148. Leastways, that's what I recall Cal telling me it costed. Despite the scratches, the carved initials RVS around the horn rim, and the fact that nobody he talked to had ever *heard* of the horn's manufacturer, Melodia— me included, but then I ain't a horn man—the instrument produced a fine and fluid sound. But it was Cal's ear for a melody that carried it through. My, but that boy could carry a tune like to make a marine weep.

Right from the start, young Cal would practice trying to get his own sound to mimic the one put out by the great players. He would sit nights, cross-legged in his bedroom, with the window open and, sometimes, Ben and Dansy sitting out on the porch listening. It didn't surprise nobody who knew them that the song Cal liked to play most of all was "Moonlight in Vermont." By this time it had become something like the Williston anthem.

Now, the Willistons had never been to any of the New England states—they hadn't hardly been out of Georgia—but Ben Williston would often tell Dansy, late at night, when young Cal was supposed to be up in his bed, how they'd one day go up to Vermont and, somewhere out beside a lake, they'd have dinner—"Macon shark, maybe," Ben would say, his arm draped around Dansy's shoulder, unawares that Cal was scrunched up somewhere listening—and then they'd sit out in the open air with "Moonlight" playing, watching the stars.

On these occasions, Cal would sneak out onto the upstairs hallway or, if they were outside, downstairs crouched against the open window, and he would sit and listen to his mommy and daddy, going back to his room only when things got a little too romantic.

And always that song would play, though, as the years went by and recollections became almost as hazy as the images of his folks' faces, Cal sometimes wondered if it had only been in his head.

Yes, sir, good days and happy times.

Fact was that maybe they was *too* good, *too* happy.

Sometimes, Cal told me one time, he got to feeling kind of guilty being so happy when there seemed so many people whose life roads were rocky and uneven thoroughfares. He always worried that God would deal him a dose of sadness to even things up kind of, so whenever the family went to church, which was most Sundays, Cal would make out he was real miserable. But one day God must've seen through young Cal's pretense and he dealt the Willistons a busted flush to end them all.

The sadness came when Cal was eleven years old and Danziel Williston was sideswiped by an eighteen-wheeler carrying huge, black, stenciled drums down to Albany. It wasn't nobody's fault, just one of those things. A combination of rain-slicked roads, a couple of worn tires, and a driver trying to make up his schedule by cutting off from a blocked I-16 through Macon, where they lived . . . and where, on Second Street, Dansy Williston was crossing over to buy some groceries.

When Cal's Aunt Gerry, a shrew-faced woman who liked to tote a Bible with her wherever she went, Sunday or any other day, told Ben that God worked in mysterious ways, Ben threw her out of the house. She was his own sister, his own flesh and blood, but there weren't no love lost there. None at all. And after the burial service—at which Ben had a bemused Reverend Spyker play Ben Webster's 1954 version of "My Funny Valentine" on a tinny-sounding cassette player, its haunting phrases drifting over the assembled mourners and mingling with their uneasy shuffling—Cal and his daddy never again attended church together. Cal only broke this tradition when Ben died.

By the time of his death, Ben Williston had become a broken and disillusioned man who had never regained his sense of humor or his lust for life. He'd been waiting a long time to die, and most everybody knew that. Dansy had been more than his wife; she had been his sole purpose for pulling in a breath on a morning. It surprised more folks than Cal that his daddy lasted so long after she'd gone.

The year was 1972. Cal was eighteen years old now. Not quite a man, but close enough for jazz. Hell, anything's close enough for that.

Well-meaning relatives failed in their attempts to have Cal move in with them, and his Uncle Gerry—who was not a relative at all but just an old friend of his father, lived over in Thomaston—helped him sort out the financial situation and legal fees and all that kind of stuff. Pretty soon everything had been put in order and Cal set off from Macon with a couple of bags—one filled with clothes and the other with record albums, mostly on the old Blue Note label, that he and his daddy had collected over the years.

Plus, of course, he took the Melodia.

The plan was to hitchhike up U.S. 23 all the way to Atlanta, and, once there, to join a band. But we all know about plans and how they have a habit of not quite working out the way folks intend.

Cal did get to Atlanta but the plans didn't travel well, and the boy drifted through a series of dead-end jobs and dead-end rooming houses until, one spring day in 1976, he saw an advertisement in the *Atlanta Journal* announcing that there was to be a musical competition over in Bremen, a small town at the crossroads of Highways 27 and 78.

Now, Bremen may only have been a small town—still is, for that matter—but back then it had big ideas.

It was bicentennial year, and there was a lot of strange things happening up and down the country in small towns—particularly small towns with big ideas. This particular idea had been hatched by the town's mayor, Rudy Fossdrake, in honor of the old fairy-storytellers the Brothers Grimm. There was no real connection other than the fact that the brothers had written a story titled "The Musicians of Bremen" and the name of the competition was The Musicians of Bremen, GA.

But the ad said only bands should apply. And, talented though he was by this time, Cal was only one man.

That was when God must have had one of his sentimental moments because, two pages away in the very same edition of the *Atlanta Journal,* there was another ad, this one from a fella name of Phil Palmer, who had his own piano trio and who wanted to extend their range by introducing an alto sax. Cal figured the idea was to turn something that probably sounded like Ramsey Lewis into something more akin to Dave Brubeck. Although Cal accepted he was no Paul Desmond—he didn't play alto sax, for a start—he figured a horn was close enough for him to waste carfare and attend the auditions.

Meanwhile, elsewhere the stage was setting. . . .

Lester "Legs" Durphy had always wanted to rob a bank.

Some kids want to be policemen or train drivers or firemen, but not Lester. Coming up to twenty-five years old in the bicentennial year, the six-foot-six onetime resident of New Jersey had spent most of the years since his fifteenth birthday in one reform institution or another.

Lester wasn't a bad boy, let's get that straight from the start. For him, crime was a way of life. He accepted pain and disappointment with the same casual attitude that he dealt it out. Thing is, you don't get no love when you're young, you don't store none up to give out to other folks. And Lester didn't get much of anything from his folks, 'cepting maybe a hardening of the skin on his face and backside from all the hitting that went on. Maybe that's why he turned out the way he did. I know this better'n most folks, but, unlike Lester, I didn't let it turn me mean.

My feeling on the matter is there's always something positive to come out of even the most negative situations, and for Lester the positive thing that came out of his fractured home life was an all-abiding love of the guitar.

Lester just loved guitar music and, most of all, he loved to hear Wes Montgomery play. Wes's music, that simple but complex picking at the chords, firing them off the neck of his guitar like gunshots, was about the only thing that could calm Lester Durphy's troubled soul. So one day he had decided he was going to learn how to play. Getting a guitar was simple. He stole one from a garage sale out in Passaic.

The thing wasn't worth but a few dollars, but it made a tune. Lester said that even a warped neck and a couple of slack strings didn't stop him from finding a chord or two that gave a momentary nod toward the great Montgomery. Necessity being the mother of invention, he went and stole himself a book on how to play in a day and, though it took him more than twenty-four hours, Lester did learn how to turn a tune.

Following his release from the Atlanta Penal Reform Farm in Marietta in March of 1976, Lester drifted into town. The only things he had with him were his beloved guitar—the book had long gone—plus twenty-three dollars and change . . . and a grim determination to rob a bank. Lester didn't care *which* bank. Money was money, no matter where it was kept. But, like I already said, plans have a habit of going sourer than last week's milk in August.

The same edition of the *Atlanta Journal* that mentioned the coming music competition in Bremen, and carried an audition advertisement for an alto sax player to join the Phil Palmer Trio, also featured an article on a Bremen insurance company—Watts, Steenhouse, and Morgann—that planned to hand out ten-dollar bills to everyone celebrating the coming special Fourth.

The idea was that each of the bills would be stamped with the company's name in gold ink, and this would be a great incentive for folks to call them up for their insurance needs . . . particularly when anyone actually taking out a new policy would receive a 10 percent discount in exchange for the company getting the bill back. The company planned to give out up to thirty-seven hundred of these bills—thirty-seven because they had been around since 1939—which meant thirty-seven thousand dollars. Even Lester could work that one out. And to Lester, an insurance company fell neatly into the category of "bank."

In the *Journal* article—which I still have—Dick Watts, the president of Watts, Steenhouse, and Morgann, responding to a question about how much financial sense such an action made, had this to say: "Sure, we recognize that some folks will use the bills to buy a burger or a hot dog, and that's just fine with us. But, in the long run, a peaceful mind is better than a full stomach. The future is a mighty long road, and a little forethought now could ease some of the pitfalls and highlight some of the ditches. Insurance is the name of the game of life, and here in western Georgia, from Columbus up to Chattanooga, Watts, Steenhouse, and Morgann is the name of insurance."

That kind of stuff might impress a lot of folks, but it like to make me feel sick to my stomach. But there was the fact that a whole lot of ten-dollar bills would be on offer and maybe, some folks got to thinking, maybe a careful person could walk away with two or three. Maybe even more.

Lester Durphy figured on walking away with a *lot* more.

Lester, who was a very "now" kind of fella, didn't have any need for insurance. But he did have need for some of those bills; in fact, Lester had a need for *all* of them, which meant him somehow getting to them before they hit the streets. And, of course, before they were stamped. Even Lester, who would never have made a sixty-four-*cent* question on the old TV show, recognized the potential difficulty of trying to change thirty-seven thousand dollars in gold-inked bills. He could be a smart boy when he put his mind to it. Trouble was, he didn't put his mind to it often enough.

Sure, he figured the bills would be consecutively numbered anyway, but that also meant that security would be modest. After all, who would even give a thought to such a thing, particularly around the Fourth of July? Lester's plan was to take the slow train up to New York and spend a couple of days walking up and down buying packs of cigarettes, gum, paperback novels, newspapers, and even an occasional McDonald's. Nobody would query a single new ten-spot, and, that way, he figured he would get back about seventy-five, eighty cents on the dollar. Plus a lot of cigarettes, gum, paperbacks, newspapers, and food. Then, when he'd cleaned up enough of that money, Lester aimed to buy a brand-new guitar all for himself.

But getting rid of the haul came later; the heist came first.

He had to get into the offices of this insurance outfit.

Flicking through the *Journal* as he pondered this problem, his eyes lit on the article of the coming musical contest. And he thought of Teddy Talese.

Edward Willem Talese had come from a wealthy Alabama farming family, spending his formative years growing up first in Mobile and then in Montgomery before he turned his back on working the land and opted instead for working the people. As he told Lester Durphy, when they shared a room at the Columbus Correctional Facility for Boys in the late 1960s—and even later, he told me—it made for easier work and more fun. And, somewhat poignantly, Talese added that, when successful, it also gave a greater sense of accomplishment.

Teddy's problem was that he was *not* particularly successful in his chosen career. Truth to tell, Teddy was not particularly successful at anything . . . save one thing: playing drums.

Teddy's hero was one Gene Krupa. He loved the way Krupa attacked those skins, pounding out those haunting rhythms. One day, he promised himself—and the rest of us—he'd get himself a job playing drums for real instead of on old covered seats and cookie tins. He didn't have no training to speak of, but he did have a natural sense of beat. You could see it in the way he moved his hips and swung his legs, like there was some distant music he was swaying to but that nobody else could hear.

When Lester Durphy called him up on the telephone early on in June of the bicentennial year, Teddy saw the possibilities right away.

"Hey, whyn't *we* enter the competition, Lester," Teddy told me he said when Lester had told him what was going to be going on in Bremen on the holiday weekend.

"You kidding me?" came the answer.

"Why would I kid you? Maybe we could do it. Maybe we could win."

"But you ain't never played no *real* drums," Lester pointed out, his voice dangerously high. "And anyways, there's only the two of us, guitar and drums. One of us don't have no instruments at all, and the other don't have no instrument to speak of. We gonna look like a couple of real hayseeds is what we gonna look like we go in for the competition. Folks are gonna fall right off of their chairs when we take the stage."

Teddy thought on that for a second or two. "Maybe, maybe not," he said at last.

"How's come?"

"Well, I seen that edition of the *Journal* and I seen there are a whole truckload of advertisements for musicians," Teddy said. "Maybe we could go along to where they're holding the auditions and make ourselves into a trio or maybe even a quartet."

I must say I had been thinking the same thing myself. Thinking maybe I could hitch me a ride on the shirttails of a couple other folks who might turn up for auditions.

Me, I was a pianist. Still am. And I'm still bringing in a little folding, good money mostly—partic'ly for a man whose big six-oh is next year—from session work and the occasional tour. Even got to play England once, Ronnie Scott's place down in Soho, London.

Now, *there's* a place! There ain't too many joints a fella can still say are jumping, but that one did, and, far as I can make out, it still does.

Anyways . . .

I was reading the *Journal,* too, hoping there'd be something for a piano player. But there was nothing. Seemed like all the folks placing the ads were piano players, so they naturally didn't want another one. But I figured I'd go along anyways and listen. Figured maybe I'd try team up with someone they turned down. It seems far-fetched, but there didn't seem like a whole lot else I could do to get into some kind of combo.

Like I say, I still have that issue of the *Journal,* though it's a little dog-eared now and well past its prime. But I guess we all are, in one way or another.

Back then, jazz was on the decline. Rock and roll—not the good old songs but some really strange stuff—was the order of the day, and the old jazz bars had given way to psychedelic clubs featuring poetry readings, a little off-key folk singing, and the occasional solo guitarist who would cover his lack of style with a mountain of feedback. The sixties had a lot to answer for.

The venue for the audition was a cellar club on Cheshire Bridge Road, and I turned up early, sat in the back of the room while a guy with white hair chatted to himself as he wiped the floor. I was thirty-nine years old and I thought I'd pretty much seen ever'thing. But I saw some sights that day. *Heard* some, too!

There were some good sounds and some not-so-good sounds, but most of the folks who turned up didn't sound like they really wanted to play. They sounded like they wanted to succeed . . . to earn. There's a difference, and it doesn't make for a good musician.

Looking back, I guess it was just one of those things that happen every once in a while. Like multiple smashes on the interstate, four vehicles coming from different places and all meeting up at the same fender-crunching instant. Cal was coming onto the stage after the guy—this Phil Palmer fella . . . nice fella, he was—had told him to play a tune seeing as how he'd taken the trouble to come down. But he told Cal he wasn't looking for a horn man, he was looking for an alto sax . . . and he'd already told one guy that the job was more or less his for the taking.

It was at this exact moment that Lester and Teddy—though I didn't know who they was then—walked in off the street and plopped themselves down at the circular stools at the bar, couple of places from where I was sat, and watched Cal Williston and his Melodia take to the stage.

Couple of seconds later, Cal commenced to playing.

Well, I tell you, a handful of notes in and, 'cepting for Cal's horn, you could've heard a roach fart in that room.

Even the old muttering guy had stopped wiping the floor and muttering to whatever demons haunted him and, instead, just leaned on his mop and stared.

Lester and Teddy, they stared, too.

And me, I stared.

And we all listened.

The sounds that came out of that instrument was living things, they wasn't just a few chords thumbed together. The notes drifted and wafted across the room like a fall breeze, filled with the burnished rusts and golds of New England's trees and the smell of maple syrup. He didn't have no accompaniment—hell, he didn't need none.

I had never heard "Moonlight in Vermont" played that way before. I don't think it *had* ever been played that way before, filling the room with something akin to a *presence* . . . though it sounds a mite flaky to put it in those words.

When he'd finished, I looked around at the two guys next to me and I saw the one of them wiping his eyes. When he saw me looking at him he sniffed and started to laugh—that kind of part-crying laugh, with saliva strings in the corner of his lips? And he said, "Sweet Jesus . . ." real soft, like he hadn't meant for nobody to hear.

I nodded to him. *Amen to that, brother!*

"Sweet holy Jesus," he said, shaking his head.

And almost as one man, the three of us got to our feet and commenced to clapping. Right about then, other folks got to their own feet, and *they* commenced to clapping.

First off, it was slow, like we all really didn't have no right being in there hearing him; then it built up and got faster until everyone was cheering their fool heads off.

And when I looked around at the two guys, I noticed my own eyes were moist and my vision was clouded. Just like theirs.

I held out my hand. "Sam Bartholomew," I said, beaming a big smile.

"Lester Durphy," said Lester Durphy, taking my hand and shaking it hard.

"Teddy Talese," said Teddy Talese.

Then we all of us went down like apostles to touch the hem of Cal Williston's sweater.

The next day was when things went wrong.

Even though Cal's rendition of "Moonlight" had pretty much affected everyone in the room the same way, Phil Palmer was not about to give back word to the fella he'd already offered the job. To his credit, I have to say, because Palmer looked like he regretted having to let Cal go.

Anyways, me and Lester Durphy and Teddy Talese was waiting for Cal when he stepped down from the stage and, pretty soon, we'd made all our introductions and discovered that among us we had the makings of a quartet. Teddy apologized for not having any skins of his own but assured everyone he'd have no trouble borrowing some for a few days for the competition. We arranged to meet up the next day for a session at a little bar in an alley off Peachtree Street.

To cut a mighty long story short, the session went well.

Teddy had managed to borrow a snare, bass, and tom-tom, plus a high hat and, although he was not Gene Krupa or Joe Morrello, he had a natural rhythm and knew how to provide a beat without drowning out the music.

Lester had a fluid way with the guitar, and he, too, was a natural, though maybe wearing his homage to Montgomery a little too clearly on his sleeve for all to see.

Me, I tinkled up and down the ivories in my customary fashion and managed to keep out of everyone else's way musically almost as much as they kept out of mine.

But it was Cal Williston who took the biscuit.

Cal was *born* to play the horn. Simple as that. If Chet hadn't lost his teeth in that fight back in '68 or Miles had maintained his modular approach, then maybe the two of them would have found what Cal Williston found. Maybe they wouldn't.

At the end of the day we went out for a few beers—to talk about what we'd achieved and arrange more practice sessions. The reality was we talked about who we were and about what we wanted out of life. That's when Lester dropped his bombshell about robbing an insurance company of thirty-seven thousand dollars in gold-painted bills and then cruising up and down Manhattan exchanging single ten-spots for packs of gum.

To say his idea sounded half-baked was an insult to every half-baked idea that had ever been thought up. This one was so completely baked it was like to explode the oven, and I told Lester as much. Cal did, too. Teddy Talese just sat and listened for the most part.

At the end of the night, slurring our words a little, we'd drifted on to talking about the great musicians and the great record albums with all the talk about the robbery gone and forgotten. Leastways, that's what I thought.

The rest of June was taken up with us practicing four songs: Brubeck's "Take Five," which was patchy at best . . . partic'ly without no stand-up bass and a trumpet in place of Desmond's alto—plus, of course, I was no Dave Brubeck; then we did a version of Montgomery's version of the Beatles' "Dear Prudence" from Wes's "A Day In The Life" album, and that was pretty neat; the third we practiced was Davis's "So What?," also good, though there wasn't much space for Lester's guitar; and, of course, "Moonlight in Vermont."

By the end of the month we'd pretty much decided on "Prudence" and "Moonlight" as being the two songs we'd do for the competition, and we concentrated on them the first couple of days in July. On the evening of the second, we drove over to Bremen and checked into a so-so rooming house on the outskirts of town. I suggested we have an early night so we'd be fresh for a full day's practice the next day, but Lester and Teddy—mainly Lester—said they was going to go out and have a few beers to celebrate. Didn't seem like we had much to celebrate yet and I told them so, but Lester's mind was made up. When they got in that night, after Cal and me had spent a few hours talking about our pasts some more, Cal was asleep, snoring like a baby. We was sharing the one room while Lester and Teddy was in another one just down the hall.

I heard them talking and opened the door. They told me they'd had a good time and they was all set for practice the next day. We split up then and went to bed. Curled up beneath the sheets, with Cal driving them home a few feet away from me, I tried to convince myself I'd been able to smell beer on Lester's and Teddy's breath. But I knew I hadn't.

I didn't sleep good that night and, come the morning, I was wondering if this thing might be awful foolish. Staring at my reflection in the mirror that morning, I even got to wondering if I'd imagined Cal Williston's talent. But, by ten o'clock, in the first run-through of "Dear Prudence," I realized I hadn't. If anything, I had underestimated it.

In the early afternoon, I suggested that we should take the rest of the day off. Sometimes too much practice can take away the soul of a performance, and we wanted to avoid that, I said. Everyone agreed. And Lester and Teddy said they wanted to go into town to hang out, take it easy. It sounded like a good idea to me.

But they didn't come home that evening.

And they hadn't come home by the time I turned off Cal's and my light and turned over to face the prospects of the coming day.

In the morning, they still hadn't shown.

I said to Cal we should go ahead anyways and check in at the contest office. We'd already booked our place and we were due onstage a little before midday. I told Cal I figured the other two had maybe had one too many beers or maybe they'd shacked up with a couple of nice Bremen girls for the night, neither of which I believed in my heart. Whether Cal believed, he didn't say. Cal didn't say much about nothing.

The sun rose high in the sky straight off and it showed signs of hanging there all day just burning the paint off of anyone dumb enough to stand out under it. There was a whole lot of dumb people that day.

The streets of Bremen itself was cordoned off and everyone just milled around taking in the atmosphere and listening to the music.

I asked at the contest office if they'd heard anything from Lester and Teddy but they hadn't. I hadn't expected they would have. Truth was, I didn't know what to think about why they hadn't showed up. But maybe there was still time, I told Cal, and he nodded.

We heard the sirens and the shots 'round about a quarter after eleven. Our spot had been moved forward to eleven thirty-five, and both Cal and me was getting a mite nervous. We'd agreed that if Lester and Teddy didn't show, we'd just bow out gracefully, although the woman at the booking desk said it'd be okay for the two of us to go on as a duo. But I didn't cotton to that and Cal said he didn't neither, so we just waited and kept our fingers crossed . . . though whether they was crossed for the boys to show or to stay hidden I wouldn't like to say.

The shots sounded like a car backfiring, only there wasn't no cars anywheres to be seen. Right away I feared the worst.

When I heard the sirens and folks shouting and screaming—because now the music had stopped and folks was just looking around in panic—I knew that Lester and Teddy had been doing more than just hanging out.

There seemed to be some activity across to our left—Cal and me was waiting over by the stage, waiting either to go on or to get out of the competition altogether—and we all of us looked around to see what was happening. There was a whole load of people in front of the stage, but we could see folks pointing across to the left.

Then there was a couple more shots and someone's voice—like from a bullhorn or something?—boomed out across the crowd for everyone to get down, down on the ground. There was screaming and shouting but everyone did as they was told and more or less just fell to the ground right where they was standing, me included. But Cal stayed right where he was, staring in the direction of the ruckus. I got up to my knees and tugged at him but he stayed put. Then, still kneeling, I glanced across toward the sidewalk and saw Lester Durphy lurching across a sea of bodies carrying a brown leather valise beneath his arm.

Right about the time I saw that he was already bleeding, the voice shouted for him to stop.

Lester didn't stop. But he saw us . . . or, more likely, he saw Cal Williston, standing right there, his Melodia in his hand, looking right at him. I looked up at Cal and shouted for him to get down, but Cal just smiled. And he opened his arms wide.

When I looked back at Lester I could see he was crying, running like a drunk, stumbling toward me and Cal Williston.

Looking back, replaying the scene in my memory, I think there was four shots, though one was unaccounted for.

Two of them took down Lester Durphy, who had already dropped the bag, and another one hit Cal Williston in the side of the head. The cops had been aiming high.

What happened next I can only guess at, even though I was a major player in the scenes that followed.

Lester flew forward like someone had given him a rocket pack, bouncing across people crouched down and lying right in front of him, his legs pinwheeling as the last of his breath just upped and left him. When he hit the ground and rolled to a stop right in front of Cal and me, Lester Durphy was as dead as he'd ever be.

Cal just fell over backward, still holding his horn, and landed on a woman I later found out come all the way from Albany for the competition. He didn't hurt her one bit, and that just about sums up Cal Williston.

I confess I didn't even think about trying to do anything for Lester—I'd seen him jump as the bullets had hit home, jump twice, and I knew there wasn't nothing could be done for the boy. Leastways, that's the way I tell it to myself late at night when there's nobody else listening. The truth of the matter was that I was a whole sight more bothered about Cal and that sound he made than I was for Lester . . . or even for Teddy Talese, who, at that moment, I didn't know what had happened to. (Turned out, I heard much later, that Teddy had been killed right on the spot when he and Lester had leaped out from the hiding place they'd fixed up for themselves in the offices of Watts, Steenhouse, and Morgann, and Lester had grabbed the bag containing the thirty-seven thousand dollars in gold-painted ten-spots.)

Anyways, me and the woman from Albany—whose brother-in-law was a veterinarian, she told me . . . and I recall that statement filling me with hope, though I can't imagine why now—discovered Cal was still breathing, though he was clearly in bad shape. I remember thinking what President Kennedy must've looked like after the bullets had taken off the side of his head in the Dallas motorcade all those years ago. A lot like Cal Williston, I imagine.

The competition was abandoned until midafternoon, and the cops came over and took away Lester's body. A couple of burly medics came across a few minutes after that and carted Cal Williston away and, as I watched him disappear through the crowd that had now got back onto its feet, I figured that was like to be the last time I ever saw him. Leastways alive.

But I was wrong, though even that's debatable.

Turned out that, while that bullet didn't take away enough of Cal Williston's head to kill him, it did take away enough to turn him into a vegetable. And that's the way he's been these past twenty years, lying in a coma, a condition with a whole lot of big words that I can't even pronounce, let alone understand.

His death on Tuesday was just a rubber-stamping exercise. The real decision was made all that time ago in Bremen during the celebrations for the bicentennial.

Now, I know I've gone on here a while—maybe a good while too long, as I now see I've been talking for almost a half hour—but a talent like Cal Williston's don't come along too often . . . and certainly not often enough.

Most of you gathered here today have never heard Cal play, and that's a goddamn shame . . . if you'll excuse me saying so, partic'ly here in the house of the Lord. But that's the simple truth of the matter.

And so it is that I've arranged for a few friends of mine to join me in giving Cal Williston the send-off I know he'd've appreciated . . . which is why, in case any of you was wondering, we've brought in the instruments you see here behind me.

Who these people are isn't important—though you'll recognize one or two of them as they come up—but, please, no applause.

What's important is we pay our respects to a magnificent talent cut down even before he'd got anywheres near to his prime.

Even more than that, it's important, too, that we recognize the wonder and the magic of music itself. And I know it exists—I saw it in the eyes of Lester Durphy two decades ago . . . when, I like to think, Lester himself could already hear the strains of Cal Williston's version of "Moonlight in Vermont" when he was stretching out his dying arms for some kind of redemption.

Nobody likes stories that don't have a happy ending, and that goes in spades for me. But this story does have a happy ending. It just doesn't have a happy middle. Cal Williston is now at rest— with his Melodia right alongside him in the casket—and the Big Man has got Himself a new horn player like to make Gabriel himself turn in his trumpet.

So this one's for Lester Durphy and it's for Teddy Talese and it's for every young man who ever took a wrong turning at the crossroads we all face from time to time. But, of course, it's mostly for Cal Williston . . . the Musician of Bremen, GA.

Our treatment of Cal's treatment of Chet Baker's treatment of "Moonlight in Vermont" . . .

It's not Cal himself but, take it from me, it's close enough for jazz. And, ladies and gentlemen . . . there ain't nothing else that matters.

A one, a two, a three . . .

Music is your own experience, your thoughts, your wisdom.
If you don't live it, it won't come out of your horn.
    —Charlie Parker (1920–55)

Audrey Peterson is an American who sets a good deal of her fiction in England. While she prefers the cozy form, she is less genteel than some other practitioners and has a keen eye for sham and pretense. Her novel Dartmoor Burial *is especially notable. One thing's for sure: When she continues the tale of "Cinderella," the royal court will never be the same.*

AUDREY PETERSON

ANNIVERSARY BALL

In a round turret of the castle, in her lavishly appointed boudoir, the queen leaned back against her satin pillows and sipped her morning tea. A tap at the door brought the maidservant, who announced, "Lady Sarah, Your Majesty."

A pretty, dark-haired young woman gave a casual curtsy. "Good morning, Your Majesty."

"Good morning, my dear. I'm delighted to see you back. Did you have a pleasant holiday?"

"Yes, lovely, thank you."

"Have a crumpet, my dear. I've had three, and I assure you Cook has done them to perfection."

Lady Sarah nibbled as instructed.

The queen gestured to the foot of her poster bed, and with the familiarity of custom, the young woman put a foot on the stepstool and nimbly climbed aboard, curling up against a cushion on the corner post. Eyeing the queen, she raised a delicate eyebrow. "Any change in the plans for the ball?"

The queen sighed. "Not a chance. You know Charmie. He still thinks last year's ball was the supreme event of his life, and he wants to celebrate it again."

"But what about Cindy? Will she be up to it?"

"She's not yet in her fourth month, and naturally, if Charmie wants it—"

Lady Sarah nodded. "The wish of her lord and master, of course. But I haven't seen her yet. Can she fit into a ball gown?"

"She doesn't show much as yet, and would you believe? Charmie insists she wear the same gown she wore last year when he first set eyes on her."

"You don't mean she's to wear the gown old Granmer Fairlie gave her from the attic?"

"The same. Granmer is putting a panel in it. She's still the best seamstress in the kingdom, so I'm sure she can make it fit."

Sarah shrugged. "Sentimentality, thy name is Charmie."

"Exactly. He gets it from his father, of course."

"And how *is* His Majesty?"

"Oh, pottering about in the gardens, as usual. Tremendously excited about becoming a grandfather. Other than his begonias, it's the first thing that's stirred him up in years."

Sarah reached for another crumpet. "I suppose everyone in the countryside is invited to the ball?"

The queen rolled her eyes. "Yes. I pointed out to Charmie that since last year was his twenty-first birthday, it was appropriate to invite *all* the gentry as well as our own particular friends, but that we need not do so again this year. No dice. He wants this to be precisely the same as a year ago."

"That means we'll have Cindy's stepmama and those two frightful girls?"

"Oh, dear, yes. I believe they treated her rather badly after her papa died, but she says they are her only relations, and her papa would want her to be kind to them."

Sarah smiled wryly. "I'd have given them the boot, in her place."

The queen sighed again. "Oh, Sarah, how I wish you *were* in her place. You know how much I hoped that you and Charmie would—"

"I know you did, but we were too much like brother and sister for that. I was ten when I came here to live, and Charmie was twelve. Once we grew up together like that, there's no place for mad passion."

The queen smiled. "Speaking of romance, isn't it time you settled on one of your suitors? Or did you meet someone new on your holiday?"

Sarah's dark eyes kindled. "Two new ones, actually. They all claim to be dying of love, so how can I choose one and condemn the others to an early grave?"

"Oh, do be serious. You will have your twentieth birthday soon. It's quite time you settled down."

"Mmm. I could line them up and have them draw straws."

At a tap at the door, the maid announced, "Prince Charming, Your Majesty."

"Good morning, darling." His mother gazed at him adoringly as he bent to kiss her hand.

"Morning, Mother. Morning, Sarah."

Noting a slight frown on her son's usually open countenance, the queen asked, "What is it, dear?"

The prince held out a sheet of rough paper with a message in charcoal. "This was brought to me this morning."

The queen took it and began to read: " 'Dere Prince . . .' 'D-E-R-E'? Oh, dear, all our efforts to educate seem to be failing. 'If you dont treat us fare and square youll be sorry.' "

The queen handed the paper to Sarah, who looked puzzled. "It's obviously one of the peasants, but what does he mean?"

The prince shook his head. "I've no idea. I had to sentence a fellow for poaching some time ago, but he admitted he'd done it, so it can't be that."

The queen sighed. "They always complain when the crops are bad, as if we could change the weather. I do think, Charmie, you ought to leave all this to the steward, as your papa has always done."

"I know, Mother, but once I became twenty-one, I felt it my duty to take some responsibility for the affairs of the kingdom."

"And now the ungrateful creatures are threatening you. I do think it's most unfair."

Sarah looked up at the prince. "Have you told Cindy about this?"

"No. no. I'm sure it's nothing, but I don't want to upset her in her delicate condition. You won't mention it to her, will you?"

"Certainly not. Well, I must go and dress for the hunt."

The prince stood up. "Yes, it's time we were off."

The queen smiled at them fondly. "Best of luck with the hunt, my dears. I shall look for you from the carriage."

In the balmy air of a perfect spring morning, Princess Cynthia drove her pony cart along the road toward the village, two miles away. If she had been any good at singing, she would have been caroling away, but her heart sang for her. She still found it hard to believe in the happiness that chance had brought her. It seemed to her that she and the prince were more in love each day, and now, in spite of upchucking her breakfast every morning, she was thrilled to be having their first baby.

From the time they had returned from their honeymoon, the princess had formed the habit of making these weekly visits to her former home, the manor house where she was born. As she approached the house, she was flooded with memories of her childhood. There had been the golden years when her mother was alive, then the sorrow of her death, and the consolation of her father's love.

It was when she was thirteen that the next blow fell. Her father announced that she was to have a "new mama," a lady with two daughters near her own age. When the three of them came to live at the manor, they were obviously dazzled by the luxury of their new home. Cindy felt faintly puzzled at why her father had chosen this vulgar person for his wife, too young to see that her stepmother was a buxom and sexy woman.

At first, Cindy tried desperately to like her new sisters, Biddy and Liddy, aged fifteen and sixteen, but while they smirked and smiled in her father's presence, they teased and tormented her when they were alone. Still, she could escape from them and take her books to a retreat in the attic. What she would not do was to call her father's wife "Mother." At his attempts at gentle persuasion, she at last agreed to address her as "Mama Myrtle." From the first, she felt the animosity of this woman, whose gushing manner belied the cold, hard gaze of her eyes.

For two years, Cindy was consoled by the times when she and

her father managed to be alone. She seldom complained to him, knowing that he still loved her but was hopelessly enamored of his new wife.

Then, not long before Cindy turned sixteen, the final blow came. After a brief illness, her father died. Now, Mama Myrtle and the girls made no attempt to hide their hatred. In her father's will, Mama Myrtle was to have the manor house for her lifetime, after which it would go to Cindy. Unfortunately, he had made no provision for an income for his daughter, naively assuming his widow would provide for her.

It was soon evident that Mama Myrtle had no intention of giving her a cent. Desperate to find suitors for her girls, she spent freely on new gowns for them, taking them to balls around the countryside and leaving Cindy at home. Plain and gauche, Biddy and Liddy, despite their finery, had no luck at all.

Meanwhile, the widow's arrogantly inept way with the servants led to their wholesale departure. Only two menservants remained, and Cindy was assigned to the role of housemaid, dusting the furniture and sweeping the hearths.

Remembering those unhappy days, Cindy pushed away the resentment she had felt at the time. Lady Sarah frankly told her she ought to ignore them, and no doubt she was right. When the queen had given her Sarah as her lady-in-waiting, she had been grateful to have a young companion in the castle, and in spite of Sarah's brusque manner, she had been more like a sister to her than Biddy and Liddy had ever been. Still, Mama Myrtle and the girls were her only family, and she felt she mustn't desert them.

Today, she was told the ladies were at the archery court, and she made her way through the garden, finding them smartly dressed in their riding habits. As Cindy approached, Biddy drew back her bow and shot her arrow into the second ring from the center.

Liddy grumbled, "Lucky shot," and Mama Myrtle said nothing, raising her bow and sending her arrow within a few inches of the bull's-eye.

Cindy called out, "Well done!" and both Biddy and Liddy

greeted her with unaccustomed smiles. Perhaps, she thought, her faithful visits were at last paying off. Even Mama Myrtle's eyes had thawed out as she said, "Do sit down, my dear. And how are things at the castle?"

Cindy gave them a glowing look. "Very well, thank you."

They laid down their bows and gathered at a round table, where cool drinks were poured.

Mama Myrtle said, "So there is to be a great ball again this year?"

Cindy blushed. "Yes. The prince wants us to celebrate our first anniversary just as it was last year. You have received your invitations?"

"Yes, indeed. Now, my dear, I am sure there will be many eligible young gentlemen present, and you will remember to see that your sisters are properly introduced."

"Yes, of course I shall."

Biddy simpered. "As soon as we heard the news, we ordered new gowns to be made."

Liddy gurgled. "Yes, with all the latest ribbons and lace."

Mama Myrtle bent forward slightly. "And what sort of gown are you having, my dear?"

Cindy blushed again. "The same one as last year."

The girls shrieked in unison. "What?"

Biddy snickered. "Can't you afford a new one?"

Liddy grinned, looking at Cindy's waistline. "Will it fit?"

"Granmer Fairlie will let it out."

Mama Myrtle gave her a shrewd look. "Surely the prince could give you a new gown? Is he—shall we say—less romantic than he was a year ago? These sudden infatuations seldom last, I've observed."

Cindy's blue eyes looked troubled. "Is that true? I *believe* he still loves me."

The old gimlet look shot from her stepmother's eyes. "With men, one can never know, my dear. I'm told he spends a great deal of time with the beautiful Lady Sarah."

"But they are old friends, Mama Myrtle."

"Of course they are. I'm sure there is nothing more than that."

Now their horses were brought by the groom, and the three waved good-bye and set off for the hunt.

Slowly, Cindy walked back to her pony cart and drove to Granmer Fairlie's cottage in the village, the second stop on her weekly visits. At the sight of Granmer's loving face, she burst into tears and threw herself into her arms.

With murmurs of "What is it, my darlin'?" and many soothing strokes on the soft golden hair, Granmer heard through the sobs what Mama Myrtle had said.

"Now, now, my little darlin'," she said softly, "you dry your tears and listen to Granmer. That wicked old woman is trying to make you unhappy, and we're not going to let her do that. I've seen you and the prince together many times for all the past year, have I not?"

A smothered gulp. "Yes."

"And if ever I saw a young man in love, it's your prince himself. And as for Lady Sarah, he thinks of her as his sister, growing up together as they did. Isn't that so?"

The golden head nodded.

"As for your stepmama and those girls, they're just green with envy at your happy life. And haven't I been at the castle these many years as seamstress, and haven't I seen the prince growing up into a fine young man, and don't I know how good and true is his heart? So let's have no more of this, my little love."

"Oh, Granmer, you've always been so kind to me. After Papa died and I was so unhappy at home, you were the one I could come to for comfort. And if it hadn't been for you, I'd never have met the prince."

And now they indulged in their ritual retelling of the events of that glorious night, how Cindy had run weeping to Granmer when the stepsisters were taken to the ball, how Granmer had taken her own wedding dress from the attic of her cottage, tucking it up here and there, how Granmer had put her beautiful golden slippers on Cindy's feet, and how she had borrowed the neighbor's ponies to draw the old carriage to take Cindy to the castle.

Eyes dancing, Cindy said, "And you told me to leave as the bell tolled midnight. . . ."

Granmer chuckled. "That's right. Everything comes so easy to a prince. All the pretty girls are after him. What he needs is a challenge, to find the girl who runs away from him."

"And then I dropped one of your slippers on the steps, and he kept it and came to find me!"

Granmer nodded. "The countryfolk say he was looking for the foot to fit the slipper, but we know he was looking for the girl herself—and he found her, my own darlin'."

Cindy's good humor restored, they set off together for the castle.

That afternoon, as Cindy stood before the long glass in her boudoir while Granmer, on her knees, worked on the ball gown, Lady Sarah burst in.

"There's been an accident in the field!"

Cindy gasped. "Charmie?"

"No, he's all right, but his groom was shot. We were scattered around in the woods, and some idiot shot an arrow where it made no sense to be. The groom was riding next to Charmie, and it went straight through his back and dropped him to the ground. The surgeon is working over him now."

Cindy said, softly, "He was close to Charmie?"

"At his side, yes."

Granmer Fairlie looked up at Lady Sarah. "Did they find the person who did it, milady?"

"No, not yet."

Presently the prince came in and Cindy threw herself into his arms, crying, "Sarah told us what happened."

The prince held her, caressing her hair. "It's all right, darling. Just a careless accident, I'm sure."

But when Cindy had retired to her bedroom to rest, and Sarah had gone, the prince drew Granmer aside and showed her the threatening note he had received.

"I don't want Cindy worried, Granmer, but I wonder if you would keep your ear to the ground in the village. We need to find out who may have written this."

Granmer gave him a level look. "You think the shot may have been meant for you, don't you, sir?"

Eyes troubled, the prince nodded. "Of course, it may have been only an idle threat."

By the next morning, however, there was no further doubt. Another note was found on the castle steps, on the same rough paper, and brought to the prince during his morning visit to his mother.

He read it quickly and handed it to the queen.

" 'Dere Prince,' " she read. " 'D-e-r-e.' It's the same fellow, all right." She glanced at the message and passed it over to Lady Sarah, who read aloud. " 'We mist you this time but there's allus anuther try.' "

Now the queen's voice was stentorian. "We must have the sheriff at once. He must find this person and have him punished."

In the room in the castle where the affairs of the kingdom were conducted, the prince sat in a high-backed chair, facing Sheriff Hawkins and a young man in woodman's clothing. Behind them sat the queen and Lady Sarah, and to the side sat the steward, a good-looking fellow in his forties.

The sheriff began in a gruff voice: "State your name for His Highness."

The man touched his forelock. "Bert Smith, sir."

"And your occupation?"

"Woodcutter, sir."

"And where have you been the past three months, Bert?"

"I bin locked up, sir, until this day week."

"And why was that?"

"Coz I were caught poaching, sir."

The prince cleared his throat. "I remember you, Bert. I sentenced you myself, did I not?"

"That you did, sir."

"And you promised not to offend again?"

"That I did, sir, and I won't poach no more, sir."

Now the sheriff held up the two threatening notes addressed to the prince. "Did you write these here notes, Bert?"

Bert frowned. "No, sir, I ain't written no notes."

"Now, Bert, you went to the village school and learnt to read and write some?"

"Yes, sir, a bit."

"And you was angry when the prince sent you to jail?"

"No, sir, only my missus and the children, they'd miss my wages, sir."

The sheriff laid the notes on the table and turned a fierce gaze on the man. "See here, Bert, you know as someone shot the groom two days ago, him as rode next to His Highness in the hunt?"

"Yes, sir, we all knows that."

"Now, we've studied the way that arrow was coming when it struck the groom, and we have a witness that says you was in the part of the forest as it come from."

Lady Sarah was asked to step forward, and in answer to the sheriff's question, said quietly, "I did see this man as I rode by. He was standing in a small clearing, holding his quiver. Then I heard the shouts and rode forward to see what had happened."

Now Bert stammered, "I did see the lady, sir, but I never shot at nobody, sir."

The sheriff now displayed an arrow that belonged to Bert, and triumphantly brought forth the one removed from the groom's back, showing their similarity.

"And so, Your Highness, I'd say we got the man fair and square."

The queen nodded. "Good work, Sheriff."

The prince frowned. "Well, Sheriff, perhaps you'd better not arrest him for the present, till we investigate further."

When Bert had been led away, the queen spoke sharply. "Really, Charmie, you don't sound very convinced. What more evidence do you want?"

The prince stood at the table, picking up the two arrows and studying them.

"But look here, Mother. These are made by the same chap

who makes my own, and half the countryside probably uses arrows like these. Besides, the fellow didn't *act* like a guilty man. Last time, he admitted what he'd done. I think he'd have done the same now."

The queen rolled her eyes. "You're too trusting, Charmie. Anyhow, I must say I'd feel better with the fellow locked up again. What do you say, steward?"

"I agree with Your Majesty, but His Highness will be cautious, I'm sure."

A week passed with no more threats, and at last came the day of the anniversary ball.

The queen lolled back among her cushions, sipping her morning tea, while Lady Sarah sat in her accustomed place at the foot of the bed, when the king appeared, clutching a bouquet of flowers.

The queen looked up in surprise, eyeing his slightly muddy clothing. "Good morning, Alfred. Did you wipe your feet on the mat?"

The king chuckled. "Yes, my dear."

As Lady Sarah began to rise, he waved his hand. "No need to get up, Sarah. I've brought you both some posies from the garden. So I hear Charmie wants everything the same as last year?"

The queen's tone was acerbic. "Even to her dashing off as the bell tolls midnight."

Sarah gave a wry smile. "She's to drop her slipper on the steps."

The king sighed. "And will she go off in Granmer's old carriage?"

The queen shuddered. "No, thank heaven, she needn't do that. The wretched thing looks for all the world like a pumpkin. No, he'll be following her down the steps, and this time he'll catch her, kneel down, and put the slipper on her foot, and they'll come back up the steps together."

Sarah added, "Everyone's been told, so they won't clutter up the steps."

With another sigh, the king laid half the flowers on the table, keeping the rest. "I'll just go along and see dear little Cindy, then. These are for her."

Finding Princess Cynthia in her boudoir with Granmer Fairlie, the king beamed joyfully at them both, gave Cindy a kiss on the forehead, and presented his flowers. She thanked him with a hug, then sat contentedly listening while the king and Granmer chatted together about old times.

Presently Lady Sarah drifted in and took a chair.

Cindy smiled at Granmer. "All of Sarah's suitors, from far and wide, are coming tonight. I do think this is the time for her to make her choice."

Sarah shrugged. "You look them over for me, Cindy, and tell me which one you favor."

As Cindy protested, Granmer studied Sarah's countenance. "Tell us this, Lady Sarah. If you really had to choose one now, which one do you fancy?"

"Well, if you put it that way, Prince Florimund is the handsomest and the richest, but his kingdom is far too distant. I've grown up here, and I'd hate to be so far away."

Cindy asked, "Is he one of those you met recently on your holiday?"

"Yes."

"Good. Then I'll pay special attention to him tonight!"

The ball was everything the imagination could desire. The torches in their sconces around the walls of the ballroom cast a magic shimmer on the ladies in their dazzling gowns and the men in their colorful uniforms. The king and queen sat in regal splendor on their thrones, while the musicians filled the air with gavottes and minuets.

Then, at the strains of a waltz, the prince and princess took the floor, making a circuit alone before the other dancers joined in. Charmie gazed down at his wife's glowing face and murmured his undying love, and she whispered hers in return.

In the course of the evening, Cindy, true to her promise, corralled various young men and presented them to Biddy and Liddy.

Each gentleman dutifully danced with the designated partner but adroitly disappeared before being caught again.

Several of Lady Sarah's suitors sought a dance with the princess, each pressing his cause in favor of the lady-in-waiting. Of these, Cindy was most taken with Prince Florimund.

"He's really quite charming," she said to Sarah.

And she was pleased to see the handsome Florimund being favored by Sarah with more dances than the others.

By eleven o'clock, the party adjourned to the adjoining rooms for the lavish refreshments that were laid out. Some then wandered out onto the terraces, and others strolled in the gardens, everyone savoring the still-balmy air.

Then came the great moment. The bell began to toll for midnight. Charmie and Cindy looked into each other's eyes, laughing, and she ran through the ballroom, out onto the terrace, and down the steps of the castle.

Halfway down, she let one of her golden slippers fall. The prince called out, "Wait!" She turned, smiling, to face him, and he picked up the slipper, kneeling reverently before her.

As she put out her foot, there was a movement in the deep shrubbery beside the steps, and the zing of a bow could be heard in the silence of the spring night.

At the same instant, Cindy cried out and fell forward.

The prince looked in horror at the arrow that pierced her back and at the red flood that poured from the wound.

The next morning, Cindy lay in her bed, chalky pale, her breathing shallow. The surgeon had removed the arrow and sutured the wound. It had been a near thing, he said, but now he predicted that with time and care she would fully recover.

The prince was still badly shaken and could scarcely be pried from her bedside, while Cindy herself was most grateful that she would not lose her baby, as they had feared in the beginning.

Meanwhile, there was an outcry to find the culprit who had shot the princess. A quiver and bows had been found in the shrubbery, but they had no distinguishing marks. The sheriff immediately arrested Bert Smith and brought him to the castle, and the king himself surprised everyone by taking the magistrate's chair.

When the queen said, "Really, Alfred, you can leave this to the steward," he said firmly, "I'll do this myself."

Before the hearing began, he called for Granmer Fairlie. "I want your opinion. Granmer," he said to his old friend.

"Well, sir, no one believes that Bert Smith did the other shooting of the groom, and he'd never have harmed the princess."

"No, but Granmer, surely the target was the prince?"

"If that's true, whoever did these deeds is a mighty poor shot. However, if you think Bert wrote those notes, there's a way to find out."

So it was that when the sheriff presented Bert Smith to the court as a suspect, the king asked that he be given a sheet of paper and a piece of charcoal.

"Now, Bert, I want you to write what I tell you."

"Yes, sir, but I ain't much good at writin', sir."

"Never mind. Write: 'Dear Prince: If you don't treat us fair and square . . .'"

Bert labored over his work, asking for each word to be repeated, until at last he had completed the text of the first note.

When the paper was handed to the king, he laid it beside the original. Bert's read: "Dear prins iff you doant treet us fare an sqare . . ."

With a glance at Granmer Fairlie, who sat in the corner, he handed both sheets to the sheriff. "Writing is different. Spelling is different."

The sheriff began, "But wouldn't he try to . . ."

With a look at Bert, he shrugged and gave up.

"Exactly," said the king. "No way."

Again, Bert was released, pending further investigation.

Now began many hours of questioning, from villagers to servants to the guests at the ball, in the hope of finding a witness or a clue to the culprit.

When the time came for Cindy's stepsisters to appear, Biddy came first and stated that she and her sister were in the garden when they heard the shouting and commotion.

"And was anyone with you?"

Biddy flushed an ugly red. "Not really. I believe one of the servants was nearby."

She was excused and Liddy came in, full of giggles. Yes, they were in the garden at the time.

"Was anyone else present?"

"We were chatting with the footman named George. He fancies me, and Biddy's ever so jealous."

The footman George was called and confirmed that they were in the cypress alley and that by the time they reached the house, the princess had already been carried upstairs.

"Mama Myrtle" came next, disdainfully stating that she could not say precisely where she was but she was certainly nowhere near the steps of the castle. She remembered sitting at a table with a plate of food and seeing people rushing past the window, but she didn't bother to see what the fuss was about.

Prince Florimund came in, looking debonair. He was in the garden, he said. A lady had asked him to take a turn with her, and he had obliged.

The king's eyes twinkled. "Was this Lady Sarah?"

"Regrettably, no. I believe I glimpsed her on the terrace with another gentleman."

In the end, no one acknowledged having seen anything of significance, and the court was adjourned.

"Come, Granmer," said the king, leading her toward his beloved gardens.

They sat on a stone bench under a linden tree. "So, what do you make of it?" he asked.

"First, sir, we must think about the notes."

"These?"

The king fished them out of his pocket and handed them to her.

"Yes. The prince showed me the threatening notes one day. Now, look at poor Bert's effort. You see that his contains neither capitals nor punctuation, while the others have both."

"So they do. Well, then?"

"It seems to me the threat notes may have been written by an educated person trying to look as if they were not. 'D-e-r-e' is possible, but notice that even Bert wrote 'd-e-a-r.' It could have been with a double 'e,' but the spelling is not so important as the other factors. Capitals for 'Dere Prince' and a comma. Then a capital in 'If.' I may be only a seamstress, but my father was a gentleman, and I was sent to a proper school in my day."

"Yes, so you were. Then, if your theory is right, it's someone who tried to imitate the writing of a simple person, someone who hated the prince and wanted to lay blame on the peasants."

"Well, sir, not exactly. It's someone who wanted us to *think* the prince was the target, but who is it who actually gets shot? First the groom, and then Cindy."

"Someone who hates them both? That seems unlikely."

"Yes, sir, it is. I believe the groom was set up to make it look as if our culprit is a poor shot. Notice that the second note says they missed this time but will try again. Now, when Cindy is hit while the prince is very close to her, we are prepared to believe it's another miss."

"Good lord! Are you saying *Cindy* was the target all along?"

"I'm afraid so, sir. The prince has no enemies. He is universally loved and admired and has never offended anyone in all his young life. Barring yourself, sir, there's no one less likely to be the object of malice."

"But who would hate dear little Cindy?"

"Ah, sir, there we have another question. Originally I had hopes of those ghastly stepsisters, but not only are they in the clear, it's also hard to see how those two dimwits could have hatched this clever plot. Now, their mama is a much better candidate. She has always hated Cindy, yet oddly enough, she would hurt Cindy more by killing the prince. If she had devised a plot, I believe that's the way it would have gone."

"She's a most unpleasant woman, I agree."

"They are an unsavory lot, those three. You notice they have expressed not a jot of concern over Cindy."

"That's true. Not a word. So where are we now?"

"I believe, sir, we must continue to look for someone who hates Cindy herself and would like her out of the way."

"Oh, dear, who could that be?"

Now, Granmer Fairlie got up from the bench and walked along the gravel path, bending over a rose bush here, a larkspur there. At last she turned and came back to sit beside the king. "It's painful for me to say this, sir, but we may have to look at someone very close to yourself."

"Surely not—?"

"I don't know, sir. It's possible."

"I know the queen has never cared for little Cindy, but Granmer, what would she gain by—well, by harming her?"

"You know how much she's always wished for Charmie and Sarah to marry. She may believe that in his grief he would eventually turn to Sarah. And she may be right."

"Wouldn't she see how terribly the prince would suffer?"

"I'm afraid she thinks of love as rather fleeting, sir. She would expect him to recover in due course."

"I see."

"The question is, do we know where she was at the time the arrow was shot?"

Granmer was surprised to see a deep flush cover the king's face. His voice was low. "Yes, I'm afraid I do know. A few minutes earlier, I saw her go down the steps leading to the steward's quarters, and I heard the door close."

"Do you mean—?"

"Yes, he's the current favorite. He's a handsome fellow, you know."

Granmer's eyes filled with tears. "Oh, sir, I am so sorry."

He patted her hand. "Never mind. It's quite all right. The queen is still a young woman, not yet forty, and I'm so many years older." He sighed. "Royalty can't always marry for love, you see. Ours was an arrangement to suit the politics of the day. I was determined that Charmie should make his own choice, and so we have our dear little Cindy."

"At any rate, sir, it seems that the queen can be struck off our list of suspects."

The king gave a wan smile. "Yes. Frankly, I rather doubt she would have troubled herself to the extent of devising an elaborate plot and so on. She's not inclined to exert herself overmuch."

Now a servant came to announce that luncheon was served, and the king put Granmer at his side at the table. The queen raised an eyebrow but said nothing.

An hour later, Granmer and the king stood at Cindy's bedside. She put up her arms to each in turn, smiling weakly, while the prince hovered on the other side of the bed, his face haggard. A nurse sat in a corner, hands busy with her knitting.

Lady Sarah came in and stood at the foot of the bed. "How is she, Charmie?"

"A little better, I think."

Granmer bent over Cindy. "Are you in much pain, little darlin'?"

Cindy whispered, "Not much." Her eyes closed, and she seemed to drift into sleep.

The prince held up a glass from the table. "We're giving her laudanum. It's good for the pain, but it makes her very drowsy."

Granmer nodded, and the visitors slipped quietly out of the room.

Lady Sarah went off without a word to the others, and the king led Granmer to a small sitting room along the corridor, closing the door behind them.

"So, Granmer, we seem to be no nearer to solving our mystery."

"Well, sir, there's one other person who would desperately like for Charmie to marry Lady Sarah."

The king looked puzzled. "I can't think—"

"You've always seen that Charmie thinks of Sarah merely as a sister, but does that mean that *she* thinks of him in the same way?"

"I don't know. I suppose we took it for granted—"

"Exactly, sir. She often says they are like brother and sister, but that doesn't mean it's *her* choice. I've seen her over the years looking at him when she thought no one noticed, and I believe she's been in love with him for years. You notice she doesn't care for any of her suitors, and I believe she has never given up hope that one day Charmie would suddenly wake up and see her in a different light. She must have been devastated when Cindy came along and snatched him away."

The king looked thoughtful. "I have observed that she and the queen often spoke disparagingly of little Cindy."

"Yes. In front of others, Sarah has hidden her feelings toward Cindy, but underneath, she must seethe with hatred."

"Do we know where Sarah was when the shooting occurred?"

"No. She wasn't officially questioned, of course, as being above suspicion. Prince Florimund thought he might have glimpsed her on the terrace, but she could have slipped away. She is certainly clever enough to plant the notes threatening the prince."

The king sighed. "Oh, dear, it's dreadful to think of. And it can never be proved, can it?"

Granmer's eyes hardened. "There may be a way, sir."

And she outlined her plan.

The king, with a rare display of authority, took charge, directing the nurse to take the air in the garden and telling Charmie to ask Lady Sarah to sit with Cindy while he went to his own room to rest.

Thus it was that Sarah sat in the darkened room, where Cindy lay in a deep sleep. All was silent except for the patient's shallow breathing.

Presently, Sarah arose and bent over the bed. Then, with a quick motion, she lifted the pillow beside the sleeping girl and laid it over her face, pressing down with both hands.

The heavy draperies that covered the tall window near the bed stirred, and the king leaped forward.

"I'll take that, if you please."

Sarah froze, then lifted the pillow and handed it to the king.

When Granmer Fairlie emerged from the window, Sarah's eyes burned with fury. "*You* did this, didn't you, you beastly old woman? You always knew, didn't you?"

The prince stepped in from the corridor, looking stunned. "Sarah," he cried out, "how could you—?"

Her anger gone, Sarah threw herself at his feet, sobbing.

Charmie simply stepped away from her and went to the bed, lifting his sleeping wife in his arms.

A year later, plans for another anniversary ball were made, but on a much reduced scale. Cindy had been told all that had happened, and in spite of her gentle nature, she felt no compassion for Sarah. She also learned of the callous behavior of Mama Myrtle and the stepsisters at the time of her illness, and she no longer felt obliged to invite them nor to visit them at the manor. Sarah had been advised to accept Prince Florimund, and it was generally agreed that the distance from his kingdom was far too great to permit visits. The queen made the journey once or twice, but no return visit ever took place.

When the expected heir to the throne had turned out to be a lovely little fair-haired girl, no one but the queen was disappointed. The king adored his little granddaughter, and the prince was ecstatic. "We can have a boy the next time," he declared.

The guest of honor at the ball was Granmer Fairlie. No reason was ever given for such an honor, and the queen, knowing the full story, made no protest beyond an exasperated groan.

The ballroom was as glowing as ever, and Cindy, wearing a stunning new ball gown, stood beside the prince as they smilingly received their guests.

Then trumpets sounded, the company fell silent, and as the musicians broke into a waltz, the king stepped down from his throne, while the queen remained in her place.

Stepping to a high chair where Granmer Fairlie sat, in a gown of lavender silk, the king bowed before her and proudly led her in the first dance.

Janet Dawson's novels about Oakland private eye Jeri Howard are a successful fusion of the traditional and hard-boiled forms. They have a nice contemporary edge while remaining very good examples of the mystery writer's art. Her Take a Number *is a wonderful novel based on its sinewy and stunning plot alone. In the following story, Hansel and Gretel go through a twentieth-century updating and take on the urban forest of San Francisco.*

INVISIBLE TIME

Greta watched the front door of the bakery on Geary Street, choosing her moment. When it came, it was brought by a middle-aged woman who wore a business suit and running shoes.

The woman stopped at the window, eyed the tempting display of cakes, cookies, and breads, then moved toward the door. Greta slipped up behind the woman, a pace back from the leather brief-case that swung from her left hand. The woman pushed open the door, her entry ringing the bell above the door.

The bakery clerk was a gangly young man wearing a silly white paper hat perched on his brown hair. He looked up from his post behind the counter and smiled at the woman. He didn't see Greta.

Fine. That's what she had in mind. Now that she was inside, Greta hovered near the door, keeping one eye on the grown-ups and the other eye on the bakery's wares. Picking a target was tough. The goods were piled alluringly on counters and shelves and stand-alone displays. Finally she spotted her best shot, bags of day-old cookies mounded high in a basket at the edge of a low table, just a few steps from the door that led out to the busy sidewalk.

The bakery clerk's head was down. He was busy boxing up a cake for a customer, a big man with a fat belly. Looked like he got plenty to eat, Greta told herself as she edged closer to the basket. Unlike some people she could name.

The customer Greta had followed into the bakery stood on the other side of the table, examining the loaves of day-old bread stacked there as she waited her turn at the counter. She hummed to herself and tapped one finger on the edge of the basket that held the cookies. Greta kept her head down, her blue eyes constantly shifting as she observed the bakery's occupants. The woman moved closer. Greta thought she smelled good, like flowers, but she didn't smell as good as the combined perfume of what came out of the bakery's ovens.

Handing the clerk a twenty, the big man put a proprietary hand on top of the box containing his cake. While the clerk looked down at the drawer of the cash register, Greta snaked her hand toward the cookies. She grabbed two bags, whirled, and made for the door.

"Hey, little girl," the woman in running shoes said, sounding surprised and shocked as she moved to stop this theft in progress. The little girl shoved the woman hard, knocking her into the table, and kept going, darting past a trio of teenagers who'd just opened the bakery door wide, giving Greta an open shot to freedom.

Once she was out on the sidewalk, she dodged to the right and ran up Geary Street, against the tide of pedestrians heading down toward Market Street, where BART and the San Francisco Municipal Railway would take them home. Intent on their own destinations, they took no notice of the skinny little girl in baggy blue jeans and a red sweatshirt, her dirty blond hair spilling to her shoulders.

Hank was waiting for her in Union Square, on the side close to the entrance to the Saint Francis Hotel and the cable cars that clanged up and down Powell Street. At his feet was a brown nylon bag with a zipper and a shoulder strap. It contained everything they owned—clothes, a couple of beat-up stuffed animals, and a picture of Mom.

"You get something?" he asked eagerly, brown eyes too big in his pinched face. He looked far more streetwise than a five-year-old boy should.

"Yeah. Cookies. Two bags. Looks like one of 'em is chocolate chip and the other is maybe oatmeal raisin. Did you get anything?"

"Pizza," he said triumphantly, displaying a dented cardboard box. "With pepperoni. Some guy was sitting on that bench over there eating it, and he didn't eat it all. He was gonna throw it in the trash. But he saw me watching him, so he gave it to me. Look, there's two whole pieces left."

"All right!" They high-fived it.

Then they hunkered down on the bench to eat their booty. People hurrying through the square paid no mind to the two children, any more than they did to the pigeons congregating around the statue of Victory atop the column in the center of the square. As she ate, Greta watched shoppers laden with bags scurry from store to store. Hank focused on the food with the single-minded appetite of a little boy who never gets enough to eat.

The store windows in Macy's and Saks were full of glittering decorations, red, green, gold, and silver, signaling the approaching holiday season, and there was a big lighted Christmas tree in the square. But the passage of time meant little to Greta. She only knew that the days were shorter than they had been. The sunshine, what little there was of it, had turned thin and weak. Nights were longer and it was harder for her and her brother to stay warm. Today the wind had turned cold. From what little she could see of the late afternoon sky, it was dark gray.

It was going to rain, she was sure of it. She didn't know what they'd do if it rained. They'd been sleeping in doorways and alleys all over the downtown area, constantly moving so the cops wouldn't find them during their periodic sweeps to rid the streets of human litter.

If it rains we'll have to go inside somewhere, Greta told herself. But it wasn't safe to go down inside the BART station to spend the night. The BART cops would catch them. And there were too many weirdos down there already. Mom had always told Greta to take care of her little brother and to stay away from the weirdos.

She was doing the best she could, but she didn't know how long she could keep it up. She was careful to limit their range to the Union Square area, north of Market Street. That's where the nice stores, restaurants, and hotels were. Greta felt safer where the people were better-dressed. Sometimes those people gave them money, or food, like Hank's pizza benefactor. South of Market and the Tenderloin were different, full of run-down buildings and scary people who would take their stuff, even during the day, though it was more dangerous after dark.

Greta couldn't remember when Mom left. A few weeks, a month, two months, it didn't matter. After a few days, the hours all ran together, like a stream of dirty water chasing debris down the sewer grate. She only remembered that it didn't used to be like this.

Once she'd had a father, though lately it was hard to recall what he'd looked like. They'd lived in a nice apartment, two bedrooms so Greta had a room of her own. She had a baby doll and a crib her dad had made for her, pretty dresses. She remembered all of this. Or maybe she thought she remembered, because Mom had told her.

She knew that one day her father hadn't come home. Although it was a long time ago, she remembered that day and the days afterward quite clearly. Mom crying, people bringing food to the apartment. They talked about God's will and a car crash. Greta didn't understand how or why God could have fixed it so that her father never came home, but no one bothered to explain it to her. She only knew that Mom missed him something terrible.

That was about the time Greta started kindergarten. Mom had a job working a cash register at some store, but it didn't pay much. Not enough to make ends meet, Mom told Greta. At the time Greta wasn't sure what that meant, but now the ends didn't meet at all, she knew. That was when she and Mom went to live with Grandma.

Greta didn't much like Grandma. The old woman seemed as ancient as a dinosaur, and not even half as cuddly as the stuffed stegosaurus her mom had given her. Grandma coughed a lot and smelled bad, puffing on foul-smelling cigarettes even if she did have some sickness with a long name. She had a sharp tongue on her, too, one she used to peel layers off Greta's mom, until Mom didn't have much spirit left.

Then Mom met Hank's dad and got some of the sparkle back in her eyes. Of course, Grandma kicked them out because Mom took up with Hank's dad. He was a different color than Mom, and

Grandma said bad things about him, but Greta liked him a lot. He drove a cab and brought her chocolate, her favorite. And when Hank was born, a year or so later, she thought the baby was beautiful. She loved him and swore she'd always take care of him, no matter what. She just didn't think it would be this soon.

Hank didn't remember his dad much. He was not quite three when the cabdriver was shot to death. Greta heard one of the other cabbies at the funeral say Hank's dad should have given the money to the punk who pulled a gun on him late one night. But Greta figured maybe the punk would have shot him anyway.

Hank's dad had left something called life insurance, which was kind of strange to Greta, seeing he was dead. She'd have rather had Hank's dad instead of money. It hadn't been much anyway, and after a while there wasn't any left.

She was nine and in the fourth grade when Hank's dad got killed. She liked school, but the rest of her life was hard. She had to take care of Hank and Mom both. Hank because he was just a toddler, and Mom, because she was drinking, cheap, sweet-smelling wine in big bottles. Greta would come home from school and find her passed out on the bed of the tiny apartment, Hank roaming around on the floor with soiled pants.

Greta stayed home from school more often, missing classes. No one ever seemed to notice she was gone. Mom got fired from her job at the store and didn't bother to get another job. She said she'd rather die than go back to live with Grandma, but as it turned out, Grandma had died by then and left all her money to some cousin.

They were evicted from that apartment. They moved to a run-down rickety hotel in the Tenderloin, where all three of them shared one room and a bath. Greta stopped going to school altogether, because looking after Mom and Hank was a full-time job. She'd cook their meager meals on a hot plate, put Mom to bed when she drank too much, and read to Hank so he could at least learn his letters. Then she'd put Hank to bed and try to get some sleep herself, which was hard to do. Down on the street, music spilled from the bars, and the hookers called to men cruising by in cars. The hookers worked for a tall man called a pimp, who hung out on the corner and kept an eye on the girls. Sometimes he hit them, and Greta would hear screams and shouts. She'd cover her ears with her hands, trying to keep the sounds out.

Then Mom started bringing men home, men who gave her money. Did that make her a hooker, too? Greta didn't like to think about that. All she knew was that Mom would shut Hank and Greta out of the ugly room. They'd huddle together on the stairs that stank of urine, dodging the other residents of the hotel, those scary-looking weirdos Mom had warned Greta about in those few times when she wasn't giggly and woozy from that stuff she was drinking.

One day Mom left. She said she was going to the store on the corner to get a bottle. But she never came back.

The manager of the hotel told Greta he was going to call social something to come and get the two children. But social something sounded like cops to Greta. She didn't want to go to jail or wherever the cops would take them. She packed what little they had in the nylon bag and they left. Now they lived on the streets and it was getting harder to find food and stay warm.

Hank, his stomach filled by the pepperoni pizza and the cookies Greta had stolen from the bakery, drowsed next to her, leaning on her shoulder. Greta put one arm around him as she savored the last bite of her chocolate chip cookie. Then she felt someone's eyes on her and looked quickly around, her senses honed by weeks of surviving on the urban landscape.

There he was, a man, staring at them across Union Square. She'd seen the man before, staring at them like this. He wore shapeless green coveralls, and stood hunched over the handle of a metal shopping cart. Inside the cart was a black plastic bag that clinked and clattered. Greta knew it was full of cans and bottles. The man had a black beard and a brown knit cap that didn't quite disguise his long black hair.

Greta didn't like the way he was always watching them. Then the man pushed his shopping cart toward them, the wheels squeaking. She jumped to her feet and shook Hank awake.

"Invisible time," she whispered.

That meant it was time for them to disappear into the shadows. She picked up the nylon bag and slung it over her shoulder, then took Hank's hand. The two children darted down the steps that led out of the square, across Geary Street, just as the green "walk" signal changed to a flashing amber "don't walk." As they angled to the left, Greta glanced back. The man in coveralls was following them, pushing his shopping cart into the crosswalk, ambling slowly as though he didn't care that the light had changed to red and the people in the going-home cars were honking at him.

Greta tugged Hank's arm and the two children rushed along Geary, dodging pedestrians. They turned right on Stockton, heading toward Market. Finally they pushed through a pair of big glass double doors and entered the first floor of the Virgin Megastore, sound pulsating around them.

They were in familiar territory now. The store was one of their favorite hangouts. It was brightly lit and full of loud music, where customers bought CDs, tapes, videos, and books. It was open late, and the children frequently spent the evening here, walking the aisles, riding the escalator up and down, and using the rest room on the third floor. Greta figured they'd lost the man with the shopping cart, but even if they hadn't, he wouldn't be able to follow them in here.

"I'm sleepy," Hank told her on their fourth trip up the escalator. "Can we find a place to spend the night soon?"

Greta was tired, too, but she didn't like to admit it. Watching and moving all the time took its toll, but she was afraid to let her guard down. She wished they could find a spot somewhere in this bright, warm store, but she knew that was a bad idea.

"Let's go to the bathroom first," she said. "Then we'll find a place."

They detoured to the third floor, past the videos and into the bookstore. The rest rooms were located down a short hallway near the store's café. Greta watched Hank dart into the men's room, then pushed open the door marked with a woman's silhouette. Sometimes, if they didn't know the place, she'd take him with her into the women's side, where they'd barricade themselves into the larger stall usually reserved for handicapped people. But they'd been here before and hadn't had any problems. Greta felt as safe here as she felt anywhere, which wasn't saying much.

When she came out of the rest room Hank was waiting for her, bouncing in time to the music that blared from the overhead speakers. Greta shifted the nylon bag from one shoulder to the other and they walked toward the café.

"You kids okay?"

The speaker was a young woman, wearing thick, clunky shoes and black tights under a short black skirt. Above that she wore a tight black T-shirt with the store's name printed across her tiny round breasts. Her hair was cut short and dyed an odd bright pink. She had little gold rings arrayed up and down both ears, and a glittery jewel in her nose. Greta had seen her before, once working behind a cash register on the second floor and another time waiting tables in the store's café.

Hank stared at her, transfixed. Greta started looking around for the quickest and shortest way out.

"I've seen you before," the young woman said, talking quietly as though she were afraid they would bolt. "You come in and wander around for hours. Don't you have any place to stay?" When neither of the children answered, she continued, her voice low and seductive. "I'll bet you're hungry. Would you like something to eat? Come back to the café. I'll give you some gingerbread."

From the corner of her eye, Greta saw something move, a skinny form in a T-shirt that resolved itself into another store employee, this one a young man with white hair. Trap, she thought. They wouldn't be able to come in here again. If they ever got out.

"Invisible time," she said with a hiss.

She grabbed Hank's arm and ran straight at the young woman, who held out her arms as though to catch them. Greta shoved her hard and the young woman fell back against a bin full of CDs. The young man who'd come to her assistance looked startled as the children darted past him. As they ran toward the down escalator, Greta heard voices behind her, all jumbled as the two sales clerks spoke together

". . . Almost had them."

". . . Told you . . . bad idea. Shoulda called the cops."

"Poor little things . . . back tomorrow night . . . try again."

Won't be back, Greta told herself as she and Hank hurried down the escalator, heedless of bumping the customers who stood still on the moving stairs. Not safe anymore. Too bad. She hated to lose any shelter, however temporary.

It had started to rain while they were inside the store. Hand-in-hand, Greta and Hank rushed along the wet pavement, until they found themselves heading up Market Street, pushed along with a tide of people. At Sixth they crossed Market, wet and cold, and headed farther away from the bright holiday glitter of the city's main shopping area and into the dingy, neon-pierced blocks where the Tenderloin collided with the area south of Market. Here were lots of people sitting in doorways, bundled up against the rain. Music blared from bars. Hookers, some of them barely older than Greta, called to the passing cars.

These grown-ups scared Greta, and she quickly detoured down a side street where it was much quieter. She found a wide doorway, recessed from the street. It looked like a good place to spend the night. She set the nylon bag down to use as a pillow. But then she spotted the man in green coveralls, back the way they'd come and moving toward them. He was close enough so that she was sure she could hear the clink and clatter of the bottles and cans in his garbage bag, the squeaking wheels of his shopping cart.

They kept moving, Hank stumbling along sleepily at her side. The nylon bag seemed as heavy as lead, and Greta was so tired she thought she couldn't put another foot in front of her. Still she thought she could hear the shopping cart following them, squeaking and rattling as they fled through the wet curtain of rain.

Then she saw something flicker. Was she imagining it? No, it came from inside a big, dark two-story building with broken glass windows. Greta crept closer and peered through the nearest window. But she couldn't see much, just something red and gold glowing farther back in the dark building. She squinted and could just make out some figures nearby.

A fire, she thought. Just the word sounded like a sanctuary, warm and inviting. But there were people, and they could be bad people.

She heard a squeaking noise somewhere back the way they had come, and made her choice. Quickly she boosted Hank up to the window, then followed him through, dragging the nylon bag with her. She held her finger to her mouth and tiptoed forward, trying not to make any noise as she moved closer to the fire.

She saw three grown-ups, two men and a woman. They'd spread big pieces of cardboard on the concrete floor of the empty warehouse to cut the chill. On top of these the grown-ups had constructed their nests of sleeping bags and blankets. In the center they'd built a fire with whatever fuel they could find. Now it danced, red and gold, crackling and popping and hissing. The grown-ups talked in low voices, occasionally laughing as they drank from a bottle, its neck visible at the top of its brown paper bag wrapping. They passed it among themselves, and one of them leaned toward the fire to stir something that was bubbling in a big, shiny kettle, something that smelled rich and savory like the soup Mom used to make.

Greta's foot encountered a piece of broken glass and sent it skittering across the concrete. The resulting tinkle heralded their arrival. The grown-ups grouped around the fire turned, seeking the source of the noise.

"Well, what have we here?" a voice boomed at them. It belonged to a big man with a white beard, bundled up in several layers of clothing, his eyes glittering in the firelight. "A couple of little angels with very dirty faces?"

"More like a couple of pups looking for a teat and a warm place to sleep." The woman who spoke had a hard face and hard eyes, but she reached for a tin mug and the ladle that protruded from the kettle on the fire. She spooned some of the hot liquid into the mug.

"Don't be feeding strays," complained the second man, a pale, skinny fellow dressed in a dirty gray sweater. He reclined on a gray duffel bag and folded his arms in front of him.

"Don't tell me what to do," she snapped. Then she held out the mug and beckoned at the children. "Come here. It's vegetable soup. We made it ourselves and it's damned good, if I do say so myself."

Hank and Greta stared, mesmerized by the smell and the sight. Then they moved into the warm circle around the fire and sat at the foot of the woman's sleeping bag. Greta reached for the mug, felt the warmth on her hands, smelled the broth. Then she held the mug out to Hank. He drank noisily, hungrily. Yet he was careful to leave half the soup for his sister. He handed her the mug and wiped his mouth on his sleeve.

"You take care of him, don't you," the woman said, as Greta sipped warm soup from the mug. "Bet you do a good job, too. My name's Elva. This here's Wally." She pointed at the big man with the beard. "And this bag of bones is Jake."

Jake snorted, and sank farther into the folds of his sleeping bag. He took a long pull from the bottle, then passed the libation to Wally. "What the hell you kids doing out here all by yourselves?"

"What are any of us doing out here?" Wally boomed, his voice echoing in the dark recesses of the warehouse. "Trying to stay warm, dry, and fed." He tipped back the bottle and grinned at the two children across the glowing heat of the fire. "Look how skinny these little angels are. Stick with us, kids. We'll fatten you up."

Wary as she was after weeks of living on the streets, Greta was also tired. She felt exhaustion creep over her as the warmth of the soup and fire crept over her body. Already Hank was asleep, his little body burrowed into her side, like a puppy pillowed on its mother's belly.

"Look at 'em," Elva said. "Just babies. What you got in that bag, girl?"

"Clothes." Greta's tongue was getting tangled up in the word.

"Not even a sleeping bag, and winter coming on." Elva shook her head. She pulled a raggedy square of cloth that looked like a piece of an old blanket from the depths of her sleeping bag. Then she scooted forward and used it to cover Hank, fussing with the edge as she tucked it around his neck, just the way Mom used to. "Where's your folks?"

"Gone," Greta said, and the word seemed to echo around the warehouse.

Elva frowned and looked at her companions. "All alone? How long you been out here, girl?"

Greta found that she didn't have strength enough to answer. She felt all her caution fall to the onslaught of sleep.

"We can't be baby-sitting a couple of kids."

Greta's eyes were shut, but she identified the voice. It belonged to Jake, the skinny one.

"No one's asking you to look after 'em. They can go with me."

That was Elva, the woman. Greta opened her eyes just a little bit. It was morning, cold gray light filtering into the warehouse. The fire was out, cold gray ashes swirling along the concrete floor. Greta felt warm, though. The children were tucked into Elva's sleeping bag. Hank was next to Greta, curled up in a ball and still asleep.

"Just slow you down," Jake growled as he rolled up his sleeping bag. "Make you a target for the cops. They don't even look like they're yours."

"What the hell do you know?" Elva scowled at him. "All anybody's gonna see is some poor homeless woman with a couple of kids she can't feed. Which ain't far from the truth. With Christmas coming on, people feel generous and guilty. I'll just park the three of us out in front of San Francisco Centre where all those rich people ride that fancy curved escalator up to Nordstrom. You just see how many handouts I get. Take my word, these kids'll be worth their weight in greenbacks."

"More trouble than they're worth, you ask me," Jake grumbled as he tied his sleeping bag with rope.

"Nobody asked you," Elva shot back.

"Now, friends, friends. Let's not come to blows, whether with words or fists." That was Wally, the big guy with the beard. "I agree with Elva. We should care for these little angels. I'm sure we'll be handsomely rewarded. Yes, indeed."

Wally laughed. He was pretending to be nice, Greta decided, but he wasn't. She didn't like the way his eyes glittered when he looked at her and Hank. She abandoned all pretense of sleep and sat up. The nylon bag was no longer beside her, but next to Elva, who had rummaged through its contents. Greta snatched up the picture of Mom and hugged the frame to her chest.

"That your mama?" Elva asked. "She was real pretty." The woman reached over and shook Hank awake. "Let's put another layer of clothes on you, 'cause it's cold out there this morning."

The three grown-ups stashed their sleeping bags in a small room in the bowels of the abandoned warehouse and set out with the two children. In the bleak daylight the south of Market neighborhood didn't look as scary as it had last night, just dirty and down at the heels.

Jake set off on his own, heading up Mission Street, but Wally stayed with Elva and the children until they reached Market. Then he bid them an elaborate and flowery farewell, lingering until Elva told him to get the hell on with it. He bowed, crossed the street, and headed for the Tenderloin.

Then Elva took Hank and Greta another block down Market and did just what she'd said she'd do. She took a position in front of the San Francisco Centre and started cadging handouts from well-heeled shoppers. Soon she had enough money to send the children across Market to the fast-food burger place. Hank ate two cheeseburgers and a big order of French fries all by himself.

"I like Elva," he declared, wiping ketchup from his mouth.

He doesn't know things the way I do, Greta thought. He's just a baby, not experienced, like me. I'm not so sure but what we're better off on our own.

She brooded as she finished her hamburger. Then she cleared off the table and stepped up to the counter to buy another one, for Elva.

But even if Greta had her doubts about staying with the trio from the warehouse, it was easy to slip into the routine, the next day and the day after. They worked the streets with Elva during the day, going from store to store, hotel to hotel, then met Jake and Wally back at the warehouse. Wally found a sleeping bag for the two children to share, and each day the three grown-ups managed to find enough food to put into the kettle. It was so easy to feel comfortable and safe, huddled in the warm circle of the fire on the warehouse's concrete floor. In the morning they'd roll up their sleeping bags and stash their gear in the little room, then head out for a day on the streets.

The two children had been staying at the warehouse for a couple of weeks when Greta saw Wally talking with the tall man from the Tenderloin, the pimp who had all those hookers working for him. She and Hank and Elva were working the Geary Theatre that day. It was a natural, Elva told them. Theater patrons left the comfortable confines where they'd seen a seasonal matinee of *A Christmas Carol,* and stepped onto the dirty city streets and came face-to-face with a couple of contemporary urchins.

"Guilt and generosity," Elva said confidently. "It'll do it every time."

After the matinee Elva led them down Taylor toward Market Street, through the Tenderloin, where Greta saw Wally. He spotted the children and waved. Why was Wally talking to that awful pimp man? Why did Wally's eyes glitter like that, above his white beard? She didn't like it. Especially since Wally came back to the warehouse that night with a big bottle of brandy, evidently the kind Jake and Elva liked a lot, because they drank the whole bottle that night, laughing loudly and acting silly, so drunk they finally passed out and Greta had to finish making dinner under Wally's watchful eyes.

When she woke up the next morning, her head pillowed on the nylon bag, Jake and Elva were still asleep, a couple of lumps in their sleeping bags, snoring like they were sawing logs.

But Wally was gone. So was Hank.

Greta kicked her way out of the sleeping bag and put on her shoes. "Hank?" she called. There was no answer. She darted around the bottom floor of the warehouse, looking for her brother, getting more frantic as she looked in all the shadowy places.

On her third circuit she encountered Wally, who was making his way back into the warehouse with a bag and a large container that smelled like coffee. "What's the matter, little angel?" he asked jovially.

"Hank's gone," she cried.

"I'm sure he's just wandered off." Wally waggled the bag at

her. "Doughnuts, little angel. Jelly doughnuts and chocolate bars. I know you like chocolate. Want one?"

"He wouldn't wander off," Greta said stubbornly. "He knows he's supposed to stick close to me."

Greta ran back to where Jake and Elva still lay snoring. She shook Elva, but the woman wouldn't wake up.

"Oh, I wouldn't bother," Wally said, placing a heavy hand on her shoulder. "When those two get a snootful of brandy it would take an earthquake to wake them. Maybe two earthquakes. Have a doughnut. We want to fatten you up."

Fatten me up for what? Greta glared at him. "I don't want a doughnut. I have to look for Hank."

"Have you looked on the second floor? Maybe he went exploring up there."

"How would he get there?" Greta knew there was another floor above this one but she hadn't seen any stairs or an elevator, not that an elevator would work in this place.

"Why, there's some stairs down at the other end, next to what used to be the elevator shaft." Wally laughed and pointed into the dark bowels of the warehouse. "Wait, I'll come with you."

Greta ran ahead, frantic with worry about Hank. She found the stairs and clambered up them, calling for her brother. She heard Wally behind her, chuckling to himself as he climbed the stairs.

Hank wasn't on the second floor of the warehouse. Or if he was, he wasn't answering her. Greta felt tears prickling behind her eyes as she searched the big empty space, skirting the hole near the stairs, where Wally said there used to be an elevator.

"Why, look at this," Wally said. She looked in the direction he was pointing. There was a doorway, open, with blackness beyond. "There's rooms back there. Maybe that's where your brother's gone."

She didn't trust the bearded man, but she had to find Hank. She walked toward the doorway and peered into the dimly lit chamber, her eyes adjusting, picking out shapes. This part of the warehouse had been used as offices, about a quarter of the floor carved up into cubicles by partitions. There was a door on the far side next to a dirty window.

"Hank?" she called, her voice echoing against the walls.

Was that a voice she heard, just a whimper? Maybe he had wandered in here and gotten hurt or something. She moved into the divided-up room, heard Wally step in after her, then whirled in alarm as she heard the door shut. Wally laughed. A few seconds later this portion of the room was brightened by the circular glow from a big flashlight.

In that instant she saw Hank. He was under an old metal desk, his hands tied to one of the legs with a length of rope. He'd been crying, but he stopped when he saw Greta.

She ran to Hank and scrabbled at the rope with her fingers. It wasn't tied very well. If she had enough time, she could get it loose. But did she have enough time?

She turned and shouted at Wally. "What have you done to him?"

Wally laughed, a nasty sound. "Caught me a pair of plump little partridges, that's what. You and him both."

"What are you talking about?" Greta demanded.

"Been talking to a man. The kind of man who'll pay good money for a couple of fat little angels like you. Oh, yes. The kind that likes little boys will have a good time with your little brother. Then there's the kind that likes sweet little virgins like you."

Wally shifted the flashlight from his right hand to his left. Greta saw his right hand go into his pocket and pull out a handful of greenbacks. "This is just seed money. I get the rest when I deliver the goods, when the man comes through that fire escape door in a few minutes."

A few minutes. That's all the time she had. Wally was between her and the door. Greta squatted and tugged at the rope securing Hank's hands, her fingers working the knot. There, it was loosening. Just a little bit more, that's all she needed.

"Look at him," she cried, making her voice teary. "You got it so tight it's cutting his hands. That's why he's been crying."

Hank didn't need to be told twice. He started to wail. Greta joined in, still fumbling with the rope.

"Shut up, both of you," Wally said, shoving the money back into his pocket. "Shut up, I tell you."

Wally walked to the desk and knelt, setting the flashlight aside so he could adjust the rope. Quick as lightning, Greta scooped up the flashlight and brought it down hard on Wally's head. He bellowed and grabbed for her as he tried to get to his feet. She slithered from his grasp, then hit him again, and he went down. She hit him a third time, and he moaned. Then she turned to Hank and helped her little brother pull free of his bonds.

She seized her brother's arm and tugged him toward the door. When they reached it, she jerked it open and they ran for the stairwell. Hank had just reached the top step when Greta was caught from behind. Wally was cursing in her ear as he lifted her off the floor. She wriggled in his arms, almost gagging at the smell of him, and sank her teeth into one of the hands that held her. He screamed as she tasted blood. He dropped her.

She regained her balance and turned to face him as he came at her again, aiming her fist at the crotch of his baggy pants, at the place Mom said it would hurt if you hit a man. He screamed again when she hit him, falling backward. But he didn't fall onto the floor. He kept going back, and down, into the open elevator shaft.

"He went splat," Hank said when she found him at the bottom of the stairwell.

"Good. I hope he broke his damn neck."

Greta looked dispassionately at the motionless body lying on top of the rusted metal at the bottom of the elevator shaft, about three feet below the first floor of the warehouse. Blood trickled from his mouth. When he didn't move, she climbed down and reached into his pocket, pulling out the folding money he'd been showing off. He wouldn't be needing it anymore.

Greta shoved the money into her own pocket, climbed out of the shaft, and took Hank's arm. They ran through the warehouse, back to where Jake and Elva were still sleeping it off next to the gray ashes of the fire. Greta scooped up the bag of doughnuts and zipped them inside the brown nylon bag. No sense letting food go to waste.

"Where we going now?" Hank asked.

She slung the bag over her shoulder and headed for the street. "Invisible time."

Kristine Kathryn Rusch spent several years editing The Magazine of Fantasy & Science Fiction. *Despite the long editorial hours, she was also able to write dozens of first-rate stories and novels in the mystery, science-fiction, and horror fields. Her latest novel is* The Consecrated Ground. *Her take on the rags-to-riches story of Cinderella finds that not everyone lives happily ever after.*

KRISTINE KATHRYN RUSCH

LOVE AND JUSTICE

Let me explain the difficulties:

1. I'm a sheriff. No title. I own land, but I work for the palace. I keep the peace and keep the peasants in line. Occasionally I investigate servants at the castle, but that's all. No power, really, except that which lies in the rules that have existed long before me.

2. The king believes in justice for all. Honest, he does. I can't tell you how many times he's said to me, "Bertrand, it doesn't matter to us if one of our lords or one of our peasants commits a crime. Criminals should be equal under the eyes of the law."

3. The king hates liars and sycophants.

All of this would have worked to my advantage if it weren't for the last item.

4. The king loves his kids.

Things would be much easier for me if he were your average coldhearted monarch. But he's not. He came into office at age thirty with reform on the brain and love in his heart. And for forty years he's stayed true to all that.

Which brings us back to number one: me. I have no power. Except the truth.

And I tell you. After that night, I hate the truth.

It begins just after sunset. I'm snoozing in front of the fire when someone pounds on the door. They pound hard, so I can't beg off. The wife has long since retired, and I'm alone with my empty glass of ale. I get up, and pull the door open only to discover a palace guard.

He's young, maybe twenty-five, and he's got that flat-faced look the inexperienced get when they're terrified.

"Need you down to the Quarter," he says.

Already I know it's bad. The Quarter is short for the Royal Quarter. It's where displaced people of the court live. The queen mother has a cottage there. (Cottage, hell. You could fit fifteen of my cottages in hers.) So do several of the royal spouses, most thrown over for the mistress *du jour*. The official spouse appears at the palace for official events, then returns to the Quarter to a life of relative ease and inconsequence until the next royal event occurs.

I hate the Quarter. Its semiunofficial status makes my job even more difficult.

I grab a torch and follow the young guard. My head is pounding from the aftereffects of the ale, and my mouth is dry. I should have taken a few minutes to clean up. As the wife says, it never pays to drink alone. Not even on Sunday.

The cobblestone streets aren't precisely empty. Several ladies of the evening try to blend in with the shadows of the tavern doorways as I pass by. Voices inside are raised in raucous song. Beggars lay against the chimney stones in a vain attempt to get warm. This part of town never sleeps.

As we cross the invisible line that separates poor from rich, the clock in the guard tower strikes ten. It's darker here, among the stately homes and manicured gardens. Private guards stand by gates, but even they don't look awake. The palace guard and I slip by with nary a notice from anyone.

Then we enter the Quarter. The palace guard makes a turn,

and as I follow, my stomach twists. I know where we are. The disgraced royals section. Not everyone who lives here is disgraced per se, but most are here because they need to pay for their quarters themselves. The "cottages" are smaller, the gardens tiny, and the guards nonexistent. If crimes are committed against royals, they happen here precisely because of the lack of protection.

The streets here are narrow and dark. The guard leads me to a tall house at the end of a road. A handful of my men pace outside it, waiting for me. Two other palace guards stand beside them, looking nervous.

The ale in my stomach churns even more. I recognize this place. I've sent men here more times than I care to count. I steel my shoulders, run a hand through my thinning hair, push forward.

"What've we got?" I ask the nearest man, his face obscured by the dark.

"See fer yerself, sir," he says, and in the lackadaisical tone I recognize the voice of Robert, one of my sharper assistants.

The gate stands open, and several torches burn in torch holders. Blood coats the bricked path. A woman is crumpled in the center, on her side, one hand extended before her. A man is leaning against a tree, his eyes open and staring, the pupils reflecting the torches in an eerie imitation of life.

I walk through the grass, careful not to disturb the blood. I've learned in my years as sheriff that crime scenes tell their own tale. A good man reads it. An inept man tramples it.

I crouch behind the woman, where there is less blood, and hold my torch close to her face. Her long blond hair obscures her features but leaves one image vividly clear:

Her throat has been cut, the wound so deep it gapes like a second mouth. I can see the bones in her neck. Whoever did this nearly severed her head from her body.

I leave her for a moment and approach the man. He's wearing publican's clothing, and his hair is longer than fashion. He's been stabbed dozens of times—torso, hands, forearms. He fought his assailant—and lost.

I order that he remain untouched. He's the out-of-place detail, the key to the whole thing. Publicans do not visit the Quarter, at least not to my knowledge. And I know a lot more than I should. Then I return to the woman.

Gingerly I push the hair out of her face. Her eyes are nearly closed, a bruise fading near her jaw. But I still recognize her.

The Princess.

The one they used to call Cinder Ella.

The whole kingdom knows the tale of Cinder Ella and the handsome prince, the one they call Charming. Little girls repeat it before they go to sleep, a hopeful fairy tale for the underclasses: If you're pretty enough, and kind enough, and resourceful enough, you can marry into royalty. Live happily ever after, guarded by your prince and his charm.

What the kingdom doesn't know is that shortly after the wedding, Charming became distressed with his wife's lack of breeding. She wore scarves to hide the bruises and, after she bore him two children and tried to negotiate things with the palace wise women, she petitioned the king for a separation.

The king is, as I said, a fair man, and he saw things a bit too clearly for Charming's sake. It didn't help that Charming was, by then, a has-been. He made his name in the wars, the expendable second son who proved to be a most able general. He kept the invaders at bay twenty-five years ago, and he earned his reputation as the most powerful general the country has ever seen.

He just didn't have anything to do when the war ended.

I've seen it before: old soldiers who don't quite know how to behave off the battlefield. Charming, who was handsome and still young, went to a series of balls, found a wife, and developed a reputation for benevolence that didn't apply at home.

The king knew that. It's hard to ignore bruises that occur in your presence. So he granted the princess's appeal for separation, and even allowed her to raise the children outside the palace. With Charming's older brother's ten children, Charming's children had no real hope of succession. The king thought: Separate the combatants and the war ends.

How wrong he was.

At least once a week, my men went to the Quarter to break up a fight between Charming and his princess.

She was trapped in a netherworld of her own making. Too famous to live in a different section of town, too disgraced to live in the protected part of the Quarter. We'd stop the fights between her and the prince, but we really couldn't do much. It was up to her, I thought, to tell the king that the war continued.

Of course she didn't.

And now she's dead.

I remain crouched even though my thighs ache. "The children?" I say.

"They're all right," Robert says. He stands off the walk, just near the gate, watching me. He wants my job, he does, and someday he can have it. "They're inside with one of the men."

"They know what happened?"

"No."

"They hear anything?"

"I don't think so."

I sigh. Too messy for me. Much too messy. I get up slowly, and my knees creak. I'm getting too old for these kinds of jobs.

I hold my torch over the walk. It tilts down. The blood from the princess ran down the walk toward the street. Behind her, though, near where I stood, is one great smear, and then small drops and several footprints. Man-sized, bigger than mine. I follow the prints. They lead to the back gate. It's smeared, too: a single handprint, large. Then the steps disappear in the dirt.

I sigh and close my eyes. There's no way out of this one for me. The princess is dead, and the king will want to know why. And how.

And by whom.

Then I have an idea.

"Robert," I say as I come back through the gate. "Who's seen the bodies?"

"Us, sir," he says.

"Anyone else?"

"Not up close."

"Good." I rub a hand over my scalp. I hate this, but I will do it anyway. It will be the best for all of us. "Find the knife."

"Sir?"

"Find the knife." I make my tone fierce.

"And if I can't?"

"You will," I say. He'll understand. Robert is one of my very best. If he finds no knife, he'll provide one. And if he provides one, I can always say that I had no knowledge of it. Such things will make all of our jobs easier.

I add, "Take care of the bodies personally."

That way no one else will see the defensive wounds on the publican. If we can, if we're quick enough, we can blame him and close the case, no questions asked.

"Yes, sir," Robert says.

"And Robert?"

"Yes?"

"Make sure no one talks. About any of it." And with that, I go into the house.

Candles are burning everywhere. A copper tub sits in the kitchen, the water cool. I look around for servants but see none. Only my man, warming his feet by the dying fire.

"Where're the children?" I ask.

"Upstairs. Asleep. Didn't have the heart to wake them."

"We'll have to do so now," I say, "and take them out the back way. We'll need a carriage."

"Aye, sir," he says, and goes to see to the carriage first.

I investigate the kitchens and the servants' area and find what I suspect. No evidence of on-premise servants. Only day servants. It confirms the rumors I'd heard, that the king had made a deal with the princess. *Leave if you want,* he reportedly said, *but if you do, you'll lose your bride's portion. The palace will pay for the children's care.*

She got by on the children's money and provided well for them. The king had forgotten, or maybe he hadn't, that she had lived poor most of her adult life. This place is incredibly big, incredibly nice for a woman without much financial backing.

But not nice enough. Overnight servants would have prevented the attack.

Or maybe they would have talked, something the king and his family did not want. It is one thing to believe in justice. It is another to enforce it strictly for one's own child.

I sigh. This, then, is what faces me. Justice and children. They do not go together.

I leave the servants' area and climb the stairs to the second story. The children are awake, huddled together in the middle of a bed, lights out. I wonder how long they've been like this. Their eyes glow in the torchlight, in an uncomfortable imitation of the dead man's below.

The girl sits up. She holds her brother tightly. He is the younger, his mouth a thin line. The children combine their mother's prettiness with their father's firm jaw. I get a sense that this pose is common to them; they've sought comfort like this before, probably whenever violence has touched their home.

"Who're you?" the girl asks. Her voice trembles.

"I'm the sheriff," I say. "I've come to take you to the palace."

The children come quietly. They ask no questions about their mother. They do not mind leaving through the back door. They are strangely calm about using the old carriage my man dug up, even though it smells of onions and dung.

I wonder at how much they know. They claim they know nothing, but their denials ring false.

When we arrive at the palace, we are shown into a small room I have never seen before. A fire burns in the grate, and candles flicker in lamps on the walls. A comfortable, well-used chair and stool are close to the fire, and a large rug made of many animal skins covers the stone floor. The room smells of old tobacco and wood smoke.

The children sit on the rug. After a moment, a servant comes and takes them to their rooms. He bids me to stay.

I sigh. I was afraid of this. I prepared my story for this moment. I am, despite the king's hatred of liars, about to lie to him: I will tell him that the publican murdered his daughter-in-law for reasons I do not yet know, and that the publican then died of the wounds she managed to inflict on him before he slit her throat. Although it's false, it is, I believe, the best for all of us, for him, for the children, and most of all, for the kingdom.

My thinking is this: The prince did it. He saw the wife with another man and lost his temper. I know. It has happened before, only not so severely. He warned her about letting it happen again.

But blaming the publican causes no dilemmas. No choice between love and justice. The guy is dead, and nothing can bring him back. He was unremarkable in life, and he'll gain a small measure of infamy in death. Infamy that can't hurt him.

Whereas the prince . . .

A door opens behind me. It's the king. He's wearing a hastily donned robe. His hair is mussed. His unusual vulnerability makes him look older than normal.

I bow.

He closes the door quietly. "You may rise," he says. "We're alone. You brought my grandchildren?"

"Yes, sire." I take a deep breath, dreading this moment. "The princess has been murdered."

"Murdered?"

"Yes, sire," I say. My hands are trembling. I clasp them together, getting ready to spring my tale.

"By whom?" he asks and then, almost as the words leave his mouth, he adds, "No. Do not tell me that."

I blink, uncertain what to say. "Sire?"

He looks away from me. "Is my son all right?"

"I—ah—do not know, sire."

"You do not know or are unwilling to say?" The king's voice shows none of the weakness of his body. It is strong, but his shoulders slump as he speaks.

"I do not know, sire. The princess died outside her home. I tended to the investigation and then brought the children to you."

"The children know she is dead?"

"I have not told them," I say. "Although they did not seem to think the trip out of the ordinary."

"I shall tend to them," the king says, "after I tend to my son. Come along, man. We shall see him together."

I do not know what the king is thinking, but whatever it is, I do not like it. I think I shall like it even less as the night goes on.

The king says nothing as he opens the door. He beckons me to follow, and we go through a maze of small corridors. As we enter a wing, a valet greets him.

The king dispenses with the usual greetings. "I have come for my son."

"He left shortly before you appeared, sire. He said he is going on a hunting trip and will not be back for some days."

"A trip?" the king says. "I was not informed of this."

"Nor I, sire. But he insisted it was long planned and that I had merely forgotten."

A shiver ran down my back. Maybe now I can try the story on the king.

But the king pushes past the valet and tries to open a nearby door. "This is locked!" he says.

"I was instructed not to touch it," the valet says, "nor to let anyone enter."

The king is paler than usual, but he bites his lower lip. He is determined. "Give me the key," the king says. The valet does so. "You are dismissed."

The valet bows and backs away. When he is gone, the king unlocks the door and pushes it open.

The room is larger than my cottage. It is the main room of a suite, the living area, with a fireplace, comfortable chairs, and thick rugs. The fire still burns, although it will burn itself out. The room is dim, but I can see rather clearly. The king grabs a torch from a nearby holder before going inside.

He stops just inside the doorway. The light from his torch illuminates the mess: clothing strewn everywhere, and fresh blood spattered on the white fur rugs. Spattered not as if someone were injured, but as if someone were wet and dripping.

I walk past the king, but he does not object to this breach of protocol. I touch the shirt lying across the rug. My fingers come away bloody.

"Now," the king says, "you shall tell me how the princess died."

I do not face him. The shirt has left a blood imprint on the rug. "Her throat was cut, and the publican who was with her had been stabbed repeatedly. Defensive wounds."

"Stabbed." The king's voice sounds strangled. It is well known that the prince collects knives. "How should I proceed, Sheriff?"

I take a deep breath. He will not believe my lie now. Still, I have no answer for him. "Sire, we do not know who killed her. We have only supposition—"

"You've hanged many men on less supposition," the king says.

I swallow, knowing as I do that the next words might condemn me or save me. "Forgive me, sire," I say. "They died by your orders."

"At your recommendation, Bertrand," he says. "If this were any other dead woman, any other husband's bloody room, what would you recommend?"

I wipe my bloody fingers on my pants. "This is not any other woman, sire, and you cannot hang a prince."

"I can do anything I wish," he says. "I am king."

"True enough," I say. I turn. The king is watching me. He is trying to evaluate my sincerity. "But you do not know how the masses feel about your son, about your daughter-in-law."

"She is—was—popular," he says. "It is why I did not let the boy put her aside."

"No, sire," I say. "She was their hope, their dreams of a better life. They do not know how your son treated her. They do not know—forgive me, sire—that her life differed from theirs only in the amount of wealth at her disposal. They believed her fortunate, your son charmed, and to disabuse them of that notion, well, sire, it will only reflect poorly on you."

"They will blame me?" he asks, clearly startled at the thought. His eyes narrowed. "What were you planning to tell me?"

I take a deep breath. I will no longer lie to this man, not even in my imagination. "I was going to make the evidence point to the publican."

"Because he is no one?"

"Because he is already dead."

The king nods. "If this man is who I think he is, he is a friend of the princess from before her marriage. A man who would occasionally bring her food and play with the children. A man who had no designs but friendship, no matter what my son thought."

He is not speaking to me. He is speaking to himself. Then his eyes clear. He frowns at me. "We shall clean up this room," he says, "and you shall bring the bodies here. Then we shall speak no more of this."

" 'We,' sire?" It does not sound like a royal "we" to me, but more like two men in conspiracy with each other.

"We," he says. "And perhaps by the time we are done, we shall have an idea about how to avenge two murders, maintain the public perception, and find an equitable way of punishing my son."

The king proved an able accomplice. He did not mind bloodying his hands.

We cleaned the room and burned the clothes, and then I returned to the crime scene, removed the bodies, and closed the house. No one spoke of the deaths again.

Except me and the king, that dawn. The truth between two men, the decision between unequals. The idea mine, the action his.

The prince is on a pilgrimage—a fancy term for exile—banished forever from this land, from his children, from this site. No public hangings, no public outcry. The public believes the princess is with him. Those who knew the publican—who was the young man the king thought—believe he has run off.

In doing this, we have achieved only one of the king's aims. We have preserved public opinion. The myth continues and may outlive us all. We have avenged no deaths and have, perhaps, caused more. And we have not punished the prince. In my heart of hearts, I believe we have rewarded him.

He was a has-been, a man without purpose, a man who would rather fight and wander than go to balls and social events. We have allowed him to fight, allowed him to roam. He still has his wealth and his position. He has merely been freed from the constraints of his cage.

I do not like the decisions we have made. I like rules and justice, just as my king does. I like the simple, straightforward way in which the world normally works.

But the shadings of power cripple me. Each time I hear someone mention the myth of Cinder Ella, I catch myself from speaking. I have told the truth once, and in doing so, I have lied. The king and I both have. We have lied to protect a man who does not deserve it.

All to maintain a popular fiction, to keep alive a belief that keeps the masses happy and the king in power.

I hope he is sleeping well, because I am not.

And after that night, I doubt I ever will.

Anne Wingate is a former policewoman who has written under two pseudonyms as well. Her books are models of construction and style, written with a gritty approach that critics have rightly praised for its honesty and warmth. In the following story, the princesses in the Grimm Brothers' "The Twelve Dancing Princesses" become the daughters of a mob boss, and the rest of the story is equally intriguing.

"The Twelve Dancing Princesses" Revisited

So da *capo,* he sez ta me, "I jus' don' get it. Dem girls, I treat 'em all like princesses . . . I mus' be da mos' unluckies' guy in da worl', ya know? I mean, not a son ta my name, so who'm I gonna han' da bizness over ta, I ast ya? And twelve, count 'em, *twelve* daughters. Like stair steps, one year apart, from Vittoria, she's twenty-five an' she shoulda been married a long time ago, down ta Ginevra, she's fourteen, an' dat's gettin' on toward ripe for marriage. And gorgeous. All twelve of 'em, drop-dead gorgeous. Damned if I know why Lucia, she say no more after Ginevra. But dere wasn't no budgin' her. She jus' *wouldn'* keep tryin' for a boy. Now, ya'd t'ink one of 'em would marry somebody wid somet'in' on da ball, now wouldn' ya? But hah! Catch 'em. Don't matter who I bring in for dem ta look at, dey won't have nuttin' ta do wit 'im. An' den a couple mont's ago dey starts sleepin' all day. I mean, *all* day, *every* day. So it stands ta reason, don't it? I mean, if dey're sleepin' all day, what're dey doin' all *night,* huh? Well, it don't take no G-man ta figure dat out. An' *shoes!* I'm tellin' ya, ever' day I got ta buy 'em new shoes. Dey wear 'em out overnight. Now, I ast ya, how could *anybody* wear out a pair of shoes *every* night, much less all twelve of 'em? Accept Sunday, dey don't wear deir shoes out Sunday night. Man, ya know what it *costs,* buy seventy-two pairs of shoes a week? I mean, bizness is good, but it ain't dat good. So dancin', I figure sure dey're dancin', but dat ain't all dey're doin'.

"So I sends one of my goons ta wait outside deir bedroom door an' follow 'em, and he don' come back. Den I sends anudder, and dat one, he wakes up dead. And I send *anudder* one, and dat one, he wakes up dead an' dis*membered.* Now I ast ya, what am I s'pozedta do now?

"So I'm tellin' ya, man, ya fin' out who dey're layin' around wit', and when ya find out, I won't take no more backtalk, da oldes' of da girls, Vittoria, I give ya ta marry, right? Ya couldn' ast a better deal dan dat—dat, *an'* my empire, when I'm ready ta hand it over. Right, ya gonna find out, right? Ya gonna find out who dey're wit'? Ya do me right and dere won't be no trouble. But if ya double-deal . . ."

By now I was noddin' my head. He was right. It didden take a G-man ta guess dat if da girls were sleepin' all day, deir nights were in'erestin'ly occupied. But it also didden take a G-man ta figure out dat if I accepted da job, which I would do if I didden wanna wake up dead like da las' two goons, or more likely jus' like da las' one, da one dat was dead an' dis*membered,* I had better fin' out who was layin' da girls, an' I better do it fast, on account of if I didden I better hope I *did* wake up dead, on account of dat'd be a lot better dan what da *capo* would have planned for me.

"I won't double-deal ya," I said. But my stomach, man, it was doin' stuff stomachs jus' ain't made ta do.

I ast ya. Is dat da sort of job ta lay on a man jus' out of da Big House? Jus' out of *six years* in da Big House? Man, I hadden even *seen* a dame for six years, accept da warden's secretary, an' she got a face like a prune. An' ever'body knows, Mafia princesses, dey don' know nuttin' about nuttin'. I mean, talkin' ta 'em, a man might as well be talkin' ta a *real* princess.

Well, maybe not dese princesses. 'Cause my guess was, da *capo* was right dat dey wasn't jus' dancin' all night. But da way dem dolls will pretend—I mean, ya can get a doll out of a guy's *bed* an' she'll sit dere and bat dem glitterin' long eyelashes at ya an' say, "*Who* do ya t'ink ya are, talkin' ta *me* like dat?"

So I did not like da next t'ing I hadda say, which was, "Boss, how am I gonna manage ta get inta where da girls sleep at night?"

Well, as I could of guessed, he swelled up like a pouter pigeon and his face looked like he was jus' about ta start screaming. "What da hell do ya mean—"

"Look," I said, soundin' patient even if I wasn't, because if ya've got good sense ya don' sound impatient at da *capo,* "ya set t'ree goons ta watch 'em from outside, didden ya? And none o' dem goons found anyt'in', at leas' nuttin' dey lived ta report ta ya, right? So it stands ta reason, where dey're goin', an' *how* dey're goin', it ain't nuttin' ya can find out from outside, right? So look, man, ya want me ta find out anyt'ing, I gotta find out from da *inside.*"

Well, as I have explained, he wasn' real happy wit' dis. But finally he had ta agree dat if nobody could track 'em from da outside den I would have ta track 'em from da inside.

So he tells me he's gonna fix up a place for me ta hide *inside* da big walk-in wardrobe, an' I try ta tell him dat don't sound like such a good idea, because if da girls is goin' dancin' an' wearin' out deir shoes every night dey would want ta get on deir fancies' gowns and when dey opened da wardrobe dere would be dis middle-aged goon wearin' a ball gown on his head, and how was I gonna explain *dat?*

So den he gets dis *good* idea.

He calls in all da girls and he tells 'em, "I t'ink somebody's kidnappin' you every night."

Da girls giggle and dey don't say nuttin'.

"So," he sez, "I'm puttin' dis-here goon in ta protec' you at night. So wear your cotton nightgowns and don't do nuttin' stupid, an' he'll be dere ta protec' you every night."

Da girls giggle and dey don't say nuttin'.

No doubt, being the perspicacious person dat you are, you have noticed dat de *capo,* he ain't yet tried ta watch 'em hisself. You ast me, he got better sense. He druther send in goons and let *dem* wake up dead an' dis*membered.* Goons is cheap. A dead *capo,* dat would start a war.

Now, my mudder, she didden raise no stupes. I t'inks dis whole t'ing t'rough. I figure, it's late at night when whatever is happenin' happens, an' it's quiet, an da udder goons, dey go ta sleep and whoever is takin' da princesses dancin' can do whatever he wantst'a ta dem goons, because dey're sleepin' hard. An' sure, da *capo* didden tell da girls about da udder goons, but girls got deir ways. Dey finds out what dey wants ta find out.

So me, I slep' all afternoon, and when I wakes up I has a plan.

If da girls turn on lights in deir room in da middle of da night, da *capo* would catch 'em for sure. So sure as anyt'ing, dey're dressin' in da dark, an' I figure dey're hidin' in da wardrobe ta put deir makeup on.

And dat ain't all I figure.

So, while da girls was at deir supper, I look in da wardrobe. Man, for twelve girls, dcy got enough clothes for twelve *dozen* girls. But in the front of each girl's section of wardrobe dere is a black velvet cape. A *long* black velvet cape, wit' a black velvet hood an' a black veil.

An dat tells me all I need ta know right den.

I figure da *capo* ain't as smart as he t'inks he is, because if he was as smart as he t'inks he is, he would have put dese girls in a room upstairs radder dan a room on da groun' floor.

I gets my long black raincoat an' my black Homberg an' da black mask I was wearin' las' time I knocked over a bank, an' I puts dem in a bag, an' I goes ta the princesses' room at bedtime with my face lookin' like the stupe dat I ain't.

Dey pretend ta be real glad ta see me. Dey gets a nice recliner chair for me ta sit in while I guards dem. Dey offer me a drink. "Real good stuff," Vittoria sez. "Not none of dat bat'tub gin."

She laughs, an' Ginevra giggles, and den all da udder girls giggle.

I let dem give me da bottle, an' I pretends ta drink out of it, an' all da girls laugh an' giggle.

Den, when all da girls go ta da bat'room togedder—I t'ink wimmen is afraid ta go ta da bat'room alone—I gives da gin ta da potted palm beside Vittoria's bed, an' I am suprised it don't start snorin'.

But like I said, my mudder didden raise no stupes. Nobody ever slipped a Mickey ta me an' got away wit' it.

So by da time dey comes back from da bat'room, I am leanin' back in my recliner chair snorin' ta wake da dead, an' Vittoria—

who I can see because my eyes is not as shut as dey look—stops and looks at me and she laughs in dis spiteful way, an' she sez, "I probably didden even have ta slip him a Mickey. He's such a stupe he'd'a gone ta sleep anyway." She laughs dis mean kinda laugh and heads for da wardrobe.

All da udder girls, dey giggle an' den *dey* head for da wardrobe.

An' I was halfway right. Dey dresses in da wardrobe, but dey don' dress in da dark. I can see little streaks of light comin' t'rough da cracks in da wood of da door—but nobody who wasn't sittin' exactly where I was sittin' woulda seen anyt'in'.

So da girls come outta da wardrobe and dey pirouette around wit' deir full skirts flyin', an' den dey do jus' what I expected dey would do. Namely, dey moves Ginevra's bed—wit' twelve of 'em liftin', it don't take no time at all—an' dey open a trapdoor, an' down de stairs dey go, one at a time, an' da las' one in line is me.

Dey go t'rough a cellar storin' more booze den a t'ousan' men could drink in a t'ousan' years, an' da las' one in line is me.

Dey go down dis long flight of wooden stairs, an da las' one in line is me.

I make only one mistake: I accidentally steps on da hem of Ginevra's cloak, an' she stops an sortta shrieks, an' Vittoria, she turns sharp and she sez, "What'sa matter wit' you?"

An' Ginevra, she sez, "Somebody stepped on my hem."

An' Vittoria, she sez, real quiet-like, "You done it yourself. You are so careless. Now, come on, an' don't make no noise."

After all da girls is out, Ginevra carefully closes the door behind her, so dat it jus' looks like anudder cellar door.

So dey walk down ta da bank of da river, which is about twelve hundred yards from da back of da *capo*'s house, an' my second question is answered jus' as I t'ought it would be. Well, almost. I figure nobody gonna use a car or a motorboat, not dis close ta da *capo*'s house, an' I was right. But what I did not expect was twelve, count 'em, *twelve* rowboats, an' in each one is one of da sons of Tony Varallo, who is da udder *capo* in town, who (da sons, not Tony) I reco'nize when da oldes' of 'em turns on a flashlight long enough ta see Vittoria. (Varallo has plenty of sons. He also has buried two wives, got one now, got one on da string, and has had t'ree molls that everybody knows about and probably a lot more dat nobody knows about. Dese sons is not all full brudders ta one anudder.)

Each of da girls goes an' gets in a boat, an da las' one in line is me. I get in da boat behind Ginevra. I figure dis is safe, because da boy, who is only fifteen, is facin' da river, and Ginevra is facin' da back of da boy wit' dis big broad grin all over her face dat I seen when she got in da boat, and so I sit down in da stern of da boat and I am facin' da back of Ginevra.

And it is a dark night and da moon is not out and dere are no lights on da water.

I figure I am safe.

But Dominick Varallo, who is rowin' da boat dat I am in, complains dat da boat is too heavy. He sez dis ta Tony Junior, and Tony Junior hisses, "Ssshut up! Sssound carriesss acrosss da water! You mus' of ate too much at ssssupper."

So Dominick, he don't say nuttin' else, an' when da boats pull up on da opposite shore all da boys an' all da girls get out and here is where cars is waitin'.

Twelve of 'em.

Every one is a long, black Cadillac.

Dey look like a funeral, which reminds me dat if I am not careful I won't live long enough ta *have* a funeral.

Da twelve boys each goes ta a car, taking one of da girls wit' him, an' da las' one in line is me.

I gets inta Dominick's rumble seat, figurin' dat is da safes' place because dat is da las' car in line, an' da procession pulls out and dey all drives about five miles ta da Varallo mansion, which is lit up like a t'ousand Christmas trees.

Da boys and girls get out of da cars, and dey all go inta the mansion, and dey all dance all night (accept for da time spent eatin' an' drinkin' an' smoochin' an' primpin') until it is almos' time ta begin ta be dawn, an' den dey go back ta get in da cars, an' da las' one in line is me.

I have one of Varallo's monogrammed wineglasses wit' me.

I let Dominick row me back across the river, he's all da time fussin' at Ginevra that she is eatin' too much, an' den while da girls an' da boys is saying good night ta one anudder I nips up ta da house, opens da door, nips up da stairs, tucks da wineglass inta my bag wrapped up in my black raincoat, an' when da girls are comin' in (each one fussin' at Ginevra for not closin' da door properly an' Ginevra cryin' so much I am almos' sorry for her), I am in da recliner, snoring ta beat da band.

In da mornin', da *capo* sends for me an' he sez, "I see you're alive."

"Yes, sir, I am," I sez. "An' I know where da girls is goin', but you won' believe me till I can prove it, so give me two more days."

He kinda gets purple in the face, but he sez, "Two more days an' no more. You sure you didden jus' sleep all night an' dream where you t'ought dey was goin'?"

"I was awake," I sez stoutly, "an' in two days I will prove it ta ya."

So da nex' night goes jus' about like da firs', accept dis time da girls go out in reverse order so that Vittoria, she can *see* that the door is closed properly because she'll do it herself, an' dis time da boys put da boats in opposite order, so dat Tony Junior's boat is las' instead of Dominick's, so I lets Tony Junior row me across da river, which is a little more dangerous because Tony Junior is a big bruiser with a few kills already ta his name (includin', I t'ink, da udder goons who try ta fin' out what's goin' on—Tony Junior is the kind of fella who'd t'ink dis*memberin'* a goon is funny), an' Dominick, he's jus' fifteen.

But, like Dominick, Tony Junior only complains dat da boat is too heavy, and he fusses at Vittoria for eatin' too much, an' Vittoria swells up like a pouter pigeon an' says, "Ya don' *have* ta take me out, ya know," an' real quick, Tony Junior apologizes. I see Tony Senior's hand in dis. Dere is somet'in' more dan a dance goin' on, an' I know it even if the girls an' boys don't, t'ough my guess is da boys mostly know it an' the girls, dey haven' a clue. Accep' maybe Vittoria.

Dis time I brings back one of Varallo's monogrammed silver platters, but dis time I almos' get caught. A servant asks me what

I t'ink I'm doin', an' real quick I say, "Da *capo,* he wants some of dem capons."

(Da buffet dat night was roasted capons. An' dat was da firs' t'ing I could t'ink of ta say. I had, of course, approached da buffet when all the girls was dancin' in da udder room. My mudder didn' raise no stupes.)

So I sits on da back steps an' eats da capons, havin' nuttin' better ta do wit' my time, until da girls an' boys come out an' get in da cars an' den get out an' walk down ta da boats, an' da las' one in line is me.

I do jus' like I done da night before, an' when da girls come up da stairs dey is arguin' again, an' Vittoria, she sez, "Dere is somet'in' goin' on here dat I do not like."

She comes over and stands right beside my chair, an' wit' a great effort, I continues ta snore until finally she shrugs and turns away.

Da nex' mornin', while da girls were sleepin' in, da *capo* sends for me again, and I tell him again dat I know where dey is going an' what dey is doing. I tell him I need one more night, and I tell him dis time, have all his goons waitin' in da front hall, real quiet-like, wit' no lights on.

Dis he is willin' ta do.

An' leave da front door unlocked.

Dis he is not real happy ta do, but finally he agrees.

Den I go and make a few preparations of my own.

An' da t'ird night goes like da firs' and second, accept dat dis time Vittoria, she watches me drink da gin, an' when da girls go ta primp in da wardrobe I go ta da bat'room and stick my finger down my t'roat and when dat unpleasant task is over wit' I take about four caffeine tablets an' den nips back ta da chair real quick ta start snorin'.

After da girls is all dressed, dey open da trapdoor and go down the stairs, Vittoria firs' an' Ginevra las', and da las' one in line is me. Ginevra, she is movin' slowly like she is still worried, an' I accidentally tread on her cloak again, an' she gives a tiny squeal.

"What's wrong?" Vittoria asks sharply but not very loudly.

"Somebody stepped on my hem," Ginevra says again.

"Silly child, you saw da goon was asleep," Vittoria says. "Who else would be followin'? You stepped on your own hem. We may have ta leave you at home tomorrow night."

"No, don't do dat," Ginevra says, and she hurries down the stairs and is very careful ta close the door behind her—wit' me still inside.

But dat is all right.

As soon as da girls see da boys an' start billin' an cooin', I open da door again an' out I nips. Da boys an girls walk down da riverbank, an' da las' one in line is me.

Dis time everybody is back in deir normal order, and I ride across the river wit' Dominick again, and dis time, Dominick, he don't say nuttin', but the line of his shoulders tells me he is almighty pissed.

I already got a goblet wit' Varallo's monogram on it, an' I already got a platter wit' Varallo's monogram on it. But Varallo is not da only person in da universe whose name starts wit' "V." Dis time I have got ta get somet'in' that proves da girls are steppin' out wit' da Varallo boys.

An' my plans is already made.

I eats from the buffet, but I drinks only water. Dis would not be a good time ta go ta sleep.

It is gettin' close ta dawn, an' da girls say dey got ta go home. Da boys is not pleased by dis—all t'ree nights dey have invited da girls ta sleep over, but da girls got better sense dan dat even if dey don't know da boys is deir papa's enemy. So after dey get outta da cars da girls walk down ta da river, each one hand in hand wit' a boy, an' da las' one in line is me. Da boys row the girls back across da river, an' Dominick, he rows Ginevra an' me, an' he huffs an' puffs like he is very tired.

But dat's okay, I t'ink. He'll get a nice long res', real soon.

Da girls head up ta the door, an da boys get in deir boats ta row back across da river, but me, I nips aroun' wit' a handkerchief an' a bottle of chloroform.

Da older boys, dey don' even notice Dominick ain't wit' dem.

Dominick is the son of the younges' moll, an da udder boys, dey don' like him much anyhow.

I tosses Dominick over my shoulder—he is only fifteen, an' he is a lightweight—an' I nips aroun' da buildin' an' carries Dominick in da front door.

As I expected, da *capo* is dere wit' his goons, an' when I dumps Dominick on da sofa da *capo* recognizes him at once an' he is not pleased. He asts me wottinhell is goin' on and do I wanna start a war?

He is even less pleased when I tell him wotinhell is goin' on. I sugges' he send a goon squad around ta guard the back door, an' ta bring da res' of his goons wit' me ta da girls' room. Of course, he comes himself, too.

Den I present him wit' da goblet and da platter.

All da girls are lookin' very pale accept Vittoria, an' she says, real sharp, "What was we supposed ta do? You wouldn' let us meet any boys we liked. All da boys ya brought ta da house was stupes. So we had ta go find our own boyfriends."

Da *capo* is not pleased. He is even less pleased when Dominick wakes up an' comes inta da girls' room, where it appears that he is not a total stranger.

So how does da whole t'ing end?

Well, you t'ink it t'rough. You got one *capo* wit' no sons and one *capo* wit' no daughters. An' neider one really wants a war.

Dey wind up mixin' it all up real good, an' dey rule da city togedder.

An' me? Did I marry Vittoria?

My mudder didden raise no stupes.

Tony Junior married Vittoria, an' maybe he's man enough ta keep her in line an' maybe he ain't, but dat ain't any of my concern.

Da happy young couples was spread all over da state, each wit' his own territory, except for da younges' boys an girls, who were sent ta boardin' school.

Now two *capos* rule da city togedder, an dey got lots of lieutenants.

An' da firs' one in line is me.

Doug Allyn's short stories are always singled out as models of the craft. He is one of a few writers who can wear many masks and speak in many voices equally well. He is also one of a handful of writers who are restoring the American crime story to its previous high standing. With this story of a mobster's twisted love, based on the fairy tale "Thousandfurs," he continues elevating the craft.

DOUG ALLYN

THOUSANDFURS

Queen was dying. Cancer. Somewhere deep inside. She didn't look bad, really. She'd been a little pudgy of late, so if anything, the approach of death actually improved her figure. Her complexion, which came in jars from Estée Lauder, wasn't affected much, either. So as her time drew near, she grew ever more lovely with each hour. Or so it seemed to her husband.

During her last days, King Costa slept in his wife's room in the oncology wing of Detroit's Samaritan Hospital. Queen never wakened when he wasn't at her side, clasping her hand. Nor was there anything she asked for that he wouldn't buy—except of course, life itself. But then, King Costa wasn't in the life business. Death was his line of work.

King was a *capo* in Detroit's East Side mob, an underboss to Don Carlo Zapone. The old mobster cut King some slack in the first month of Queen's illness, but as the weeks passed he found his *capo*'s devotion to his dying wife an annoyance, almost an embarrassment.

"It ain't right," Carlo complained to Joey Segundo, his number three man. "I can see a guy goin' bonkers over a teenybop topless dancer or somethin'; middle-aged crazies do it every day. But over his wife? After twenty-five years? It ain't natural, Joey. What's up with King?"

"He's been crazy about Queen since the first time he saw her," Joey said with a shrug. "King spotted her shoppin' at Hudson's one day, walked right up and said his name's King and she's gonna be his Queen and that was it."

"You mean she just married him?"

"Hell, no, she thought he was nuts and called security. She's a society dame from Grosse Pointe. Old money, Dodge family, I think, so it ain't like she didn't know the score. Still, she was flattered by him comin' on so strong. King ain't a bad-lookin' guy if you like the Jack Palance type."

"I always figured he looked more like Dracula. That's why he's so good at collectin' money people ain't sure they owe us."

"Dracula, Palance, whatever. Either way, he's tall, dark, and not too beat up, and some women dig it when a hardguy like King gets the hots for 'em. Queen did, too, at first, but when she found out what a serious badass he really was, she tried to break it off. He lost it. Flipped right out. Killed her dog, threatened her family. She ran away to Europe, hid out for a year. He had to pay the Corsican mob a bundle to find her and bring her back. After that, she gave in and married him and they ain't been apart since. King always gets what he wants, Mr. Zapone."

"Right now I'm more interested in what *I* want," Zapone said. "And what I want is for King to quit mopin' over his old lady. Either he gets back on his game or I'll cash in his chips for him. You tell him that, Joey."

"Yes, sir, Mr. Zapone," Joey lied. There was no way he'd say a thing like that to King Costa, orders or no. Life is too short. Which is why he never had to pass the message. Two days later, Queen, whose given name was Angela, passed away.

As a gesture of sympathy, Don Carlo Zapone offered to foot the bill for a mob funeral: limousines, flowers by the truckload, hired mourners to wail and faint, the works. King refused.

His Queen was buried quietly in Grosse Pointe Meadows with only King and Joey Segundo present. A stone tower of black granite, taller than a man, marked her final rest. It was engraved with a crown, her name, the year, and this inscription: Love is stronger than death. Wait for me.

King Costa never wept for his wife. Not when she was dying in his arms as he held her fiercely, trying to keep her in this world by the sheer power of his own will. Nor did he cry at her funeral. Outwardly, he seemed little affected by her death. But over the next few days, Joey noticed a change in him, a coldness that hadn't been there before. Strong men stepped aside at King's approach. And they were wise to do so.

He spent most days at Queen's grave, brooding at the foot of the black stone in silence, staring off into some immeasurable distance.

Don Carlo Zapone tolerated King's crap for exactly a week. He left a dozen messages on King's machine but got no replies. Enough! His patience at an end, he sent Joey to muscle King, to order him on pain of death to be at Carlo's penthouse office in the Renaissance Center at noon the next day.

To Joey's surprise, King arrived promptly at the appointed hour. He stalked into the don's luxurious office and, without a word, seized the burly crime boss by his lapels and pitched him through the picture window. A forty-five-story drop. Then King calmly sat down at Carlo's desk and tried out his leather executive chair for size.

"Jeez, King," Joey said, stunned. "Don't you think that was a little hasty? I mean, old Carlo wasn't the most sensitive guy in the world, but he was a don, you know? The other mob bosses aren't gonna like this."

"Carlo Zapone hasn't done a dishonest day's work in twenty freakin' years," King said. "Somebody should've tossed his fat ass out a window a long time ago. Screw him. And screw the other bosses. This is my mob now, and Detroit's my town. You got a problem with that, Joey?"

King's eyes were as dark and flinty as Queen's gravestone. "Hell, no, boss, it's fine by me," Joey said. "Far as I'm concerned, Don Carlo's dead, long live the King."

"They'll kill him, you know," Jake Cohen said. Fortyish, switchblade slender, with a taste for brunettes and tailored double-breasted suits, Jake was the *consigliere* to what had formerly been the Carlo Zapone mob. Jake was a blueblood hood, third-generation Motown Mafia. His father'd been a notorious machine-gunsel with the Purple Gang, but Jake's law degree made him a far more dangerous man. Don Carlo may have been the boss of the Motown Mob, but Jake had always been its brains.

"The other bosses may try to hit him," Joey Segundo agreed. "Lotsa luck. The King won't be easy to kill."

"In which case, they may decide to send him a message by whacking one of us."

"That'd never work," Joey demurred. "The King wouldn't give a shit."

"Somehow I doubt my fatherless children would find much comfort in that."

"C'mon, Mr. Cohen, you're a well-known lawyer. The Syndicate wouldn't dare rub out a guy like you."

"No? Does the name Jimmy Hoffa ring a bell?"

"Yeah, I see what you mean. We're in trouble, aren't we?"

"In a word, yes. Of course, they may not try to assassinate King or even one of us. Maybe they'll only threaten him."

"With what? They can't scare King. I think maybe he wants to die."

"Which I'd be happy to arrange," Jake said. "Only with King and Carlo both gone, the Syndicate will just send some Mustache Pete from Chicago or New York to take over. They'll bring in their own people and we'll be unemployed, my friend, and in this town, that's a damned unpleasant prospect."

"You're supposed to be the big brain, Jake. What can we do?"

"The way I see it, we've got to get King's head screwed on right before we both end up dead or on Hastings Street selling our blood. You know him better than anyone; what'll it take to straighten him out?"

"Queen," Joey said simply. "He was nuts about her, and now he's just nuts. Our only chance is to find him a new Queen."

"Get serious," Jake said with a snort. "Love's a mystery of the soul. Moondust and roses and a million ballads. It's a very complicated business."

"Maybe it is sometimes, but not with King," Joey countered. "I've been thinkin' about it. You see, he flipped for Queen before he knew a damn thing about her, who she was or anythin' else. It was love at first sight with him. The lightnin' bolt. He spotted her in that store and jumped on her case like a Rottweiler at lunchtime."

"I've heard the story," Jake said thoughtfully. "So you're saying it wasn't Queen he fell in love with, it was her . . . looks, her smile, something like that?"

"That's how it was. And if it happened once, maybe we could make it happen again. I hired an imitation Elvis for my kid's tenth birthday party. Is there a way we could hire ourselves an imitation Queen?"

"Maybe." Jake's litigious mind was already spinning off schemes like sparks from a pinwheel. "Maybe there is."

The next day, Jake Cohen caught a flight out of Detroit Metro direct to LAX. By two o'clock he was in the office of Mona Steinmetz, head of the biggest theatrical casting company in the City of Angels.

"Actually, locating a double is a common problem," Mona said, waving Jake into one of the overstuffed leather chairs that faced her massive desk. "Actors occasionally get ill or temperamental when a picture's nearly finished. Psychologically, it's very unsettling to have look-alikes hanging around the studio at contract time. It makes the stars feel a little less special, you know?"

"It beats stashing a horse's head in their sheets," Jake agreed, glancing around. Mona's office appeared to have time-traveled from the past century at great expense. Her desk, carpeting, and all the furnishings were genuine Victorian antiques. Only the computer console beside her was modern.

The lady herself was a mare of a woman, long-jawed, with incisors the size of teaspoons. Her hair was knotted in a messy bun, but her eyes were like gimlets. Jake recognized a kindred spirit.

"Let's cut to the chase, Mona. Can you find me a match or not?"

"That depends," Mona said. "Do you know the woman in the photograph you faxed to me yesterday? Personally, I mean."

"I knew her," Jake amended. "She passed away."

"Then you'll have to make the final call for yourself," Mona said, dealing out eight-by-ten glossies on her desktop like tarot cards. "A camera only sees in two dimensions. Do any of these photographs look like her to you?"

Jake frowned over the color shots, started to shake his head, then hesitated. "This one does, but her hair is wrong. The woman in question was a blonde."

"Long hair or short?" Mona asked. She pressed a button on her desk, and her computer blinked to life. She slid the photo into a slot in the computer console and the woman's face immediately appeared on the screen.

"Her hair was platinum blond and worn fairly short," Jake said. Mona tapped a few keys, and the image's hair changed from brunette to blond. Another tap cropped it to the proper length. A third tap lightened her eyebrows to match.

"Make her hair a little longer," Jake said, leaning forward, eyeing the screen intently. Mona tapped another key. "Good. That's very good. With a little work, she might do."

"I was afraid of that." Mona sighed. "If it's a speaking part you'll need to hire someone to do voice-overs. This girl's got an accent."

"What kind of an accent?"

"French. She grew up in Paris."

"I don't think that'll matter. When can I see her?"

"Now," Mona said, flicking on her intercom. "You said it was a rush job so I took the liberty of having all six of the girls come in. Send in number four, please."

Jake swiveled in his seat to face the door. The statuesque woman who sauntered in nearly took his breath away. Not only with her beauty, though she was unquestionably fine as a fox. But up close and personal, her resemblance to the dead Queen was startling.

"Miss Millie Pelleterie, this is Mr. Cohen," Mona said.

"*Bonjour,* Mr. Cohen," Millie said. "Nice to meet you." Her accent was distinct but not unpleasant.

"My pleasure, ma'am," Jake said. "I, um, really hate to rush things, but this is kind of an emergency. Are you free to fly to Detroit with me this evening?"

"I'm never *free,* Mr. Cohen," Millie said sweetly. "But for the right price, I may be available."

The following night, Jake took King Costa and Joey Segundo out to dinner at Reggio's, an exclusive Italian restaurant a few blocks from the Renaissance Center. King was morose, picking at his food like a raven and acknowledging Jake's glib attempts at conversation with only an occasional monosyllable.

And then Millie walked in. Her hair was newly blond and restyled à la Queen. Even her clothing had been carefully chosen to resemble something Queen might have worn. She was in the company of two other girls, and a waiter escorted the trio to a prearranged table in King's field of view.

The effect on him was electric. King went rigid, his eyes zeroing in on Millie like laser gunsights. For ten minutes he completely ignored both his meal and his tablemates, gazing hungrily across the restaurant. Then he rose suddenly and made his way through the crowd to Millie's table.

Joey and Jake exchanged knowing grins as King knelt at Millie's knee and spoke to her at some length. But their smiles froze when she slapped his face, hard, and stalked out of the restaurant without a backward glance.

"What the hell did you think you were doing?" Jake demanded later, in Millie's suite at the Pontchartrain Hotel. "Slapping King? Do you have any idea who he is?"

"I know he isn't the big-time independent producer you said I'd be meeting," Millie shot back. "Some guy accosts me in a public place, says he wants to marry me, what am I supposed to do? Say yes?"

"He asked you to marry him?" Jake echoed in disbelief.

"Actually, begged and pleaded might describe it better," Millie said smugly. "So how about it, Mr. Hotshot Lawyer? Are you going to be straight with me about what's going on here?"

"I didn't lie to you, my dear. Or at least, not entirely. You really are up for a part. In fact, it could be the role of a lifetime."

"You mean as an actress? Or a fancy dress . . . how do you say? *Putain?* Hooker?"

"I don't know what you mean."

"Let's cut the crap, counselor. I was born at night but not *last* night! That guy was no movie producer. His name's King Costa and he's a mobster."

"You . . . know? But how?"

"Because I've been carrying his face around in my purse for the past twenty years." She rummaged through her handbag, came up with an old snapshot, and handed it to Jake. The photo was of King, decked out to disco down in a vanilla polyester jacket, bell-bottoms, and a broad paisley necktie.

"I don't understand," Jake said. "Where did you get this?"

"From my mother. The information on my bio sheet isn't totally accurate. It says I'm an orphan, but that's not exactly true. I've always known who my parents are; I've just never lived with them. I grew up in France with relatives."

"But why did your mother give you King's picture? Who was she?"

"It's a long story, and I promise to explain everything," Millie said, "but first things first. I think we should discuss the financial arrangements."

"What financial arrangements?" Jake was completely at sea.

"My dowry, of course. When King asked me to marry him, I slapped his face. But I didn't say no."

"What the hell do you mean, she's my daughter?" King roared. "I don't have a daughter!"

"Apparently you do, boss," Joey explained hastily. "You remember back when you were courting Queen, she took off for Europe and hid out? Well, she was pregnant, and she had the kid there. She figured if you knew about it then you'd . . ." Joey swallowed.

"I'd what? Spit it out, Joey."

"That you'd make her marry you. But that was before she got to know you, boss. She didn't realize what a great guy—"

"Don't try to sugarcoat it, Joey," King said, snarling. "I know how she felt about me back in those days. Queen never cared about me the way I cared about her, not ever. I admired her for it. It proved she had good taste. But why didn't she tell me about the girl later on?"

"According to Miss Pelleterie, Queen was trying to protect her from the life you were in, King. I mean, we're not exactly members of the Chamber of Commerce, you know."

"I see," King said. He strolled over to the window he'd tossed his late boss through and stared out over the Detroit skyline for what seemed like a very long time. "It doesn't matter," he said at last. "I want her anyway."

"Want her, King?" Joey gulped. "What do you mean?"

"To be my love, my own, my soulmate. Do I have to draw you a picture?"

"But she's your daughter, King."

"So? It's not like I ever bounced her on my knee or changed her didies. Dammit, Joey, she looks so much like Queen that it's almost like having her back. I want her and I mean to have her and that's it. Fix it."

"But King, havin' a . . . relationship with your own daughter is illegal."

"So? Since when did we give a rip about what's legal?"

"But it's a sin. A mortal sin!"

"Joey, I just don't care. If I have to burn in hell for eternity, so be it. It's not like I'm asking her to shack up or anything. We'll have a fancy church wedding, cake, bridesmaids, an accordion player, the whole schmear. Now, are you gonna fix it for me, or do I get somebody else?"

Joey Segundo was no coward, but he noted King's eyes measuring the shortest distance between Joey and the newly repaired picture window.

"No, boss, whatever you want's fine by me," Joey said with a sigh, caving in. "The fact is, Millie's already a step ahead of you. Knowing the family history and all, she thought you might feel this way. And, um, she says she's willing to marry you. For a price."

"Pay it."

"It ain't that simple, King. See, Millie remembered this fairy tale she read when she was a kid."

"What fairy tale?"

"A story called Thousandfurs. The way it goes, this king wants to marry his own daughter, so the girl asks him for a really expensive wedding gift, hopin' to change his mind."

"What kind of a gift?"

"A fur coat," Joey said, swallowing. "A custom job, made out of a thousand furs. Only since Millie grew up in France and all, she's naturally a big fan of Brigitte Bardot, the animal-rights bimbo? So she doesn't want one coat made of a thousand furs. She wants a thousand fur coats, all top of the line, and all made of *faux* mink."

"*Faux* mink? You mean phony?"

"That's right, boss," Joey said desperately. "And I've already done some checkin'. Top-grade fake furs can cost even more than the real thing, fifteen, maybe twenty grand a pop. And anyway, there ain't a thousand phony mink coats in the whole U.S. of A., to say nothin' of Detroit."

"So?" King asked, genuinely puzzled. "What's your point?"

The manager of the Pontchartrain was close to a coronary. They began arriving at midnight, and by 10:00 A.M. the spacious hotel lobby was jammed and they were still rolling in, racks and racks of *faux* furs, luxurious mink coats that filled the lobby until there was scarcely room to move.

Each coat had its price tag and provenance prominently displayed, designer labels from Paris and Rome and Bangladesh; Cardin, Armani, Cathy Lee. Only the best of the very best.

The manager rang Millie's room at eight, begging her to make them stop, but Millie didn't deign to appear until noon. She sauntered grandly down the main staircase, calmly evaluating the lustrous sea of mock mink as though she saw it every day.

The telephone on the desk rang. "It's for you again, Miss Pelleterie," the manager pleaded. "A Mr. King. It's the tenth time he's phoned."

"Tell him I'll be unavailable this afternoon," Millie said coolly. "I have to try on a few paltry fur coats some admirer sent me. Oh, and while you're at it, tell Mr. King the answer is yes."

"They're both nuts," Joey said grimly. "And they're gonna get us all killed."

"Probably," Jake agreed. "The story's all over the papers. Millie auctioned the rights to the *Enquirer,* the *Star,* and Geraldo. Have you seen the headlines? 'Mob King Will Wed His Own Princess.' 'Mob Boss to Boff Own Offspring.' Sweet Jesus, even O. J. never got coverage like this."

"Maybe the cops will stop it somehow," Joey said hopefully.

"No chance. After getting whipped in three Kevorkian cases in a row, the prosecutor isn't interested in any more high-profile morality crusades. Besides, King's not pretending the marriage will be legal. They aren't using a real priest, only an actor who plays one on TV."

"So there's no way to put the kibosh to it?"

"Oh, it'll be stopped, all right. I've been hearing rumors all week, none of them good. Did you know King's invited the mob bosses of every crime family in the country to the wedding?"

"You're kidding," Joey said. "Are any of 'em coming?"

"All of them," Jake said. "But not for the reason King thinks. They're going to convene a meeting of the Syndicate council the day of the wedding. They're saying the meet's only to confirm King as Carlo's successor, but I doubt that. A lot of the bosses are Sicilian Catholics. A guy marrying his own daughter is an *infamia* to them, a mortal sin. They won't stand for it. They're going to confirm King, all right. They'll elect him to that big mob council in the sky. And maybe us along with him."

"But what can we do?"

"Considering how well our last idea worked out, we're probably better off doing nothing." Jake sighed. "The way I see it, we may as well dust off our tuxes, go to the wedding, and have one hell of a good time, my friend. Because it's probably going to be our last night on this earth."

But for once, Jake Cohen, the brains of the Motown Mob, was dead wrong. At the Syndicate council meeting the day of the wedding, not a single boss mentioned the morality (or lack of same) of King's marriage.

True, most of the bosses were Catholic, and a few were even devout. Sort of. In fact, it was their religious convictions that decided King's fate.

Being a mob boss is a macho profession, like bull-riding or selling encyclopedias door-to-door. The bosses considered themselves brave men, and admired *coraggio,* courage, above all things.

As good Catholics, sort of, they knew that King's marriage would guarantee his soul an especially warm corner in the fires of hell. And a man who could face an eternity of flames for a woman, *any* woman, must truly be the bravest of all. A man to be feared by hoods, cops, and straight citizens alike. And since fear is the stock in trade of the crime business . . .

The council took a voice vote two minutes after being called to order. Their decision was unanimous. They elected King Costa to be their new *capo de tutti capi,* boss of all bosses. Each mobster knelt to kiss his ring, and then they all adjourned to dance the tarantella at his wedding.

King had won.

And yet his lot was not a happy one. Whether from some instinctive Freudian compunction or because he was, after all, old enough to be her father, King wasn't quite up to consummating his marriage to Millie. Before long, their relationship was in big trouble.

The bottom line was: Millie simply wasn't Queen. She was only an imitation, like the faux furs of her dowry. Venal and ill-tempered, she was soon cuckolding King with rock drummers and aluminum-siding salesmen and suchlike. Her lack of character should have come as no surprise to her husband. After all, what can one expect from a girl who'd marry her own father for a fur coat? Or for a thousand of them?

So despite their grand wedding and great power, King and his bride never even came close to living happily ever after. Which is as it should be. Because in this life, happy endings are rare indeed, and should be reserved for children, and true, true lovers, and fairy tales.

Sharyn McCrumb is a best-selling author whose books have now reached readers around the world. She works in a style and voice all her own, telling us about worlds that are at once familiar yet unlike anything else. She is that rarest of literary beings, a true original. Her remake of "The Snow Queen" updates a classic fairy tale while maintaining its sense of wonder.

GERDA'S SENSE OF SNOW

"Gerda! Kay's gone!"

"Kay has been gone a long time, Niels," I said wearily. "And you're dripping snow on my rug."

Niels Lausten just stood there blocking my fireplace with his shivering body, while his parka rained on my caribou skin rug. I could tell that he wasn't going away, despite my apparent lack of interest in his news. I took a sip of my tea and read a few more lines of my book, but the sense of them never quite reached my brain, so I gave it up. I would have to hear him out, and I knew it was going to hurt, because it always did, no matter how many times I told myself that the Kay I once knew, my childhood best friend, was gone forever. I wrote him off every time one of the old gang showed up to tell me the latest about poor Kay—shameful stories about a life going down the drain in a haze of vodka, in a swirl of drunken brawls, and petty acts of vandalism that seemed to gain him neither profit nor comfort. It had never made sense to me. I had tried to see him a couple of times, early on, to see if he'd accept my help, but the bleary-eyed lout who leered back at me bore no resemblance to the quiet, handsome boy next door whose hobby had been growing roses in the window box. In the winter we used to heat copper pennies on our stoves and hold the hot pennies to the glass to melt the ice so we could look through the peepholes and wave to each other. I thought we'd always be together, our lives as intertwined as our rose trees, but a thicker sheet of ice had grown up between us as we grew older, and noth-

ing seemed capable of melting it. The old Kay I'd loved was gone.
I knew it. I whispered it over and over to myself like a litany. Why
couldn't I believe it? Why couldn't Niels leave me alone to mourn?

"He's gone, Gerda. Really." Niels had peeled off his gloves,
and now he was blowing on his fingers to warm them. He was
still shaking, though, and his white face went beyond a winter
pallor.

It wasn't that cold outside. About average for a Danish winter.
I wondered what else had been going on in town while I was escap-
ing the winter at my fireside, engrossed in a book. Now that I
looked at him, Niels seemed more frightened than cold. He was
always a follower, always the first one to run when trouble appeared. I wondered what trouble had appeared this time.

"All right," I said with a sigh. "Tell me about it."

"We were just horsing around, Gerda. Kid stuff, really. We'd
had a few drinks, and somebody said, 'Wouldn't it be fun to swipe
some of the kids' sleds and hitch them to the horse-drawn sleighs?'
That would be a real fast ride—and you wouldn't have to keep
climbing a hill in between rides. So a couple of the guys tried it,
but the sleds skidded, and they fell off in a minute or so. Then we
saw a different sleigh. We'd never seen it before. It was painted
white, so that it blended in to the snowdrifts, and the driver was
wrapped in rough white fur, with a white fur hood covering the
head and hiding the face. The rest of us hung back, because the
sleigh was so big and fast-looking, and we couldn't tell who was
driving it. But Kay laughed at us, and said that he wasn't afraid of
a fast ride. Before we could stop him, he'd tied his sled to the
runners of the white sleigh, and the thing took off like a thunder-
bolt. The sled was sliding all over the road behind that sleigh, but
he managed to hold on. We yelled for him to roll off. He almost
got run over by the horse of an oncoming sleigh. He wouldn't turn
loose. Then the white sleigh got clear of traffic, and Kay was gone!
We followed the tracks outside town a mile or so beyond the river,
until the snow started up again, and then we lost the trail, so we
came on back. . . ." He shrugged. "So—he's gone. I figured you'd
want to know, Gerda."

"Yeah, thanks," I said. "Maybe I'll ask around."

"He's probably dead," said Niels.

"Yeah. He's probably dead." I went back to my book.

I tried to put him out of my mind, and I nearly succeeded for the rest of the winter. I kept thinking that Niels or Hans would turn up with some new story about Kay—that he was back after robbing the rich owner of the sleigh, and wilder, drunker than ever. But the town was silent under the deepening snow. I waited out the silence.

In the spring the thaws came, and the sun coaxed people back out into the streets to pass the time of day with their neighbors. They started asking each other what had become of that wild young man Kay. Nobody had seen him since midwinter. His friends told their story about the sleigh ride and how he never came back. "Oh, well, he must have been killed," people said. When the ice floes broke up on the river outside town, people said that Kay's body would come floating to the surface any day now. Surely he had drowned while crossing the river ice, trying to make his way back to town after his reckless sleigh ride. A few days later they had found the wooden sled buried in a snowbank farther still from town. Kay's hat was in a clump of melting snow nearby, but there was no sign of his body. But maybe the wolves had gotten him. They wouldn't have left anything, not even a bone.

"He's dead," I said to the old street singer who appears on the corner even before the birds come back.

"I don't believe it," he said, and went on with a warbling tune about sunshine.

"I'll ask around," I said. And this time I meant it.

I didn't go to the town constable. If Kay had died in an accident, the constable would have discovered it already. If something more sinister had happened to him, the constable would be the last to know. I didn't waste my time with official inquiries.

I went to the river. My grandmother used to tell me that the river would answer your question if you threw in one of your possessions as a sacrifice. I was tempted to try it, but before I could work myself up to that stage of desperation—or belief—I saw the old man I had come looking for. He lived in a shack downstream from the brewery, and I always wondered how he made it through the winter, dressed in his layers of reeking rags, with skin as translucent as ice under his matted hair. He grinned at me with stumps of teeth that looked like the pilings of the dock. I used to dream about him. I thought he was Kay in thirty years' time. Maybe dead would be better. But I had to ask.

"You remember Kay? Young, blond guy. Drinking buddy of yours. He's been gone since midwinter."

The bloodshot eyes rolled, and the old man gave a grunt that was more smell than sound. I took it to be a yes.

"He hitched a child's sled onto the back of a white sleigh, and it sped away with him. The word around town is that he drowned— only his body hasn't turned up. Or maybe the wolves got him." I could taste salt on my tongue. "Not that it matters," I whispered.

The old derelict wet his lips, and warmed up his throat with a rheumy cough. I fished a coin out of my pocket and handed it to him. "Get something for that cough," I muttered, knowing what he would prescribe.

"I know the white sleigh," he said with a rasp. "I wish it had been me."

"You know it?"

"Ar—they call her the Snow Queen." He flashed a gap-toothed smile. "She brings the white powder to town. Ar. Kay would like that. White powder lasts longer than this stuff." He dug in his overcoat pocket for the nearly empty bottle, and he waved it at me. "And it's the only thing that would take the hurt away. You know about the crack, do you?"

I shook my head. "I knew Kay was in trouble. I never cared what kind of trouble. If I couldn't help him, what did it matter?"

"The crack. That wasn't the Snow Queen's doing. They do say it's mirror glass from heaven. Trolls built a magic mirror that made everything ugly. Took it up into the clouds so they could distort the whole world at once. Got to laughing so hard they dropped the mirror. Shattered to earth in a million tiny pieces. Crack of the mirror. They do say."

"Sounds like my grandmother's tales," I said. It was a lot prettier than the truth.

"They say if the mirror crack gets into your eye, then you see everything as ugly and misshapen. Worse if it gets into your heart. Then your heart freezes, and you don't feel anything ever at all. From the look of him, I'd say that Kay has got a piece in his eye and his heart. And nothing would make the coldness pass, except what the Snow Queen has—that perfect white powder that makes you dream when you're awake. He won't be leaving her, not while there's snow from her to ease his pain."

I hadn't realized it was this bad. But maybe, I told myself, he's just sick, and then maybe he can be cured. Maybe I can get him past the craving for white powder. I knew I was going to try. "Where do I find the Snow Queen?" I asked the old man.

He pointed to a boat tied up at the dock. "Follow the river," he said. "She could be anywhere that people need dreams or a way to get out of the cold. Give her my love."

"You're better off without her," I told him. "You're better off than Kay."

There wasn't much to keep me in town. For a long time I had needed an excuse to get out of there. Too many memories. Too many people who thought they knew me. It took less than a day to tidy things up so I could leave, and there wasn't anybody I wanted to say good-bye to. So I left. Looking for Kay was as good a reason as any.

I spent most of the summer working as a gardener on an estate in the country. The old lady who owned the place was a dear, and she'd wanted me to stay on, but the roses kept reminding me of Kay, and finally one day I told her I had to move on. I had enough money by then to get to the big city, where movies are made. That's where they sell dreams, I figured. That's where the Snow Queen would feel at home.

I got into the city in the early autumn, and since I didn't know anybody and had no place in particular to go, I just started walking around, looking at all the big houses, and all the flowers on the well-tended lawns. A gardener could always get a job here, I thought. It was always summer. I stopped to talk to one guy in shabby work clothes who was busy weeding a rosebed near the sidewalk.

"New in town, huh?" He was dark, and he didn't speak the language very well, but we managed to communicate, part smiles and gestures, and what words we knew in each other's tongues.

"I'm looking for a guy," I said.

He grinned. "That—or a job. Aren't they all?"

I shook my head. "Not any guy. One in particular. A guy from back home. I think he's in trouble. I think he has a problem with . . . um . . . with snow. Know what I mean?"

"A lot of that in this town," said the gardener. By now I was helping him weed the rosebed, so he was more inclined to be chatty. "He hooked on snow—why you bothering?"

I shrugged. "We go back a ways, I guess. And he's—well, he was an okay guy once. Tall, blond hair, good features, and a smile that could melt a glacier. Once upon a time."

The gardener narrowed his eyes and looked up at nothing, the way people do when they're thinking. After a moment he said, "This guy—does he talk like you?"

"I guess so. We're Danish. From the same town, even."

He looked at me closely. "Danish . . ." Then he snapped his fingers and grinned. "Girl, I know that fellow you're looking for! But I got some bad news for you—you ain't gonna get him back."

I wiped rose dirt on my jeans. "I just want to know that he's all right," I mumbled.

"Oh, he's better than all right. He's in high cotton. He's on the road to rich and famous. See, there's a movie princess in this town, getting ready to shoot the biggest-budget picture anybody's seen around here in a month of Sundays, and she was looking for a leading man. Not just anybody, mind you. She had to have a fellow who talked as good as he looked. Well, that's not something easy to find in anybody, male or female. But they had auditions. For *days,* girl. Every beach bum and pool shark in this town showed up at the gate, ready to take a shot at the part. Most of them talked pretty big to the newspapers. Pretty big to the interviewers. But as soon as they stood beside Miss Movie Princess, and the cameras were rolling, they started sounding like scarecrows. She was about ready to give up, when all of a sudden this guy talks his way past the guards, without even so much as a handwritten resumé. 'It must be boring to wait in line,' he told the receptionist, and he smiled at her, and she forgot to call security. I got a lady friend, works for the movie princess, so I get all the news firsthand, you know what I'm saying?"

I nodded. "Most of it," I said. "Listen—this guy—was he tall and blond? Regular features?"

"Oh, he was a hunk, all right. But the thing was, he talked just like you do."

"It's Kay!" I said. "I know it is. Look, I have to see him."

"Well, the thing is, he got more than just the part in the movie. He got the girl, too. So now he's living up in the mansion with Miss Movie Princess, and my lady friend says it looks like it's going to be permanent."

"I have to know if it's him," I said. "Please—he's like—he's like my brother."

The gardener believed that—more than I did. "All right," he said, "let me talk to my lady friend, see what I can do. They'd never let you in the gate, dressed like that, and with no official business to bring you there. But we might be able to get you up the back stairway to see him. I got a key to the servants' entrance."

He took me back to the gardener's office and fixed me something to eat. Then I helped him with the bedding plants while we waited for dusk. That evening we went up to the mansion in the hills, in through the back garden, and through the unlocked kitchen door. I just want to see that he's all right, I kept telling myself. Maybe he's happy now. Maybe he's settled down, stopped the drinking. Maybe he's got his smile back, like in the old days, before it became a sneer. If I see that he's all right, I can go home, I thought.

At least I'd know for sure.

I didn't notice much about the house. It was big, and the grounds around it were kept as perfectly as a window box, but it didn't make me feel anything. I wondered if living in a land without seasons would be as boring as a long dream. I don't have to stay, I told myself.

"In there." My new friend had stopped and shined his flashlight at a white and gold door. The bedroom. "You're on your own from here on out, girl," he whispered, handing me the light. Soundlessly, he faded back into the darkness of the hallway.

I waited until his footsteps died away, and then I twisted the doorknob, slowly, as soundlessly as I could. Another minute passed before I eased inside. I could hear the regular breathing of the sleepers in the room. In the moonlight from the open window I could see two large pillars in the center of the room, and on either side of the pillars were white and gold water beds in the shape of lilies. I crept closer to one of the beds. Long blond hair streamed across the pillar, but the bare back and shoulders were muscular. Surely it was Kay. I switched on the flashlight and let the light play over the features of the sleeping man.

"What the hell!" He sat up, shouting in alarm.

It wasn't him.

The movie princess was screaming, too, now, and she had set off the alarm that would bring her security guards into the room. Suddenly everything was noise and lights—like a very bad dream.

I lost it.

I sat down on the bed and began to cry, for the hopelessness of it all, and because I was so tired of noise and lights and a world without seasons. The movie princess, seeing that I wasn't a crazed admirer, told her guards to wait outside in the hall, and she and the man asked me what I was looking for. When I heard the blond man speak, I realized that he was from Minnesota—"Close, but no fjord, my gardener friend," I thought. I guess we all sound alike to outsiders.

I told them about Kay's disappearance, and about my need to find the Snow Queen, which appalled them, because they were not into that sort of lifestyle, but they agreed that my purpose was noble, since I was trying to save a friend from the clutches of the powder dreams. They gave me money and jewelry to help me on my trip, and the movie lady insisted that I put on one of her dresses, and take her "wheels," as she called them, to speed me on my way. They didn't have any advice for me about where to look, but they told me to stay cool. A funny wish, I thought, from people who choose to live where it is always hotter than copper pennies on a wood stove.

I sped away through the night, not really knowing where I was going, and wondering who to ask about the Snow Queen. I found myself going down streets that were darker and narrower, until I no longer knew which way I was going and which way I had come. I came to a stop to think about what to do next—and then the decision was no longer mine to make.

A shouting, screaming mob of people surrounded me, and hauled me out of the vehicle.

"She's wearing gold!" one of them shouted.

A dozen hands pawed at my throat and my wrists. I struggled to throw a punch, to kick at my attackers, but I was powerless in the grip of the mob. They pinned my arms behind my back and stuffed a dirty handkerchief in my mouth. I watched them dismantle the wheels of the movie princess until it was an unrecognizable hulk in a dark alley. The crowd began fighting among themselves for my money and for the jewelry the princess had given me. I figured I wasn't going to live much longer, but nobody would come looking for me.

A large woman ambled over to me and peered into my face. "She like a little fat lamb," the woman said. I stared at the stubble beneath her chin, hoping to distract myself from her dead eyes. "She looks good enough to eat, doncha, baby?" She pulled a hunting knife from the folds of her skirt and began running her finger along the blade.

I struggled harder to break free from my captors, but it was no use. All I managed to do was spit out the gag. I swore in Danish: "*Pis og lort!*"

"Iddn't she cute? She just say '*Peace, O Lord!*' Never had anybody pray before."

I didn't give her a Danish lesson. Let her think I was praying. Maybe it would help. She edged closer to me, the knife wavering at my throat. I had closed my eyes, wondering if I should have chosen prayer, when suddenly the fat woman drew back and screamed.

I opened my eyes and saw that a small brown girl had jumped on the woman's back and was biting her ear. The woman began to swing around, waving the knife and swearing. "Get down, you devil of a child! What you want to do that for?"

"Give her to me!" said the girl. "I want her. She can give me her fancy clothes and her rings, and she can sleep with me in my bed!"

The men began to laugh and nudge each other. The fat woman shook her head, but her daughter bit her ear again, and she screamed, and everyone laughed even harder. "She's playing with her cub!" somebody said.

The small brown girl got her way. They bundled us into the set of wheels, and we took off through a maze of streets, all neon and no stars. The girl was about my height, but stronger, with nut-brown skin, big dark eyes, and white wolf teeth. "She won't kill you as long as I want you!" she told me. "Are you a movie princess?"

"No. I'm looking for somebody."

The dark girl cocked her head. "You lookin' for somebody? Down here? At this time of night? Girl, you were looking for Trouble, and you sure enough found him. You ain't goin' nowhere, but at least you're safe with me. I won't let nobody hurt you. And if I get mad at you, why, I'll just kill you myself. So you don't have to worry about none of the rest of them. You want a drink?"

We stopped at the curb in front of a ruined building. Some of the windows were boarded up, and some had the glass smashed from the panes, and birds flew in and out of the dark rooms. A sign on the double front doors said "Condemned," which was true enough, I thought. This was the place the gang called home. As they marched me into the building, lean, snarling dogs clustered around us, but they did not bark. One looked up at me and growled.

"You will sleep with me and my little pets tonight," said the brown girl, patting the snarling dog. We went inside the derelict building. The gang had built a campfire on the marble floor of the entrance hall, and they were cooking their evening meal. I was given something greasy on a sort of pancake, and when I had eaten as much of it as I could, I was led upstairs and through a dark hall to the girl's room. There was no furniture in the room, only a sleeping bag on the floor, and some straw. Holes had been punched in the walls of the room, and the windows were empty squares looking down on the lights of the city. Pigeons milled around on the floor, occasionally rising to sail out the glassless window, then drifting back in on the next puff of breeze.

"These all belong to me," said the girl. She reached out and grabbed a waddling pigeon from the floor and thrust it into my face. "Kiss it."

I pulled away, and worked on the rope binding my hands.

"The pigeons live in the hole in the wall," she said, smoothing the bird's feathers. "They come back at night. But I got to keep old Rudy tied up, or he'd run off for sure, wouldn't you, Rudy?" She opened the connecting door to another empty room. A frightened boy shied away from her as she approached him, but he couldn't go far, because he was chained to the floor by a copper ring encircling his neck. His face and ragged clothes were caked with dirt. The dark girl drew her knife. "Rudy's a special pet. I'm saving him. Every night I got to tickle him a little with my blade just to remind him what would happen if he tried to run." She passed the knife gently across the boy's throat. He struggled and kicked at her, but she laughed and turned away.

"Are you going to sleep with that knife?" I asked her as she climbed into the sleeping bag.

"I always sleep with the knife," she said. "You never know what's going to happen—do you, Sunshine? Now why don't you tell me a bedtime story? Tell me what you were doing out here all by yourself with no more protection than a pigeon got?"

"If I tell you, will you untie me then?"

She shook her head. "Make it good, and maybe I'll untie you tomorrow."

I started telling her about Kay, and how he had hitched his sled to the sleigh of the Snow Queen. The dark girl laughed, and said in a sleepy voice, "Boy strung out on the powder. Sure is. I heard about buying a one-way ticket on an airline made of snow. Old song. Never heard it called hitching a ride onto a sleigh before. Guess that's what they mean by cul-tu-ral di-ver-si-ty." Her voice trailed off into a slur of sounds. Soon her breathing became slow and even, and I knew she was asleep.

"I've seen her," said a soft voice in the darkness.

It was the boy. I heard the rattle of his chain as he edged closer.

"You can talk," I said. Somehow I had thought he wasn't quite right in the head, I guess. But he sounded okay—just scared to be talking with his tormentor so near.

"Yeah, I can talk. I been around. After I ran away from home, I lived on the street for a while—until *they* got me and brought me here—and I used to see her—the one you call the Snow Queen. She'd ride by every now and again, and there was always a good supply of that white powder on the street after she'd been around. Oh, yeah, the Snow Queen. I know her, for sure."

"But do you know where to find her?"

"She got a place up in the hills. Couple of hours from here, where it's so high up it stays cold. She likes the cold. Big white showplace in the mountains, all by itself. I never been there, but I heard talk. I could find it."

"I wish I could let you try." I eased out of the sleeping bag and leaned back against the wall, listening to the pigeons cooing in the darkness, but I didn't sleep. I thought about Kay.

The next morning the dark girl crawled out of the sleeping bag. "I dreamed about that guy you talked about," she said. "Dreamed he was sitting on ice somewhere, trying to spell some big word with a bunch of crooked pieces of glass. Kept trying and trying to spell that word, and he couldn't do it. You believe in message dreams? I do. He's in a bad way, all right. Yes, he surely is that."

I nodded. "Rudy says he knows where to find him."

"What? Chain-boy? He don't know nothing." She reached for her knife and scowled at her prisoner, but this time he did not cringe.

"I do know," he said. "I seen a lot. Seen her on the street. I can find her, too."

"Maybe that's what your dream meant," I told her. "Maybe you're supposed to send us after the Snow Queen."

The dark girl looked afraid. "Even us don't mess with her."

"She won't know you're involved. It'll just be Rudy and me. We'll go after her." I stared at her until she looked away. "You've been told to let us go," I said. "Your dream."

"Yeah, okay. What do I need you two for? It's not like you were any fun or anything. Go chase the Snow Queen. Get yourself killed in a cold minute."

The boy and I waited in silence while she made up her mind. At last she said, "Okay. The men are all out for the day, but Mamacita is downstairs, and she won't like it if I let you go. So you have to wait a little until she goes to sleep, and then I'll lead you down the fire escape so she won't see you."

The boy and I exchanged smiles of relief.

The dark girl pulled on Rudy's chain. "I'm gonna miss tickling you with my knife, boy," she said. "You look so cute when you're scared, but never mind. I'm gonna let you go, and I want you to take this lady to the house of the Snow Queen, and you help her get him out of there. And if you run out on her, I'm going to come and find you myself. You got that?"

He nodded. "I'll take her there."

"Okay. I'll get you some food." She moved behind me with her dagger and cut the rope that bound my wrists. Then she handed me the key to the boy's copper neck ring and nodded for me to unchain him. "Okay," she said with a hiss at us. "Get over to the fire escape. I'll come back with the food when it's safe for you to go. After that—anybody asks, I ain't seen you."

Rudy took me back to the part of town where he had been before the dark girl's gang had captured him. "There's an old lady here who might help," he said. "She's been on the street so long she knows everything."

He led me down an alley to an old packing crate propped up

against the side of a Dumpster. The sides of the crate were decorated with faded bumper stickers, and an earthenware pot of geraniums stood by the opening, which was covered with a ragged quilt. "This is her office. Well, it's her home, too. We have to knock."

We got down on our hands and knees to enter the tiny hovel that was home to Rudy's friend. When my eyes adjusted to the dim light, I saw a grizzled old woman cooking fish in a pan on a camping stove. She wore a grimy Hermès scarf wrapped around her head, several layers of cast-off designer clothing, and a pair of men's Nike running shoes.

Rudy gave the old woman a hug and immediately begin to tell her the long tale about his troubles, which he apparently considered much more important than mine. At last, though, he had run out of complaints to make, and the woman's sympathetic clucks were becoming more perfunctory. Then Rudy said, "And this is my friend Gerda. She got me away from the gang, but she's looking for a guy named Kay, who went off with the Snow Queen. You know what I'm saying?"

"Poor thing!" said the old woman, nodding. "You still have a long way to go! You have a hundred miles to run before you reach the hill country. The Snow Queen lives up there now, and she burns blue lights every night. I will write some words for you on a paper bag, and you can take it to Finnish Mary. She never could get the hang of city life here, so she lit out for the mountains. She lives up there in an old mining ghost town now. She will advise you better than I can."

She gave us a little of her fish, and some produce from the grocery store Dumpster, and then she scribbled some words on the paper bag, gave Rudy directions to the mining town, and sent us off to the hill country, wishing us luck in our quest.

We walked out to the big highway and started thumbing for rides. We were able to hitchhike most of the way into the hill country, so we made it by nightfall. The evening light was soft and silvery as we walked the last couple of miles from the highway into the ruins of the old mining town. We found Finnish Mary's shack by following the trail of wood smoke back to a crumbling hovel that was built over the basement of a demolished house. We crept into the hot, dark room. Finnish Mary was huddled next to her stove, wearing an old cotton caftan over a layer of dirt. On a clothesline close to the ceiling hung bunches of dried herbs and crystals suspended from bits of fishing line. Finnish Mary was obviously into New Age arts and holistic medicine.

Rudy explained who had sent us, and handed her the paper bag bearing the message from the packing crate lady in the city. With her lips moving, Finnish Mary read the words on the paper bag three times until she knew the message by heart, and then she opened the door of the wood stove and tossed the bag into the flames. "Paper is fuel," she said with a grunt. "Never waste anything."

We nodded politely.

"Talk," she said.

Rudy told her his story first, and then mine, and Finnish Mary smiled a little but didn't interrupt or ask a single question. When Rudy had finished explaining, he asked, "This is a dangerous job. Is there some kind of herbal medicine or maybe a crystal that you could give Gerda to help her? Maybe something to make her stronger in case she has to fight her way into the Snow Queen's estate? I figure she needs to be about as strong as twelve men to get her friend out of there."

Finnish Mary smiled up at him. "The strength of twelve men. That would not be of much use!" She took a parchment scroll down from a dusty shelf near the door and read it silently, while beads of sweat ran down her forehead. We edged away from the woodstove, but it wasn't much cooler anywhere else in the shack. We waited.

Finally she said, "The Snow Queen isn't home right now. She's gone South to make another delivery of the white powder. Probably took most of her guards with her. So you won't have much trouble getting up there, but getting what you want is something else again. Kay is going to stay with the Snow Queen because he's hooked. He's got that mirror crack inside him, and as long as he's into that, then he will never feel like a human being again, and the Snow Queen will always have him in her power."

"Right. That's clear enough. What I'm saying to you is: Can you give the girl something so she can cut him loose from the habit? Some kind of potion that will break the spell, you know. . . ."

Finnish Mary shrugged. "I can't give her any power greater than what she already has—it takes love to break a spell like the Snow Queen's. And sometimes even that won't do it. Gerda has to get into that house, and then try to get Kay to see what he's doing to himself. If that doesn't work, there's nothing else you or I can do to help her. Here's what you do, boy: Walk Gerda down the road until you come to the iron fence. That's the garden of the Snow Queen's estate. Leave her by the bush with the red berries on it. You going in with her?"

"Me? No!" Rudy's voice trembled, and for the first time I could see how afraid he was. It had taken all his courage to get me this far. "The Snow Queen may be gone, but who knows how they've booby-trapped that compound! I already lost one fight with a gang like hers. I'm playing it safe for the immediate future."

"You don't have to go with me," I told him. "I'm in this alone."

"Then leave her at that berry bush and get back here fast, before anybody sees you. I'll come outside with you and show you the way."

It was nearly dark by the time we started on the dirt road that led up into the hills. I could see blue lights up ahead of us, and I knew that we were going in the right direction. I was a little bit afraid of the Snow Queen and the guards she might have around her estate, but I had come so far that I was eager now to reach journey's end and to find Kay at last. I didn't know if I could save him, but I wasn't going back without trying.

Rudy walked with me as far as the berry bush beside the wrought-iron fence. He kissed me on the cheek, but before I could thank him, he turned and began to run back down the hill toward Finnish Mary's ghost town. I was alone.

As I slipped between the bars of the iron fence and began to creep toward a thicket of shrubs, I noticed that it had begun to snow—a welcome change to me from the hot, dusty city down on the plains. Maybe the snow helped me get past the Snow Queen's guards, too. As the wind picked up, it became darker and colder, not a night to be out patrolling a peaceful compound. I decided that they didn't get too many visitors in this remote mountain outpost. Or maybe there weren't any guards. Maybe they all went with her, for I sensed from the silent, dimly lit grounds that Finnish Mary had been telling the truth: The Snow Queen was not at home.

Within a few minutes I was within sight of the house. It looked like a palace made of drifted snow—very white, probably stucco, or adobe, or whatever it is they use to build in these unforested mountains. Spires and turrets spun out of the main building like icicles, and through the glass patio doors I could see soft blue lights illuminating the interior. I still didn't see any guards around, so I ran from one thicket to another until I reached the side of the house. I edged close to the glass doors and looked inside.

The great room beyond the doors was vast, empty, and icily white. In the center of the room stood a blue-lit ornamental pool that was frozen—the Snow Queen's "signature," I supposed. But I had little time to notice any more of the details of that vast, cold room, because by then I had caught sight of Kay, paper thin and blue with cold. He was sitting in shadow at the edge of the frozen pool, hunched on the floor, concentrating intently on some small pieces of ice. He was moving the broken shapes into one position and then another, as if he were trying to put together a pictureless puzzle. He was so absorbed in the complexity of his task that he did not even look up when I slid open the glass door and eased into the room.

As I came closer, I could hear Kay muttering, "I have to spell *eternity*. She said she'd give me whatever I wanted if I could spell it out with ice." His hand was shaking as he pushed more bits of ice shards together. I could not make out any shapes at all in the design, but he seemed to think he was making a sensible pattern. This is what the Snow Queen's powder has done to his mind, I thought, and suddenly I felt so tired, and so sad that it had to end this way that I began to cry. I thought that nothing could make this shell of a man recover his health and spirits.

I knelt down and put my arms around him. "I've found you, Kay!" I said, holding my wet cheek against his cold face. He felt like a sack of bones wrapped in parchment when I hugged him. "It's going to be all right. I've come to take you home."

He looked up at me then, and at first his stare was cold and emotionless, as if he had trouble remembering who I was, but I got him up and made him walk around, and gradually his eyes cleared a little, and he began to mumble responses to my questions, and before long we were both crying. "Gerda," he whispered. "Where have you been all this time? And—where have *I* been?"

He was like somebody waking up from a long nightmare. At one point he looked around the room and said, "This place is cold and empty. Let's get out of here!"

"The sooner the better," I said with a nod. The Snow Queen could come back anytime now, and since I wasn't armed, I wanted to be gone before she returned.

We had a long way to go to get back home, and Kay had an even longer way to go to get the craving for the Snow Queen's powder out of his system, but we took it slowly. First, out the garden and down the mountain, where Rudy met us and helped us back to the highway. Then back to the city, and finally the long journey home to Denmark, where Kay could get long-term medical care for his condition.

It is spring again now. More than a year has passed since Kay took off on the wild ride with the Snow Queen, but he is almost his old self again. He grows stronger every day, and he's talking about getting out of therapy soon, and looking for work. Maybe he'll become a gardener in the country. He's growing roses again.

I looked at him, tanned and fit in the warm sunshine, with roses in his cheeks as pink as the ones on the rose tree, and I whispered, "Peace, O Lord." This time I wasn't swearing.